TALK OF TOKYO

Tokyo Whispers – Book One

Heather Hallman

www.BOROUGHSPUBLISHINGGROUP.com

TALK OF TOKYO
Copyright © 2021 Heather Hallman

ISBN: 978-1-957295-02-2

For Candler who loves me, warts and all

4

ACKNOWLEDGMENTS

I'd like to thank Boroughs Publishing Group, and especially Michelle, for taking a chance on a debut author. Working with my editor, Jack, was one of the most enjoyable parts of the writing process. I learned tons.

Thank you to my beta readers who reviewed this manuscript, and others, including Mira S. Park. You picked out mistakes, omissions, and poor prose. Your advice has been enormously helpful.

Much gratitude for the love and support of my parents and in-laws. Special thanks to my parents, Holly and Norman Spector, for having bookshelves full of Danielle Steele, Judith Krantz, John Jakes, and James Clavell. Obviously, I read them all thoroughly. To my in-laws, Peggy and Ed Hallman: Thank you for caring for me like a daughter.

Lots of hugs and kisses to Candler and the girls for tolerating all the time I spend staring at screens. My love always.

TALK OF TOKYO

CHAPTER ONE

Tsukiji, Tokyo

April 1897

Shaky hands and racing heart notwithstanding, Suki gave herself a fighting chance. The incorrigible rake might have accusations, threats, and plans for retaliation, but she had feminine cunning. While she lacked familiarity with the mechanics involved in that sort of cunning, she'd seen how furtive glances and teasing words reduced men to foolishness. The basics of flirtation rivaled neither the complexity of French verbs nor the convolutedness of English spellings, both of which she'd mastered with ease.

A maid hastened across the garden and opened the front gate. "Mr. Spenser is expecting you," she said in the clear, precise English of servants in Tokyo's foreign quarter of Tsukiji.

Suki followed the maid through Spenser's front garden, past azalea bushes boasting radiant displays of scarlets, lavenders, and magentas. Flurries of pale pink temple bells burst forth in a graceful arrangement that bore a decidedly feminine touch.

Of course it did. Spenser's gardens would've been planted by his former wife.

Suki pictured the fair-haired young woman vigorously fanning herself at last summer's festival. She'd worn one of those heavy dresses that trapped sweat and exacerbated the summer itch. Several months later, news had traveled through Tsukiji that Spenser's bride had returned to England for good.

As Suki stared up at the Japanese-style wooden beam home with the gingerbread trim and second-story dormer windows favored by Tsukiji's British residents, dread once again grew in the pit of her stomach. If Spenser had seen fit to alienate the woman he'd pledged to honor and protect, what did he have in store for the woman he most certainly despised?

"The door is over here," a man's voice called from the house.

Had Emperor Mutsuhito been standing on the front porch, Suki wouldn't have been more surprised. The irate gentleman she'd been expecting was looking at her with an expression of mild amusement. Up to now, she'd only caught glimpses of the incorrigible rake in passing. Closer examination revealed an angular jawline that an aspiring journalist might wish to trace with her finger and cheekbones ordinarily found on statues of world-conquering kings. Pillow-like lips, one touch of which would make a woman's insides melt, were already having that very effect on her.

Griffith Spenser was downright handsome. But not in a way that made Suki swoon into the azalea bushes. A crease lined the middle of his chin, and his nose could be described as a bit wide, his brow as a bit too high. The caramel-colored hair atop his head hadn't been set with a pomade but permitted its thick waves, adding a few inches of unruly height to the already tall, lean gentleman.

Given his reputation, she should have been prepared for a strong dose of masculine appeal. But her head felt light and airy, and her breath had all but disappeared. In its place, a bubbling sensation portended a spell of the giggles. Gripping her satchel, she took in enough air to restore her powers of reason. Unless she got to work, Spenser was going to be the instrument of her undoing. Fortunately, she knew his weakness. Like most foreign men who arrived on Japan's shores, Spenser was enamored with the nation's beauties. And although her chignon had loosened to lopsidedness, and her kimono bore the marks of a full day's teaching, and she was, in fact, only half-Japanese, she could muster enough charm to make Spenser reconsider his plans.

Fluttering her eyelashes in a coquettish manner, which had much in common with trying to dislodge a flying insect, Suki faced the man who held her fate in the palm of his rather well-shaped hands. "I was admiring your fine home."

"I quite like it myself."

"Was it constructed after the quake of '94?"

"We commissioned its construction when we arrived in '95. I'm assured by its builders it could withstand another earthquake of that intensity. Japanese-style homes fare better than brick and stone."

"Mother Nature has given us many opportunities to rebuild."

"Mother Nature?" Spenser furrowed his brow. "I thought it was the giant catfish residing under Japan flipping its tail that caused all these earthquakes." His tone was teasing, while the observation revealed Spenser as the type of foreigner who bothered learning about traditional culture.

"You know your Japanese folklore," Suki replied.

"I like to be prepared for all the dragons and ghosts I'm certain to encounter," Spenser said with a smile that brought out creases along his soft brown eyes. "I should introduce myself, although introductions are probably unnecessary. I'm Griffith Spenser, arrived from England, resident of Tsukiji for almost two years."

Suki mentally added to the introduction: Spenser counted minor members of the British aristocracy among his family, although he himself had no chance of inheriting a title; his company was the most highly regarded foreign-owned trading firm in Tokyo; he'd arrived with a new bride who left him a year later; and he now graced the bed of war widow Natsu Watanabe. Also, he played lawn tennis.

The Tokyo Tattler's job was to know these facts about Tsukiji's most illustrious residents, and Suki needed to continue doing this job, which was why she couldn't let Spenser's allure compromise her defenses. The man had asked her to his home without explanation. Although she'd like to imagine he'd summoned her to discuss the modern significance of Japanese mythology, she was a realist. Spenser had a score to settle with the Tokyo Tattler, and all this pleasant banter about earthquakes was merely diversion.

"It's an honor to make your acquaintance, Spenser-*san*." She bowed low and rose slowly, presenting him with downcast eyes and a curl of the lips, a pose meant to convey both shyness and carnal desire. Rakes liked that combination.

"I appreciate your coming on such short notice," he said with a heavy sigh. "The events of the past few weeks have left me no choice. I find myself scrambling for any means to rectify the situation."

Spenser was going to rectify her? What could that possibly entail? She'd be fortunate to leave his home in one piece. Steeling her nerves, she gave Spenser her most accommodating smile. "I'd be pleased to oblige in any way I can."

His shoulders relaxed by degrees. "I'm much relieved to hear that."

Was Spenser already caving to her charms? Truly, men were like flower petals in the hands of an eager child.

Stepping aside, he motioned for her to enter the house. Like a chivalrous Western gentleman, he was content to let his female companion be the first to confront whatever danger, disaster, or vengeful demon lurked inside. A Japanese man would have taken the lead, not stood so close behind her, bringing heat to her cheeks as she removed her shoes and stepped into the home's interior.

A middle-aged Japanese woman appeared and gave a low bow before offering Suki a pair of slippers.

"This is the housekeeper, Rei-*san*. In the event you have any misgivings about our conversing alone, she'll act as chaperone. I realise it's a bit unorthodox inviting a woman I've never met to my home. But these days I find it difficult to present my face in public."

Suki heard sadness—profound sadness, to be exact—weighing down his voice. How could he have been so offended by her writing? All she'd done was spread a bit of gossip. Her readers had questions as to why Spenser's wife had suddenly departed Tsukiji and how he'd ended up with everyone's favorite war widow on his arm. As their Tattler, Suki was duty-bound to provide answers, all of which had ample verification.

Granted, there'd been times when she'd presented a luscious *on-dit* based on weak sources, which had later proved false. But those incidents bore no relation to Spenser. Everything she'd written about Tsukiji's Lothario had been obtained through trusted sources. Had she really made it impossible for Griffith Spenser to present his face in public?

Rei-*san* led them to a parlor at the front of the house. Here, Spenser's former wife had left her mark in the form of rural scenes in gilded frames, luminous bronze sconces, and a carpet that resembled a field of daisies.

Spenser motioned to a high-backed chair and took the one opposite. "I'm told this is an excellent variety of green tea," he said while Rei-*san* poured a cup for Suki.

"I enjoy all varieties of tea," Suki said, her voice lilting with her best attempt at deferential sweetness. Truthfully, she preferred black tea with milk and sugar like the British, which was also how her Japanese mother took it. His people had won the tea battle; he might as well gloat.

Spenser forged ahead with his cup of Japanese tea, his nose crinkling as the earthy brew neared his lips. After a short sip, he returned the earthenware cup to its tray and sat back. "Shall we discuss the reason for my requesting your presence this evening?"

To expose her identity, to chastise her for what she'd written about him, to describe how he planned to denounce her to all of Tsukiji as the shrew who was penning their gossip.

Using flirtation to charm this rather serious, seemingly intelligent man into abandoning his plans for her demise no longer seemed the wisest course of action. Fortunately, she had other means at her disposal: apologize, grovel, offer to extol his virtues for the next five columns. Strike first with her own blistering interrogation. How had

Spenser discovered she was the Tokyo Tattler? Who were his spies? How did he dare attack Tsukiji's favorite columnist?

Spenser was a member of civil society, which meant he appreciated the idea of rights. She could plead freedom of the press and the public's right to knowledge. Those were British notions, too.

The teacup nearly slipped from her trembling fingertips as she lowered it to the tray. Whatever it took, she'd placate Spenser. Otherwise, every word she'd written, every source she'd cultivated, every piece of journalistic advice she'd taken to heart would be for naught. "Please tell me, Spenser-*san*, why you summoned me to your home."

"I asked you here to request your assistance with my wards."

"Your…" The word fell on her ears, devoid of meaning. Did wards refer to Tokyo's administrative districts? Why would Spenser possess urban administrative districts? And why would he need her assistance with such possessions?

"My wards."

She stared at him, unable to fathom what he possibly meant by wards.

"I'm not planning on plundering their inheritance or any such nonsense. I'm concerned with their future care once they arrive in Tokyo."

Wards, as in children. He was a guardian, and wards were the children under his guardianship. An entirely unexpected revelation, but not unwelcome.

Feeling compelled to provide explanation for her confused response, Suki grabbed at the first word that came to mind. "Warts. I thought you said you had warts. Now I realize you said *wards*. T-sounds and d-sounds at the end of a word can create much confusion for the listener."

"Warts? You thought I'd ask a beautiful, intelligent woman of no prior acquaintance to my home to discuss my warts?"

A feather could have knocked Suki to the floor. Not only had Spenser summoned her for a most innocent reason, but he also thought her beautiful and intelligent, two words no one ever associated with her person save well-meaning family when they thought she needed a boost.

Suki, on the other hand, had associated his obviously handsome person with warts. It was a positively ludicrous explanation. But like the British say, "in for a penny, in for a pound."

"Please understand. English is not my first language, nor is it really my second. My father spoke French with me when I was a child, and I've always spoken Japanese, though I never learned all the characters necessary to read and write properly. I suppose having grown up in an English-speaking household, and having spent all my life in Tsukiji, and the fact that I am an English teacher makes it my best language; but it is not my first."

Spenser lurched forward while gurgling noises issued from his mouth. Spasms racked his torso, and his head jerked side to side. The plate of biscuits on the tea tray remained untouched, yet something substantial must have gotten lodged in his throat. The housekeeper-chaperone was nowhere in sight. Suki would have to save him from choking to death, and the only thing she could think to do was give his back a firm wallop like her sister-in-law when her son attempted to inhale a plate of tangerines.

Suki fisted her hand and rose, prepared to strike, when Spenser reeled upwards. Tears brimmed in his eyes, and his face was a brutal shade of red. The menacing grimace contorting his mouth reminded her of the angry-god statues standing guard outside Buddhist temples. But at least he was breathing.

Rapid hiccuppy gasps finally revealed the frenzied fit for what it was. Spenser was laughing.

No human being laughed in this fashion. Mirth of this degree could kill a man. What if he fell off the chair, hit his head, and ended up maimed for life, or worse? And she'd be the one responsible. Acting as though she'd heard the word "warts" instead of "wards" had been a means of rescuing the conversation. Instead, she'd caused him to produce sounds not found in the natural world, like that of a frog wrestling a turnip, which would simply never occur.

The more he laughed, the harder it was to restrain her own. Eventually, she surrendered and joined in the hilarity. Let him think she was laughing at her supposed linguistic foible, which, thankfully, seemed to be amusing him to no end.

"For the record, I don't have any warts," he sputtered, and another bout of laughter commenced.

That would have been her guess. Spenser didn't appear to have any blemishes to speak of. Likely, he was as pleasing to look at in the flesh as he was fully clothed, which was the very last place her thoughts should have gone. They had wards to discuss.

"I appreciate your honesty about the warts, and the wards." Suki tilted her head to the side. "Perhaps you could tell me more about the latter?"

Spenser dabbed his eyes once more and cleared his throat. "I apologize for not being more specific in the invitation to my home. But it is a private matter, and in this town, the truth quickly becomes twisted into all manner of gossip."

Suki nodded her understanding.

Folding his hands, Spenser exhaled with a sigh. "A few months ago, my eldest brother passed away. An illness took him. He was a widower, and his wife was French. They met when he was working at a trading firm in the south of the country. They raised their two children on the continent and visited England periodically. My nephew Lucien is seventeen, no longer a child, really. His sister Marianne is fifteen, and I'm most concerned about her education and other aspects of a young woman's life."

Finally, Spenser's invitation made sense. Suki happened to be a teacher of fifteen-year-old girls. Naturally, her name would have come up when Spenser mentioned needing assistance with his niece's education. "That is a tricky age for a young woman."

"I last saw my brother several years ago when he was in London on business. I informed him of my intention to marry Victoria, a family friend with whom we'd been close as children. He thought her a lovely woman, which she is, even if she didn't care for Japan." A pained expression settled so briefly on Spenser's face that if Suki hadn't been staring, she would have missed it entirely.

"My brother believed Victoria was still with me in Japan when he directed the children into my care. Since his passing, I notified Marianne and Lucien of Victoria's absence, but they are determined to honour their father's wishes and reside with me in Tokyo."

"On the other side of the world. They must be brave."

"I suppose the desire to venture abroad runs strongly in our family. A great-grandfather of many centuries ago was a pirate. His wealth bought us a title, a manor, and respectability. Nevertheless, my brother and I, along with quite a few uncles and cousins, have set our sights on places far from England."

"How did you end up in Japan?"

Other questions begged to be answered: Why did you stay? Why didn't you leave when your wife departed? Was it because you fell for the irresistible beauties of the Orient? Did their company ease your loneliness? Or were you already in love with Natsu Watanabe? And when might we expect your fickle eye to stray from her the way it did from your wife?

Suki chastised herself for being cynical. A real journalist collected facts before drawing conclusions.

"My company presented me with the opportunity to oversee East Asia trade at our Tokyo offices. I thought it sounded like a splendid adventure. Even with the upheavals of the previous year, I think everything turned out for the best."

The dreamy look in Spenser's eyes told Suki everything she needed to know about his relationship with Watanabe. He was enamored. The loving ministrations of the impeccable war widow must have been the perfect salve for the end of his marriage and the death of his brother. No wonder he was glad to be in Tokyo. Their love was something to be admired, an aspiration for Japanese women and foreign men who couldn't resist their mutual attraction.

Suki felt a pang of guilt for the many words she'd written against the match. Henceforth, the Tokyo Tattler would refrain from malicious gossip about Griffith Spenser. Straightening her posture, she smoothed her kimono skirt and gave this exceptional man her full attention.

"How might I be of assistance with your wards?"

CHAPTER TWO

Griff forced down another sip of the green brew and returned his teacup to the table between him and Miss Malveaux. He should have served black tea. Everyone in the foreign quarter drank black tea, and if he'd served it for his meeting with Miss Malveaux, he wouldn't be trying—and failing—to disguise his aversion to the pungent infusion.

But he'd been determined to impress the schoolteacher as the sort of foreigner who ventured beyond the foreign quarter and embraced Japanese mores. While he was that sort of foreigner when it came to travelling the countryside, attending cultural performances, and learning the basics of the language, he could not stomach the murky concoction. Hopefully, that would not damn him in Miss Malveaux's eyes because she was the perfect fit for the position: teacher at a prestigious girls' school, fluent in French, English, and Japanese, and quite good company.

Although a bit nervy at first, perhaps owing to a bug in the eye that caused her lashes to beat with unusual fury, she'd proved her humour by joining in his laughter, which could be off-putting. Griff had it on good authority that his hysterics resembled the sound of feral cats mating.

Clearly, she was a good sport, and he'd regret her slipping through his fingers. "I was hoping you'd consider accepting the position of governess for Marianne and Lucien. This isn't a formal governess position. You wouldn't be required to take residence in our home, only to direct their education and engage them in various cultural activities. With your facility for languages, I thought you'd be best suited to introduce the basics of Japanese." He fiddled with the fringe on the arms of the upholstered chair. He'd served an easy ball into Miss Malveaux's court. All she had to do was tap it back over the net.

Once again, an expression of incredulity swept across Miss Malveaux's face. Everything he said seemed to cause her surprise.

"I appreciate your thinking of me in this capacity," she said kindly but firmly. "Unfortunately, I'm unable to assume the responsibilities such a post would entail. I have employment at the Ginza Girls School, which keeps me very busy."

She was too good to be true, and too good to concede the point. "We could adjust to your teaching obligations. Hopefully, the children will be in some form of schooling themselves."

"I work the length of the day. There would be no time for me to provide your wards with adequate guidance."

He pulled the final arrow from his quiver. "Might I inquire about your current salary? I may be able to offer greater remuneration."

Miss Malveaux folded her hands. "I'm fully committed to the school. I couldn't consider it."

Griff added loyalty to the list of Miss Malveaux's fine qualities alongside grace, elegance, and dark brown eyes that made him wonder what it would be like to lose himself in their depths. "Your loyalty is commendable. I apologise if I offended in seeking to lure you away from the school. Anna Yamashita thought you might be persuaded to take the governess position."

Miss Malveaux's posture somehow straightened even farther. "Yamashita-*san* has many ideas about the young women of Tsukiji."

"She is a matchmaker by trade, is she not?"

"Her specialty is Japanese men seeking foreign wives. She's among those who believe this generation's sons need a well-educated foreign mother to instruct them in the ways of the modern world."

"Then you must rank high on her list of foreign women. Are you contemplating marriage?" Immediately, he regretted the question. They'd only just become acquainted, and Miss Malveaux was giving him a look that would bring any unruly student into line.

"I have no interest in Yamashita-*san*'s services. As I said before, I'm fully committed to my work at the girls' school."

"You'd be wise to give much consideration before agreeing to a match. Marriage is a difficult bargain, as I recently learned." Why was his voice brimming with such remorse? Usually, he managed a stiff upper lip on the topic of his failed marriage. Was he trying to court her sympathies?

Miss Malveaux nodded and murmured her approval. "I've heard the same."

Relieved at being restored to her good graces, Griff sank into the chair and continued, "I apologise for inquiring about your status. It was impolite of me to ask."

"There's no need to apologize. I, too, ask many questions. I've found it's better to follow where curiosity leads."

"I'm relieved to hear you say that. I promise I'm not usually such a muttonhead. Truth be told, I'd feared you'd refuse an invitation to my home. Thanks to the scandalmonger of Tsukiji, some people in the community have a rather negative impression of my character."

Miss Malveaux cleared her throat. "The scandalmonger of Tsukiji?"

"The Tokyo Tattler. It's a gossip-filled column in the *Tokyo Daily News*. Whoever is penning the worthless drivel has painted me as one of those foreign devils whose favourite pastime is the corruption of Japanese women."

"How appalling."

"My former wife Victoria's departure generated many falsehoods that proved damaging to my reputation, which I've since compounded by spending time with a Japanese woman rather well-known around Tsukiji. But…" Griff stopped himself before launching into all the reasons why he was desperate to distance himself from this popular Japanese woman. "I beg you to disregard any scandal sheets with my name on them."

"I never read idle gossip."

"That's good to know. I remain convinced you'd be the perfect candidate for the governess position, but I fully understand your commitment to the girls' school. Might it be possible, however, to ask your advice on finding a suitable governess?"

Rustling in the back garden followed by a plaintive mew like that of a woodland creature with its paw caught in the trap drew his attention to the window. Miss Malveaux furrowed her bow in a puzzled expression. "There's always something lurking back there," he remarked.

"That's what happens when you fill in swamps to build the foreign quarter. Creatures of all sorts find their way to dry land." Miss Malveaux took a long sip of tea and gave her teacup the sort of approving smile he could never muster. At least he'd served a pleasing variety of the leaf. Placing her cup on the tray, she continued, "I can think of several young women in Tsukiji who might be interested in the position. They're in the stage of life between schooling and marriage and would be capable of guiding your wards in their educational pursuits, as well as help them adjust to their new lives in Tokyo. Would you like me to contact them on your behalf?"

Griff let out a bated breath. Miss Malveaux was going to make his life much easier. "I'd greatly appreciate your assistance. Any chance these women also speak French? My niece might wish to have someone with whom she can comfortably confide."

Miss Malveaux shook her head, and the firelight brought out flecks of gold in her hair. "None of those women speak French," she said. "A close friend of mine is French and in service to an American family. I don't think she knows anyone who could serve as governess, but she might be able to direct you to a maid who could converse with your niece. An English-speaking governess and French-speaking maid might prove ideal.

"As for Japanese instruction, perhaps you have a Japanese acquaintance who could conduct lessons? Outside Tsukiji's gates, your wards would benefit from speaking the native tongue."

Griff should be thinking of Natsu, who'd told him the previous week that Marianne and Lucien's first Japanese word should be "mother," so they'd know how to address her. He'd added the comment to his list of reasons why he must be finished with Natsu before his niece and nephew's arrival. "One of my secretaries at the company can instruct Marianne and Lucien in the language."

"You've given much thought to their needs. I'm sure they'll flourish in your household."

They'd flourish like little maple saplings if you were their governess, he wanted to say, but held his tongue. The best he could hope from Miss Malveaux was a solid recommendation for the position. And perhaps her friendship going forward. She might be the type of friend who took meals with the family on occasion and afterward joined him in the study to inquire about his niece and nephew's progress. There, she might release her chignon from its clips and let him run his hands through her silky tresses.

With a firm shake of the head, he dismissed the thought. He shouldn't be getting worked up over a fine schoolteacher like Miss Malveaux. She deserved better than a so-called friend speculating about her person. "Thanks to your advice this evening, I believe Marianne and Lucien will adjust to Tokyo life splendidly."

Miss Malveaux finished her tea to the god-awful dregs, then hovered her hand several inches above the empty cup, a Japanese signal that acknowledged their conversation had reached its conclusion and she required no more refreshment. "I'll inform you as soon as I hear of any potential candidates for the positions." She smiled amiably, her full, pink lips still moist with tea. The luscious sight sent a jolt of desire coursing through him.

A woman that fetching was opposed to marriage? Dedicated to her work, she'd said, but that didn't preclude a lover who had the privilege of running a thumb across that ample bottom lip. Lucky chap.

Miss Malveaux cleared heir throat. Had she seen him staring at her lips? How often he complained about his reputation as the rake of Tsukiji, and here he was confirming it. He stood and motioned for her to precede him to the parlour door. "I'm looking forward to learning of your results."

His housekeeper, Rei-*san*, had arranged Miss Malveaux's *geta* sandals in the entrance. She stepped into them and pushed a loose strand from her face. Utterly adorable. Envy for her lover—how could there be no man with a claim on her?—caused him to clench his jaw.

"Thank you, for the tea, Mr. Spenser." Miss Malveaux bowed to him, and he bowed back, probably too low for a man bowing to a woman, but she was an extraordinary woman, and he wasn't a very good bower.

"It was my pleasure. I'll be awaiting your response about the candidates." And he very much hoped this response would serve as an excuse for him to once again request the pleasure of Miss Malveaux's   company.

CHAPTER THREE

Suki hurried up the staircase to her room, her mind still turning over the visit with Spenser. Moments from their conversation had assailed her during the evening meal, particularly the part when Spenser had called her "beautiful" and "intelligent." They'd been spontaneous words. He'd said them right as he'd launched into that appalling laughter. Not mere platitude, Spenser actually believed her beautiful and intelligent, which made her giddy and lightheaded, and left her wondering what else he'd thought of her, and what she made of him.

But she couldn't afford to spend another minute ruminating. The Tokyo Tattler column was due the following morning, and if she didn't make haste on the revisions, she wouldn't get a wink of sleep.

Increasing her pace up the flight of stairs, Suki glided her fingers along the bumps and ridges in the worn banister. Mother Garrick's latest wallpapering, a cheerful rendering of periwinkle morning glories on tangles of bright green vines, served as background for the Garrick family photographs. Suki's gaze passed over the Garricks' wedding portrait, taken in the United States, and photographs of the family as they made their life in Tsukiji where Papa Garrick was a professor of the biological sciences at St. Paul's University. With each successive photograph, the number of children increased until a few years before Suki and her *okasan*, mother, came to live with the Garricks and made the family "perfect," as Mother Garrick liked to say.

By the time Suki reached her bedroom at the end of the second-floor hallway, the dining room conversation had faded to a low rumble save for peals of her sister-in-law Rosie's laughter. When Suki had made her escape, the household—presently consisting of the elder Garricks, their son, Roger, his wife, Rosie, their two boys, Suki, and her *okasan*—had been discussing an ornate metal rain chain that had gone missing from their Canadian neighbor's home. Everyone around the table had agreed it made the loveliest sound of all the rain chains in Tsukiji; certainly, anyone would covet the piece. Had it been a slow week for gossip, a stolen rain chain of such renown would've made it into the Tokyo Tattler column. But not this week.

A rush of air tinged with the scent of rosewater lotion greeted Suki as she opened the bedroom door. The night was warm enough to make a fire unnecessary; even so, a chill seeped in through the large windows facing the street. Suki closed the curtains against the cold air, changed into a heavy flannel nightgown and robe, and sat at her writing table. Under the lamp's glow, she looked over the sheets of paper that would become this week's Tokyo Tattler column.

Thanks to a marquis' ball, the Tattler had not been wanting for gossip. Naturally, Suki hadn't been in attendance. Rarely was she present at the illustrious events about which she reported. Maids, housekeepers, gardeners, grocers, delivery boys, and occasionally her sister-in-law, Rosie, who often attended such affairs, provided details down to the silky undergarments Tsukiji's ladies had worn to the gathering, to the silky undergarments Tsukiji's gentlemen had pulled from their lovers' hips after the gathering had concluded.

News from the ball filled the first paragraphs of the column. According to Tattler sources, titled Japanese and Tokyo's elite foreign residents had filled the marquis' dance floor in an array of dress that had celebrated and transgressed the day's fashion. The Tattler praised several well-attired women who hadn't received previous Tattler mention—Suki aimed to be inclusive—and several whose labors had earned them a place of recognition. A few Tsukiji residents whose pride could use a tweaking had either chosen attire too flouncy for their age or had worn their weight in headpieces and jewelry. The Tattler limited her tsking to them.

Far and away, the high point of the ball concerned a recently arrived American divorcee in residence at the Hotel Metropolis. Her lavish attentions to a Russian naval officer—one of Suki's informants reported the divorcee's tongue finding its way into the officer's ear—had stunned foreign attendees and positively horrified the Japanese nobility, many of whom still considered men and women dancing together a violation of public decorum.

Not that the Japanese nobility was beyond reproach in their flirtations and bed-hopping. They were, however, exceedingly private about their affairs. Divorce was too shameful to contemplate, and jealousy a pointless indulgence. Provided they exhibited utmost discretion, high-born wives who desired a diversion could indulge in amorous encounters without fear of neglect or abandonment.

The Tattler happily turned a blind eye to affairs that brought women no harm, even when multiple sources provided tantalizing tidbits that readers would've feasted upon for days. Japanese women of lesser status seduced into foreign men's beds endured an altogether different fate. To these affairs, the Tattler invariably applied her pen.

Suki paused to rub her toes. Her writing table faced the bedroom window, which afforded her the opportunity to observe her neighbors' comings and goings. This was especially helpful for avoiding undesirable encounters with people such as the ever-annoying matchmaker, Yamashita-*san*, whom Suki had successfully avoided earlier that day. But the draft from the broad window turned her toes to icicles.

Recalling Yamashita-*san* reminded Suki of the redness that had sprung to Spenser's cheeks when he'd inquired about her marital interests. Had he pushed further, she would have told him what she told others: she was happy with her teaching and couldn't give a husband and children the care they deserved.

Truth be told, she'd stopped thinking about marriage when she'd seen how other half-Japanese women from Tsukiji had struggled in Japanese households. Any future mother-in-law was bound to be disappointed when Suki spoke out of turn and neglected to scold a servant for failing to heat her husband's bath to the ideal temperature. As for a foreign husband, that was beyond consideration.

Suki returned her attentions to the column. After discussion of the marquis' ball, she'd written about a group of German engineers who'd been seen at all times of the night and early morning with their Japanese translators, young women who presented easy targets for foreigners intent on seducing the native women. Such women hailed from families that decades before had been among the samurai and landholding castes. Their fathers filled Japan's modern bureaucracies and journeyed abroad to learn how Western schools, hospitals, and militaries functioned. The daughters grew up speaking English, French, and German; they read romance novels wherein they learned of the foreign man's seemingly unique capacity for unbridled passion and devoted love.

Time and again, Suki had seen aspiring modern women rush headlong into affairs with these mythical foreign creatures. Shocked and devastated when their beloved sweethearts departed Japan for wives, lovers, and other obligations, these women were left with limited prospects for the future. Tainted by their association with the foreign devils, they had no hope of marrying Japanese men anywhere near their social standing; they were fortunate if their parents acknowledged their existence. Often, a young woman's midsection noticeably swelled about the time her lover felt compelled to leave.

The thought made Suki's stomach turn on the grilled fish and roasted potatoes she'd eaten at supper. *Okasan* had been more fortunate than other women who fell for a foreigner. She'd been disowned by her father when she refused his choice of husband to marry the foul-smelling, large-nosed, hairy demon whose child she carried in her womb. Her French husband, however, remained in Japan long enough for her to discover a passion for Western-style dress and hone her skills as a modiste. Neither she nor Suki ended up in a factory or brothel.

Suki was five years old when her father returned to France to attend his grandfather's funeral. Gifts of children's toys and letters describing how he was going to shower her with kisses arrived regularly at first, then slowed, then ceased. *Okasan* supported them by taking commissions for ball gowns but couldn't afford their Tsukiji home. Eventually, they moved to a small room outside the foreign quarter's gates.

At the age of seven, Suki was entering Tsukiji each morning to attend the missionary school when *Okasan*'s gowns caught the eye of an American professor's wife in need of something special for the university's Regent's Ball. Upon hearing how the talented modiste and her daughter had been abandoned, Mother Garrick invited them to live in her home. The Garricks furnished *Okasan* with a studio where she created gowns that earned her a reputation as one of Tsukiji's foremost seamstresses. Suki got a set of American parents and seven American siblings.

When Suki was fifteen, *Okasan* asked friends returning to France if they would inquire after the status of her former husband. A letter arrived months later with news that Suki's father was a civil servant in Paris with a wife and children.

"I hope this brings peace to your heart," *Okasan* said after sharing the news.

Suki shrugged her indifference. "He's like every other foreign man who goes back home. It's not as though I thought he was coming back."

Okasan returned to her stitching, and Suki's throat swelled. She understood the reason *Okasan* had shared the uneasy truth of her father's contented Parisian life: the wish for his return had colored her thoughts and imaginings for ten long years. It was now up to her to find peace, somehow.

Jiggling her pen, Suki found ink enough to finish the column. Any woman, regardless of family history, strength of character, level of education, or determination to succeed where others had failed, could fall into the trap of believing in the foreigner's strength of commitment. The Tattler's job was to remind Japanese women what happened when they lost their heads in the throes of foreign male seduction.

This week war widow Natsu Watanabe was in need of reminding.

Griffith Spenser had put Suki under his spell simply by the way he'd gazed upon her while she'd spoken. So badly she'd wanted to think him sincere in calling her beautiful and intelligent that she'd ignored the most obvious explanation for his flattery: Spenser was a rake whose primary reflex was to lure women into his bed.

Suki could only imagine the flattery he'd used on Watanabe. She was probably head-over-heels in love and completely devoid of wits. Most fortunately for Tsukiji's favorite war widow, she had a Tattler looking out for her best interests.

Of late, Suki's informants hadn't provided any gossip on Spenser and Watanabe, but the absence of news was worthy of reflection. She concluded the column:

What has become of the incomparable war widow, Mrs. Natsu Watanabe? The Tattler misses her gentle smile and impeccable taste. Who can forget how she shone at the British Legation's breakfast in the pale-yellow day dress with its generous bustle?

Might she have grown weary of Mr. Griffith Spenser? All for the best, says Tattler readers who have become the wiser. Foreign men are not always the dream they seem.

Upon rereading the conclusion, Suki found it a touch disingenuous. She knew why Watanabe and Spenser hadn't been seen recently in public: he was grieving his brother and preparing for the arrival of his niece and nephew. But she couldn't very well write as much since this had been revealed to her by Spenser himself. Were he to read the column, he'd know the identity of Tsukiji's gossipmonger, and she had little doubt he'd expose her to the foreign quarter as retribution for christening him the foreign quarter's incorrigible rake. Which he was: all evidence pointed in that direction. Any gossipmonger would have concluded that Spenser had driven his wife from Japan on account of him having taken a lover. When he later stepped out with Watanabe, he'd given Suki all the confirmation she'd needed to accuse him of indecent behavior.

Spenser had every right to be angry at his portrayal, and she couldn't have him retaliating by sharing her *nom de plume*. Many a night she'd lain awake, heart racing, covered in sweat at the thought of her family, friends, neighbors, and, worst of all, the Ginza Girls School, learning that she penned the column. She hated the lie, but she wouldn't be the Tattler forever, and anonymity was paramount.

Suki rose from her chair and paced her small room. Being the Tokyo Tattler was a necessary step in becoming a journalist, which meant reporting gossip, even when the delectable tidbits concerned persons whose character had made a favorable impression. In truth, she'd found Spenser kind and personable. Her brother Roger regarded Spenser highly based on their acquaintance at the lawn tennis club. There was a chance Spenser might be the sort of foreigner who fulfilled his pledge of marriage, who stayed in Japan and provided for his children. Several such families were her neighbors, and they were happy.

Watanabe could be one of those rare women who had a chance at the dream of a devoted foreign husband. Thanks to her deceased husband's role as liaison between Japan's naval officers and foreign officers serving as naval advisers, she'd been a fixture on the Tsukiji social scene long before she'd become attached to Spenser. Desirable for her charming companionship and well-established in the foreign community, Watanabe must have had her choice of suitors, and she'd chosen Spenser. Suki's informants, who'd spotted the pair at Rokumeikan balls, on strolls through Hibiya Park, watching the circuses at Shimbashi, or dining at the Imperial Hotel, reported the couple appeared quite smitten. All signs pointed to

Watanabe having the upper hand with Spenser, which boded well for her romantic aims.

Slumping on her bed, Suki considered the possibility of giving Spenser and Watanabe the Tattler's blessing. She couldn't simply ignore them; they were popular figures in the foreign quarter, which was why it had been necessary for the Tattler to pursue the mystery of why Spenser's wife had abandoned him in Tokyo. At the time, there had been rumors of her aversion to the food, the climate, the earthquakes, the sweaty backs of the rickshaw runners. But any of those things could be overcome in time with the care of a devoted husband. The Tattler could only conclude that Spenser had taken a lover. It made sense then and continued to make sense now. Spenser was a rake.

A sudden realization brought Suki upright on the heavy cotton coverlet. Earlier that evening, Spenser hadn't mentioned marriage, except to inquire whether *she* had been using a matchmaker's services. Had he been planning to marry Watanabe, wouldn't she have been present at their meeting to discuss his wards' care? A future wife would want a say in who'd be acting as governess in her home.

Then there was the way Spenser had looked at her before bringing their meeting to an end. She'd caught him staring at her hair with that heavy look in his eyes. She'd seen that look before and knew what it meant: Spenser desired her. Even worse, her body had responded with a warm tingling sensation as though welcoming his desire. One look from Spenser and she'd yielded like freshly pounded mochi rice.

The man was a rogue, plain and simple. And the Tattler owed it to Tokyo's modern, young women to hold such a man in check.

CHAPTER FOUR

Suki passed Tsukiji's Anglican church, its steeple aimed toward the dense clouds hovering over the foreign quarter, and entered the university district where cafes and booksellers awaited the day's flurry of activity. Between a French wine shop and a store specializing in wood-pulp paper stood Ned Taylor's home, the first floor of which housed the *Tokyo Daily News* offices.

Owner and editor, Ned had built the newspaper from a weekly business report into the most widely read English-language newspaper in Tokyo. A darling of the Tsukiji community, he'd earned the respect of the Americans and Germans for his entrepreneurial prowess, and deference from the British, French, and Russians for having the good fortune of being born the nephew of a British duke. Close to forty, he remained unattached, but his entanglements with Japanese and foreign women were legion. None of which made it into the Tokyo Tattler column.

Two years ago, Suki had proposed an arrangement between her and Ned: she'd give him the Tokyo Tattler, a weekly column of frippery and flirtation that would increase female readership and broaden his appeal to advertisers. In exchange, he'd tutor her in the field of journalism to prepare her for a post among the male reporters at the *Tokyo Daily News*. So far, she'd kept her end of the bargain.

A few minutes after seven, Suki rang the doorbell. A metal cadence echoed through the house. According to Ned, reporters spent the latter part of the night building rapport with their sources, usually at entertainment venues across the city. Hours after she departed, they'd show up for work at the newspaper offices, no one the wiser as to the Tattler's identity.

A maid greeted Suki and motioned her to Ned's office. The odor of male bodies and tobacco intensified as she passed the reporters' room. Doubt pricked at her. Could she work alongside those men deep into the night, puffing on a pipe and musing about whether the police would bother making an arrest in the latest prostitute murder?

It was a man's world. Ned would have to issue threats for Suki to gain entrance to their hallowed domain. They'd resent her. But resentment faded over time.

Suki entered Ned's office to find him poring over a newspaper. Without looking up, he waved her to the chair in front of his desk. "You're not going to believe this." Ned folded his hands across a page of newsprint from one of Chicago's newspapers. English-language periodicals from around the world arrived daily at the office. From their society pages, Suki had taken lessons on how to write the Tattler column. Elsewhere, she'd discovered an increasing number of women's names in article bylines.

"Brace yourself, Suki." He gave her a teasing grin. "This might be the most exciting news the world has seen. An alien airship has crashed down in the small town of Aurora, Texas. More accurately, it crashed into the windmill of a local judge and destroyed his flower garden. The airship was crafted from an unknown metal, and the pilot was in possession of papers written in mysterious hieroglyphics."

Suki placed the envelope containing the folded pages of this week's Tattler column on Ned's desk and poured herself a cup of tea. "Might the airship have been Japanese?"

Ned let out a laugh. "That would explain the unearthly symbols."

"Was the alien's hair dark and straight, his eyes reminiscent of the Far East?"

Ned scanned the page in front of him. "The alien pilot was burned beyond recognition, then given a Christian burial."

"How convenient, and sad."

"For Japanese and aliens alike. Both parties seem to have their designs on the great United States of America." He looked Suki up and down with the carefree smile of a man unapologetic in his admiration for the female form.

Suki had been expecting the look, since he always gave her the look. And, as always, she stifled the urge to squirm in her seat and calmly sipped her tea, reminding herself that Ned was still smarting from a heartbreaking rebuke. Few details had circulated through Tsukiji about what had transpired between him and his lady love. The previous August he'd boarded a ship to Hong Kong a day after she'd left Tokyo for the same destination. Three weeks later, he'd returned alone. Judging by the intensity with which he threw himself into his work at the paper and debauchery with the Hotel Metropolis crowd, everyone in Tsukiji concluded that Ned had been broken.

He sat back in his chair and crossed his arms. "So, what does the Tattler have for me today?"

"A divorcee arrived at the Hotel Metropolis a few weeks ago, seemingly intent on putting her former husband's infidelities to shame with her own spree of East Asian affairs. Tattler sources reported she was behaving badly at the marquis' ball."

"I was there. It was a sight to behold."

"I heard she was a rare beauty."

Ned let out a low whistle. "Exquisite. Less diligence on her part would have achieved the desired effect. Even so, the Russian naval officer was not disappointed in the attention."

"Another successful night for the divorcee, then?"

"If the officer's wife's face was any indication, there was no success for anyone."

"His wife was there?"

"Present and accounted for."

"Angry?"

"Livid. If I were him, I would have slept with one eye open."

Familiar pangs of guilt struck Suki at the prospect of making the officer's wife—the innocent party—suffer once more when she encountered her humiliation in the Tattler column. Had Suki known of the wife's fury, she would have omitted, or at least softened, description of the divorcee's advances. She had no choice but to put the incident on record. Tattler readers who'd attended the ball would expect to read all about the *on-dit* in this week's column. "I assume there were many corroborating witnesses to the event."

"It was the talk of the ball."

Suki sighed away her reluctance. "Then to the newsprint it goes."

"Spoken like a true journalist, Miss Malveaux."

"That's the goal."

"Anything else?"

"About my being a journalist?"

"Any other treats for your readers?"

Suki told him about a group of German engineers who'd been seen around Tsukiji alongside their adoring translators.

Ned ran thumb and forefinger along his moustache. "Having read the Tattler for some time, I have a feeling this situation won't end well for the young ladies involved."

"I wrote as much. Hopefully, they'll read the column and reconsider their romantic whims. I ended the column with speculation about Griffith Spenser and Natsu Watanabe."

Suki rested her eyes on the envelope containing the Tattler column. The previous evening, she'd gone to sleep satisfied with the column's final paragraph. Upon waking, she'd determined to leave it out. Spenser was still grieving the loss of his brother, and the last thing he needed was to have his affair with Watanabe questioned by the town gossip. The Tattler's role was to entertain with news about the fashionable men and women of the foreign quarter, not to aggravate a man's grief.

Then, over breakfast, she'd reflected on her responsibility to Tokyo's women. No matter how decent and forthright Spenser might have come across the previous evening, he was still a rake whose wife had left him and whose designs on Watanabe were typical of the foreign man: trick his lover into a passionate affair, then leave her to suffer the consequences.

Suki continued, "As you may recall from previous columns, Mr. Spenser has been escorting the lovely Mrs. Watanabe about town. Recently, however, they haven't been seen together. The Tattler thinks Watanabe-*san* deserves better."

Ned shrugged. "If the ending fits, we'll keep it, though I may have to cut some of your copy this week."

"Plenty of ink was spilled on the fashion choices at the ball. You can have your way with as much of that as you wish. Just save the Tattler's praise for Maeda-*san*. According to various sources, she's been enduring hours of gown fittings and painstaking jewelry selection for meals at the Imperial Hotel."

"Let me guess: she's in love with an American railroad magnate currently in residence."

"A Dutch arms merchant. Thus far, he seems to be restraining himself. Maeda-*san* is married to a Japanese bureaucrat, and they have a half-dozen children. I've noticed that attention from the Tattler can be adequate replacement for attention from distant husbands and amorous targets."

Ned raised a brow. "I've always suspected that all women wanted was a little attention."

"Recognition is more like it."

"You know I'm a supporter of women's rights." A shadow crossed Ned's face, and his gaze moved to the window overlooking the university district. Like Suki, the woman he'd chased to Hong Kong had been an aspiring newspaper reporter committed to women's betterment.

"What about equal work at the newspapers?" Suki asked gently. "I know a member of the fairer sex who's been learning journalism's methods under your generous tutelage for almost two years."

Ned faced her with one of his charming grins. "I walked straight into that one."

Suki tilted her head to the side. It was time for Ned to talk, and her to listen. He knew she wanted to be done with writing about ball gowns and stolen kisses. She was ready for the opportunity to better her city and country by reporting on the abuses that threatened the fragile relationship between the foreign and Japanese communities: the bribery and blackmail, the secret agreements undermining the rule of law and spirit of economic freedom, and the everyday accusations, insults, and deceits that eroded mutual goodwill. Ned needed to do what was fair and uphold his end of their bargain.

He placed his reading glasses on the desk and rubbed his eyes. "You think you've got the…spirit for the job. But a reporter has to be willing to take risks, to dig deeper, to take on the ugly side of life, and there's plenty of ugliness in this city. My men don't give up. They don't take 'no' for an answer." His gaze fixed on her kimono. "Japanese women are too obliging when sources don't wish to talk."

Biting anger on behalf of Japanese women broke through Suki's calm demeanor. "Don't let the kimono fool you. There are plenty of Japanese women talking back to men. Women are protesting in factories. They're working as train conductors and salespeople where they exercise as much authority as men."

"I'll grant you that point, Miss Malveaux." Ned pulled a letter-size envelope from the pile of correspondence on his desk and placed it in front of Suki. "I received this yesterday. It might give you a chance to prove your abilities."

"You want me to investigate the conservative faction?"

Ned had presented Suki with similar envelopes before. Usually, these contained missives from conservatives who loved—and loved to hate—the Tattler. They loved her column for giving them a window into how the country's elites had succumbed to decadent Western lifestyles by committing outrageous offenses like dining on roasted meats and allowing their wives and daughters to wear gowns that hinted at the shape of a woman's bust and hips. Or, even better, how these modern Japanese had flirted, kissed, and cavorted with the foreign devils.

They hated the Tattler because they couldn't abide a foreign newspaper columnist bringing shame to *their* people in a foreign language for a foreign audience. The Tattler turned the upper classes' dalliances into a form of entertainment; the conservatives wanted to use these as ammunition for social revolution.

Ned handed Suki the envelope. "I doubt the conservative faction wrote this one."

The message had been penned in neat English script:

Please inform your Tattler to look closer at the activities of Baron Umezono. If it is scandal your Tattler wants, then it is scandal your Tattler will find.

It was a gossipy tip, and the conservative faction had sent her tips before, but they'd never attempted to turn a clever phrase. "The author is an English speaker of high, if not native, abilities. The conservatives could have hired someone to write it, perhaps a sympathizer among the foreign population."

Ned pointed to the envelope. "The postmark is from Tsukiji."

"That would fit, if they received foreign assistance. Have you heard of Baron Umezono?"

"I've heard the name. He is one of the more debauched members of the nobility. Even if you find simple gossip about an affair here and there, verification for any claim against him must meet a higher standard than anything involving our Tsukiji neighbours. You'd be able to exercise your investigative skills."

Ned was stringing her along. Adding a journalistic twist to her work on the Tattler was a poor substitute for giving her a story of social importance. "This message is just the conservatives making noise about profligate Japanese. They are the same people who were thrilled when I wrote about the vice-minister who'd groveled an apology to the British Legation's doorman for being unable to repay his gambling debts."

Ned tilted his head back in laughter. "He thought the doorman was that Irish cardsharp."

"I believe the cardsharp forgave most of the vice-minister's debt when the story came out."

"You did well with that piece. Why don't you follow up on this tip about the baron? See what you can find."

If Ned needed a demonstration of her abilities to go deep with a story, then she'd go deep with Baron Umezono. "I'll investigate the baron and provide you with an article of the highest journalistic merit. Afterward, I'd like to assume responsibility for a story your regular reporters would cover."

"Impress me with your journalism and we'll talk about your future at the newspaper."

CHAPTER FIVE

Natsu Watanabe fanned her décolletage. "Western theater is awfully stuffy," she said, her crimson lips in a pout that demanded Griff probe her discontent.

"You thought *The Importance of Being Earnest* was too reserved?"

"People were laughing." She directed an expansive wave of her fan at the audience leaving their seats. "The play wasn't reserved."

"Then it's the theatre building you find stuffy?" Of course, she was referring to the humidity generated by a hundred or so audience members milling about the Tokyo Player's amateur performance hall. Nevertheless, Griff played his part; teasing out English meanings was their habit.

"Griff-*san*, you know very well I speak of the theater," she said with a laugh that would signal amusing banter to those around them.

He offered her an arm as they exited the aisle, which she used to pull herself up against him, her breasts pushing into his biceps. "If 'stuffy' isn't the right word, you must teach me the right one later."

That was the line she'd fed him the first night he'd spent at her apartments. Earlier that evening, he'd escorted her to an exhibit of Greco-Buddhist art, where she'd told him she had a "penchant" for a stucco frieze.

He responded with a confused expression, which must have stayed with her because later that evening in the rickshaw, while her fingers traced circles on the top of his knee and his untended erection practically tore a hole in his pants, she requested a substitute for "penchant." All Griff could do was growl, "'Like' is decent. Say 'I like it very much.'" Which she did many times that night and had done many times since. Now he couldn't hear the phrase, even incidentally, without wincing.

"I don't think there will be a *later* tonight," he said.

"But, Griff-*san*," she whispered into his neck. "You must be in need of love."

"We can talk about it later."

Natsu winked. "Then there will be a later. I'm so glad you changed your mind."

Griff glanced longingly at the lobby door, ready to put the night behind him. He'd brought her to *The Importance of Being Earnest* to fulfil a promise he'd made to show her the play that had all of London, and Tsukiji, abuzz. He'd also wanted to submit his feelings to one final test: did any desire remain for Natsu?

She was a gorgeous, enticing woman. Accompanying her to concerts, suppers, hot-air balloon launches, flower viewings, and the newest French restaurants had made him the envy of every man in Tsukiji. More than a few chaps at the lawn tennis club had told him they'd give an eye, a leg, even one of their balls to be in Griff's place. Had they any idea of what Natsu was like in the bedroom, the shedding of appendages would have cost the tennis club half its membership.

Natsu was the dream of his horny, unsatisfied, younger self, who would have cherished every moan at his touch and every protest against the torment his large member caused when it breached her delicate quim.

"What kind of woman must I be to want something that brings me such pain?" she had to know each and every time they made love.

Inevitably, the novelty of their coupling wore off, and he came to realise Natsu's sole interest in life was him. She only ever wanted to talk about his genius at work, although she didn't seem certain of what he did. Or his prowess on the lawn tennis court, even though she'd never seen him play. Or the admiration he garnered from

Tsukiji's residents. Given his reputation as the town Lothario, he highly doubted that one.

A recurring topic of conversation was how their meeting at Tsukiji's moon-viewing party had been fate intervening to save both their lives: his generous care had rescued her from devastating grief over the loss of her husband; her gentle touch had restored him after Victoria's ruthless departure. Over time, Natsu had embellished the story of their mutual sadness to the point that he half-expected her to describe them meeting on the banks of a rushing river prepared to fling themselves into the abyss.

One night, after nearly causing penile damage with a set of spirited pelvic twists, she'd needed to know if he'd noticed that she'd been wearing the gown he'd praised a few weeks before. She also wondered whether he appreciated having been served his favourite beef dish for the evening meal. Was he pleased when, following the meal, she presented him with the tobacco he most enjoyed smoking?

"I've studied you, Griff-*san*. I know your every need and desire even better than you know them yourself. Imagine our future together," she said with a triumphant grin.

They hadn't slept together since.

Over the past month, they'd dined at Natsu's favourite Chinese restaurant, gone to a cherry blossom viewing picnic, and taken a stroll through Shinjuku's gardens, but he hadn't been back to her apartments. She attributed his lack of interest to grief over the loss of his brother, and he let her believe the fiction. In truth, he yearned to lose himself in a woman's tender affections. Most recently, his need had grown into a distraction he should have banished on Natsu's willing body. But he hesitated. No matter how much he craved release, her clingy attentions and presumptions about their imminent marriage made their outings a chore he had no desire to prolong.

The lobby filled with Tokyo Players greeting their audience. Natsu nodded at a Japanese count known for his theatre patronage and animated retellings of the several boisterous years he'd spent in

London. "Might I speak with the count? He's so good at explaining these plays to me."

"By all means," Griff replied.

Natsu fluttered her lashes and stuck out her lower lip, a gesture that meant she was sorry for something that one needn't be sorry for, like when she poured too much of his favourite whisky into the glass or straddled his hips when it was time for him to leave in the morning. The present look of contrition on her face probably referred to the sorrow she felt for his inability to understand the count's rapid Japanese. Or she felt sorry for the envy she would induce as he watched her listen to another man's brilliance. Were he to spend the rest of the night with Natsu, she would turn to him while releasing her hair or removing her undergarments and ask whether he hated her for talking with the count.

No, there was no desire left for Natsu Watanabe.

***

Griff dismissed the rickshaw runner in front of the redbrick building that housed Natsu's apartments. "Shall we take a stroll?" he asked, betting that passersby and the open windows of homes in the fashionable Ginza district would temper her response when he ended the affair.

"Do you want to hear more of what the count thought about tonight's play?"

"No, I want us to talk."

Natsu took his arm. "I have whisky waiting upstairs that you could enjoy while we talk. But the night air is refreshing. We should stroll. Although that may make you hungry. There's a delicious soba restaurant on the next block if you wish to eat."

"Let's just walk."

At the end of the block, Griff stopped and faced her. "I want to explain why I cannot come to your apartments tonight."

"Do you have an early morning appointment? My maid will wake you."

"I don't have an appointment. My life is very full right now with my niece and nephew arriving. I need time to prepare."

"I can help. How about a French meal for their first evening in Tokyo? They'll feel more comfortable with a taste from home. I'll decide on the menu. But you must tell that housekeeper Rei-*san* to obey my instructions. She never listens to me."

The suggestion that loyal, efficient, conscientious Rei-*san* needed correction strengthened his conviction to get the deed over with as soon as possible. "There will be no menu, Natsu. Our affair has reached a place where it can go no further. I cannot be your husband."

Natsu covered her open mouth as laughter spilled forth. "Griff-*san*, I don't need to marry you. I'm an independent woman. Marriage is not necessary for me."

Was this a joke? Was he supposed to laugh? One of her dearest pastimes was waxing lyrical about how happy they'd be spending the rest of their days together, the beautiful children they'd have, the entertaining she'd do in his home. She'd even had the gall to ask his friends' wives to advocate on her behalf. In a single week, three of his mates had demanded to know when he was planning to propose a lifetime union with Natsu so their wives would quit harping. Now she would dare deny that she'd ever wanted marriage. "But you've always talked about us marrying."

She took his hand in hers and squeezed. "I'm sorry to have given you that impression. I didn't mean to hurt you. The truth is, I'm happy with our being lovers. Come to my apartments, and I'll show you how happy I am to be your lover."

"I'm not coming to your apartments tonight."

Dropping his hand, Natsu lifted her chin, turned on her heel, and hastened back to the redbrick building. He followed in the wake of her cloying, floral scent. At the entrance, she turned to face him.

Tears filled her eyes. "You have another lover. She was at your house two nights ago. I saw the two of you together."

His mind went to an image of Suki seated next to the parlour windows. Had Natsu been spying on him? "That woman is not my lover. She's helping me find a governess for the wards. How did you know she was there?"

"I came to your house because I wanted to present you with a box of ripe strawberries. They were perfect strawberries."

"Rei-*san* never mentioned your coming to the house."

"I couldn't ring your bell when I saw you with that woman. You were laughing in such a foul manner." She pulled a handkerchief from her reticule and wiped her eyes. "I know you're sad because of your brother's death, and you have many obligations with his children coming to Tokyo. But I cannot accept your apology, Griff-*san*. Not now. I'll retire to my apartments and think about it."

The doorman gave Natsu a deep bow and opened the door.

Griff couldn't believe what he'd just heard. Natsu expected him to apologise for her spying. Granted, it might have been upsetting for her to see the way he'd been looking at Miss Malveaux in her proper teacher's kimono with strands of hair framing a face neither European nor Japanese, but more beautiful for being both. But had Natsu been sincerely troubled at having seen his reaction to Miss Malveaux, she would have sought clarification earlier. Instead, she'd stored the incident to wield when she'd needed an advantage.

Rickshaws lined the block, but Griff walked in the opposite direction. As much as he wished to be home sipping whisky, he needed to spend his agitation. Several blocks later, he reached the Tsukiji gates, his head cooled by the crisp night air and his mind eased by the realisation that soon enough he'd be through with Natsu's antics. As he passed the stone façade of the Anglican church, its steeple taller than Tokyo's highest buildings, his thoughts drifted to the questions that had plagued him since Victoria had departed for England the previous year: why hadn't she been more amenable to Japan? Why hadn't she been more amenable to him?

They'd been sweethearts in the blush of first love when he'd proposed they shorten their courtship and she join him for the new posting in Tokyo. The tentative smile she gave in response was the best surprise of his life. Victoria was not the kind of woman who travelled well. She balked at the notion of stepping foot in London. Whenever they mused about their wedding trip, she described a fortnight in Blackpool while he envisioned a tour of the continent. Nevertheless, she gazed upon him as though he'd invented gravity and her much beloved Stilton cheese. On their wedding night, he lost himself between her thighs and declared himself the happiest man in the world.

She boarded the ship to Japan with professions of excitement and a belief they would produce a baby while at sea. The mission hospitals in Tsukiji offered superior care, she'd heard. If she fell pregnant on the ship, it would only be a few months in the new country before a tiny bundle of joy arrived to calm her nerves. Yet, with each nautical mile that accrued between themselves and England, their lovemaking became less frequent, and her trepidation more paralysing.

Their lives in Tsukiji centred around her discomfort. They constructed a home meant to relieve her fears of earthquakes and floods; they avoided Japanese foods to protect her weak constitution. On those innumerable days when she couldn't leave her bed for the harsh cold of winter or the unbearable heat of summer, he remained by her side, pining to explore the vast city before him, to sink into the hot waters of the famed spa resorts, to inhale the wonders of the country that fascinated him more with each passing day.

The annulment of their marriage had stung like a slap in the face and left him with several uncomfortable truths. He hadn't been enough; their love hadn't been enough; and he should have known better than to bring her to Tokyo.

Although it was nearing midnight when he returned home, Rei-san greeted him with soft slippers and a warm towel. He accepted both gratefully and retired to his study, where she'd placed his whisky and glass. He stewed over the business with Natsu until the whisky eased her into a minor annoyance. In short order, he'd end their affair once and for all, and she was going to accept their parting.

Fortunately, Tokyo was not London. Natsu's reputation wouldn't suffer for having stepped out with him for the previous half-year. She was yet a respected war widow and the ideal wife for a man who relished the weighty attentions of a beautiful woman. One day, Natsu would thank him for releasing her to find someone with whom she was better suited.

As for his reputation, there was nothing to lose. According to the Tokyo Tattler, his wild lust for Japanese women had already driven a new bride from Tokyo. Abandoning Natsu would merely confirm his rakish character.

He took a long sip of whisky and snippets of the Tattler's words came back to him.

Who else saw the dashing couple exchanging looks of love at the officer's club in Ginza? ... Griffith Spenser and his lovely mistress Mrs. Natsu Watanabe, widow of the late officer Gentaro Watanabe... the widow in light blue silk... neckline not too low as to scandalize, but low enough to tease her lover with the bountiful breast beneath. So unlike a Japanese woman to possess such a breast!... your Tattler must wonder what will happen to our dear war widow in the clutches of the foreign Lothario?... the incorrigible rake... whatever happened to the bride who accompanied Mr. Spenser less than a year before?... did Mr. Spenser's roving eye force her return to Mother England?... the Tattler can only imagine how many lovers Mr. Spenser has taken... what will Mrs. Watanabe do when his roving eye alights on another of our native beauties?

The Tattler would devise all manner of lies about how the affair with Natsu ended. He bristled at the thought of Marianne and Lucien arriving in Tsukiji to learn of his skewed reputation. At least his close friends laughed off the portrayal of Griffith Spenser, incorrigible rake. They assured him that everyone knew the Tattler was an opportunist who exaggerated the smallest rumour for the sake of attracting readers to her column.

Unfortunately, it worked; the Tattler was widely read. Even friends who dismissed the rumours had read the drivel in the first place. Natsu relished showing him what the Tattler had written, brandishing descriptions of her necklines as though she was appalled at having been noticed. Indeed, the Tattler wrote so glowingly of Natsu that he often wondered whether Natsu knew the witch personally. Requesting the Tattler publish stories of their affair was exactly the sort of means Natsu would use to stake her claim. The more public the relationship, the higher the price for any woman who would dare set her sights on Griff, and the greater the pressure on him to make Natsu his wife.

Of course, Natsu herself could very well be the Tattler. Her English was good enough; she knew everyone in Tsukiji. Ned Taylor was never one to resist a woman's charms. What were the chances that Natsu had spread her legs in a bid to author the column?

That would mean Natsu was the one who had turned the private shame of his marriage's end into a public scandal. Had she thought that devastating his character would make him an easier catch? He couldn't even contemplate having slept with someone so vile.

He finished off the glass and poured himself a second. First Victoria, then Natsu. Both proved to be far more difficult than he'd bargained for. He was through with difficult women. He needed someone easy to be with, easy to talk to, easy to laugh with. Like Suki Malveaux.

Whisky's familiar dizziness settled into his head, and the sound of his yawn filled the study. He ought to retire to his room and spare Rei-*san* the sight of him passed out on the settee. But he had thoughts left to think, particularly thoughts about the woman who had been at his home a few nights before. Miss Malveaux was uncomplicated, yet intriguing. And quite attractive, which he could overlook for the sake of their being friends.

Because friendship was what he needed, and Miss Malveaux would be a marvellous friend. Marriage didn't interest her. That was the type of woman he needed. Someone with no designs on him. Someone who paid no attention to the Tattler's idle gossip.

First, he'd get rid of Natsu, then he'd spend more time with friendly spinsters like Miss Malveaux. Griff finished the glass of whisky, then stretched out on the settee to bathe in the warmth of the fire's last embers before his heavy eyelids shut.

CHAPTER SIX

Suki arrived at the wrought-iron gates of Tsukiji's largest home at the same time as the dairy delivery. She engaged the young man carting the family's considerable haul in conversation as they walked past the tall white columns to the servants' entrance in back where freshly washed linens dried in the sunshine's abundant rays and the scent of greens unfurling from the damp earth filled the air.

Today was the first day of the Ginza Girls School's spring holiday, and she foremost wished to catch up with her dearest friend, Marcelle Renaud, lady's maid to the American envoy's wife. Aside from Ned Taylor, Marcelle was the only person who knew Suki was the Tokyo Tattler, and her connections among those in service were a rich source of gossipy tidbits.

A gathering following the Tokyo Players' final performance of *The Importance of Being Earnest* had already yielded a few tasty morsels for this week's column. If Marcelle were to provide Suki with a few more titillating *on-dit*, she'd have gossip enough to bask in the luxury of having four full days to sharpen her word selection and apply the most apt phrasing. This week's Tattler would reach new levels of journalistic excellence, insofar as society pages could be considered journalism.

Learning about Baron Umezono's scandalous activities was another of Suki's aims for the spring holiday, and she was hoping Marcelle might have a tip. She'd tasked her *bonne amie* with learning anything she could about the baron, and the previous evening Marcelle had sent a message that she was in possession of *une grande rumeur* that Suki had been waiting for.

As it turned out, Suki had *une grande nouvelle* of her own, for which she needed her best friend's unfailingly sage advice.

Marcelle called a greeting from the kitchen garden. She wore a linen maid's apron over a day dress the color of a cloudless sky. Atop her dark curls sat a sunbonnet covered in wild irises that spilled stylishly over the rim, and a basket of leafy plants with pink stalks hung from her arm. "*Rhubarbe, ma chérie amie.*"

"*Rhubarbe*," Suki repeated.

"In English it's rhubarb." Marcelle inflected the word with her employer's American accent. "The master of the house loves rhubarb pies."

"Who in the world would think to make a pie out of those things?"

Marcelle gave the greens a look that should have made them shrivel on the spot. "The chef was not French, I can promise you that."

"Is it awful?"

Marcelle shrugged at the stalky plant. "Actually, it's passable, but why bother with rhubarb when you have plums and pears?"

"And apples."

"Now you sound like an American." Marcelle put down the basket and looped her arm through Suki's. "You're half-French, *ma chérie amie*. Must I always remind you?" she said with an exaggerated eye roll.

They'd been friends since Marcelle arrived in Tsukiji three years before. The American envoy's wife, whose upbringing dictated she employ the services of a French lady's maid, had recruited Marcelle straight out of a dress shop in Paris. An orphan from infancy, Marcelle spent her childhood being tossed between family members for whom it had been most convenient to accommodate the child. Nevertheless, she received an adequate education and set her sights on becoming a Parisian modiste and marrying a certain Parisian gentleman. All hope for a lifetime of wedded bliss was lost when her lover left Paris one week with a passionate kiss and returned the following with a wife. Soon thereafter, the envoy's wife invited Marcelle to join her family in Japan.

The timing of the offer couldn't have been better for all parties, Suki included. Tattler reports on Tsukiji's fashion choices owed much to the envoy's wife. Her discerning eye sorted every fringe, feather, button, and bauble at Tokyo's glamorous events into those she requested Marcelle to procure for her, those that meant nothing to her, and those she hoped her Tsukiji neighbors wouldn't dare try again.

Marcelle pulled Suki over to the pathway through the garden. "We should walk. The daughters' French has greatly improved, and they always want to know what we're whispering about."

"Do they suspect I'm the Tattler?"

"They're not clever enough to suppose. But they accuse me of being secretive and having a lover from Japan's upper classes. They've decided you are the go-between. As if I would need a go-between."

Suki leaned toward her best friend until the modest assortment of roses on her sunbonnet met the spectacular irises of Marcelle's. "Mademoiselle Renaud, have you taken a lover and not told me?"

"I would always tell you in the event. So far there's only been the Japanese colonel, and that was only a handful of times. And the American doctor who was still a bachelor at the time, which everyone knew about, and those glorious nights I spent at the Dutch envoy's residence when the queen's cousin was visiting, which no one knows about except you and the queen's cousin's valet."

"I'm glad to be kept apprised. Now what is the *grande rumeur* you spoke of in yesterday's message?"

"It will be the centerpiece of this week's column."

"Baron Umezono has earned a place in the Tattler column?" Suki asked hopefully.

"Not the baron."

Suki groaned inwardly. Her wish that the baron investigation would be simple and straightforward was clearly not coming true. "I thought this week's centerpiece story was Madame Clark teaching the Tokyo Players how to mix the martini cocktail." A maid at the home of a principal actor had passed along several scintillating tales about the gathering that had followed the Players' final performance.

After tugging a few violet blooms from a rosemary bush in the herb garden, Marcelle held the tiny petals up to her nose, then scattered them along the pathway. "From what I heard, Madame Clare drank more than all the others combined and still stayed upright. The esteemed Madame Harrison, however, had to be carried home by three of the younger Players, who were as drunk as she."

Picturing several young Players hoisting the rotund woman admired for her vocal range onto their shoulders reduced Suki to giggles. "What could you possibly tell me that would surpass that?"

"The next chapter in the ongoing saga of incorrigible rake meets war widow." Marcelle gave Suki a sly smile. "Natsu Watanabe has been inquiring about wedding gowns."

Suki's world spun. Griffith Spenser and Watanabe were getting married. How was this possible after the message he'd sent her?

The previous afternoon, Suki had received a message from Spenser about accompanying him to Ueno Park to see the carp streamers displayed in honor of Boys' Day. He'd wondered whether she might enlighten him on the reason for the gigantic fish waving in the breeze.

It may prove enjoyable for us to discuss the care of my niece and nephew out of doors, he'd written.

Her first impulse had been to dance about the back parlor, message held aloft, while gleefully shouting to Rosie and her sons about a park invitation from Spenser. Surprised at her girlish response, she'd retreated to her room and collapsed on her bed to consider the reasons why she'd nearly lost her senses over the prospect of strolling the park with Spenser. *He was a bona fide rascal.* He was also the epitome of a gentleman in taking care of his niece and nephew. And so downright appealing that recalling the way he'd looked at her while she'd spoken sent weakness through her limbs and made her skin burn.

He was also having an affair with a gorgeous war widow. So, why had he decided on meeting to view the carp streamers? He must have understood that an afternoon in Ueno Park would mean spending hours in one another's company and possibly taking a meal together, depending on the timing. Moreover, requesting a Japanese woman's explanation of cultural traditions was a ploy of many an interested foreigner. Was Spenser committing an act of seduction?

Propped up on her bed pillows, she'd reread the message and grown increasingly bothered by its impertinence. He was suggesting a public outing that would appear to any onlooker like a romantic occasion. This, while escorting an upstanding war widow around town, was not within the bounds of propriety.

Suki's sources had reported seeing Spenser and Watanabe at the final showing of *The Importance of Being Earnest*. Although an unremarkable sighting as the couple didn't attend the raucous post-performance gathering, it nevertheless bore mention in the column after what the Tattler had written the previous week about their absence from the public eye. The fact was that they were very much a couple, and Spenser shouldn't be asking for another woman's company in Ueno Park no matter the depths of his cultural curiosity about Boys' Day celebrations.

Marcelle, wise about everything that occurred between the sexes, was supposed to enlighten Suki as to how she should respond. Her present disappointment owed much to the fact that she'd fully anticipated her best friend would insist she enjoy Spenser's company under the colorful streamers, his motivations be damned and his relationship with Madame Watanabe notwithstanding. A promise of marriage would certainly change that.

"Are you surprised?" Marcelle asked.

Suki gazed at the cherry trees stripped of their glorious pink blossoms and still unsure about the bright green leaves unfurling on their branches. "Well, yes. How did you find out?"

"Yesterday, I was looking everywhere for lilac blue lace that I could use to create an eye-catching detail on the elder daughter's dress. Madame Pennington, owner of Dress American, and Mademoiselle Lowell, the seamstress for Madame Shearer, both mentioned Madame Watanabe had come around to ask what kind of wedding dress they might envision for a summer affair. That gives you two reports, which must meet the Tattler standards. Although with those two gossips spreading the news, everyone in Tsukiji will know about the engagement by next week's publication. But your readers won't believe it until they hear it from the Tattler. It's such a dramatic finale to Monsieur Spenser's woes, don't you think? With his wife leaving and his niece and nephew soon to arrive."

Suki swallowed hard and summoned all the indifference she could muster. "How fortunate for the family."

Marcelle pulled a handkerchief from her apron and patted her brow and the damp hairs framing her face. "Truthfully, I'd thought after your meeting with Monsieur Spenser the other evening, he was going to pursue the charming Mademoiselle Malveaux."

"What could possibly make you think so?"

"You accused him of having warts, and he nearly fainted with laughter. Then you said he was giving you the eye. Obviously, he took pleasure in your company. Anyone with sense would conclude you'd become the Englishman's object of desire." She gave Suki's arm a gentle squeeze and led them toward peach trees growing heavy with buds.

"Apparently, that was not the case," Suki replied.

"Now, what was this *grande nouvelle* you received? Something to do with that Baron Umezono?"

"No," Suki said, her voice wobbly with dashed hopes that she never should have hoped for to begin with. "It had to do with

Monsieur Spenser. He sent a message requesting that I take a walk with him in Ueno Park to view the carp streamers."

Marcelle glared at Suki as though she'd been the one who'd committed an unspeakable offense. "Monsieur Spenser requested an afternoon stroll with you, a woman he finds beautiful and intelligent. Those were his words, correct?"

"He said that."

"While his future bride is searching for a gown to wear at their wedding?" Marcelle's gaze smoldered. "He ought to be punished, whipped, flogged."

"He wants to discuss his wards," Suki said meekly, figuring Marcelle should be fully appraised of the circumstances before passing judgment.

Marcelle walked several paces ahead of Suki as they rounded the bushes at the back of the garden, while grumbling about the various punishments Monsieur Spenser had earned, several of which involved inflicting irreparable damage to the place between his legs. "There are other ways to discuss his wards." She finished with a wag of her finger.

Suki sighed. Marcelle's logic was sound, but Suki felt an irresistible pull toward an altogether different logic—never minding that it might not make a lick of sense. "He wants to learn about the cultural significance of carp streamers, too."

Marcelle rolled her gaze as she retook Suki's arm and led them along the pathway. "Monsieur Spenser wants to stare at your pert breasts."

"My brother Roger believes Monsieur Spenser is a good fellow. Seeing as Madame Watanabe has been inquiring about wedding gowns, he's obviously committed to her. I'm inclined to give him the benefit of the doubt. After all, I do have a reputation around Tsukiji for being expert in translating Japan's cultural traditions. Madame Yamashita must have told him as much when she recommended me for the governess position."

Marcelle gasped. "Then you're going to accept the invitation?"

"The carp streamers are a magnificent sight, and if the weather is as nice as today, it should be spent out of doors. I doubt under the circumstances of his impending nuptials he'll turn into a flirtatious rake." Indeed, the more she thought about Spenser's motivations, the more innocent his invitation seemed.

"He'll flirt. Men cannot help but flirt with women they find beautiful. But you must flirt back. You need the practice. That way when the perfect man comes along, you'll have him wrapped around your finger in no time."

An afternoon in the park giggling, flattering, and presenting Tsukiji's Lothario with come-hither expressions would serve to hone her skills. And when the perfect man failed to come along, her new powers of persuasion might serve her journalistic endeavors. "I'll do just that."

They returned to the kitchen garden, and Marcelle picked up the basket of rhubarb. "Don't forget to tell him about the two French women in Yokohama who are interested in the maid position."

"I'll pass along their qualifications during our walk in the park."

Marcelle narrowed her eyes. "On second thought, don't tell him about the younger one. She isn't trustworthy, and we need a spy in the house."

"A spy is no longer necessary. Monsieur Spenser is going to marry Madame Watanabe. There won't be any more gossip."

"Imagine the people who will pass through their doors, the stories his servants will overhear. A spy would be invaluable to the Tattler."

"I like to think my days as the Tattler are numbered."

Marcelle pouted. "Don't you *dare*. Tsukiji would be so boring without the column. Every woman in town tears open the newspaper on Wednesday morning to read about who wore the right gown, who chose the most brilliant jewels, who had her hair styled to perfection. That's why French maids are in such demand. No one dresses a woman more elegantly or provocatively."

"Someone else can write the Tattler. I plan to become a journalist, which is why I had been hoping your *grande rumeur* concerned Baron Umezono."

"Aah, the baron." Marcelle shifted the basket of rhubarb to her other hip. "I did learn something of the *bon vivant*. A maid at the British Legation has a sister who is a maid for a different baron, and she asked around and learned that your Baron Umezono is not especially awful. Visits brothels and gambles away his money at the Hotel Metropolis even though he doesn't have much of it."

Suki's ears perked up at the hotel's name. "Why does everyone seem to get in trouble at that hotel?"

"It's international. People can be whoever they want and do whatever catches their fancy. Japanese aristocrats pretend they're cosmopolitan gentlemen in the clutches of world-class courtesans."

Drawn by the rhubarb's surprisingly sweet scent, Suki picked a stalk from Marcelle's basket and held it near her nose for a long inhale. "If only misbehavior at Metropolis made for serious investigative journalism."

"You could visit the baron's favorite brothel." Marcelle drew Suki in closer. "The British Legation maid told me it has a spa where multiple women take turns giving him a soapy massage."

"Very clean, yet also very dirty."

"I have the name of the place if you'd like it."

Suki shook her head at the suggestion. "Then I could discover the shocking news that Baron Umezono is a man who takes pleasure in being handled by multiple women at the same time. That letter about the baron is feeling more like the work of the conservative faction."

"Aren't they the ones who send you all that mail?"

Suki rolled her eyes. "They despise me for putting their countrymen's sins on display for anyone who can read English. I dread the day they find out I'm the Tattler. A woman and a half-breed, contaminated by foreign blood."

"They're bloodsucking leeches. Benefiting from foreign-learning while crying for foreigners to leave."

Suki agreed. "They want to send Japan back to the dark ages of warlords and samurai and women waiting on their every move."

Marcelle threw her hands in the air. The basket leapt from her hip, sending its stalky contents in every direction. "A delicious fantasy that has only ever existed in the minds of lustful young men. Conservatives must accept that Japan is becoming more modern every day. Are they unaware the emperor wears Western dress, drinks coffee, and eats meat at his evening meal?"

Suki picked stalks off the pathway and returned them to the basket. "They're the first to show up at St. Luke's Hospital when their families are suffering lung disease or dysentery."

"Hypocrites all of them." Marcelle huffed and returned the basket to her hip.

"Baron Umezono is probably a fine man with a weakness for certain vices. Most of the Hotel Metropolis's guests seem to fall into the same boat." Suki grabbed Marcelle's elbow. "We should go there and witness the baron's behavior for ourselves. Then I can tell Ned I've exhausted all possible routes of investigation."

"Oh yes. We must do something outrageous. It's been far too long since I had any fun. Let's go tonight."

"Tomorrow would be better, I need time to plan, consider the questions I'll ask if the baron is in attendance. Even in his absence, I could inquire among employees at the hotel about his reputation. There is a chance, a remote one to be certain, that this will be the first step in my journalistic career."

"I'll select a few gowns the mistress wore last season and make the necessary adjustments."

"Excellent. Then we'll blend in with the other revelers."

"*Au contraire.* We'll stun them all with our *beauté française.*"

Suki grumbled in protest. "We have to proceed with discretion, preserve our anonymity, immerse ourselves in the crowd."

Marcelle patted Suki's hand. "I'm going to put you in the gown the mistress wore to the opening of the Tsukiji Art Museum. By the end of the night, the name Suki Malveaux will be on everyone's lips."

An image flashed through Suki's mind of Spenser staring agape at her pert breasts straining the neckline of a scarlet tulle concoction. Heat sprang to her cheeks. She had to cease this knee-jerk fascination with the man and resolve herself to plain facts: Spenser and Watanabe were getting married, and she was getting a walk in the park.

CHAPTER SEVEN

The doorman at Natsu's building eyed Griff as though he'd emerged from a fetid bog. Whenever Griff accompanied Natsu back to her apartments, the young man practically fell over himself to assist her with shopping items and lead her to the elevator, with no regard to a perfectly capable Griff who stood right there. Natsu, in turn, would lavish praise on the lad for his assistance and later complain to Griff about the excessive care beautiful women had to endure.

Griff could well imagine Natsu inviting the doorman up for a cup of *sake*, then letting him take his pleasure. Griff hadn't made love to Natsu for a month, and she often told him how much she craved a stiff serpent.

Bravo for the pair.

Unfortunately, no matter how well the strapping young man twirled his serpent, he wasn't going to satisfy Natsu's desire for a place in Tsukiji. She wasn't going to let Griff go without a fight.

Natsu's maid led Griff into the parlour to wait for Natsu. He walked to the window overlooking Ginza Boulevard. The day's last rays of sunshine cast a soft light on shoppers, students, and servants, breaking away from the gaslit streets towards the narrow residential blocks as the nighttime establishments came to life. He almost made out the pub that served the best grilled chicken in Tokyo.

He'd written to Natsu that he wished to speak with her before an event with the lawn tennis club. That way, she had ample warning that his time with her was limited. When he finally put an end to the affair, she'd only have a fixed amount of time to exhaust her tears, shouting, pleading, self-flagellation, attempts at seduction, or whatever else she came up with in response.

In truth, there was a farewell celebration for a fellow at the lawn tennis club who was returning to London, and Griff very much looked forward to losing himself in the festivities as soon as possible.

"Griff-*san*," Natsu said from the doorway, her voice husky and seductive. "I've been waiting for you." She glided over the thick Persian rug to the ivory settee with the intimidating gilded arms. As usual, her lips gleamed red and her choice of dress, this time a peach and lace flouncy gown, was too extravagant for the occasion. Running a hand across the silk upholstery, she motioned with the other for him to sit. "You must join me."

Griff took one of the high-backed chairs opposite the settee. "I'll sit here."

"As you wish." The affair with Natsu had been going on long enough that he recognized tension in the lines of her beatific smile, and right now there was much tension on display.

The maid placed small puff pastries on the table between the settee and Griff's chair while Natsu poured Griff's tea. "I thought it was too early for whisky, but I have chilled champagne, if you prefer. Shall I light a pipe for you?"

"Natsu, there is something I need to say, and I don't want there to be any misunderstanding between us."

She handed him the tea with a heaping tablespoon of sugar as he preferred. "I've been waiting days to hear you apologize for that visitor last week. You don't know how much it hurt me to see that woman at your home." Her voice quaked with the words.

Griff sipped his tea while Natsu, who had conveniently forgotten that she'd been spying on him under the pretence of delivering strawberries, pulled a handkerchief from her sleeve and wiped her eyes. Placing his teacup on the bone china tray, he addressed her in a firm, even tone, "I'm sorry to have upset you in that case. But that's not the reason for my visit this evening. I came here to tell you that the time has come for our relationship to end."

She lifted her brow ever so slightly, and the inkling of hope that Natsu was going to quietly accept the end of their relationship gave way to hardness in the pit of his stomach. He continued, "It's been a pleasure to spend these past months in your company. You've treated me better than I deserve and for that I'm grateful, but I don't see a future between us. The last time we spoke, you said that you didn't wish for us to marry. I hope that didn't mean you were opposed to the institution, because I believe you'll be most happy when you find a man to marry. Your husband passed away only a few years into your marriage. It'd be a shame for you not to marry again. You've spoken of how much you want children." Sweat formed on his brow at even mentioning the word "children" in front of Natsu. Through the course of their relationship, he'd been careful to use a condom or spill his seed outside her body. Even when he was genuinely enamoured with her, the thought of her bearing the Spenser progeny had given him the sense of being in the thick of a maze with no foreseeable exit. "Wouldn't you like to marry again?"

Her eyes filled with tears. "If that is what you wish."

"I wish for your happiness, and I'm sorry to see you saddened."

"Sorry? There's no need for sorry. I'll find another man and take him as a husband." She pressed the handkerchief against her eyes, then twisted her mouth into a smile that sent chills down his spine. "The truth is, I never really cared for you. The hairs on your arms and chest hurt me, and the smell of those horrid meats you eat makes my stomach turn. You took me places, and that made me glad. Yes, I'll marry a foreign man who will give me the best life. And he'll be much better than you. I hate to disappoint you, Griff-*san*, but it's no matter to me if you leave my apartments this instant or spend the night in my arms."

He rose from the chair. "In that case, I'll take my leave."

"*Wait.*" Natsu reached across the table and grabbed the sleeve of his jacket. "Don't go. I didn't mean what I said." Tears made their way down her cheeks. "The truth is, I love you and I can't live without you."

Griff retook his seat. His jacket was rumpled from where Natsu had held it in her grip. "I know you have strong feelings, but time will ease your sadness. When Victoria left Tokyo, I was devastated. I'd known her my entire life. We'd been married."

Natsu sat bolt upright and wagged a finger at him. "I saved you from sadness. I helped you, and you used my body for your manly whims. Have you forgotten?"

Yes, he'd taken pleasure in her body, and every time she'd insisted he do so. "We have many fond memories. But there is no future for us."

"We can have more fond memories, many more. Don't you want to come home every night to whisky and lovemaking? Isn't that what all men want?"

Griff could grant that a man might content himself with whisky and lovemaking. But true contentment was having a woman by his side who possessed a depth of heart and mind with which to face the joys and travails of their lives together. "Men appreciate those things."

Natsu dug her nails into the settee cushion. The white-knuckle grip made Griff break out in a sweat. "Can't you see? I make you happy. You shouldn't leave me."

"It's time for me to go."

Her bottom lip trembled. "I've listened to every word you've spoken. I know what foods you like, what drinks you prefer, when you need to eat, sleep, bathe, and read alone in the study. I know how to touch you to make those deep sounds come from your mouth. I'll be the perfect wife."

Griff stood, needing a break from Natsu's histrionics. He walked over to the window. Outside, gas lamps twinkled in the darkness and illuminated the passers-by still crowding streets. Sighing, he turned back to her. "Natsu, you're young and spirited. You'll be the perfect wife for another man."

"No woman will ever treat you as well as I." Her words came out like a rattlesnake's hiss.

Griff summoned his most placating tone. "Yes, you've treated me well, but there's no future for us. You have your choice of men. Nearly everyone in Tsukiji wants to be your husband."

Natsu stood and fisted her hands. "But I only want you. I cannot live without you, Griff-*san*. I cannot go on."

"You'll find happiness again."

Her eyes narrowed. "Only you," she said. Spittle gleamed on her lips. She reminded him of his sister's three-year-old daughter the day he'd eaten the last butterscotch. No amount of apologising or promising had consoled her.

At least he could reason with Natsu. "You had a successful, loving union with Watanabe-*san*."

Natsu stomped across the room until she was standing directly before him. "I had a rabbit in the garden when I was a child. I loved that rabbit more than I ever loved my husband." Her voice was pure venom.

He couldn't be cornered by her. If she raised a hand at him, he'd have to stop her from committing a violent act, and he couldn't lay a hand near her. She'd scream in pain no matter how gentle his touch. God, he had to get away.

Manoeuvring around Natsu, who thankfully stayed in place with a mixture of scorn and disbelief on her face, Griff took long strides to the other side of the room and stood behind the settee. That put three pieces of furniture between them, which he found reassuring. "You said your marriage had been a love match."

"My husband meant nothing to me. We never spent more than a few days under the same roof before he went to war and got himself killed."

Time and again, Natsu had talked about how her husband had not only been a hero to the Japanese people but also the centre of her universe. Griff's despondency in the wake of Victoria leaving was nothing compared to the profound sorrow Natsu had experienced in losing her beloved husband. "But you were devastated by grief when we met."

"I had to grieve because you were grieving. Everything I've done has been for you, Griff-*san*. Everything," she said, her voice barely a whisper.

What kind of woman manufactured grief for a man she never loved in order to seduce another? Griff walked to the doorway. "I'm leaving now. I can show myself to the door."

Natsu didn't reply; her head remained bent and tears darkened her bodice.

Griff made it down the hallway to the entrance when a hoarse cry followed by a slew of Japanese filled the apartments, and rapid footfalls preceded Natsu.

She fell to the floor in a deep bow of contrition. "Please don't leave me," she sputtered through tears.

"It's time for me to go."

"But I cannot live without you."

"You're a strong woman, Natsu. I'm not the man for you."

Heaving a few breaths, she rose from the wooden floor and smoothed down her skirts. "You know nothing about me. I've had many lovers since you shared my bed. You thought it was only you, but I had men stronger than you, wealthier than you. You were never enough for me."

Whether those affairs were proof of him being the biggest fool in Tokyo or a fiction she'd devised to save face mattered little. Natsu had paved the way for his exit, and he wasn't about to dawdle. "It sounds like you have plenty of activities to occupy your time. I won't keep you another minute." Griff closed the door behind him.

CHAPTER EIGHT

Breezes off Tokyo Bay wafted through the Hotel Metropolis lobby, lightening the scents of tobacco smoke and perfume. Little about the lobby had changed from when Suki had pranced around the reception area and bounced off the cushioned chairs as a young girl. The walls bore the same paintings of foreigners opening trade between Japan and the Western world. On one canvas, they frolicked in Yokohama's pleasure quarters; on another, they attended a sumo exhibition. In recent years, the sprawling new hotels of Roppongi and Western Tokyo had started attracting the visiting princes, heads-of-state, foreign generals, and wealthiest scions. The Hotel Metropolis nevertheless still claimed its share of dignitaries, diplomats, missionaries, speculators, sightseers, and pleasure-seekers. Its restaurant and bar remained a vital part of Tsukiji's social life.

A first glance provided no hint as to why the hotel had recently become the setting for the Tattler's most salacious gossip. Revelers in silky gowns and well-pressed suits took seats on the lobby sofas, where they sipped from tall glasses and engaged one another in conversation. Suki noticed a reporter from the *Tokyo Daily News* speaking furtively with a Japanese man whose pomade-slick hair and broad moustache marked him as a bureaucrat. Near the grand piano, a Ginza Girls School alumnae conversed with a fair-haired gentleman. Although Suki could only make out his broad, suited back, judging by the enraptured expression on her former student's face, she had to conclude the gentleman was nothing short of a heavenly sight. She noted the young woman's aubergine gown with sheer overlay for mention in the column. The girl would be terribly pleased, and she could use a warning about the foreign male's otherworldly allure.

Marcelle nodded at a group of several women standing near the terrace doors. "Look at the fringe on that rose-colored gown. I'll have to copy it for Madame. And do you see how that bustle sits on the Japanese woman in the dark blue tulle?"

"Too high?" Suki guessed.

"Absolutely not. Look at the balance between her bust and derrière. A truly skillful modiste must have put the gown together. I wonder if *Okasan* did it."

"You must ask her."

"Champagne," cried Marcelle as a waiter passed with a tray of the bubbly amber liquid.

They took seats near the terrace where some rather notable incidents documented in the Tattler column had occurred. As the champagne danced on Suki's tongue, she felt drawn to the gaiety.

Tonight, however, wasn't about tipples and chatter. She was on a mission to observe, and hopefully make the acquaintance of, a scandalous baron. "Half of Tsukiji must be here this evening. I wonder if Baron Umezono is among the crush."

Marcelle glanced at the groups of people talking and strolling the terrace. "How will you find him?" she asked.

The baron was in his thirties and partook of pastimes associated with nighttime hours. A third of the men in the lobby were Japanese, half of whom appeared to be around thirty, and all were partaking in drink. "I'll have no choice but to inquire. I could ask a waiter."

Marcelle leaned into Suki until their bare shoulders touched. "I just saw an Italian gentleman who dined at the envoy's house last week. He was quite insistent that I join him for a late night on the town. Should I pester him about whether he knows the baron?"

Marcelle's bosom threatened to spill over the gold trim along the edge of her bodice. "In that gown? He'll end up pestering you all night. Why don't you stroll the terrace? Listen for any French being spoken. A fellow countryman would be most approachable."

"I shall seek out a citizen," she declared, and returned the look Suki had given her breasts. "And you, *ma chérie amie*, must watch out for the incorrigible rakes as they will certainly be pestering you."

Marcelle had put Suki in a coral taffeta gown her mistress had commissioned when she'd been fond of outlandish sleeve decorations. Suki had been taken aback at how the volume of the layered tulle lent her the appearance of a shapely bust and small waist. "This gown belongs to an envoy's wife. Hardly worth a second glance."

"Madame looked like a giant nectarine in it. You are the ripest peach."

Suki glanced down at the shimmering fabric. "Perhaps an admiring fellow will lead me to the baron? Until then, I'll be questioning the waiters."

She felt for the notepaper and the pencil stub in her reticule. Tonight could be the start of her journalistic career. She must take care to record the facts and be willing to take risks in obtaining them. Catching the eye of a waiter, she summoned him toward her. "Cultivate your sources," Ned said whenever she mentioned befriending a new house servant. A waiter at the Hotel Metropolis would be an invaluable contact for Suki, the Tokyo Tattler, as well as Suki Malveaux, Tokyo's foremost, and only, female newspaper reporter.

The pockmarked youth bowed and offered his assistance.

"I was hoping you could help me in locating a member of the nobility. I heard he frequents the hotel."

The waiter craned his neck while surveying the lobby. "I believe the man seated near the terrace is a marquis."

"Any barons?"

He looked around a second time. "Not that I can see."

"What about the clubrooms?" Suki raised her voice to make herself heard over the rousing start of a piano sonata. "Are many illustrious Japanese playing games this evening?" On one occasion when her family was greeting a foreign professor residing at the hotel, curiosity had led young Suki to a smaller room off the lobby where various games of chance were taking place. Mother and Papa Garrick had the "shock of the summer" when they found their precious Suki questioning a burly Russian on the rules of whist.

"There are plenty of gentlemen in the clubrooms. The good weather seems to have attracted a lot of guests this evening. Your baron may be among them."

Seeing as this waiter had only a vague idea of who was among the hotel's guests, Suki doubted he was going to be her invaluable contact. "Thank you for your help. I believe I can continue the search on my own."

High-pitched laughter from the lobby sofas punctuated the din of conversation. A gorgeous woman was pressing the front of her dress against the sleeve of a naval officer's jacket. Was that the divorcee in residence at the hotel? With the Russian officer she'd pursued at the marquis' ball? Suki's sources would tell her about it tomorrow.

The waiter looked Suki up and down. "Your Japanese is much better than most foreigners."

Earlier that evening, Suki had caught a glimpse of herself in the mirror and noted how the gown's snug fit emphasized the several inches of height she claimed over a typical Japanese woman, and how the bright color made her eyes appear a lighter shade of brown. Wishing to spare the youth any confusion, she admitted, "My father was French and my mother Japanese."

"You look a little of both," he said, giving her another full appraisal.

"Is there a problem, Nakai?" Suki nearly jumped at the barked question from the man who'd suddenly appeared beside her. He was about her height and, like her, appeared to have parents from both East and West.

The waiter bowed low. "I was helping the honorable guest locate a baron."

"Get back to work. I'll help our guest." The man bowed to Suki. "I apologize for the waiter's rudeness. Did he cause any offense?" His refined English contrasted with the guttural Japanese he'd spoken to the waiter.

"None at all. I apologize for having disturbed his work."

The man's stern expression gave way to a solicitous grin that made Suki feel like the most important guest at the hotel. "Perhaps I can help with the search for your baron. I'm the hotel's proprietor, Chase Norton."

Suki's heartbeat quickened. The man offering his help was none other than the mysterious hotelier who'd purchased the Metropolis a few years before. All she knew of Norton was his national origins—American by birth with a Chinese mother—and his success as a man of business with hotels across East Asia. "Pleased to meet you, Mr. Norton. I've visited the Hotel Metropolis over the years and always found it an outstanding establishment."

A bundle of skirts pressed against Suki's gown, sending her out of kilter. Behind her, a trio of Tsukiji matrons, two of whom Suki knew by name, had their ears trained on her conversation with Norton. Before they could launch into pleasantries that would oblige Suki to introduce the hotelier, she issued a glare that would bring immediate silence to a classroom of chatty young women. Normally, she wouldn't be so impolite, but a journalist needed access to her sources.

Norton paid the women no heed. "I appreciate your compliment. I don't spend nearly enough time here as I would like. Too many demands in places far away."

"I've gathered as much from your reputation."

Norton heaved a dramatic sigh. "One endeavors to achieve an unremarkable reputation and becomes known for his absence. And you are?"

"Suki Malveaux, resident of Tsukiji."

"And an American like me?" Norton's poise as he awaited her answer belonged to a man used to being obeyed.

"French father, Japanese mother. When my father returned to France, my mother and I took up residence with an American professor and his family."

"That explains the accent. What an unusual life story."

"I'm sure you've heard stories far more unusual than mine."

"Each accompanied by its own joys and sorrows, which is why we must attend to our own needs first. So please tell me more about this baron you're seeking."

Ned spoke at length about how a reporter had to trust his gut. Right now, her gut was telling her that Norton was the type of hotelier who kept tabs on men with reputations like the baron's. Her gut was also telling her that the rather private hotelier was not likely to welcome newspaper reporters conducting investigations at his hotel. A woman dressed like a delectable peach, however, might not be as objectionable.

Suki took a small step toward Norton. Her gaze caught on the exquisite stitching of his fine wool jacket. He was the sort of man who stayed on the edges of the crowd and no one paid a bit of notice until calamity broke out and he was the one who took control. She curled her lips into her best seductive smile. "I'm looking for a Baron Umezono. I have a message that must be delivered directly to his person."

Norton nodded slowly. "Such a message should be delivered forthwith. I believe the Baron Umezono is in one of our clubrooms this evening."

The baron was at the hotel. Everything was falling into place. "I would greatly appreciate your pointing me in his direction."

"The last time I saw the baron, he was in the clubroom at the far end of the terrace. One of my waiters will direct you."

"Thank you, but I know where the clubrooms are located," Suki said as though she was well-practiced at seeking out barons at hotels.

Norton inched toward her. "Go easy on the baron," he said with a lingering glance at her neckline that left Suki pleased to be taken for a seductress and perturbed that her best friend had dressed her like a harlot. "His arm is in a sling."

A sling raised more than a few questions of journalistic interest. Suki gave her most gracious thanks to the hotelier and cut through the terrace crowd to locate Marcelle. It didn't take long to find her. She stood under a gas lamp near the hotel bar. The men seated at the tables nearby seemed to be keeping tabs on her from the corner of their eyes. But judging by the way Marcelle gazed at the dark-haired man with whom she was speaking, those other men were out of luck. And judging by the way her gentleman's gaze was so riveted on her face that he wouldn't notice an earthquake until he was flat on the terrace flagstones, Marcelle was decidedly *in* luck.

Marcelle nodded to her companion. "I'd like to introduce Vasu Chakrabarti. He's a trader from India. This is his first visit to Japan."

"It's my pleasure," Mr. Chakrabarti replied.

Suki shook his proffered hand. "It's a pleasure to make your acquaintance, Mr. Chakrabarti. I hope you don't mind if I have a word with Mademoiselle Renaud."

Marcelle promised to seek out Monsieur Chakrabarti later and took hold of Suki's arm. "Isn't he charming?"

Suki led them across the terrace. "He finds *you* charming."

"In spite of my terrible English. If only the French had taken over the world."

"They've taken over much of it. You're just in the wrong country."

"Don't *ever* say that." Marcelle gave Suki a playful elbow in her side. "I'm never leaving Tokyo. It's far better than Paris, except I miss *brasillé*, although the French baker in Ginza makes a tolerable version. But who needs *brasillé*? This gown is already too tight."

"We can discuss the fit of your mistress's gowns another time. I was just told by none other than Chase Norton, owner of the Hotel Metropolis, that Baron Umezono is in the clubroom on the far end of the terrace."

"What are you going to do?"

"Exactly what I told Mr. Norton I would do: present the baron with an invitation for a stroll on the terrace in the company of a pretty mademoiselle."

Marcelle looked back to where she'd been standing with Mr. Chakrabarti. He hadn't moved an inch. "I refuse. What if Monsieur Chakrabarti sees us? He'll think I'm the worst sort of Frenchwoman."

"Fret not, *ma chérie amie*. All you have to do is *deliver* the message. I'll be the one doing the walking and the talking," Suki said with a suggestive raise of brow.

"The schoolteacher is planning to seduce the baron?"

Marcelle didn't have to say that with such utter disbelief. "Only a little to earn his trust, as is sometimes necessary for reporters. Then I'll ask him the questions I've prepared."

"That gown has turned you into a coquette. Baron Umezono will want to devour you."

"He may have difficulty holding me down. His arm is in a sling."

"Lucky you."

The hum of low voices and laughter drifted from the clubrooms onto the terrace. Suki peered inside. The hotel's guests, men with a few women among them, puffed on tobacco and lazed about on thick upholstered chairs, occasionally reaching out to move cards, dice, and Japanese yen. Only one guest wore a sling.

The baron's tobacco pipe burned on a holder next to his good hand. He turned several cards over and gave the dealer a nod. The dealer collected cards from around the table and presented the baron with his winnings.

When the next round ended, Suki nudged Marchelle. "Go inside and tell him a female admirer is waiting on the terrace. Her name is Ame."

"Ame, as in candy?"

Suki gave Marcelle her best eyelash-batting, come-hither look. "What man in his right mind would refuse himself sweets on the scandalous Hotel Metropolis terrace?"

Marcelle approached the baron slowly. Reaching his side, she leaned down and whispered into his ear. He blinked, then shook his head. She persisted in her whispers, and they exchanged a few words that made her eyes narrow. Finally, the baron raised his hand in dismissal. Undeterred, Marcelle gestured to the terrace with a rush of whispers that made the baron's eyes bulge. He stood from the table and followed her out the door.

CHAPTER NINE

Suki waited for the baron next to the balustrade separating the terrace from the dark waters of Tokyo Bay. A light sweat broke out under her gown, and she tensed against the shiver. All she had to do was persuade the baron to tell her why someone wished to expose him for scandalous behavior, and she'd have the beginnings of an impressive newspaper article. Persuading him to speak was the challenge. He had no reason to trust her. She'd have to capture his attention so thoroughly that the words spilled from his mouth without him realizing. Fortunately, she was dressed like a harlot and Baron Umezono had a fondness for ladies of the pleasure quarters.

As the baron approached, her thudding heart jumped in her chest. Marcelle, who walked several paces behind the baron, gave a fling of her hand in a signal that she was tossing the baron Suki's way, then scurried to the other end of the terrace where she'd left Mr. Chakrabarti. Suki would have to thank her best friend later, provided she hadn't already disappeared with her monsieur.

The baron murmured what sounded like approval as he came upon the balustrade where Suki was planted to the ground. "What an unexpected treat." The tip of his thick tongue jutted out to wet his upper lip.

Suki hid her disgust with a flirty tilt of the head and a seductive smile that might be perceived as strained by a perceptive viewer. The *sake* coming off the baron's breath, however, suggested he was not that sort of viewer, at least not tonight.

"Ame-*chan*." The scents of lemony hair oil and incense wafted off the baron. He gazed from her bust back up to her face. "A half, are you?"

"Half-Japanese," she replied slowly, drawing out the syllables. He was intrigued, and she needed to keep him that way.

"And the other half?"

"Russian."

"Well," he said, his lips curled into a wolfish grin, "I've never had the pleasure of a Russian woman."

She had to get him talking, and she couldn't do anything as foolish as reveal her revulsion at his hot breath and the enlarged pores dotting his brow. The baron had to be the object of her desire, the man who made her pulse race and her knees weaken. There must be a face she could substitute for the rather nauseating one before her.

Spenser's came immediately to mind. Imagining him leaning against the balustrade, gazing at her with that desirous stare he'd given her the other evening, summoned a luscious heat that brought a flush to her chest and an inviting smile to her lips.

The baron wagged a finger. "It was Kato-*san* who sent you, wasn't it?"

Having the baron believe she'd been sent as a gift from an acquaintance might put him at ease and get him speaking. But if she feigned knowledge of this Kato-*san*, and the baron called out her ruse, she'd lose any chance of earning his trust. "Does it matter?"

"I'd like to express my appreciation to whomever sent such a sweet package." The baron let his hand descend to the side of her neck. Without thinking, Suki batted the beefy monstrosity away. But the baron didn't seem to notice. He fixed his gaze on her neckline, and before she realized what was happening, he'd stuck a finger inside the front of her gown. Suki gasped at the shock of his cold, damp digit against her skin, and leapt away before he could go any farther.

Tittering to make light of her prudish response, she explained, "I'm quite ticklish." With several hand lengths between her and the baron, she gave him a bright smile. "Who do you think sent me?"

He moved forward, erasing the distance between them, and bent down to her ear, his whiskers scraping her jawline. "At this point, I don't give a damn who sent you."

Something thick and hard pressed between her legs. Suki froze. The baron had breached her skirts with his thigh. "What is this?" Her voice was high and shrill, but the baron, seemingly unaware of her discomfort, nudged her toward the balustrade. With each small step, he lifted his thigh higher until it struck the sensitive place between her legs.

Suki flinched at the violation. Clearly, the baron wasn't interested in conversation, and she wasn't interested in spending another second in any kind of proximity to his thigh. "I was hoping to learn more about you, Baron Umezono," she said while inching herself off his leg. "Perhaps we could take a stroll along the terrace."

The baron clenched his brow. "You want to talk? Personally, I don't prefer it." The baron stopped her with his arm and returned his leg to its previous position.

"What are you doing?"

"This," he said and cupped the front of her gown along with her breast. "Do you like it?"

Suki slapped his hand away. No newspaper article was worth letting this beast paw at her. "I'm sorry, but I have to—"

He pulled her against him before she could say "leave," and pain slashed through her breast. The baron had clasped his thumb and forefinger around her nipple.

"*That hurts.*" She gave him a push that would have sent one of her brothers—in their younger years—to the floor. The baron reeled, yet stayed upright, and Suki got space enough to maneuver out of his reach.

"What the devil is wrong with you?" he growled. "Is this some kind of joke?"

Ned liked to say, "when in doubt, tell the truth." Reporters were entitled to their stories. Since charming the baron was no longer an option, the truth was her best hope for salvaging something from this fiasco. "I'm sorry. Fulfilling whatever perversions you have in mind is not why I sought you out tonight. I work for a newspaper, and someone asked us to look into your affairs. I was hoping to learn who would make such a request."

"A newspaper?" he snarled. "My affairs aren't worth a fig. They pale in comparison to the dealings carried out in this town."

"Are you a target of the conservative faction?"

"That's preposterous. No one cares what I do as long as I stay out of trouble and don't waste too much money." His gaze wandered to the clubroom, then back to Suki. "I'm thirsty, Ame-*chan*. It's time to get a drink."

He was speaking to her with full knowledge that she was a reporter, and there were questions she'd like to pose, provided she was posing them somewhere in full view of her Tsukiji neighbors. "Shall we share a drink at the hotel bar?" They could sip one of those new-fangled cocktails, and he could tell her who he thought had sent the letter to the *Tokyo Daily News*.

"That won't do." His eyes snagged on her breasts. "But a hotel room might be just the place." The baron stepped toward Suki; she moved back. "I take great pleasure in feasting on a woman's sweet candy, Ame-*chan*, and you are a delicious confection." His words seared her ears. "How about we retire to one of the hotel rooms, and you let me taste your delights?"

Suki stepped backward again with her hands raised, unsure that he'd ever take the hint that she didn't want him anywhere near her. "I'm not that type of woman. I don't go to hotel rooms with men." Backing up several more paces, she knocked into a wall of a body. Someone clasped her upper arms and pulled her in close, away from the baron. She looked down at the long, tapered fingers and sent a prayer to gods East and West: *please let it be Spenser*. As she faced the newcomer, relief flooded her body. Spenser's breath against her cheek smelled of alcohol and something cloying, but she was in his arms, and he was helping her.

"I…" Suki inhaled deeply and steadied her voice. "I didn't know you were standing there."

Fire lit Spenser's gaze. He released her and took a wobbly sidestep that nearly had him tripping over his own feet. "I saw you on the terrace and thought I'd wish you a good evening. Then I noticed you were talking with that man." Spenser looked at the baron as though he was about to toss him into Tokyo Bay.

The baron raised his hand and backed away. "I'm leaving. We'll pretend this conversation never took place." With a final lustful glace at Suki, he scampered back to the clubroom.

Suki watched with a tinge of regret as her newspaper story departed for the betting tables. Apparently, Baron Umezono didn't think that Ame-*chan* was worth an international incident at the Hotel Metropolis.

"Did that man hurt you?" Spenser asked through clenched teeth.

He'd bruised her nipple, which she wasn't about to admit. Nor was she going to confess the other awful things the baron had said and done. Knowing that she'd endured any discomfort at the baron's hands might compel Spenser to take decisive, and highly embarrassing, action. Fisticuffs at the Hotel Metropolis between Griffith Spenser and Baron Umezono over the latter's treatment of schoolteacher Suki Malveaux would make for a scandal Spenser would deeply regret when tomorrow brought sobriety, and she would never, ever live down. She'd have to come up with a more benign explanation for what he'd seen of her and the baron.

"There was a misunderstanding between myself and the gentleman." Suki's voice hitched on the last word. Baron Umezono hardly qualified. "My dear friend, Marcelle Renaud, thought he'd cheated her in a deal for the purchase of silk. Renaud-*san* is a lady's maid for an important American family. She wanted me to speak with the baron in Japanese."

Spenser shook his head. "That's not how it looked to me. He was getting quite close." His eyes narrowed. "Did you say something about going to a hotel room with him?"

Panic seized Suki's insides. She'd rather face an international incident than have Spenser think she'd been about to share a hotel room with the baron. She'd have to give him an ounce of truth at the risk of sending him into the clubroom with fists blazing. "The baron assumes that any woman who wishes to speak with him also wishes to share a hotel room. I do not."

Spenser clenched his jaw. "That lout. I ought to have a word with him."

"I told him in no uncertain terms that he was incorrect in his assumption," she said in her best "this discussion is over" schoolteacher voice because avoiding an international incident was her preference.

Spenser grumbled something unintelligible and angry. But seeing as he was struggling to remain upright, she didn't suppose there was a good chance of him carrying out an immediate assault on the baron. Feeling greater concern that he might hurt himself if he attempted an unaided step, Suki wound her arm through the crook of his elbow to give him support. He swayed at her touch, and she tightened her grip to prevent them from going down in a heap of silks and wools.

"I appreciate—" he began, then his gaze fell on their entwined arms. The front of her gown pressed against his jacket sleeve; only a few layers of fabric separated her breasts from his arm. She stiffened at the memory of the baron's fingers twisting her throbbing nipple. But she wasn't with the baron; she was with Spenser, and he wasn't going to hurt her. He wanted to help her and protect her. He was kind and generous, and someone—may gods East and West help her—she wished was not already betrothed.

Spenser's gaze moved from their hands to her eyes; his were dark and heavy with that ardent look he'd given her in his parlor. The terrace, the hotel, the whole of Tokyo faded into the background.

There was only the two of them, standing before one another, their eyes locked, their breaths releasing as one.

His gaze went to her lips, and she had the distinct impression their bodies had grown closer. He was about to kiss her; she felt certain of it. And she wanted it. She wanted to feel his breath's caress on her cheek as his mouth neared hers. She wanted those pillow-like lips pressing into hers. She wanted him to take away the ugliness of Baron Umezono and give her a moment of pure bliss.

One that would no doubt be the talk of Tsukiji tomorrow since there were at least a dozen of her neighbors on the terrace who could discover them at any moment. All they had to do was drift over to the corner of the terrace, and she could never show her face in public again. He was getting married, and schoolteacher Suki Malveaux didn't have moments of bliss with anyone, anywhere.

Suki turned her head away. "We should find my friend, Miss Renaud," she said, her voice thready. After clearing her throat, she continued, "I must tell her about the baron and introduce you. She's the friend who's been inquiring about candidates for the French maid position."

"Yes, I'd like to thank her." Spenser exhaled a stuttering breath and regarded her with the same seriousness he'd regarded her with when he'd proposed to hire her as a governess. "I'm much obliged for your help with preparations for my niece and nephew's arrival."

To Suki's relief, Spenser's steps steadied as they proceeded along the terrace. "I apologise for my state," he said. "I drank too much whisky after a misunderstanding of my own tonight."

A misunderstanding that had driven him to drink? Had this misunderstanding occurred between him and Watanabe? A gleeful smile nearly came to Suki's lips, which made her feel rotten. "I'm terribly sorry to hear of your misunderstanding."

"Well," he said matter-of-factly, "there'll be no more misunderstandings after tonight."

Spenser seemed quite untroubled. Had they argued and made up, resolving all points of conflict between them once and for all? But having come dangerously close to losing his love, had the fear of a life spent without her sent him to the bottle? How fortunate for Watanabe.

Suki caught sight of Marcelle walking toward them and pulled her arm from Spenser's. Marcelle flashed her an impressed look before exchanging pleasantries with Spenser and appraising him of the candidates she'd found for the maid position.

Spenser's whole body swayed with each nod at her words. He needed to be shoved in a rickshaw homeward or left to rest on one of the lobby sofas. Once Marcelle had concluded her description of the merits each maid would bring to the position, Suki turned to Spenser. "I believe we'll be departing the hotel shortly."

Marcelle opened her mouth as though to object, and Suki responded with the stern look she saved for students who interrupted lessons.

Spenser bent forward in a Japanese-style apology. "I'm sorry for any rudeness on my part. It wasn't my wish to offend you." He deepened the bow, which added sincerity, but seemed to threaten his compromised sense of balance. Tilting precariously to the side, Spenser shot out his arms and lifted his leg in what appeared to be an attempt at an upside-down ice-skating maneuver. "Whoa," he called out, his head inches from the terrace flagstones.

Suki grabbed his waist. Marcelle secured his shoulders, and they managed to bring him upright. His face went from purple to red to a peculiar grayish green.

"Are you well?" Suki asked.

He stepped back and smoothed down the front of his jacket. "Thanks to your efforts, I didn't meet my end on the Hotel Metropolis terrace."

"We're pleased to have helped," Suki replied in a lighthearted manner as though there was nothing amiss about two women in evening gowns saving a gentleman from planting his face into the stones.

"I've made an utter fool of myself," he said with obvious self-disdain. "But I still very much hope you'll accompany me to Ueno Park." His eyes met Suki's. "I've been looking forward to spending the day with...the carp streamers, of course."

For a second, Suki thought Spenser was going to say he was looking forward to spending the day with her, which was completely ridiculous, seeing as he was planning to spend the rest of his life with the most desirable woman in Tokyo. "Of course." Disappointment tinged her voice because she truly wished he was looking forward to spending the day with her. And she shouldn't be wishing for such things. "I'll bring details on the candidates for the governess position."

Spenser bid them good night and shuffled toward a jocular group of men seated at the hotel bar.

Marcelle gave Suki a playful tap on the shoulder. "I leave you with the baron and you return with Monsieur Spenser. Truly you are a woman of the night."

"I was trying to keep Monsieur Spenser from falling flat on his face."

Marcelle's nose wrinkled. "Did he bathe in whisky?"

"He said he was drinking due to a misunderstanding."

"With Madame Watanabe?"

"One can assume," Suki said. Not that it signified since they'd settled matters. "In any event, the situation has been resolved. He said there would be no more misunderstandings in the future."

Marcelle placed her hands on her hips, sending her chest jutting out. Immediately, a group of gentlemen standing nearby paused their conversation to stare. "Nothing save a lover's quarrel could drive a man to drink like that. She probably wants a quick wedding so she can move into his home before his wards arrive, and he wishes to wait until after they've settled. Then again, maybe he wants to marry quickly to secure his catch, and she wants more time to prepare a large wedding party. Or there could be a baby on the way, which is often the cause for any number of misunderstandings before vows of marriage have been recited. I wonder what color the child's hair will be. Monsieur Spenser's hair is quite light. Maybe the child will have hair like roasted chestnuts. How lovely."

Even as Marcelle talked about Spenser's marriage and children with Watanabe, Suki's mind wandered to how it'd felt when her gaze had met Spenser's. How could he look at her like he was going to kiss her when he was planning to start a family with Watanabe? Only a thoughtless and insincere man would indulge in tender feelings toward one woman while pledged to another. And although she'd only made Spenser's acquaintance on two occasions, she felt certain he was, in fact, thoughtful and sincere. Even more so, he proved himself the consummate gentleman in rescuing her from the baron. Spenser was hardly a rogue, which was why his actions made no sense.

Marcelle leaned closer. The suddenness of the movement caught Suki off guard, and she jumped back. "Are you well?" Marcelle asked.

Suki's hands shook from the rush of defensiveness against another attack like the one she'd received from the baron. But this was Marcelle, her best friend. "Only startled."

Marcelle wrapped an arm around Suki's side, and she relaxed into her friend's secure embrace. "It has been a startling night," Marcelle continued. "But this could be good for the Tattler. Between the search for a wedding gown and a misunderstanding on drunken display at the Hotel Metropolis, this week's column will have paragraphs about Monsieur Spenser and Madame Watanabe."

Suki placed her arm in the crook of Marcelle's elbow and led them on a stroll across the terrace. "I cannot mention anything about Monsieur Spenser's misunderstanding unless we hear about it from other sources. Doing so would be tantamount to revealing the Tattler's identity." Then Spenser would realize that he'd rescued the Tokyo Tattler, the despised gossipmonger, from a baron's attack.

And, for that, she owed him a favor—going forward she would refrain from gossiping about him in the column. Spenser and

Watanabe were marrying. She would share news of their engagement and write columns about their beautiful nuptials, then never mention them again.

"How fortunate for him to escape the Tattler's tentacles," Marcelle replied. "What about the baron? Has the Tattler snared him at last?"

"The baron is nowhere within reach of the Tattler's tentacles. His tentacles, however, touched my breast."

Marcelle stopped. Her nostrils were flaring. "What did you do?"

"I behaved as though he'd violated my person, which wasn't how he expected Ame-*chan* to behave. After that, I had to tell him I worked for the newspaper, and he still wanted me to join him in a hotel room. Then Spenser came along and rescued me."

"What did Spenser do?"

Took me in his arms and pulled me to his chest, she almost said. But she couldn't say as much without turning a hot scarlet at the memory and revealing her feelings for Spenser. And Marcelle, rightfully so, would tell her to stifle those feelings because he was about to walk down the aisle.

Besides, where could those feelings ever lead? Even if he weren't engaged to Watanabe, Suki couldn't marry him, or any foreigner for that matter. An affair was another matter. She wasn't opposed to carrying out a love affair with someone who made her feel even a hint of what she felt for Spenser. Marcelle had fabulous affairs, the details of which she shared with Suki, and those details had piqued Suki's curiosity. But the idea of Spenser conducting an affair with the Tokyo Tattler was laughable.

She should be grateful to Spenser for having saved her from the baron and return the favor by leaving him alone. "He scared off the baron, who fortunately prefers the gambling tables over making an international incident out of a foreigner running off with the woman who was trying to flee his advances."

"That *horrible* man grabbed your breast while you were trying to flee his advances. He should be castrated and quartered. No woman should have to endure such filth."

"If only you were judge and jury. Fortunately, Spenser took care of the rascal."

Marcelle hummed a few notes that sounded like a woman proven right. "Very fortunate you are to have him looking after you. Speaking of rascals…." Marcelle looked up and down the terrace. "I've seen several rendezvous that would be perfect for the Tattler column. An American woman was dragging a rather swarthy gentleman into the far corner, and the way they were moving suggested they might not be waiting for a hotel room. There's something mysterious in the hotel ambiance. I could stay and find out more."

Suki heard her best friend's plea loud and clear. "The Tattler would appreciate your efforts. Might you require Monsieur Chakrabarti's assistance in collecting gossip?"

"I'd been thinking he'd make a good companion in seeking out improper behavior. It would be odd to do so alone, don't you think?"

Suki gave a solemn nod. "You ought to find the monsieur right away. I assume he'll be able to escort you home safely once you've exhausted your gossip-collecting."

"I can already tell he's going to take very good care of me," Marcelle said with a mischievous smile.

Suki bid Marcelle good night and passed through the lobby with her gaze averted from the hotel bar where Spenser and his friends were carousing. In a few days, she and Spenser would meet in the park for her explanation of the carp streamers, and she'd inform him of the candidates for the governess and maid positions. Thereafter, there would be no reason for them to continue their acquaintanceship, and her heart would cease longing for something it should never have desired in the first place. And that would be a welcome relief.

CHAPTER TEN

The following afternoon, Suki gathered around the table with the Garrick family for a Sunday supper of roasted chicken and asparagus, grilled yellowtail fish, onions boiled in a sweet soy sauce, miso clam soup, and pickled-plum rice. The table had been set with gilded, flowery porcelain dishes the Garricks had brought from America and earthenware bowls and plates they'd acquired since arriving in Japan. Tapers in sterling silver holders lit their feast on the rainy afternoon.

Mother and Papa Garrick took their usual places at opposite ends of the table. On one side, Roger and Rosie sat by themselves. Baby Charlie, still short of his first birthday, napped upstairs, and their three-year-old son, Henry, sat on the other side of the table between Suki and her *okasan*.

"We'll use it for the Christmas dresses," Mother Garrick replied to *Okasan*'s request for suggestions about how to use the several crates of Belgian lace she'd recently acquired.

"What a splendid idea!" *Okasan* said, the golden thread of her fichu enhancing her glow at the prospect of making dresses for the family. "I'll begin work on the designs. Who will be joining us this year?"

Suki braced for Mother Garrick to give an accounting of where each of her seven children, save Roger, were spending the holidays. "I'm hoping Patricia and Elizabeth, and their families will attend. But don't bother with new dresses for them. I would like one, and we'll need ones for Suki and Rosie."

Suki sighed inwardly. Mother Garrick's accounting of everyone's holiday plans would have inspired Henry to throw his rice or spill Suki's wine as he became agitated when a single person around the table garnered all the attention, and that person wasn't him.

"Please don't make me a new dress," Rosie said. "My shape hasn't returned, and I cannot do justice to your work."

Roger put down his bowl of miso soup after a large gulp. Like their Japanese friends, the Garricks dispensed of spooning when it came to Japanese soups. "Rubbish," said Roger. "You look the same as always."

"Don't use crass language at the table," Mother Garrick scolded.

"I'm sure you'll have returned to form by December," *Okasan* said. "In the meantime, I can accommodate a changing shape. Panels and stitching do wonders."

Ever since Marcelle had brought up Watanabe's wedding gown search, Suki had been waiting for a chance to introduce the topic into the flow of conversation. Although Marcelle had heard from two sources about Watanabe's search, if she hadn't solicited a gown from *Okasan*, who dressed more Tsukiji brides than any other modiste in the city, the story might be false, and Suki had sworn not to report any more stories on Spenser and Watanabe that didn't celebrate their fine persons and forthcoming wedded bliss. "Speaking of gowns, I heard someone was looking for a very special one. You know Natsu Watanabe, wife of the late officer Watanabe, who served as military liaison for the foreign officers."

"The woman who has been stepping out with Griffith Spenser?" Rosie asked.

"The very one. As it turns out," Suki began, infusing her words with a lighthearted, gossipy tone, "several people have said that Mrs. Watanabe is on the hunt for a wedding gown."

"Watanabe-*san* sent me a message several days ago with a request to meet about her wedding gown," *Okasan* said.

Suki swallowed the pang of disappointment—merely a lingering weakness that would soon pass—and gave *Okasan* a hearty nod. "That would be a very good commission."

"Unfortunately, I don't think I'll be able to accommodate Watanabe-*san*'s schedule. I'm quite busy over the next few weeks. I offered to meet her in a month's time, but she hasn't responded."

"She's a widow, and he's divorced," Mother Garrick replied. "They'll marry soon. No need to drag it out and make a spectacle."

"I've heard nothing about upcoming nuptials from Griff," Roger said. "He was at the lawn tennis tournament today. Granted, he wasn't chatty. He's our best backhander and could barely lift a racket. Apparently, he went a little heavy on the spirits last night."

"Men don't talk about love and marriages to one another," Rosie said.

Papa Garrick wagged his finger. "The male would absolutely share news of a promise to marry. It's a means of demonstrating claim to a certain female."

"The chap didn't mention a word of it," Roger said.

"A summer wedding sounds romantic, if it's true." Rosie looked across the table at Suki and gave her a sympathetic smile.

According to Rosie, every time they discussed finding a governess for Spenser's niece and nephew, Suki got a "dreamy look" in her eyes. Rosie was convinced that Suki was enamored, and all of Suki's protests had only made her feelings all the more obvious.

After the meal, Suki excused herself with pleas of exhaustion. Almost as soon as she shut the bedroom door, someone knocked.

"May I?" Rosie asked as she came in and took a seat on the chair in front of Suki's writing table. Suki sat on the bed and braced herself for a dose of Rosie's encouragement.

"It must have been difficult to hear Natsu Watanabe was looking for wedding gowns," Rosie began.

Suki moved to rest against her pillows and stretched out her legs. "They'll have a wonderful life together, a dozen children with hair like roasted chestnuts." The cynicism in her voice made her sound petty, and she was determined to be happy for the newly engaged couple. "And his wards will have a mother at home," she added, this time with brightness.

"You've looked smitten since you returned from his house last week. Anyone could tell he appealed to you."

"Men promised to marry have no appeal for me."

"Then there are other men who appeal?" Rosie widened her hazel eyes like a pampered pet waiting for treat.

"At this time, there is no one."

"I can't even count the number of men who've inquired with Roger about your status. You could marry tomorrow if you wanted." Rosie sighed bitterly as she propped her legs on the bed. Suki's reluctance to engage in courtship rituals was a source of great aggravation to her sister-in-law.

"If I married tomorrow, everyone in Tsukiji would think I was in a family way or possessed by a ghost."

Rosie nudged Suki's toes with her own. "You'd be sent to one of those mountain temples where they would exorcise your ghost."

"It's not as though I'm avoiding men. I *have* agreed to an afternoon in the park with a man in just a few days' time."

"I'm surprised Mr. Spenser would request a walk in the park at the same time he is readying to marry." Rosie pursed her lips like Henry refusing a serving of cabbage. More than Suki, she'd been convinced that Spenser's invitation to Ueno Park indicated romantic intentions. "I hate to think he's like those foreign men who take liberties with the hearts of Japanese women."

Spenser wasn't the sort of man who took liberties; he was the sort of man who rescued women who were under siege from barons who couldn't keep their hands to themselves. Moments of shock and disgust had gripped Suki throughout the day when she'd recalled how the baron had cornered her on the terrace. She'd also recalled the relief of being in Spenser's arms and his gaze on her lips.

She would have loved to share the entirety of the previous night's events with Rosie, who would sympathize and offer wise advice. But doing so would mean inventing a story about how Suki the schoolteacher had ended up with the baron in the first place.

So she offered a defence for Spenser. "He wants to talk about the carp streamers."

"An afternoon in the park with a beautiful young woman gives a man the chance to appraise her figure and experience the feel of their bodies accidentally touching as they stroll the pathways. It's not an activity for an engaged man."

"Then I should beware. Griffith Spenser is, after all, a man. As Papa Garrick says, 'monogamy is man's greatest struggle.'" Suki tilted her head forward and raised her brow in imitation of Papa Garrick.

"But monogamy is what separates man from the beasts," Rosie replied with her own imitation, and they fell into a spell of giggles, the backs of their feet beating in time against Suki's mattress.

After their laugh, Rosie poked Suki's foot with hers. "Don't be cynical about love. You'll end up sounding like the Tattler."

Suki covered her wince by acting as though a loose string in her quilt had to be pulled at that very moment. Many times, she'd wanted to confide in Rosie about her authorship of the column, but she'd never been able to bring herself to say the words. She'd told herself that she was sparing Rosie from shocking news when she was pregnant and overcome with motherly duties. Now it was too late to reveal her *nom de plume* without admitting to a deception that Rosie would find as troubling as learning that her dear, sweet Suki was a gossipmonger. "I doubt the Tattler has known true love."

Rosie's eyes lit up. "What if the Tattler sees you at the park with Mr. Spenser? You'll end up in the column for sure."

"I'm sure our walking together will appear as chaste as it truly is."

"Imagine! Schoolteacher Suki in the scandal sheets."

"That's the last thing I'm worried about," Suki replied with a reassuring smile.

After Rosie left to put the boys to sleep, Suki settled behind her writing table to work on the Tattler. This week's column was already longer and more scandalous than usual. The length could be attributed to her having time to indulge in writing during the Ginza Girls School's spring holiday. Good weather bringing out Tsukiji's friskiness likely contributed to a few of the romantic intrigues. Goings-on at the Hotel Metropolis were responsible for a good many of the rest.

Suki scanned the first few paragraphs, which contained the week's lighter items. She'd written about the sighting of the Garners' daughter walking with the distant cousin of the Austrian royal family and the Bianchi widower presenting flowers to the Montanari family's widowed matron. A servant in the Martinez household had told Marcelle about the Silvas' youngest daughter's adoration for a Japanese university student who paid little attention to her. The Tattler devoted several sentences to the lovely ivory dress with apricot detailing the youngest Silva daughter had worn to the Tsukiji Ladies' Luncheon. Hopefully, seeing her name in the column would give the young woman confidence enough to confess her affections.

The Tattler was usually keen to encourage foreign women in their pursuits of Japanese men. According to the ever-annoying, but sometimes correct, matchmaker, Yamashita-*san*, a foreign woman found a devoted spouse in the modern Japanese man. These gentlemen treated their foreign wives with as much, if not more, respect than they could expect from a husband of similar background. And foreign wives were given more freedom than Japanese—or half-Japanese—women in the same household.

In the next part of the column, Suki had recorded the most recent happening in the riveting saga of the American divorcee in residence at the Hotel Metropolis. This time, the temptress had been caught in an illicit embrace with a Portuguese trader visiting from Macao. The story came through a German missionary's wife who shared it with

Marcelle's mistress in a bid to persuade her, or her husband the envoy, that their citizen needed correction.

Marcelle overheard the German woman relating how the fifteen-year-old son from a New England whaling dynasty had seen the couple on a secluded end of the Metropolis's terrace. The lad spared no detail in reporting to every other young man at the mission school how he'd been drawn to the couple by the divorcee's loud moans, then saw the divorcee's quivering thighs and the man's hands making vigorous motions between them. Suki had turned the moans into "sounds of delight" and the movement of thighs and hands into a "wanton moment."

She replaced the word "wanton" with the word "risqué," as that seemed less judgmental and the divorcee was already the object of much judgment from Tsukiji's matrons. Then she put down the pen. Her mind wandered to the previous night on the hotel terrace. What would have happened if she and Spenser had been alone in a faraway corner? And he hadn't been thoroughly squiffed? Would that kiss have happened? Would she have let him touch her, let his hands move down her body as his lips left a trail of kisses on the bare skin of her neck? A pleasant throbbing sensation took hold between her thighs.

Suki shifted in her chair in an attempt to undo the feeling. She was being absurd. Had Spenser been able to string a sentence together, he wouldn't have been leaning toward her like he wanted to taste her; rather, he'd have been boasting about his bride-to-be.

The column followed the divorcee's moment on the Metropolis terrace with news of a fight at the hotel's roulette table between the scion of an American oil family and the scion of an American railway family. According to bystanders, the two disagreed over a baseball umpire's call in favor of the New York Giants over the Boston Beaneaters. Blows were exchanged. A cut over the eye of one scion and an elbow to the other's nose sent blood flying across the clubroom. Finally, none other than Chase Norton, hotel proprietor, broke up the fight.

Suki hesitated to mention his name in the Tattler. He'd spoken of avoiding a reputation, which was a sentiment she fully appreciated. She finished her report of the incident with a sentence about fists being thwarted by one of the wiser men in attendance.

Between the divorcee, the gambling, and the fighting, the Hotel Metropolis was looking like Tsukiji's den of iniquity. Changing mores among world travelers must have been behind the recent debauchery: instead of hiding their impulses toward sex and aggression, people were now celebrating these most basic of human instincts, as Papa Garrick would call them. Fortunately, standards existed to spare the innocent from harm. Suki ended the passage of Metropolis gossip with a recommendation that hotel guests practice greater discretion for the sake of the more sensitive among them.

The story of Watanabe's search for a wedding gown would bring the column to its conclusion. Suki lifted her pen, then put it down. Multiple sources, *Okasan* included, had confirmed the *on-dit*. Verification was not the issue. What was at issue was her determination to present Spenser and Watanabe's union in a flattering light. But that was not how the Tattler approached news of an engagement between a foreigner and his Japanese lover. The Tattler was a skeptic in these cases. That was the role Suki had dedicated herself to. To fail in performing that role was a betrayal to her reader and to the countless young women who'd had their lives ruined by foreigners.

Even so, the previous night Spenser had rescued her like a gallant knight; therefore, tonight, she would soften her words.

All of Tsukiji will be thrilled to learn a wedding appears to be on the horizon. Have you seen the signs of the pending nuptials? A joyous countenance on the future bridegroom? A lightness in step from the bride-to-be? Did your thoughts turn to the esteemed Griffith Spenser, who contributed to our lawn tennis club's swift and certain victory over the team from Yokohama? Did you think of the enchanting Mrs. Natsu Watanabe, widow of the late Captain

Gentaro Watanabe, who gave his life for his nation's victory over China? If so, dear reader, you are most perceptive.

Tsukiji's most talented seamstresses have been receiving inquires this past week about creating a wedding gown for the vivacious Mrs. Watanabe!

The Tattler urges all to be mindful as no formal announcement has been made. No mention of a date has circulated through Tsukiji's parlors. The commission of a wedding gown, however, presents a most encouraging sign that the announcement of a proposed marriage is imminent.

Now, dear reader, as much as we wish to raise our voices in rejoicing at a match between such outstanding persons, we must instead hold our breaths. What do we know about the inclinations of the foreign man? Recall the many times your Tattler has shared stories of the volatility of their promises, of their roving eyes, of the kith and kin in their home countries who demand and deserve their affection and loyalty. We wish nothing but the best for our dear Mrs. Watanabe but urge her to prepare for an outcome that in the tender throes of love may seem unfathomable.

Fondness and Friendship Always,
Your Tattler

CHAPTER ELEVEN

Not until Griff squeezed into a rickshaw beside Miss Malveaux did he realise the tests of endurance and restraint his invitation to Ueno Park would entail. First, there was the problem of concentrating on Miss Malveaux's ongoing commentary about Tokyo's sights while trying not to notice the sprinkling of light freckles on her high nose, each one begging to be kissed. Then he had to keep his mind from wandering to how her soft lips would feel on various parts of his body. *Very, very good*, he decided before forcing himself to listen more closely to her words about a temple they were passing. Then there were the various efforts at keeping his eyes averted from the swell of her bust under a lacy pale-yellow frock he continuously, shamelessly imagined himself removing from her body.

The reward for his almost-good behaviour came each time their eyes met. A light flush would spring to her cheeks, and he became increasingly convinced she felt the same desire as he.

After the fool he'd made of himself at the Hotel Metropolis, having her beside him was nothing short of a miracle. Snippets from that night had returned the following day at the lawn tennis tournament while he'd been trying in vain to connect racket to ball. The lads assured him that he'd spent his time at the hotel wandering the terrace and imbibing several glasses of something called a Manhattan before passing out on a lobby sofa.

But he recalled head-spinning rage and an overwhelming desire to slam his fist into the face of that miscreant leaning over a stunningly attired Miss Malveaux. It had taken him a dizzying five minutes of staring at the familiar-looking woman in the gown that revealed a pert bust and hinted at full hips before recognising her. He'd been drawn to her corner of the terrace like a bee to fragrant gardenias. Then he'd seen that rogue forcing himself nearer to Miss Malveaux while she'd backed away. Griff could have sworn he saw her give the overbearing lout a push, which had been enough for Griff to swoop in with fists at the ready.

Also clear in Griff's mind was the subsequent realisation that chaste friendship with Miss Malveaux was impossible. Whatever impulse had driven him to nearly plough a stranger into the terrace flagstones wasn't going to be satisfied with a casual acquaintanceship.

And he had a nagging recollection, which might just be the fragment of a dream or a fleeting wish, that they'd almost kissed. They hadn't actually kissed; he would have remembered as much, but for some reason, he felt as though their lips had nearly touched.

Since he had no memory of Miss Malveaux berating his lack of manners or slapping him for misbehaviour, he'd shown up at her home that afternoon as planned. Relief poured through him when she'd greeted him as though nothing was amiss. Parts of him, however, had stiffened right back up when she'd seated herself without complaint in the rickshaw, even though it had been obvious his Western-size body would take up more than half of the bench and they would invariably make contact during the ride.

Despite their forced proximity—or perhaps because it demanded a distraction—Miss Malveaux was proving to be the consummate Tokyo guide. She gave the names and histories of the grand temples with their heavy copper roofs and entrances flanked by rows of vendors selling medicines, amulets, and fortunes. She knew which members of the nobility resided in the high-walled estates of the hill district and regaled him with each neighbourhood's distinguishing characteristics.

"We've entered Asakusa," she said over the traffic's din of horse-pulled omnibuses, rickshaw runners calling out signals to one another, and cart-vendors hawking their wares. She pointed to an octagonal, towerlike building. "This is the *Ryounkaku*. You may know it as the Twelve-Story Tower for the number of its floors. At the time of its construction, it was the second tallest building in the world after the New York World Building."

"I've visited the tower in spite of the lean." The '94 earthquake had left the tower with a tilt, but Griff had been game to climb its stairs to the top. "The views of Mt. Fuji were truly spectacular."

Miss Malveaux nodded. "I perfectly agree. Did you have a chance to visit Asakusa's Sensoji temple?"

"Actually, I've been there twice. The incense and all the sellers around the temple make for a particularly Asian experience. It's a far cry from Ginza and Tsukiji with all the redbrick European buildings."

"Asakusa also has significant popular history. It was the most important district for theater, musical performances, archery contests, and other entertainments during the shogun's reign." She pointed to tall, wooden gates marking the entrance to stone-paved streets lined with wooden structures several stories high. "Those are the pleasure quarters. During the shogun's era, it was the only licensed area for prostitution in the city and, notably, far removed from the shogun's palace so as not to tempt his retainers from their duties. Now, as you are most certainly aware, such quarters are found throughout the city."

After their encounter at the Hotel Metropolis, Miss Malveaux had every reason to believe he was a drunkard, but he wouldn't have her thinking he was also a punter. "My experience with Tokyo's houses of ill repute is limited to the single occasion when friends dragged me there unawares."

"It must have been shocking," she said as though playing along with the fiction of him having had a single brothel experience in a city where prostitution was hardly a sin and wives went to brothels alongside their husbands to select their spouses' entertainments.

"Believe it or not," he said with more defensiveness than he'd have preferred, "I was surprised at the cleanliness."

"Cleaner than those in England?" she said with a challenging glimmer to her eye.

"Based on what I've heard from others, much." He needn't admit to any experience in an English brothel.

Miss Malveaux let out a short burst of laughter, and he grinned ear-to-ear. The connection he'd felt when she'd visited his home hadn't been a wishful illusion. There was an ease between them as though they'd known each other for longer than a week, and it did nothing to diminish the sparks that filled the air when their gazes met.

"Oh no," she said and covered her mouth.

Griff peered out her side of the rickshaw and understood her shock. Several dozen naked men danced and chanted before the tall vermilion gates of a shrine. "Is that some kind of ritual?"

Miss Malveaux shook her head. "More like a protest, and a dramatic one at that."

The men's loins were jiggling quite furiously. "What are they saying?"

She bent her ear toward the commotion. "They're saying something about foreigners bringing about the end of the world."

"I've heard of native populations doing the same after the arrival of Europeans. They lose their land and culture at the hands of colonial powers. No wonder they think it's the end of the world."

Miss Malveaux furrowed her brow. "But Japan has never been under colonial rule. Those men are angry about all the new taxes and blame the foreigners for showing Japan how to be a modern nation."

"Are they farmers or peasants?"

She shook her head. "People on the land are too busy to protest. Those men are likely from poor samurai families who became poorer after the emperor took residence in Tokyo. With little education, they ended up doing the same menial labor as men from the other classes. Stripped of their swords, they have nothing to pride themselves on."

"That's not all they've been stripped of," Griff observed. "The towels wrapped around their heads notwithstanding, why are they naked?"

"Men traditionally dance naked at festivals. You know we Japanese aren't ashamed of nudity."

Griff was well-aware of the lack of inhibitions Japanese people felt around naked bodies. "I've been to a few public baths during my travels and have yet to feel comfortable with the mixed bathing."

"It can be difficult for foreigners."

The rickshaw lurched to the side and Griff grasped at the metal bar in front of them, sparing Miss Malveaux the burden of him landing on her lap. "I take it you're not embarrassed by nudity?" Griff immediately flushed with embarrassment. He hadn't meant to ask about her feelings toward nudity, although he was plenty curious. The conversation had just veered in that direction.

Thankfully, Miss Malveaux didn't seem to notice his blush. She simply nodded, which he found very stimulating. "Even the mixed baths I find relaxing," she said. "*Okasan*, my mother, always took me to the public baths, even after we moved to the Garricks' home. That was how we maintained our connections with Japanese friends. But we haven't gone in many years. It's been a while since I've attended a festival with that much nakedness. Those men were quite a surprise."

"Were they of the Buddhist faith or the native Shinto?"

"Most foreigners have no idea about Japanese religions," she remarked with a small smile. *Was that a look of admiration?*

Compelled to earn even more of her admiration, he continued, "I only know there are two types, which is far fewer than we have in England."

"I've heard there are many types in your country. There must be as many in Tsukiji, although nearly everyone is some kind of Christian. Those men were demonstrating in front of a Shinto shrine, and their dancing was of Shinto origin. But the language of the protests sounded like Buddhist chants. There aren't the same barriers between Buddhism and Shinto as among the European faiths."

"Which do you prefer?" Again, his questions were overstepping the bounds of propriety. But he had this irrepressible need to keep Miss Malveaux talking. He enjoyed listening to her light, melodic voice and watching her pink lips move with the words. And he truly wanted to learn more about her. "I apologise for such a rude question."

"It's not rude. We Japanese are practical people. We take aid from Buddhist, Shinto, or Christian faiths whenever these may assist in the travails of life. As for me, I pray at the shrines and purchase charms, usually when we visit my *okasan*'s family. In Tsukiji, I tell everyone I'm Christian, a Presbyterian like the Garricks. I attend church when I'm not too busy on Sundays preparing for the week's work. I like all kinds of religious celebration. Christmas is a particular favourite."

"You like the presents."

"The cake."

Griff would have liked to see her eating cake. More precisely, he'd have liked to see her licking the sweet morsels from her fingers. Adjusting himself on the rickshaw's cushioned seat, he vowed to refrain from wicked thoughts. So far, the excursion had gone brilliantly, and he didn't want Miss Malveaux to catch him eying her like the indecent dunderhead he was reputed to be.

He'd already come dangerously close to confirming his reputation as an incorrigible rake when he'd asked Miss Malveaux to join him in Ueno before ending the affair with Natsu. But when a chap from the lawn tennis club had recommended that Griff take a look at the extraordinary display of carp streamers, his first thought had been to request Miss Malveaux's companionship. They would discuss his wards, he'd told himself, even though everyone knew an invitation to the park was an overture from a man planning to woo his companion. He'd been in denial then. But no longer.

Sitting beside her in the rickshaw, her dress brushing against his leg while he tried to refrain from picturing himself removing that dress and kissing every inch of her naked body, had left him convinced that he should be wooing Miss Malveaux. Nevertheless, he had to proceed with caution. Heaven forbid Natsu learned of today's excursion. Upon leaving the house this morning, he'd taken care to walk around the garden and look up and down the street before exiting the gate. He wouldn't put it past her to hover in the bushes like some overzealous female ninja.

As long as the blasted Tattler didn't learn of his afternoon with Miss Malveaux, Natsu should be none the wiser.

Shortly after arriving at Ueno Park, they found seats on a bench near the carp streamers. Gazing up at the billowing lengths of fabric against the clear blue sky, Griff pictured hearty fish braving the river tides.

"We hang the streamers on Boys' Day for our sons to grow up strong like the carp," Miss Malveaux said and pointed to a cluster of streamers on a tall pole. "The larger carp are the parents, and the smaller ones are the children."

"How long will they fly at the park? I'd love to show them to my niece and nephew."

"Boys' Day is next week, and they'll take them down shortly thereafter."

"Then I suppose I'll have to come up with something else."

"I can recommend several places to visit upon their arrival," Miss Malveaux said brightly, and a vision came to his mind of her showing Marianne, Lucien, and himself the sights of Tokyo, which he liked very much.

After finishing boxes of rice balls and pickled radish that Miss Malveaux had been thoughtful to bring, they strolled along broad pathways lined with clusters of cherry, plum, and ginkgo trees. Deeper into the park, swaths of bamboo and cypress cast cool shadows on the pathway. Although he had no recollection of how it happened—whether he'd stepped closer or she'd moved nearer—or why—was it to avoid disturbing the peaceful forest or to better hear one another speaking?—they came to be walking as near to one another as possible without touching. Their steps slowed, and they spoke in low voices meant only for one another. He told her about growing up in the English countryside and his years at Oxford. She answered his questions about her childhood in Tsukiji. Hours later he couldn't say how many people they'd passed, which flowers had been in bloom, or whether there had been dozens or hundreds of carp streamers. There was only Miss Malveaux in a pale yellow dress, their words mingling, and their hips and shoulders occasionally touching.

Miss Malveaux was telling him about teaching at the Ginza Girls School, and the conversation was proceeding with so little reservation that his thoughts found their way into words before he considered whether he was probing too far. "I know you don't wish to marry, and your teaching is of foremost importance, but you're young and attractive. There must be a fellow who escorts you around town, someone you have feelings towards."

"There's no man like that in my life," she said softly, her footfalls light on the packed earth.

Griff turned his head to hide the ridiculous grin on his face. "I would have thought otherwise."

"I've been busy with teaching, and other activities, and haven't had the time."

"Your teaching must be very demanding," he said. Yet, she was spending most of the day with him. That must count for something.

They continued along the pathway until it ended at a small greenhouse. Miss Malveaux stopped. Several times she opened her mouth as though readying to say something, then seemingly changed her mind. Finally, she took a deep breath. "Very few people know this, but I feel we're becoming friends, and you seem open-minded about other cultures and ideas. The truth is that I'm studying to become a newspaper reporter. I know it's not a woman's place, but I think that women have much to contribute."

London's newspapers allowed women journalists, but they were few and usually in the mould of the Tokyo Tattler. "What kind of stories do you wish to report?"

She wiped her hands along the side of her dress, and he imagined her ridding her hands of chalk while presenting a lesson to her students. "I'd report on happenings between the foreign and Japanese communities. Japan wants to be a modern nation, which means allowing foreigners to live in concessions like Tsukiji and doing business with foreign companies, like yours. Most of the time, relations between the communities proceed honorably. There are times, however, when deceit and corruption take place among men with less honorable intentions. I believe it is the responsibility of newspapers to expose such malfeasance and light the way forward."

He hadn't thought he could find her more impressive, but once again she'd succeeded in exceeding his expectations. "That's quite brave of you. Most women wouldn't dare involve themselves in such unseemly matters."

"Most women don't know they can choose a path different from finding a husband and bearing children," she responded quickly as though she'd given the retort before.

Griff glanced away. Hearing Miss Malveaux reject the necessity of a husband and children felt like a reproach to the intimacy growing between them. Was she uninterested in intimate relations? Or was she the type of woman who'd allow affections to progress without the prospect of marriage? Facing her again, he replied, "I'm beginning to suspect you're a bluestocking."

Miss Malveaux gave a small laugh. "I'm beginning to suspect you know too much about me."

The sun tucked itself behind the mountains, and the winds picked up with the darkening skies. Despite the keen desire that had started licking at him when he'd greeted Miss Malveaux at her home and had only grown stronger, he sensed a chill in the air. Because he didn't want Miss Malveaux to suffer the cold, and because he'd been waiting all day to do it, Griff took her arm, placed it within the crook of his elbow, and prayed she wouldn't pull away.

She didn't.

They walked away from the greenhouse and down the park pathway. Neither of them said a word. In her soft, shallow breaths, desire crossed her lips, and if that desire amounted to even one iota of what he was feeling, this was not going to be their last walk in the park. "I've been wondering about something. You mentioned becoming a newspaper reporter, and I truly believe it's a noble pursuit. I was only thinking about whether you might be able to make reports on the news and go for walks in the park on occasion."

Even in the dwindling light of day, the pink on her cheeks deepened. "With the right man, I'd consider taking walks in the park on a more regular basis."

"What kind of man might that be?"

"Well…it would be someone who was easy to talk to, someone with whom I could roam around the park for hours on end without any wish to leave."

He could pull her to him now and kiss her tenderly, deeply so that neither of them would ever hear the name Ueno Park without thinking about their kiss in the waning light of day, under trees thick with leaves. But he wanted her to know that this kiss signified more than a commemoration of their walk through the park. "The truth is, when I heard about the carp streamers, I immediately thought of us viewing them together, not because you'd make the perfect guide— though you certainly are—but because I wanted to spend the day in your company, and I hope very much this is the first of many days we spend together in the park."

Stopping abruptly, Miss Malveaux removed her arm from his. Her head cocked to the side, and she looked at him as though he were a puzzling riddle she'd failed to solve. "I'm surprised to hear you say that. Frankly, I'm surprised at myself for getting carried away with a man who has pledged himself to another."

Her words were like a punch in the gut, a well-deserved one. Of course she was aware of the affair with Natsu. He'd admitted to stepping out with someone when Miss Malveaux had visited his home, and thanks to the Tattler, all of Tsukiji thought he and Natsu were the picture of love. "You probably heard I've been escorting Natsu Watanabe around town. But there has never been any kind of pledge between us. In fact, we recently decided to part ways."

"Recently?" She seemed to choke on the word.

"This past week, actually."

Miss Malveaux looked positively incredulous. "You and Mrs. Watanabe are no longer a couple?"

"She deserves a man who can return her affection in equal measure. I'm not that man."

"That is…honest of you." Miss Malveaux made approving sounds. "It was yet early in your relationship. It's far worse for a woman when her sweetheart decides he cannot fulfil his commitments after they marry and bring children into their union. It makes for a very bleak future."

"Only a truly despicable man would abandon his family. But I doubt Mrs Watanabe will ever have to suffer such unkindness. She knows what she wants and is extremely resourceful."

"She's a vibrant woman, then."

Vibrant was an accurate description of Natsu. Indeed, she was vibrant, and also manipulative, demanding, and extremely focused on the target of her affections. "She has much attention to give."

The park gates came into view. Griff couldn't let their afternoon end with talk of Natsu. He stopped under a cluster of cherry trees cloaked in shiny new leaves. "I hope I'm not being too forward, but I was wondering if I could address you by your Christian name."

A brilliant smile creased her face. "I'd like that. Please call me Suki."

"Please call me Griffith, or Griff, as my friends call me."

"Griff."

He loved how his name lingered on her lips.

The pathway was deserted, and the cherry trees afforded them a modicum of privacy. He could kiss her now or spend the rest of the night, week, month, or whole of his life regretting it. "I was also wondering if I might kiss you."

Suki turned her face up to his. "A kiss? I've never been kissed."

Never been kissed, never been touched. Gentle, he had to proceed gently. "Would you like to be kissed now?"

Slowly, she nodded. "Very much so."

Griff leaned down and brushed his lips against hers in the lightest of kisses. She didn't move an inch. Again, he caressed her lips, gently teasing them, rousing them until she discovered her way into his kiss. She moved her lips beneath his, taking what he gave and giving it back in kind. He pulled away to see how she was affected, and there it was: her radiant smile.

"I'm suddenly quite happy," Suki said, her smile growing even brighter.

"As am I." Cupping her face, he kissed both sides of her smiling mouth, then tasted the succulent lower lip. Her breath fell lightly on his cheek, and he buzzed with delight. She'd given him her first kiss. Griff had a claim to Suki Malveaux.

Their lips pressed together in full kisses, each one like a light on the path to an unimaginable, and unimaginably desirable, destination.

"I've never…" she began, then teetered and stumbled.

Griff pulled her back to standing. "I've got you," he whispered.

"I lost my footing on the tree roots."

Placing his hands around her waist, he held her with enough space between them that she wouldn't think he was taking advantage of her misstep. "Does this work?"

"Yes." She tilted her head, presenting him with her sweet, ripe mouth.

As their kisses deepened, desire flared in him with each touch of her hands along his cheeks, his neck, and the back of his head. Her fingers threaded his hair, sending waves of pleasure rippling down his spine. Tentatively, he moved his hold from her waist to the small of her back. Warmth radiated through the fabric of her dress, bidding him to stroke small circles. She arched into his palm as light purrs erupted from her throat and hummed against his lips. There must have been dozens of ways to make her moan and gasp in his arms, and he was going to learn each one.

Griff parted his lips slightly, an inquiry as to her interest. She stilled, then her lashes fluttered open. His pulse quickened at the sight. Suki was undone. The schoolteacher who could speak for days about the city sights had given way to a woman enraptured by a kiss. He loved it. Her lips opened for him, and he dipped inside. Soon her succulent, velvet tongue was swirling with his and their hips were swaying to the of their joining mouths.

As though sensing his wish, Suki wrapped her arms around his midsection and brought him closer. The feel of her skirts against his stiff cock sent merciless heat through his core. A deep, lusty groan escaped him.

She pulled away. "Did I hurt you?"

"Not at all," he said, his voice a low rumble. "Is this too much?"

"Not at all," she said, returning to his embrace.

He left her divine lips to trace kisses down her chin and neck. Revelling in the flowery, citrusy scent of her smooth skin, his addled mind somehow made way for reason. "Suki, I must return you home before we commit terribly indecent acts in the park."

Giggling, she took a step backward. "We should probably stop."

"Only for now," he said firmly.

"Only for now."

CHAPTER TWELVE

Suki looked down at her fingers entwined with Griff's and willed the rickshaw runner to make haste. She longed to relive every moment of the glorious day from the boxed lunches under the carp streamers, to strolling along the pathways for hours, to the strands of conversation that had flowed so freely yet weaved together. And the heavenly kisses that had left her so weak in the knees that she'd had to lean into Griff's sturdy side all the way to the rickshaw. But those musings would have to wait.

All she could think about was getting to the *Tokyo Daily News* offices as soon as possible and telling Ned Taylor to stop the presses on the Tattler column. Otherwise, tomorrow morning every Tattler reader in Tokyo would be under the impression that Griffith Spenser and Watanabe were about to be married.

Griff would have to spend the foreseeable future explaining to well-wishers that in fact the affair had ended. Worse would be the humiliation for Watanabe. Suki couldn't fathom the misunderstanding that had culminated in Watanabe searching for wedding gowns while Griff was ending their affair. Unfortunately for Watanabe, the Wednesday morning edition of the *Tokyo Daily News* was going to make that misunderstanding a very public one.

Suki turned to Griff. He faced the street, but she could tell from his cheek's light creasing that a smile played on his lips. How she hoped he could carry this feeling with him for the rest of the night and into tomorrow, and for however many days one typically spent reliving the splendor of a lover's first kiss. If only this heady feeling wasn't going to evaporate as soon as he opened tomorrow morning's newspaper.

Getting to Ned as quickly as possible was of utmost importance, and the most expedient way to reach his offices was to part from Griff near Tsukiji's gates. "I've asked the runner to deposit me on the east end of Ginza Boulevard," Suki said, keeping her voice steady and light. "There's a French bakery I wish to visit on the way home."

"I'd be glad to join you. I was planning to escort you home."

"Perhaps another time? The baker's wife gave birth last month, and I promised to visit during the spring holiday and never made my way there. Tomorrow is the final day of the holiday, and I would be remiss not to visit now."

"I didn't know there was a French bakery in Ginza."

"The baker studied in France for years. I promise to take you another time."

He leaned closer. "I'm going to hold you to it. I happen to be a fan of the croissant."

His breath on the shell of her ear sent a tingling sensation down her side. She glanced at his lips and blushed. Oh, those kisses. Their lips and tongues, the lengths of their bodies pressed together, the stiffness of his desire against her hip, all of it utterly sublime. "The croissants are delicious."

"I trust you would know."

Excitement pulsed through her as he caressed her hand with his thumb. An affair with Griff would be delightful. How lovers carried out their affairs was a complete mystery, but based on what she knew of Griff, he had the experience to guide them every step of the way. Whatever was going to happen to her heart by surrendering to their attraction had already occurred; they'd kissed, and she was still in control of her faculties. An affair with him was not going to destroy her.

They bid one another good evening with promises to meet soon for the purpose of discussing candidates for the governess and maid positions.

Griff took her hands in his. "I wonder how long this is going to hold up as an excuse."

"It's going to be a very long process…" Suki said with a shy smile. Their eyes met and affection welled within her. Had he asked her to join him on a trip to the other side of the world, she would have said yes, especially since that would put them far from Tsukiji tomorrow, which was where she wanted to be if Ned couldn't halt the presses on her column.

Inside the bakery, Suki greeted her old friend and apologized for not being able to visit over a cup of *chocolat chaud*, as was their usual custom. She chose a dozen choux cream pastries, accepted the weighty box, then rushed through Tsukiji's gates toward the *Tokyo Daily News* offices.

The house was quieter than she'd expected. There was only one occupant in the reporter's room, and he was scribbling furiously while wiping away ashes from the rolled cigarette dangling between his teeth. Suki sat on her usual chair in Ned's office and waited for nearly half an hour before he entered the room, bearing the tang of fresh ink.

He greeted her with one of his head-to-toe appraising looks. "Whatever brings Miss Malveaux to the *Tokyo Daily News* in the dark of night?"

Gritting her teeth against the urge to request he cease eyeing her in such a fashion, Suki began, "I realize you must be busy preparing the papers for tomorrow, but I need to make an amendment to the Tattler column."

Ned fell into his chair and took a cup of tea from the pot his housekeeper had brought for Suki. "I'm afraid changes would be impossible. Those sheets have already been printed."

Suki gripped the arms of the chair as though that would keep the world from crumbling beneath her. There must be something Ned could do. This problem must have occurred before. Newspapers received new information all the time. "Why can't you simply reprint those pages?"

"What's going on? This morning you brought me a fine column, some of your best writing. A dalliance here, a promise to marry there, some mischief at the Hotel Metropolis. You accused the Metropolis guests of insensitivity, but that's what the Tattler does."

"I'm not concerned about the hotel. I wrote a falsehood about the impending marriage of Griffith Spenser and Natsu Watanabe."

Ned shrugged. "That's gossip. Some of it turns out to be false. As a newspaperman, I've resigned myself to it."

"I just learned this afternoon that there is no engagement."

"But you had sources telling you otherwise when you wrote the column, right?"

Suki nodded.

"Print now, apologize later," Ned said with one of his indifferent shrugs.

She let out an exacerbated sigh. Ned was being stubborn. Were the mistake regarding a member of the peerage, British or Japanese, he wouldn't say, "apologize later." Griff may not be a nobleman, but he was well-known and highly respected in Tsukiji. "Mr. Spenser is an important member of our community. He's going to be furious when he reads about his supposed engagement in tomorrow's edition."

"Mr. Spenser is a man of business, and this newspaper is a business. He'll understand the costs involved in a reprint. We're not correcting those pages." Ned leaned forward on his desk. "Besides, I know Mrs. Watanabe, and I doubt she'd mind a little public attention."

Griff had said something similar about her. "How well do you know Mrs. Watanabe?"

Ned gritted his teeth against a long exhale. "Well enough."

Irritated at trying to do the right thing and being called unreasonable for it, she allowed herself the question any properly trained journalist would ask in response. "Have you ever been Mrs. Watanabe's lover?"

"Miss Malveaux." Ned threw the pencil on his desk. "You've got the reporter's edge. Perhaps you will get a byline soon."

"You evaded the question."

Ned grimaced the way he'd been grimacing since he'd returned from that trip to Hong Kong. Did Watanabe have something to do with the falling-out between Ned and his love? "No, I've never had the pleasure of being the object of Mrs. Watanabe's desires. But she is a lovely woman who's made plain her intentions to snare a foreign husband. Have you considered that the information you received today about Spenser and Watanabe may be mistaken? A man in his position knows a good deal when he sees it. Heck, most men would give one of their testicles to wed Mrs. Watanabe."

Suki felt the blood drain from her face at the word testicle. "I see."

"Pardon me for the coarse language. But that's the kind of talk you get in the newsroom. If you want to be a part of the boys' club, you'll have to get used to hearing about certain male body parts."

The university district's cafes buzzed with students and their tutors partaking in meals, ales, and conversation. "I'm fine with testicles," she replied loud enough for passersby to hear, and there wasn't a hitch to her voice. "What bothers me is the publication of a lie that may ruin Mrs. Watanabe's marital ambitions. We owe it to her, and to her late husband who sacrificed his life for this country."

"We can print a retraction in tomorrow's evening edition." Ned shuffled around his desk and picked out paper and the pencil he'd thrown a moment before. "Why don't you write one now, and I'll be sure to work it in?"

Suki accepted the paper and pencil and paused. The retraction would appear only hours after readers first learned of Griff's engagement to Watanabe. The gossip would be cinched almost as soon as it started. If she didn't issue the retraction, and waited until the following week to correct the erroneous news, then Griff and

Watanabe would have to spend an entire week explaining their dissolution of their relationship. It would be most convenient for them to have the retraction immediately. But she had no way of knowing how many people he'd told about ending the affair with Watanabe. Likewise, there was no knowing whether Watanabe had shared the news of her parting from Griff. A retraction this soon could reveal Suki as the column's author, and she couldn't let that happen

The pencil slipped from her hand and landed on the carpeted floor. She picked it up and held it between her fingers. As much as she wanted to spare Griff the discomfort of having to respond to the false news of his engagement, she couldn't have him learning she was the Tokyo Tattler. He could never know. He'd be furious if he ever found out he'd kissed the gossipmonger he despised.

Suki felt as though the wind had been knocked out of her. What had she gotten herself into? Kissing a man she'd called an incorrigible rake? She owed him an apology, many apologies, for what she'd written about his wife leaving him and his malicious intentions toward Watanabe, simply because he was a foreigner. She had every reason to believe Griff was better than other foreign men; he hadn't deserved to be treated in such a derisive manner.

Writing the retraction right now was the least she could do for him. But she couldn't do it because she had to protect herself.

In a way she was protecting Griff, too. He didn't want to know that he'd kissed the Tokyo Tattler. And he'd made it clear that he wanted to continue kissing Suki Malveaux. Just as she very much wanted his kisses, and more. This taste of passion he'd given her at Ueno Park promised horizons she could only imagine. But engaging in a love affair without disclosing her *nom de plume* felt wrong. Someday soon, she would have to explain why she'd started writing the Tattler column and, more importantly, why she'd written about him in such a disrespectful manner. Until she figured out how best to give these explanations, she needed the protection anonymity afforded.

"A retraction won't be necessary." Suki placed the paper and pencil on Ned's desk. "The information I received this afternoon can be written into next week's column."

"As you wish." Ned leaned back in his chair and raked a hand through his hair. "By the way, have you turned up anything on Baron Umezono?"

"I asked around this past week, and he sounds like a typical *bon vivant*." Ned didn't need to know about her failed attempt to seduce information from the baron.

"You should cast a wider net. This arrived today." Ned handed her an envelope similar to the first one she'd received about the baron. "I've been thinking about giving the story to one of the boys in the other room. They'd love sinking their teeth into a scandal concerning the Japanese peerage. But it seems to be beckoning you."

Suki accepted the letter.

The Tokyo Tattler appears to be squandering an opportunity to expose Baron Umezono's misdeeds. Progress in this regard will give comfort to his victims. How many more need suffer to appease this man's demons?

"Victims?" Had she almost become one of his victims at the Hotel Metropolis? Had Griff not been there, would the baron have forced her into a hotel room? Many a woman, no matter how much she abhorred the idea of spending the night with Baron Umezono, would be wary of making a scene at an illustrious hotel while he half-carried her away.

"So the letter says. We could be dealing with more than the innocent peccadilloes of a *bon vivant*. I can give the lead to another reporter if it's too much for you."

"No," Suki said firmly. This article on the baron could free her from the Tattler column, which had become vitally important. "That won't be necessary. I've already begun investigating and have every intention of continuing."

"Learn who's writing these letters as well. There's a story in here. I can feel it."

"And if the reporting is satisfactory?"

Ned leaned forward and placed his elbows on the desk. "Do this well, and I may be the first newspaperman in Tokyo with a regular female reporter."

"Then, when you find a new Tattler, you'll have two women employed at the newspaper."

"Who knew the *Tokyo Daily News* would be so progressive?"

***

Suki braced herself as she did every Wednesday morning. The Tattler column invariably provided topics for breakfast conversation, and Suki had no doubt today's topic would be Spenser and Watanabe's forthcoming nuptials.

She'd already told Rosie the truth about the engagement. The night before, after a dessert of choux cream pastries and copious amounts of tea, Rosie had followed Suki to her room for details about the afternoon with Griff. She regaled an appreciative Rosie with description of carp streamers, boxed lunches, and hours of conversation that included Griff's confession of having parted from Watanabe. Even without revealing the kisses, her breathless retelling of the afternoon, and the flush on her cheeks—which could very well have been an effect of the pastries and tea—must have made her seem like a "woman in the throes of love," because that was what Rosie accused her of being.

The rest of the night, Suki spent mostly awake, her heart fluttering with delight as she recalled the afternoon at the park, then thudding erratically as she imagined Griff discovering her *nom de plume*. The announcement of his engagement to Watanabe was going to compound his grievances against the Tattler. He would never forgive her. She could explain how the column was a way of warning Japanese women who pledged themselves to the worst sort of foreigner. She could tell him how his goodness and affection were making her less cynical. But stacked up against the damage she'd done to Griff's reputation, her reasoning would carry little weight.

If only she could finish her tenure as the Tattler before anyone learned she was Tsukiji's gossip, her authorship would remain secret, and Griff would never be the wiser. Then they could become lovers and do the things Marcelle had told her lovers did to one another, things that she wouldn't mind trying for herself. As long as she kept in mind that Griff was a foreigner and could leave for England at a moment's notice, he couldn't hurt her, and their affair could be quite satisfying.

Suki wished the family a good morning, then walked over to the sideboard. Much to her relief, Mother and Papa Garrick were trading rather loud opinions on the future site of the American Legation from opposite ends of the table. Rosie was asking Henry about which friends he would like to visit that afternoon, and *Okasan* had baby Charlie on her lap while she sipped a cup of green tea, which was how she finished every meal. No one was talking about Spenser, Watanabe, weddings, or any other of the week's gossip. Had Ned pulled the column or managed to insert a revision?

Relieved to the point of giddiness, Suki happily gathered a bowl of rice porridge topped with runny egg and a plate of buttered toast from the sideboard and took her seat next to *Okasan*. Resting a napkin on her lap, she looked up to find herself the object of Mother Garrick's scrutiny. A surprised and delighted gleam suffused the matron's eyes. All hope faded. Legation conversation had been a false flag; the Tattler column had gone to print.

"Did Mr. Spenser say anything yesterday about marrying Mrs. Watanabe?" Mother Garrick asked.

"Not a word," Suki replied and took a small bite of toast.

Mother Garrick placed a finger on the newsprint laid out beside her teacup. "We were discussing this the other day. The Tattler says Mrs. Watanabe has been asking around for wedding gowns, a sure sign of their upcoming marriage. But you and Mr. Spenser went looking for furnishings for the wards' rooms only yesterday. It really should be Mrs. Watanabe's decision. She should choose what kind of furniture ends up in her home."

Suki had excused her lateness the previous evening by telling the family that after viewing the carp streamers, Mr. Spenser had taken her on a shopping expedition to outfit rooms for his wards. In truth, Griff had asked her to assist him with that very task at a future date, and her body temperature rose every time she imagined them walking side by side along Ginza Boulevard, their hands brushing as they inspected the curtain fabric.

"Perhaps they're not marrying." Rosie winked at Suki from across the table, which, thankfully, no one seemed to notice. "If you recall, Roger said he'd heard nothing about marriage from Mr. Spenser at the lawn tennis tournament."

"Then the Tattler would be mistaken, which would be quite rare," Mother Garrick said and gave the newspaper another jab. "Whoever is writing the column has a reputation for accuracy."

"It has to be Mrs. Pennington. She hears everything in that store of hers," Rosie mused.

Mother Garrick made a tsking sound at Rosie. Discussion of the Tattler's identity tended to start a series of speculations that veered far from the subject at hand. "Mr. Spenser should marry for the sake of his wards."

"His niece and nephew need someone to help them adjust to life in Tokyo," *Okasan* added as she jiggled Charlie, who cooed his approval.

"They'll have Suki." Rosie shot Suki a sly grin.

Suki glared back. "They'll have a governess and maid attending to their needs."

"I bet he marries her," Papa Garrick chimed in.

"Marries Suki?" Rosie asked with exaggerated innocence, which made Suki nearly toss a slice of toast straight at her sister-in-law.

"Of course not Suki," Papa Garrick grumbled as though that was the most ridiculous suggestion he'd ever heard. "Mrs. Watanabe. Now that the cat is out of the bag, he might as well claim his kitten."

Mother Garrick murmured her approval. "I'm sure there is an agreement between them. The news has appeared in print. There is no backing out now. That would be humiliating for Mrs. Watanabe."

The toast Suki had just swallowed seemed to catch in her throat. Griff had said in no uncertain terms the affair with Watanabe was over. But might he reconsider in order to spare her, and himself, the embarrassment of a broken engagement? Suki coughed and grabbed her teacup. The warm brew freed the dry bread from her throat.

"An appearance in the scandal sheets is no reason to pledge your life to another," Rosie said.

Papa Garrick tilted his head forward and raised his brows. "Men marry for the shape of the breast and hips. That's how they know the wife will be good for childbearing."

"Men choose wives for their high moral character," Mother Garrick retorted. It was a familiar argument.

"So they say," Papa Garrick replied with obvious disbelief.

"Well, I've never noticed the shape of Mrs. Watanabe's hips," Roger said.

"They're hardly worthy of note," Rosie said and winked again at Suki.

***

Most mornings during the spring holiday, Suki had been helping *Okasan* sew an intricate seed-pearl embellishment on a gown commissioned for the British envoy's midsummer ball. Resuming her place from the day before, Suki rolled an ivory bead between her fingers and wondered whether it was possible Griff would marry Watanabe simply because everyone in Tsukiji believed they were engaged.

Yesterday, he'd talked about her being better suited for another man. He couldn't match Watanabe's affection, he'd said, which Suki had taken to mean that he'd been the one to initiate their parting. His mind about Watanabe was made up. Marrying her because of a rumor regarding their engagement was unfathomable. Griff had been married before. After the dissolution of one marriage, would he make such an inauspicious start to another?

Suki doubted it. But did Watanabe? Ned had said Watanabe was determined to marry a foreigner. By all appearances, she'd decided that foreigner would be Griff. In her desperation to save the affair, might she have tried to force a commitment by inquiring about wedding gowns?

Surely, she knew such a stratagem would backfire. A worldly woman who spoke multiple languages and had already been married would realize that she cannot trap a man into marriage and then expect his devotion and esteem. But if all she cared about was status in the Tsukiji community, then she might not mind a cold husband.

Even if Watanabe failed to win back Griff, rumors circulating about her search for a wedding gown made it look like he'd given her the impression of their being engaged. A woman who'd believed she was heading down the aisle, but was tossed aside instead, could garner allies to condemn Griff and rebuild her reputation.

No matter Watanabe's reasoning for her wedding gown search, the Tokyo Tattler had taken her bait, and once again the column was going to make Griff suffer.

After several hours of sewing, Suki headed toward her room to return overdue correspondence. Passing the front hall table, she noticed a long package. The attached letter, addressed to Suki Malveaux, bore a man's handwriting. Hands shaking, she turned it over. The sender's name brought a smile to her lips.

Dear Miss Malveaux,

Thank you for the pleasure of your company yesterday. Please find a small token of appreciation for all you have done for my niece and nephew. I hope it will not be too much of an imposition to request your further assistance.

This Friday evening, the headmaster from Tsukiji Secondary School and his wife will be dining at my home for the purpose of discussing prospects for Marianne and Lucien's education. I would be grateful if you could attend. Your insight will be invaluable both as a secondary schoolteacher and family friend.

Warmest regards,
Griffith Spenser

The package bore the insignia of Ginza's most prestigious boutique. Inside was a European-style parasol of light indigo silk with a lace overlay, and it was breathtakingly beautiful. Grasping the smooth handle, she pushed open the ribs. The color reminded her of a bright spring sky marked with carp streamers.

More thrilling was the invitation to dine at Griff's home. With only vague plans for their next meeting, she'd felt like a fisherman's boat bobbing offshore. Now she had only two days to wait until they were together again. Then she could look into his gaze and know that the attraction between them, which was so overwhelming that she sometimes suspected it was merely a dazzling figment of her imagination, was, indeed, real.

Collapsing the parasol, she ran a hand from the wooded nub at the top, down the lacy silk, to the firm bamboo handle. Granted, the exquisite parasol was a very good sign their attraction was real for Griff, which was exciting and terrifying, because any tender feelings he felt for her would be multiplied in hate if he learned she was the Tattler.

She wanted to believe that soon she'd produce a spectacular article on Baron Umezono and give up the business of gossip. But what if the baron didn't give her a story worthy of print? What if he did, and Griff, along with everyone in Tsukiji, learned she was the Tattler anyway?

After returning the parasol to the box, she tucked it under her arm and walked toward the stairs. In truth, part of her welcomed being revealed. It was going to entail a lot of difficult explaining, especially to her family. But she'd been preparing to weather that emotional tumult for the past two years and had strategies in mind.

It would also mean receiving credit for creating the column, for all the work she'd put into obtaining and presenting the town's gossip. The column was precious to her. She took pride in its success. Tsukiji's women loved the gossipy talk, and the Tattler was a much-needed voice warning young Japanese women against the world of hurt that came from losing their hearts to a foreign man. Sometimes she'd made mistakes, as she had in maligning Griff, but her mistakes were no more frequent or severe than any other reporter's at the *Tokyo Daily News*.

She ought to tell Griff sooner rather than later, before they grew fonder of one another, before the betrayal of his trust became profound. Let him direct his anger at her, not at a faceless Tattler, and be done with it. He would probably despise her for all that she'd written, but if he didn't… That would be too good to be true.

Taking the stairs to the second floor, she considered penning Griff a letter confessing all. But it was still too early to confess. She was yet the column's author, and protecting her anonymity was paramount. Maybe once his niece and nephew had settled into their new lives in Tokyo, she'd tell him. By then, she should have impressed Ned with her top-notch reporting and moved on to more important journalism, and Griff and the rest of Tsukiji would better understand why she'd come to write the column in the first place.

But none of that was possible until she uncovered something of significance about Baron Umezono. The Ginza Girls School resumed classes tomorrow, and she hadn't begun considering how to investigate the victims mentioned in the letter Ned had shown her the previous day. She needed to stop mulling over the handsome, upright Griffith Spenser and direct her thoughts to the lustful, profligate, and possibly criminal, Baron Umezono.

CHAPTER THIRTEEN

Determined to find the perfect gift for Suki, even if it took him all day, Griff was at the Ginza boutique when its doors opened. The parasol caught his eye almost as soon as he entered the store. Nevertheless, he asked to see nearly all the proprietor's Japanese-crafted, Western-inspired goods. Suki's gift was in there somewhere.

"She must be a beauty," the proprietor said when Griff finally decided on the parasol.

"Beautiful, but also witty and clever."

"It's good when a woman is more than beautiful," the proprietor said, his English as confident as his store was popular with the Tsukiji crowd. "She will make a good—" He pursed his lips. "—companion, is that the word?"

Companion brought to mind an elderly woman beaming at her helper. But it rang of suitability, and he and Suki were in many ways suited. "A companion in a sense. She's not interested in marriage, as she is busy with her work."

"She's a working woman, then…" the proprietor murmured, as though he well understood the appeal of women working in the pleasure quarters.

"She's a teacher," Griff corrected.

"Teachers work hard. You're an understanding man."

"I've been married once already."

The proprietor sighed. "Then you know what happens a few years into marriage. You're right to take her as your lover. Marry for the children."

"Quite true, old chap," Griff replied, although he disagreed. The idea of pledging himself to a lifetime of loyalty and love appealed even after a failed marriage. Funny how the woman he fancied right now seemed to think so little of the institution.

He left the boutique mulling over the indeterminate place he'd found himself with Suki. He couldn't put his finger on what he wanted from her. Nor could he say for certain what she wanted from him. She'd told him that night at his home that she didn't wish to marry, but women only said that when they were obliged to care for parents or other relations, or couldn't bear children, or found men's company repugnant. None of these seemed to apply in Suki's case. She'd said her mother was in excellent health and had a thriving business. Physically, Suki seemed in good health herself, and based on their interaction in Ueno Park, he would guess she found the company of men satisfying.

Suki simply wanted to work. Other women wanted the same. It was the modern world, after all. Eventually, though, she'd want a husband and children, wouldn't she?

Griff reached the crossing before Tsukiji's gates and stepped into the muddy road. A rickshaw runner shouted warning before swerving to avoid ploughing Griff to the ground. A cyclist, in turn, had to swerve to avoid the rickshaw and a cascade of shouts went down the street. Calling out apologies to everyone near and far, Griff made his way on the other side. And his mind returned to the question of what Suki wanted.

He supposed she wished for them to be lovers. He was willing— no, eager, unreasonably eager—to accommodate that wish. But what would that make them? Companions? Gladly, he'd escort her to events around the city, and she could accompany him on those occasions when a partner was needed. Then they could spend the remainder of the night at a hotel or the love nest he would set up outside of Tsukiji.

But what of her family? Would they approve, however tacitly, of an affair? The Garrick family had lived in Tsukiji for decades, and were well-respected, highly involved members of the community. Suki might be able to offer excuses for the occasional night away from home, but anything more might threaten the Garrick family's reputation. He couldn't even fathom what her Japanese mother would think.

As much as it frustrated him to have no clear idea about how they would proceed, he wanted her more. Provided their liaison involved kissing, much more kissing, and all the tugs, nibbles, licks, caresses, and bites she desired, he'd accommodate whatever arrangement she preferred.

***

Griff's secretaries, two young Japanese men educated at Tsukiji's St. Paul's University, rose to greet him with a bow when he entered the firm's offices. The morning custom made him feel like he'd ascended the English throne, but it was the Japanese way.

Today, they wore broad, foolish grins.

"What the devil is going on?" he asked.

"You're getting married. Congratulations!" Ichiro said.

"Congratulations!" Tsuyoshi echoed.

Griff shook his head at the absurdity. He'd been married, that much was true. But he was not presently readying for another journey down the aisle. "I'm afraid there's been a mistake. I'm not getting married."

Ichiro pointed at the newsprint on his desk. "But it says right here in the newspaper that you've promised to marry Watanabe-*san*."

Although he suspected who was responsible for the misinformation, he braced himself to utter the she-devil's name. "I take it this is coming from the Tokyo Tattler?"

Ichiro nodded. "Of course."

Griff accepted Ichiro's copy of the newspaper and took it to his desk. It was already open to the Tattler column. His gaze scanned the usual drivel until reaching the final paragraph. Yes, apparently, he was getting married. Natsu was looking for wedding gowns, so a wedding was on the horizon.

Damn Natsu, conniving woman knew she could ask around for wedding gowns and the news would spread straight to the town gossip. Had she thought he'd reconsider their parting once he'd seen news of their impending lifetime union in print? Did she think he was the sort of man who thought it a splendid idea to spend the rest of his life with a woman who'd trapped him into marriage?

Let everyone in Tsukiji condemn him for escorting her around town and giving her the impression she should be inquiring about wedding gowns. They could join the blasted Tattler in damning him as an incorrigible rake who humiliates and deserts his Japanese lover. He would not be bullied into marriage.

He didn't know who he wanted to curse more: Natsu or the Tattler. Unless they were one and the same. Then he could take care of two birds with one stone. Not that he should be throwing stones at Natsu. She was part of his past. He had Suki now. Who was probably at this very moment listening to someone spouting the Tattler's lies. She might not be a reader of the gossip column, but its contents spread through Tsukiji like a bad flu.

Even though he'd told Suki the affair with Natsu had ended, she might hear the news of his upcoming marriage and think him a liar and seducer who would say anything for a passionate interlude in the park's shadows.

He should go straight to her home and explain Natsu's manipulation, and his suspicions that Natsu was the Tattler, or at least familiar with the scandalmonger. But what would the Garrick family make of Tsukiji's incorrigible rake storming into their home with wild accusations against Tsukiji's favourite war widow? What would Suki think?

Better to pen a message with assurances that he and Natsu had parted, then attempt to focus on his work while awaiting her response.

Much to his relief, a few hours later, he received Suki's reply. She'd never doubted his affair with Natsu was over. Newspaper reports, she explained, sometimes lacked a full grasp of the story. Surely, the Tattler would learn he and Natsu had parted and correct the false story in a future column.

Included in Suki's reply was her thanks for the elegant and stylish parasol, and acceptance of his invitation to dine with the headmaster two days hence. In the privacy of his home, they'd be far from the public eye, and he wouldn't have to worry about the Tattler getting wind of him and Suki dining together. Then again, his home wasn't entirely safe. Natsu had spied on him when Suki had last visited. He wouldn't put it past her to do it again. Nor would he put it past her to punish him for ending their affair by spreading rumours about him and Suki that would eventually end up in the Tattler column. He could already imagine the condemnation of Mr. Spenser, town Lothario, for snaring another Japanese woman in his evil clutches. Then how would the Garrick family feel about letting their daughter spend time with him?

Ignoring the Tattler was no longer an option. The damnable gossip's fascination with him needed to cease, or he would never be free to pursue his companionship—if that was how to describe it— with Suki.

Speaking directly to Ned Taylor was one way to end the madness. Foremost he wanted the Tattler to refrain from reporting on his life. Also, he wanted a correction to this week's column. Although Griff and the *Tokyo Daily News* owner weren't on familiar terms, they had mutual acquaintances. A friend could direct Griff to a restaurant or pub Taylor favoured, and Griff could pull him aside for a word. The newspaper's proprietor should feel obliged to heed Griff's request, since the item about his impending nuptials was so far removed from the truth. Or a mate from the lawn tennis club could contact Taylor on Griff's behalf. A practice session started in a few hours. After fending off his teammates' congratulations on his engagement, he'd ask someone who knew Taylor well enough.

Then he'd be able to focus on important matters, namely how he would finagle time alone with Suki at this Friday's supper with the headmaster. Perhaps he had a French missive that needed translation? Naturally, the letter was in the study, which was as good a place as any to relive those moments under the shade of Ueno Park's cherry trees. This time he'd pay more attention to her neck and venture to the curve of her shoulder. He could already hear those sweet purring noises she'd made in the park. The cut of her dress permitting, he'd venture to her plush breast and tease her nipple to a peak. What kind of sounds would she make then?

"Spenser-*san*, here is the assessment of the Indian cotton deal you asked about." Tsuyoshi placed several sheets of paper on his desk.

"Right, thank you. I'll look at it shortly."

The assessment should keep him at his desk for the next fifteen minutes, which was about the length of time needed before he could rise without an embarrassing admission of what happened when a man had sordid thoughts about his companion.

CHAPTER FOURTEEN

From the Ginza Girls School, Suki went home to change into a Western-style dress before heading to the American envoy's home. She and Griff had exchanged several messages since Wednesday concerning preparations for his niece and nephew's arrival. He'd been under the impression that she had a comprehensive understanding about what it was like growing up in France. Each time he asked about schooling, childhood amusements, or churchgoing, Suki sent a message to Marcelle for an answer. After several rounds of acting as go-between, Suki suggested she bring Marcelle to supper with the headmaster. Griff agreed, and, fortunately, Marcelle's mistress didn't require her services.

Suki, on the other hand, very much needed her best friend's services. The mere thought of seeing Griff cast a sensual weight upon her, leaving her unbalanced and easily distracted. She paused in the middle of grading students' papers, lifting chopsticks, or brushing her hair to ponder how it'd felt to be caught in the gaze of his soft brown eyes and caressed with his gentle, but eager mouth. What would she do when she finally encountered him in the flesh? Lose her breath? Forget her name? Faint outright? Marcelle, with her volubility and humor, would divert attention from Suki's unraveling.

They met at the front gates of the envoy's home. With her dark hair piled atop her head and an emerald-green dress showing off her ivory skin, Marcelle was easily the most stunning woman in Tsukiji. Even in the bright blue evening dress with crimson ribbons around the hem and neckline that *Okasan* had made specially for her, Suki felt like a houseplant yet to bloom. At least she'd know for certain whether Griff truly had eyes for her.

Marcelle gave a twirl. "Twice in less than a week I get to wear one of madame's dresses. The maids are probably mad with jealousy. I know they say terrible things behind my back. My Japanese is still dreadful. You must come to one of their late-night gatherings and listen to what they're saying."

"Everyone adores you," Suki reassured her best friend in all honesty. She didn't know anyone who would decline the opportunity to bask in Marcelle's glow.

"Only because I flirt shamelessly with anyone who will speak to me."

"That doesn't hurt."

Suki set off at a slow pace so that Marcelle's excitement wouldn't have them in front of Griff's house inexcusably early. "Perhaps you might flirt with the headmaster this evening?" Suki teased, although that could give her and Griff a chance to converse alone.

"I don't wish to upset the headmaster's wife."

"You're French," Suki said, using the excuse Marcelle herself gave for her exuberant flirting. "That gives you license to bat your eyes at every man in the room."

"You're French too," Marcelle pointed out. "I'm not the only one who'll be flirting this evening. I cannot wait to see you and Monsieur Spenser together."

"What are you talking about? We're not a couple."

Marcelle shook her head, and the golden earbobs she'd borrowed to match her dress shifted with her, catching light from the gas lamps lining the street. "You spent the entire day with him at the park. He gave you a parasol worth more than I earn for a year's worth of work."

"It was a gift for helping him find a governess and maid."

Marcelle wrapped an arm through Suki's elbow and pulled her closer. "Or a kiss in the middle of the woods?" she asked.

"It was a few trees in a public park."

"You kissed."

"We did, and it was marvelous." Heat poured through Suki, no doubt turning her face an unholy color of red that needed to subside before they reached the Spenser home.

Marcelle squeezed Suki's arm. "You're a couple."

"We're friends, close friends."

"Exactly," Marcelle said as though she'd won the point.

Griff stood waiting in the entrance as they arrived. At the sight of her, his eyes lit up and a private smile crossed his lips, giving Suki every confidence he reciprocated her feelings, the gorgeous Marcelle notwithstanding. When the beauty turned to accept slippers from Griff's housekeeper, he brushed his fingers against Suki's. Electricity pulsed across her skin and a delicious, wanton sensation stirred in her innermost places. Heat sprang once again to her cheeks, leaving little doubt that she was going to be an embarrassing scarlet for the entirety of the evening.

They'd arrived earlier than the headmaster in order for Marcelle to make recommendations about the rooms for Griff's niece and nephew. While he showed them the front and back parlors and dining room on the first floor, Marcelle regaled him with descriptions of French homes and meals and informed him of the colors that might appeal to his niece and nephew and the flowers they might miss during the month of May. At times, Suki supplied Marcelle with an English word, but mostly she stayed silent, admiring the way Griff treated a woman in service.

They were heading down the second-floor hallway to the room that would be his niece's when the front bell sounded. Griff excused himself to greet the headmaster and his wife, and Marcelle tapped Suki on the arm. "How dare the Tattler gossip about that wonderful man? He'd sooner commit *harakiri* than hurt a woman. All those words about him being an incorrigible rake were absolutely false."

Suki pressed a finger to Marcelle's lips to get her to speak softer. They were still near the stairs, and there was no way of knowing how sound traveled through the Spenser home. "After he saved me from that disgusting baron, I had no doubt of the monsieur's integrity." Of her own, she was continually uncertain, but so far that evening, Griff hadn't mentioned the Tattler column, which meant it wasn't foremost in his mind. "Thankfully, he seems to be in good spirits. I'd been worried he'd be upset because of the marriage announcement."

"That detestable Tattler would be best to mind her own affairs," Marcelle said with an imperious raise of brow. "We should go downstairs to greet the headmaster. He's about to become the object of a Frenchwoman's designs."

Suki turned toward the stairs. "And his wife? What will she think?"

"She'll clutch him all the tighter tonight," Marcelle said with romantic wistfulness.

"Lucky man," Suki replied.

At the bottom of the stairs, muted voices from outside filtered into the home. "Monsieur Spenser must be giving them a tour of the garden," she said to Marcelle.

Suki was nearly finished lacing her short leather boots to join them when the conversation grew louder. "I'm meant to be here," a woman said, her English inflected with a Japanese accent.

"No, you're not," Griff replied, his words slow and deliberate. "Our relationship is over."

Suki and Marcelle exchanged wide-eyed glances.

"I can help with the children," the woman said. "I'll teach them everything they need to know. They must learn Japanese customs and manners, and the best places to shop, who they should talk to, who they should be seen with. Remember how much I taught you? You were lost before you met me."

"Let me assure you, I have plenty of help. You must go."

The door opened, and Suki was face-to-face with the woman she knew from having seen a handful of times in passing. In a heavy, silk kimono the color of red hibiscus, Natsu Watanabe looked as though she belonged in the empress's retinue. Their gazes met, and an ugly expression flashed across Watanabe's impeccable features.

Suki turned to Griff. "I'm sorry. I thought you were touring the garden with the headmaster. We were about to join you."

Watanabe stepped up to the front door and bowed deeply. "I must apologize for disturbing your evening. I'm Natsu Watanabe. It's a pleasure to make your acquaintance." Her gaze traveled from Suki to Marcelle, then back to Suki and narrowed as though having discerned a blemish. "Are you among the headmaster's party?" she asked in Japanese.

"I'm Suki Malveaux and this is my friend, Marcelle Renaud," Suki replied in Japanese. "I'm a schoolteacher, and Spenser-*san* requested my assistance in finding an English governess to help with his wards' education. Renaud-*san* is in service at the American envoy's home and is helping Spenser-*san* locate a French woman to serve as maid."

"I can see all is well at Spenser-*san*'s home," Watanabe replied in English with a pleasant smile.

"I told you everything was taken care of," Griff said as though speaking to a misbehaving child. Then he turned to Suki and his eyes softened.

Her heart fluttered, and she could feel that persistent flush spreading up her neck.

"In that case, I'll bid you good night," Watanabe said and bowed.

She exited the front gate with a light step, her shoulders relaxed, the pleasant smile yet on her face, seeming for all the world as though departing after an ordinary visit to a friend's home.

Griff shut the front door after she and Marcelle entered. "I apologise for the intrusion. Mrs Watanabe wishes to be of assistance, and I was trying to make her understand that her assistance is not needed. She doesn't seem to have accepted our parting. I feel like I've spent the entirety of this week clarifying the status of our relationship to everyone in Tsukiji. Yet she, who knows better than anyone what occurred between us, cannot grasp the truth." A grimace creased his face. "The Tokyo Tattler really set me up this time."

Suki swallowed against the lump in her throat. "The Tokyo Tattler will certainly issue a correction in the coming week. As you have spread the word through Tsukiji, the author must know of your parting from Mrs Watanabe."

"Frankly, I wish whoever was writing that wretched column would just leave my name out of it. I can't imagine I'm the most fascinating individual in this town."

"Some people like to see their name in the newspaper," Marcelle said soothingly.

"I'm not one of them. Mrs Watanabe likes the attention. As for me, I want the Tattler out of my life."

Suki's gut twisted into knots.

"But let's not dwell on that unexpected visitor," Griff said. "I still haven't shown you the front parlour and—"

The bell at the front gate rang.

They fell silent and remained that way until the sounds of lively English conversation between an older man and woman filtered into the entrance.

Griff released a long breath. "Our guests have arrived. I'll have to show you the rooms another time."

***

For the evening meal, Griff presented a rich, earthy bouillabaisse and cheesy mushroom croquettes, two of the French dishes his cook had recently mastered. But Marcelle took center stage with teasing comments, probing questions, and lavish compliments for the affable headmaster. His wife seemed to delight in the adoration heaped upon her husband and thanked Marcelle on giving the headmaster the most pleasant dining experience he'd had in ages.

And no one seemed to notice Suki's and Griff's gazes meeting, and the air humming with the electricity between them that made her limbs feel like melting candle wax. Nor did they notice that Suki only managed small bites of the succulent fish and tiny sips of the fragrant broth, as she felt suffused with longing to satisfy an entirely different appetite: she craved Griff's lips on hers, his hands moving along her body as they had at Ueno Park.

Following supper, they retired to the front parlor, and conversation turned to French methods of education. Marcelle recalled her years in school and made observations about the French school system more generally. Neither the headmaster nor his wife gave Griff and Suki a second glance when they excused themselves for Griff to show Suki letters of recommendation he'd received on behalf of candidates for the governess position.

"Letters of recommendation, already?" she whispered as they walked down the hallway.

He placed a hand on the small of her back, sending waves of warmth through her body. "So many letters it's going to take hours to go through them all," he whispered back.

Like the front parlor, the study faced the home's bountiful garden. Suki walked over to the window. Moonlight left silver slashes on new leaves rustling in the wind. Griff came up behind her. Taking a small step backward, she leaned into the firm muscles of his chest. His arms circled hers, and her body went slack. She'd reached her destination. It smelled of exotic spices and dark wine, and it felt like abundance.

Leaning down, he caressed the skin of her nape with his lips. Her head lolled, and sturdy hands tightened around her waist. Griff wasn't going to let her fall.

"These past few days provided one infuriation after another," he said, his voice husky. "At the same time, nothing mattered but seeing you again."

Regret gnawed her insides. If only she'd been able to stop the column, then Griff wouldn't have been forced to endure infuriation after infuriation. "I'm sorry the week has been so difficult."

"It's not your fault," he said. Ugly pangs of guilt turned her stomach. How could she let him hold her when she'd caused him so much aggravation? He settled his lips on the shell of her ear. "You were my saving grace. I had our kisses to remember."

She shivered at his breath on the tiny hairs of her lobes. Griff didn't deserve to suffer such anguish, and she wasn't innocent enough to revel in his embrace. But she was here, and their kisses had given him comfort. She turned in his arms. His remained wrapped around her, holding her close. Then she gazed on his lips. He closed his eyes and lowered his head, and she met his lips with a pressing need to ease his distress, but even more so, with desire built up from days of imagining their next kisses. Every nerve in her body danced as their lips joined and nagging thoughts about gossip columns and unintended consequences disappeared like the moon behind a cluster of dark clouds. After bringing her arms around his neck, she drew him closer and pressed her lips harder. Their tongues mingled, and a flame ignited within her that summoned a wanton creature who delighted in the force of his mouth and the feel of his body against hers.

"You're driving me to madness, Suki," Griff whispered and traced kisses along her jawline. The brush of his upper lip, rough with stubble, was irritation and raw pleasure.

"That was my intention."

He pulled back. Desire burned in his gaze. "I want to hear all your intentions."

"Kisses," she said in a breathy voice. "I intend to have many more of your kisses."

He responded with plentiful kisses—slow and purposeful—down her nape to the crimson ribbons of her bodice. Delectable heat gathered between her legs. Grabbing the arms of his jacket, she pressed into him. Her nipples tightened against the jacket's wool and the pressure building inside her burst forth in light purrs.

"I love that sound," he said, his voice ragged.

He stopped the gentle strokes to her back and traced his fingertips to the swell of her breast. She braced, her body anticipating the pain she'd experienced at the hand of Baron Umezono. But Griff's touch was lovely. Gently, he kneaded the silk of her dress and the flesh beneath it. Like a contented feline, she purred again.

On her puckered nipple, he rested his palm and turned circles, each whirl making her breath quicken and her head light. Sensation ricocheted through her body, then gathered in her deepest reaches as a heavy, throbbing ache that propelled her toward him. She dug her fingers into his shoulders at the same moment his hot mouth came down on the silk over her hard nub. She gasped, then shuddered at the utter joy of it.

Releasing her breast, he looked up at her with a wide, satisfied grin. Then his shameless mouth came down on the other side, and her hands reached into the thick locks on the back of his head, pressing that mouth deeper into her bosom. Head thrown back, she freed her hips to move of their own volition. And their primal dance brought the ridge of his manhood to the inside of her thigh.

The length of him rubbed against her leg as his mouth roamed the exposed skin at the top of her chest. Letting out a long groan, he squeezed her waist. "I want you, Suki, every part of you."

"I want…." She struggled for words. She wanted to explore him, to give him the pleasure she'd felt, to touch him as he'd touched her. So she dared to brush her fingertips against the stiffness jutting from his trousers.

Griff groaned a rush of damp heat into her nape, then stepped away from her touch. "Wonderful Suki." Bringing her fingers to his lips, he planted soft kisses on each one. "If only guests weren't sitting in the other room."

Her fingers trembled under the care of his lips. "If only."

"Next time?" he asked, a devilish twinkle in his eyes.

The riotous passion that had consumed her moments before quieted to a low hum of anticipation. "Next time," she echoed.

Griff pulled her to his chest. "And when might that be?"

The question hit her like a splash of cold water. Tomorrow's faculty meeting, preparations for next week's lessons, classroom duties, grading, and reporting students' marks demanded her time; she also had the Tattler column due in four days and the investigation of Baron Umezono's favorite nighttime establishments. Of all her commitments, the only one she could reasonably toss aside was the investigation of Baron Umezono, which amounted to giving up her best chance to become a reporter and cease gossipmongering.

She hated to think of Griff being alone and wanting her company, but she had no company to give. "I'm sorry, but I'm quite busy until the end of next week."

"Then we'll meet at the end of next week. We can discuss my niece and nephew's furnishings more extensively then. I seem to be making so little progress," he said with mock dismay.

Relieved, she kissed him tenderly, but firmly in the hope of giving him another kiss to remember for the week they'd be apart.

Griff ran his hand down her back. "I'll be counting the days until we can continue with our illicit courting…" He paused and the expression he'd given the green tea they'd drunk when she'd first visited his house home returned. "No, we can't call it that. Sounds too much like we're planning to elope. How about our romantic interludes? No, that sounds boring."

Nothing between them could ever qualify as boring. "An interlude does sound terribly brief."

He pushed away a strand of hair that had loosened from her chignon. "I'm not letting you go anytime soon."

The words vibrated through her. How she wanted to continue this seductive embrace. "A lengthy interlude, then?"

He shook his head. "Too contradictory. How about a flirtation of uncertain duration?"

"That's a mouthful," she said, and the words instantly brought to mind the mouthful he'd taken of her breasts, which made her heart race and another intractable flush rise to the skin of her chest.

"We could say a fling, with no specified time limit," Griff suggested.

"A fling…I like that." It fit well enough, as it appeared they were going to be lovers, a thought that made her feel giddy and hopeless at the same time. She was yet the Tattler and had many amends to make if anyone ever found out. And he would always be a foreigner who might board a ship back to his home country tomorrow. Not that she expected he would take such drastic action with his niece and nephew arriving. And his work, and the lawn tennis club, seemed to bring him great satisfaction. But he was a foreigner, and she was Japanese, even if she had a foreign father and lived in the foreign quarter and spoke several languages. How could she trust him with the truth? Did he even want to know? After their kisses tonight, she could reasonably surmise he preferred ignorance.

Griff took her hand and studied the palm, then leaned down and kissed its center. "I'm going to spend the week thinking of nothing else but this fling."

The feel of his lips lingered as he withdrew. Already she longed for him. Was she being foolish to make them wait a week? Should she forget about Baron Umezono and his misdeeds?

No, she wasn't going to let her feelings for Griff overcome her good sense. She had priorities, and a fling ranked among them, but couldn't be the most important.

Shortly after eleven o'clock, the headmaster and his wife took their leave. Suki and Griff walked Marcelle back to the envoy's home and bid her good night at the wrought-iron gates. On the way to Suki's home, they walked with a respectable distance between them, their steps slow.

"How is it," he asked, his voice rising with a suspicious lilt, "that Marcelle handled the headmaster like a professional geisha yet spoke like a bureaucrat on the fundamentals of France's educational system?"

"I've often wondered similarly. She went to good schools. Her father was from an aristocratic line, but poor, even before the revolution. From what I understand, she was orphaned as a baby and lived with various relations during her childhood, usually those who needed the allowance she received after her parents' passing."

"How sad," he said, his tone sympathetic.

Was he thinking of his niece and nephew, who'd lost their parents and were now traveling around the world to live with him in Tokyo? "I suspect it was quite difficult for her. Eventually, she moved to Paris and lived with cousins. Then she fell in love with a man who ended up marrying another. The American envoy's wife offered her employment when they were visiting Paris on a diplomatic tour. Marcelle accompanied them from Paris to Tokyo about two years ago."

"She's brave to have come all this way and started a new life."

"Very brave, and wise. She knows everything, especially about fashion." Marcelle also had vast knowledge about all the naughty things men and women did to bring one another pleasure, but that wasn't something one mentioned on the streets of Tsukiji, even at this late hour when there were few people about to eavesdrop over the croaking frogs and the whirling gusts off Tokyo Bay. Nor did Suki feel quite ready to discuss such things with Griff.

She continued, "I don't think Marcelle will be a lady's maid much longer. I imagine her becoming a modiste with her own store in Tsukiji. She talks about staying in Tokyo when the envoy's family returns to the United States."

"I imagine she would do well with her own boutique," he said, then turned his gaze to Suki. "How about you? How did you end up working at the girls' school?"

"I attended the missionary schools in Tsukiji. Everyone told me I should train to be a teacher of languages. Very few Japanese can read, write, and speak several languages."

Griff gave a short laugh. "Not many British can, either. Some can speak French or the ancient languages, Latin or Greek, but those aren't very useful. Your school is fortunate to have you."

"I'm fortunate to be there. The headmaster was a professor of languages at the Imperial University before accepting the position at Ginza Girls School. He places great emphasis on language-learning and offered me an apprenticeship as soon as I graduated secondary school. Three years ago, I was appointed to the school faculty. It's a good place for the girls. Most of them are attentive and curious about the world. Their families are among the nobility, as well as the new class of industrialists and government bureaucrats. They want educated daughters who will raise educated sons."

"It sounds like an important position."

A powerful gust sent a shiver through Suki despite her heavy satin cloak. "I enjoy it." She didn't often reflect on her work at the girls' school as a source of enjoyment. She had always been quick to tell others—Griff included—how important teaching was to her and how busy it kept her. This had become a way of excusing herself from assuming other responsibilities like marriage and being the governess for a handsome man's wards. But she did enjoy working at the school. Her teaching responsibilities had become easier over the years as she'd learned how to better communicate with students and faculty alike. If she ever became a newspaper reporter, she would miss it. "I feel like I make a difference. I teach my students about the rights of women in the modern world, and some of them choose to work. They become teachers and take roles in their family enterprises. With their determination, it's only a matter of time before women can vote and enroll in the same university courses as men."

"Your students must admire you." Griff kicked a large stone out of Suki's way. The recent rains had made a mess of the streets; pedestrians were fortunate not to twist an ankle, and Suki was fortunate to have such a considerate escort.

"I'm not sure they would admit to admiration. They look rather horrified when I give them my hard face." Suki lifted her brow, widened her eyes, and pressed her mouth into a straight line.

"That is rather frightening," Griff said, and gave her a scared face that looked more like the face of a horrified foreigner tasting fermented soybeans for the first time.

Suki laughed. "The truth is, I wouldn't mind leaving the school for another type of work."

"You said before that you wanted to be a newspaper reporter?"

Griff remembering those words she'd been so afraid to say aloud was like receiving ten parasols from Ginza's finest store. "I'm beginning work now on an article that I hope will earn me a place among the reporters."

"Might I ask about the subject of this article?"

Seeing as Griff had rescued her from the baron on the Hotel Metropolis terrace, he would likely be surprised and even concerned for her safety if he learned that the baron was the subject of her journalistic pursuits. In truth, she was a bit concerned about having anything to do with the baron. She would have to be circumspect. "It's a member of the nobility who has a rather sordid reputation."

"Have you learned something scandalous?"

"Nothing extraordinary. Truthfully, I'm at a loss about how to get information on him."

"I might have heard something about this nobleman. Does he have a name?"

That night at the Hotel Metropolis, Griff and the baron hadn't recognized one another, which meant they hadn't been introduced. But he might know something of the baron's reputation. By virtue of his cavorting at the Hotel Metropolis, she could assume the baron was deeply involved with the foreign community of which Griff was a prominent member. It would be foolish not to inquire whether Griff knew of him; she couldn't be on a wild-goose chase forever. "Baron Umezono. Have you heard of him?"

"Umezono..." A gas lamp flickered overhead, sending shadows across Griff's face. "I've heard the name. Isn't that one of the families that control most of Japanese industry?"

"A lesser branch of those families. I suspect he's their black sheep."

"Baron black sheep?" Griff replied with a questioning grin.

"That has a nice ring to it." The steep roof of her home came into view, and Suki slowed her pace. "I suppose I'm trying to find out what he did to deserve such a title."

Griff nodded. "Now I remember why I've heard of him. He has railway companies and invites foreigners to invest. I could ask around about his ventures, unless that would be overstepping the bounds of our fling?"

Railway deals weren't the usual Tokyo Tattler fodder, and the letters about the baron had been addressed to the Tattler. But if Griff's information amounted to a lead, as the word implied, it could lead toward the baron's more unseemly pastimes. "I believe asking about the baron is well within the bounds of our fling."

"I'll let you know as soon as I hear anything." Griff stopped. Suki's house was only a few steps away. Turning to face her, he took a deep breath. "There's something I've been wanting to say."

An ominous buzz seemed to join the frog's croaking. Suki nodded.

"You may think that because of my reputation around Tsukiji I'm often engaged in flings, but I wanted you to know that I've never done something like a fling in Tsukiji, or anywhere else in the world, with a woman of your upbringing and education. I understand you're a modern woman who is committed to her work at the school and who wishes to be a newspaper reporter, which I very much respect. That's why I'm interested in exploring our affections, even if that means a fling."

Suki cringed at Griff suffering from a reputation she'd been responsible for creating. "I understand you are a vastly different man than your reputation has suggested," she said brightly. "And I, too, want to explore our affections. It means a great deal to me that you understand my work commitments, and that you're willing to assist in these by asking about the baron."

Griff closed the distance between them. If she were inclined to risk her reputation as an upright schoolteacher, she would have run a hand across the swell of his chest. "We'll have to meet forthwith to discuss my important findings," he said in a voice that seemed to warm the bracing bay winds.

"I'd always wondered how lovers found excuses to meet. I had no idea how important barons and wards would be."

"There must be an entry in the Handbook of Flings that details their importance."

"If not, I suppose we'll have to write it."

"Gladly," Griff said, his lips brushing her cheek as he stepped back. "Anything to spend more time with Suki."

CHAPTER FIFTEEN

Griff's lawn tennis partner had a smile, win or lose, and was always ready for a London Gin with a splash of lime juice, a drinking habit he'd acquired while serving in the British Royal Navy. He slapped Griff on the back. "I say that earns us a glass of the club's finest."

They'd bested their opponents in a fierce two-hour bout that had given Griff the physical release he'd needed after spending the previous week correcting the Tattler's mistaken news of his betrothal. No, he'd told neighbours and friends, he was not marrying Mrs Watanabe. Yes, that meant the relationship was over. And no, he was not interested in meeting their daughters, nieces, or neighbours of fine character and outstanding pedigree.

Griff ran a towel over his forehead. "A toast is in order," he agreed. Members of the lawn tennis club were known for occasional drinking parties and forays to night spots, but they weren't the sort who remained until dawn at the Hotel Metropolis gambling tables or the Ginza brothels. They preferred the exertion of sport to clear their heads, followed by strong beverages and raucous conversation in the tennis club parlour before returning home to dine with their wives and children.

Griff and his partner retired to the club's bar: a table set with spirits and glasses, an arrangement that apparently hadn't changed since the club's founders had placed the table there a decade before. They poured hearty glasses of gin, added the lime, and toasted their victory. A group of fellows whose matches had concluded well before Griff's two-hour contest of strength and will were already seated at the parlour tables. Griff and his partner joined them in reliving last week's victory over Yokohama's lawn tennis club. Among those sharing tales of glory were several club members known for investments in the railway industry. After a second round of drinks, Griff shifted the topic of conversation. "Has anyone been investing recently with Baron Umezono?"

"You mean the bawdy baron?" one of the members at the next table asked with a snicker that was echoed by the other members.

A fellow who thought his backhand rivalled Griff's rapped his fingers against the worn wooden table. "He goes to clubs where the dollymops cater to every, and I mean every, need."

"The ones who bend over like Greek slaves?" Griff's partner inquired as he finished off his second glass of gin.

"That's only the beginning," Griff's rival replied

A member at another table twisted around. "Does he go to those clubs where they chase you around with a leather strap?"

"I've been there," Griff's partner interjected. "Had to leave before the chits raised welts on my back. What would my dear wife think?"

A member at the table farthest away placed his glass on the table with a definitive thwack. "I've heard the bawdy baron likes several toffers at a time."

"One is never alone in a crowd," a scarlet-faced member called out. Everyone roared with laughter. "The Japanese don't have the same sensibilities as our Christian nations," he concluded with a shrug.

Griff's partner took a long sip of gin. "The Japanese leave a man to his own devices. Let him do as he wishes. Just because the baron likes full attendance at his bedroom events doesn't mean we have to join the crowd."

"We can thank the good Lord for that," the scarlet-faced man said, and the lawn tennis enthusiasts broke into another round of laughter.

Several members walked over to the bar to replenish their glasses, and Griff took advantage of the pause in conversation. "Although I find the baron's nighttime activities intriguing, I'm more curious about his railway ventures. I've heard his proposals are attractive, but I've yet to delve into the business of rail."

A Scotsman recognised as one of Tsukiji's shrewdest men of business raised his glass from the next table. "Twice I've invested. Each time it's promises of ten, fifteen percent return and I end up settling for seven at most, which isn't terrible in our corner of the Orient. The government has its reach so far into the railway business that contract bidding is mere pretence. The baron gets his contracts because he has an uncle or cousin who is a cabinet minister or some high-level bureaucrat to whom favours are owed. So, if you want to invest, you have to deal with the baron."

The Umezonos sounded like the other prominent families who controlled Japan's government and supported offshoots like Baron Umezono with business contracts. "So he's generous enough with investors."

The Scotsman laughed. "Get him into a game of cards and you'll see generosity. What he lacks in talent he makes up for in stupidity."

The man next to the Scotsman swirled the clear liquid in his glass. "You better believe some of those missing railway percentage points are financing the baron's losing streak."

Griff addressed the Scotsman. "Does he have any rail construction going on now?"

"He's building a line in Saitama, north of here. It's going to be extensive, going all the way into Gunma."

"Have you invested in it?"

"Enough to keep me in the Umezono family's good graces. You never know when one of them will end up being prime minister. Mostly, I'm concentrating on ventures in western Japan. I've been permitted to join a gold mining group. They might let me make up to nine percent on this one," he said with a roll of the eyes. "Getting into rail isn't necessarily a bad bet. Is it your money or the company's?"

Griff moved his seat forward for a fellow to pass behind him. "Mine. It would be a private investment."

"You could go to Saitama and check it out yourself. Find out who the baron has managing the project. If any of them have the last name Umezono, run the other way. Nepotism has no place in day-to-day operations. Spend enough time in the rail business, and you'll learn that lesson."

Sounds of agreement followed the Scotsman's pronouncement, and the club members launched into stories of rotten investments wherein the sole purpose had been to funnel money into poor aristocratic families. Griff nodded at their tales while his mind wandered to the possibility of accompanying Suki on an investigative trip to Saitama.

She would want to see the site once he told her about it, and there was no way he was letting her travel alone. A day of work and preparations for Marianne and Lucien's arrival would have to be sacrificed for the sake of accompanying her on the trip. But he was quite willing to make the sacrifice, particularly if the trip involved spending the night at a cosy country inn. After all, it was best to avoid travelling in darkness on uncertain roads.

Spending the night at a country inn would only mean one thing, however, and Griff was yet wary of a fling with a virgin like Suki. It wasn't inconceivable that there were virginal women from good families who disdained marriage but still wanted to experience the pleasures of romantic love. As a forward-thinking, modern man, he could imagine that sort of woman. But he'd never entertained the possibility of him being that sort of man. Indeed, his impulse with Suki was to request a proper courtship. Not only was she the type of woman whom one ought to marry, but she was someone with whom he could imagine a happy union. That, unfortunately, was not an option.

He would be settling for stolen nights at cosy country inns, one of which might be in his near future. And despite his misgivings, every ounce of his being hoped that it would come to pass. Then Griff might end up owing the bawdy baron a debt of gratitude. Perhaps he would be investing in the railway business.

***

After a satisfying meal of Windsor soup and rice, Griff retired to his study. Rain falling in the garden sluiced the leaves and rocks with steady tapping that threatened to lull him into a stupor. The whisky Rei-*san* had set on the table by the fireplace beckoned, but there was a task he needed to complete first. Selecting an ivory sheet of paper, he picked up his fountain pen and addressed Suki. In the letter, he told her of his success in learning about the baron's reputation and business dealings. On neither topic did he elaborate. He could explain the baron's railway dealings more fully when they met. How he would describe the bawdy baron's other dealings flummoxed him. One didn't discuss risqué sex acts with a woman whose first kiss had only recently occurred. Perhaps when they met, he would simply tell her the baron was known for outrageous private behaviour, and she wouldn't inquire further.

After all, Suki wasn't going to make the baron's private affairs the subject of journalistic inquiry. That was more the Tokyo Tattler's style. Suki was a serious journalist. She'd never stoop so low as to concoct stories from a man's suffering the way the Tattler had when Victoria left, and then paint him a Lothario for having stepped out with Natsu. Suki said she never read the gossipy drivel. It was below her, and for that Griff was grateful.

He finished the note with an offer to have their discussion about the baron in his study or at dusk under the cover of cherry trees. After sending the message, he fretted about whether he'd been too presumptuous in suggesting places where they'd kissed. Would she think he didn't respect her journalistic endeavours?

Her reply came early the following morning. She appreciated his efforts and would be pleased to meet on Friday evening at his home.

Were the meeting to take place in the study, all the better. Being a teacher of foreign languages, I appreciate being surrounded by tomes of various linguistic tongues.

By happy chance, he was alone in that very study as his thoughts drifted to the places on Suki's body he'd like to surround with his tongue.

He was lacing his shoes in the entranceway, weighing the benefits of walking to the office versus taking a rickshaw, when a messenger arrived with a letter from Natsu. In it, she requested they meet that afternoon. This was the first he'd heard from her since she'd shown up the previous week to play the role of wife at the headmaster supper. His housekeeper, Rei-*san*, had taken the blame for Natsu learning of the event. She and the cook had enlisted the aid of several Tsukiji grocers in obtaining the right spices for the bouillabaisse, and consequently spread word of the occasion. Rei-*san* had vowed to exercise more discretion in the future, and he'd vowed to put the entire incident out of mind.

Ignoring Natsu's existence until she found another man was the best course of action. It also ran the risk of prompting her to take desperate measures for the sake of getting his attention. Nevertheless, he disregarded Natsu's morning message.

For the midday meal, his secretaries took him to the home of an elderly woman who'd turned her first floor into a small eatery. They feasted on tempura-style shrimp, whitefish, seaweed, sweet potatoes, and leafy vegetables, along with pickled vegetables, steaming rice, and miso soup. Full, and content to rest for an hour before continuing with the reading on his desk, Griff closed his eyes only to open them a moment later when Ichiro came to his desk with a message.

"I believe this is private," he said and handed the envelope to Griff. The sender was Natsu. This time she requested he contact her with haste, as she had something of dire importance to share about the horrible Tokyo Tattler.

That Natsu thought he would forgo an afternoon of work to meet with her about the Tokyo Tattler spoke to the depths of her delusions about their parting. And the request struck him as odd. Natsu calling the Tattler "horrible" was puzzling since she'd never uttered a contrary word against the gossipmonger who regularly described her as the most beautiful, gracious, and admirable woman in all of Tokyo.

As far as he recalled, this morning's column had been no different. Much to his relief, the Tattler had started the column with an apology for having incorrectly reported on his engagement to Natsu. Wanting to give it another read in case he'd missed something the Tattler had written about Natsu, he called out to Ichiro for a copy of the *Tokyo Daily News*. Scanning the column confirmed his impression. Her name only appeared in connection to the false betrothal. The Tattler had written:

Your Tattler has learned of an unfortunate mistake in last week's column. To clarify, Mr. Griffith Spenser and Mrs. Natsu Watanabe are NOT engaged to be married. Indeed, the Tattler has learned the two have parted to their mutual satisfaction. Hence, the Tattler predicts that a woman as stunning, vibrant, and elegant as Mrs. Watanabe will find a worthy suitor in short time. Mr. Spenser, on the other hand, may need privacy to recover from the loss of this rare find. The Tattler can only hope these two fine people will accept this author's most sincere apologies for any distress the mistake may have caused.

What objections could Natsu possibly have to the column? As usual, the Tattler had fawned over the wonderful Mrs Watanabe. There was no embarrassing speculation as to why she'd been searching for wedding gowns or how the affair had ended. So why would Natsu call the Tattler "horrible"? He remained convinced that if Natsu herself wasn't the Tattler, she was at least friendly with whoever was penning the gossip. Maybe they had a falling-out? It would be like Natsu to reveal the Tattler's identity to a sworn enemy and let him take care of exacting punishment.

In truth, he was feeling less vindictive about the Tattler since his afternoon with Suki in Ueno Park. Tenderness, apparently, had softened his edges. The previous week he'd asked a friend from the lawn tennis club to speak on his behalf with Ned Taylor if he happened to cross paths with the newspaperman. Griff had yet to hear from the friend about whether he'd spoken with Taylor. But the Tattler's statement about Griff needing privacy aligned so neatly with his wishes that it must have been written on Taylor's orders. The editor had gotten the message, and Griff had a sense of resolution about the column. He was ready to give it no more thought.

Nevertheless, he would be wise to make certain the nosy gossip had moved on from harassing him. Suki wanted her name listed as author of newspaper articles, not splashed across the scandal sheets. She shouldn't have to worrying about courting gossip every time they stepped out together. If his suspicions proved correct, and Natsu was going to offer him the Tattler's identity, he could speak with the gossipmonger directly and demand she leave him alone.

Besides, he'd received two messages from Natsu in less than six hours. If he didn't agree to meet with her soon, she might be tempted to surprise him at the office, or in the front garden of his home, or inside while holding Rei-*san* and the cook hostage until he agreed to a moment of her company.

He returned her message with the suggestion they meet at Shimbashi's indoor market. This would put them in a public space where they could speak freely, as they were unlikely to encounter anyone they knew. Tsukiji residents and the Japanese with whom they mingled sent servants to do the shopping. Hopefully, Natsu wouldn't think it beneath her.

***

"A *foreigner*," Griff overheard a servant girl say to her companion as he approached the broad plaza in front of Shimbashi's market.

He was tempted to reply—he could confirm the obviousness of his being foreign in the rudimentary Japanese he'd picked up from lessons with his secretaries over ales at Ginza's pubs. But were Natsu to arrive while he was in conversation with the servant girl and her companion, also wearing the simple kimono worn by servant girls, she would do something petty and spiteful. Most likely, she'd leave without acknowledging him or withhold her news until he'd grovelled an apology for not keeping his eyes peeled for her arrival.

So, he waited on the plaza, observing the flow of patrons with empty baskets entering the market under its green tiled eaves and leaving with baskets full of produce and packages wrapped in woven dried rice fronds and hemp.

He'd first come to Shimbashi's indoor market during his early forays around Tokyo when Victoria had refused to leave their home, and he hadn't wanted to venture too far from his new bride. He'd bought her decorative pots, wooden dolls, and Japanese hair ornaments in the hope of inspiring interest in their new surroundings. She hadn't budged, but Griff had continued visiting Shimbashi's, always finding items for family and friends in England.

He was considering the wisdom of foraying inside and possibly missing Natsu's arrival when, looking for all the world like a giant grape in a bright purple dress with matching parasol, she sashayed toward him.

"Spenser-*san*, it's been too long," she said, her words soft and measured. Rising from a bow, she nodded towards the market. "Shall we shop while we chat? I hear there's a man who produces covers for windows."

"Do you mean curtains?"

"That sounds like the right word," Natsu said with a kiss-me-now rasp to her voice. "Perhaps you will find something for your niece and nephew's rooms."

Griff let Natsu take the lead through the lower floor of the market, around stalls offering bolts of silks, cottons, and hemps, glass figurines, wooden toys, ceramic dishes, rows upon rows of lacquered chopsticks, raw produce, and fishes, dried and smoked. Over the din of vendors and patrons, he picked up every other word Natsu uttered while she pointed to rice crackers he recalled being served at her apartments and a seaweed tea he'd been unable to swallow. In her banal observations, he sensed smugness at having succeeded in piquing his interest with information about the Tattler. He would grant her a few more meaningless remarks before telling her she needed to convey the information, or he was walking away.

They climbed a wide staircase to the market's upper floor, where renowned sellers of kimonos, cabinetry, and watercolour scrolls had three times the space to show off their wares. This part of the market could be Japan's version of Harrods. An investment scheme took shape in his mind: a department store for Japan's growing middle and upper classes backed by several foreign trading companies, and naturally led by his firm. The support of a major Japanese conglomerate with government connections to secure the seemingly endless permissions and licenses would give them the means to bring an authentic European department store to Tokyo.

At the display of British window furnishings, Natsu stopped. "Wouldn't this be lovely for your niece's room?" She ran her hand around a bolt of cotton stamped with pink roses. Biting her lower lip, she gave him a penetrating stare as though they were about to remove their clothes in the middle of the market and fornicate on a pile of curtain fabric.

"I'll have to discuss the curtains with Rei-*san*," he said, hoping that would put a damper on Natsu. Her barbs at Rei-*san* had made obvious her dislike of his housekeeper. That he got along so well with another woman, even one twenty years his senior and a mother-figure, had somehow been a threat.

"Your housekeeper would approve. She has simple tastes."

With that, Griff reached the limit of his patience. "What do you wish to tell me, Natsu? You said you had something to share about the Tokyo Tattler."

"You're no fun for me, Spenser-*san*. Is it so terrible to look at curtains?"

Griff turned away from Natsu and headed towards the staircase.

Natsu followed on his heels. "I was only trying to help. I have much to tell you."

"Then talk," he said snappishly.

She motioned to the balcony circling the upper floor. "Let's speak outside."

Griff found space next to the balcony railing where they could converse without disturbing other shoppers chatting outside. "What do you have to tell me, Natsu?"

She grinned like a puppy eager for a round of fetch. "I know who the Tokyo Tattler is."

But did she? Or was this just another one of Natsu's games? "Who might that be?"

She rested an elbow on the balcony railing and cocked her head to the side. "Wouldn't you like to guess?"

So, this was another of Natsu's games. "I'd rather you tell me."

"You've stopped being fun," Natsu whined. "I really don't understand what's happened to you. It must be because of her."

"Of who?"

"I saw her enter the *Tokyo Daily News* offices. I heard the Tattler goes there every Tuesday morning to turn in the column. Yesterday, it was her."

Griff said nothing in reply. He wasn't going to say another word until Natsu 'fessed up.

"You know her...quite well." Natsu paused, eyeing him.

Griff supposed she wanted to see his jaw drop and his outrage explode in a flurry of curses. That was not going to happen. "I do?"

"She's been to your home."

"Really?"

"Twice. Once when I was there to bring you strawberries and then again last week when I came to help you with the headmaster. She introduced herself as Suki Malveaux. Her friend was a French servant."

Griff shook his head. Natsu had been so jealous of Suki being at his home that she'd made up this ridiculous lie to disparage her. "You're talking about Suki?"

Natsu banged a clenched fist against the railing. "I knew it by the way you looked at her. Now, you use her familiar name. Did you know she was the Tokyo Tattler?"

Natsu was unbelievable. This was how she'd planned to vanquish her rival for his affections. "What makes you think Miss Malveaux is the Tattler?"

"It makes sense, doesn't it? I heard her speak English. She sounds like an American, and she is part-Japanese. Judging by the woman she brought to your home, she counts servants among her friends. A woman like her can get gossip from every home in Tsukiji."

"All that is true. But it's also true of other women. Like you. You speak English and Japanese well enough to order plenty of servants around."

Natsu looked at him as though *he* was the one sputtering inane accusations. "I have proof."

"What proof?"

"I saw her entering the office yesterday, on *Tuesday*, the day before the column gets printed."

Relief washed over him. "She doesn't go to the *Tokyo Daily News* to turn in a column. She's studying to be a newspaper reporter. That's why she goes to the newspaper offices."

Natsu huffed and chewed her lower lip. "No. It must be her. It was the right time and the right place."

Natsu was realizing her error, and he felt more pity for her clinging to the ridiculous falsehood than vindication over her error. "You're mistaken," he said softly. "Miss Malveaux is going to be a reporter."

"She has you trapped, Griff-*san*." Natsu grabbed the lapels of his jacket. "You must free yourself from her."

Griff remained still, not wanting to lay a hand on Natsu for fear of her taking it as a hint that he was relenting or declaring loudly that he was causing her pain. "I have no intention of freeing myself. You're making a false accusation against an innocent woman."

Still clinging to his lapels, Natsu pressed her face into his chest. "I understand you're angry," she said, her voice wobbly, "but I'm willing to give you another chance."

"There aren't any more chances."

"*Please,* Griff-san," she cried into his shirt. Usually so elegant and composed in public, Natsu was fraying at the seams.

"No, Natsu. And this is the last time I'm going to meet with you. I'm leaving now. I have an appointment at the lawn tennis club."

He escorted Natsu as far as the line of waiting rickshaws and bid her farewell.

"I'm afraid I've made you sad," she said after taking her seat. "You cared about that Malveaux woman, and she betrayed you. What a terrible thing."

"Miss Malveaux has done nothing to betray me."

"You're confused." She lifted her chin haughtily. "The truth is sometimes difficult to accept. But I wanted you to know before everyone else in Tsukiji finds out."

"Nobody is going to find out anything."

Natsu gave him a sultry look. "Let me know if there's anything I can do to take away your sadness."

He wasn't sad; he was perturbed at Natsu. Foregoing a rickshaw, he walked in the direction of Tsukiji. The notion that Suki Malveaux was the Tokyo Tattler was utterly absurd. She was studying to be a reporter, and the *Tokyo Daily News* was the foremost English newspaper in all of Tokyo. She hadn't mentioned where or how she was studying to be a reporter, but it made sense that she would be taking lessons there. He'd ask her about it when they met on Friday.

How she would laugh at the preposterous suggestion that she was the Tattler.

Meeting Natsu had been a mistake. She was a desperate, attention-seeking, venomous woman. The Tattler, whoever she was, had been incredibly generous with Natsu in calling her a *rare find* and…

"*She's a vibrant woman, then,*" Suki had said in Ueno Park.

It'd struck him as the most generous way to characterize Natsu, and it wasn't a word one heard often.

Griff frowned and pulled the *Tokyo Daily News* from his satchel. He reread the first paragraph. *Mrs. Watanabe… stunning… vibrant.*

No. He shook the thought away. Plenty of people used the word "vibrant." Maybe it was a word they favoured at the *Tokyo Daily News*. Sweat broke out on his brow. What kind of man was he to think that a woman as gentle and kind as Suki Malveaux was a hateful gossip?

CHAPTER SIXTEEN

Ned was at the front door of the *Tokyo Daily News* offices when Suki arrived. His resigned expression made her insides clench. Reasons why he'd requested the early morning meeting sprang to mind: he'd decided to shutter the newspaper; he'd sold it to someone who had no interest in the Tokyo Tattler or female reporters; advertisers had revoked their support for the absurd gossip column; or, worst of all, everyone in Tsukiji was about to learn she was the Tokyo Tattler.

"What is it?" she asked.

"Come in, and I'll show you. The editor visited last night to give fair warning, and the newspaper just arrived."

Suki took her usual seat in front of his desk, and Ned placed a copy of the *Tokyo Tribune* in front of her. On the front page, in the bottom right corner, ran the headline "Tokyo Tattler Revealed." The brief article named Suki Malveaux, teacher at the prestigious Ginza Girls School, as purveyor of Tsukiji's sensational gossip.

She couldn't move, couldn't even tell whether there was breath in her body. All of Tokyo knew she was the Tattler. It was the end of Suki Malveaux, schoolteacher. To family, friends, neighbors, and the Ginza Girls School, she'd forever be the gossipmonger who divulged intimate details about people she'd never met and events she'd never been to.

Everyone knew, all at once. She'd always thought that she'd be revealed in conversations spread house-to-house through Tsukiji. She was prepared for that. She'd spent countless hours coming up with the right words for each person in her life to explain her reasons for writing the column and why she'd never told them. She'd anticipated their reactions, complaints, and objections, and had a plan for responding to each one. But she hadn't thought the end would come on the front page of the *Tokyo Tribune*. To tell them all at once was impossible.

As for begging Griff's forgiveness, she had no hope. At least if she'd been the one to tell him, his adherence to gentlemanly politeness would've compelled him to listen while she explained. Now he had no reason to receive her; he'd probably never speak to her again.

Her throat swelled, and tears pooled in her eyes. Taking a deep breath, she kept them at bay. She would not lose her composure in front of Ned. "It's over," she said, her voice hollow.

Ned scowled. "What do you mean it's over? Just because you've been recognised doesn't mean you can't write about ball gowns and parties and a few kisses here and there."

Suki shook her head. "Find a new Tattler. I can't do this any longer."

"Why not?"

Ned was being flippant, but his question was reasonable. "I always thought that if everyone found out, it would be over. I proposed writing the column because I was assured of my anonymity."

"I never thought anonymity was necessary. Still don't. Why would your sources care if it was Suki Malveaux writing the column? Provided you protect them, they'll still talk to you."

Ned had a point. Her methods for acquiring gossip wouldn't have to change. But the fear of losing sources wasn't the cause for her resistance to writing as Suki Malveaux. It was the writing part. "The Tattler's voice isn't my voice."

"Change the voice. Make it more your own."

She could never be Suki, the Tattler. The Tattler was a role she'd played to prove her worth to the newspaper. Granted, she liked playing that role, liked losing herself in the Tattler's voice. Over time, the column had become an art she practiced, an entertainment she enjoyed. Others enjoyed it, too. The Tokyo Tattler had given Tsukiji's Wednesday mornings a dose of intrigue and amusement.

Might there be a way she could write as herself? What would her family think if she did? And if she didn't continue the column, what was she going to have left once someone from the Ginza Girls School read the morning paper? "I don't know if it's possible to continue the column, but I'll consider it."

"Excellent. Take a few weeks' holiday from collecting gossip. You can pen a confession, tell everyone how you managed to keep your *nom de plume* secret for so long. It'll be brilliant. I'll inform the advertisers. They'll love it."

Once again, the Tattler would attract the readers and revenue. She'd made the column—a column for women—indispensable, and she'd established a female voice at *The Tokyo Daily News*. She was proud of her accomplishments and wished for the column to continue, but how could she be the one to write it? How could she maintain that voice her readers loved? Surely, the teasing, catty, gossipy voice would get submerged in serious Suki Malveaux. It was the voice she'd hid behind to warn Japanese women against foreign rakes. What voice would she use now? Could she be cynical and hurtful toward foreigners while writing as herself? What about the damage she'd done to men like Griff? Would they be justified in seeking revenge? Those questions would have to wait.

Today she had to face her family and the Ginza Girls School. Her throat went dry at the thought. She was expected at work in less than an hour. "Ned, might I have a cup of tea?"

Ned left the office, and Suki picked up the *Tokyo Tribune* article. After reading each of the hundred or so words twice, she thought about how the school's headmaster was reacting to it, how Mother and Papa Garrick, Rosie, and Roger were taking the news.

Rather than ushering the maid into his office with a tea service, Ned himself brought in a pot of black tea and poured her a cup with milk and sugar as she usually took it. The warm brew relieved the scratchiness in her throat and made her realize how cold she'd gone at learning of her exposure. But how did the newspaper learn of her identity? "The *Tribune* article doesn't say how I was found out."

Ned pursed his lips and looked down at his desk. "I'm sorry, Suki. As it turns out, it's entirely my fault. I had a friend—a lover, really—at the beginning of the year. It only lasted a few months. Her husband was in Ibaraki conducting training exercises for the army. We ended up spending a lot of time together. At some point, she came to notice I always left early on Tuesday mornings."

"The morning I deliver the column."

"She used to joke that I had a Tuesday morning mistress. Towards the end of the affair, she actually accused me of meeting another woman on Tuesday mornings after I'd exhausted myself pleasing her." He paused. "Apologies for the crudeness."

"I've heard worse."

"Indeed, you have, and I suspect you're going to hear even cruder language once you take a place in the reporter's room."

Was Ned finally going to grant her request to report on regular news stories? Was this going to be her reward for sticking with the column? Or was he trying to atone for revealing her identity to his lover? "So, how did your lover-friend find out I was the Tattler?"

"One night she tried baiting me into admitting the affair. I had drunk quite a bit, and in the course of our argument, I said that yes, I did meet a woman on Tuesday mornings, but she was not my lover. She was a writer for the newspaper. The following day, it occurred to her that I was referring to the Tattler. I attempted to lie my way out of it, but she had me pegged. I thought I was a better liar."

"But why did you tell this woman my name?"

"I would never do that," Ned said defensively, then his sheepish expression returned. "I made her promise she'd never say a word of it to anyone. Then, the other night, this friend paid me a visit, very apologetic because she'd told Natsu Watanabe about the Tuesday morning mistress."

Suki pictured Watanabe in that stunning kimono, the color of hibiscus, and the ugly expression that had flashed across her face. "Why did she tell Watanabe?"

"Their husbands fought together in the war with China, and they were close. Watanabe knew about my…relationship with her friend. From what I understand, Watanabe became quite the bully. She threatened to reveal the affair to my friend's husband unless she told her everything she knew about the Tattler. So my friend told her about the Tuesday morning meetings. I reckon Watanabe noted your coming to the house one Tuesday morning and disclosed the information to a reporter at the *Tokyo Tribune*. Last night, the editor came by to warn me about the story. It was the gentlemanly thing to do. We foreign newspapers must ally ourselves, or the Japanese will run us out of town. He wouldn't name the source of the article, but when I asked if it was Watanabe, he didn't deny it, which is as good an admission as you're going to get."

Watanabe was a woman scorned. But to threaten a friend with exposing her affair was inexcusable. "Clearly, Watanabe was intent on learning the Tattler's identity at all costs."

"I was curious as to why Watanabe would be so determined to learn who was writing the column. She couldn't hold a grudge against you. Every woman in this town loves the Tattler. The men of Tsukiji, however…"

Suki would bet Watanabe had sought out the Tattler's identity as a way of endearing herself to Griff. He hated the Tattler. How thrilled Watanabe must have been to see Suki on Tuesday morning after meeting her at Griff's home the previous Friday night. Now Watanabe could position herself as his defender, the one who helped him weed out the gossipmongers in his life.

Suki clenched the thick cotton of her kimono skirt as the realization hit her: Griff already knew. He hadn't sent a message yesterday after she'd accepted his invitation to dine the following evening, which was unusual since he'd been sending her messages at least twice a day about the governess position and his niece and nephew's arrival. Watanabe must have gotten to him during the day.

Suki trembled with anger at Watanabe for being so devious and at herself for letting Griff believe she was a passionate teacher of languages and aspiring newspaper reporter, knowing full well he'd never have requested her assistance with his wards—much less kissed her under the cherry trees at Ueno Park—had he known she was the Tattler.

Taking a sip of tea, she willed herself to be strong. Fate, and more accurately, Watanabe had chosen this day for her to face the consequences of being the Tattler. She would have to accept it. "Whatever her reasons for revealing the Tattler's authorship, Mrs. Watanabe has succeeded brilliantly."

"Women will forever confound me," Ned said with a shake of the head. "But you're different, Suki. You've been doing that column for almost two years and you're good at it. Last night the editor of the *Tokyo Tribune* asked me where he could find a Suki Malveaux. You're a better writer than half my reporters, and your instincts are sharper than the rest. I may have been reluctant to consider having a female reporter on the job, but that was old-fashioned thinking. Use these next few weeks to work on that article about Baron Umezono. What have you learned so far?"

Suki took another sip of tea. Ned's praise gave her a jot of hope, but she had nothing to give in return. "Nothing to write an article about."

"Stick with this story about the baron. Stick with the Tattler. It'll pay off, I promise."

***

The Ginza Girls School bell chimed the conclusion of the final lesson period. For the first time in her teaching career, Suki wished for a few more hours of lessons. The classrooms full of eager young faces had given her moments throughout the day when she'd been so immersed in her instruction that she'd forgotten about the *Tribune* article, about how she'd deceived everyone she cared about, about how angry they must be, about how they were waiting for an explanation as to why she'd kept the column a secret.

The faculty's cold politeness had struck her from the moment she'd stepped foot in the office. No one said a word to her about being the Tattler. As usual, her fellow teachers were engulfed in a myriad of duties. But absent were the smiles of support in acknowledgment of their work's demands and the amusing comments they would mutter to Suki under their breaths that were meant to give them both a much-needed laugh.

Suki was erasing conjugation drills from the backboard when the calligraphy teacher dropped by her classroom. Students had already departed to take their midmorning tea, and in the silence that followed, Suki was fighting feelings of dread by trying to focus her thoughts on the English lesson she would teach during the next period of study.

Suzuki-*sensei*, the calligraphy teacher and a dear friend who'd entered the school's faculty in the same year as Suki, closed the door behind her. "Can we talk?" she asked, her stunned expression leaving no doubt about the question that would follow.

Suki put down the cloth she'd been using to wipe the blackboard and sat at one of the students' desks in the front row. Suzuki-*sensei* took the one beside her. "Is it true?" she asked, eagerly tapping her ink-stained fingers on the wooden desk. "Are you the Tokyo Tattler?"

Maintaining her composure took every ounce of effort Suki could muster. Her friend was kind to a fault and a generous listener: the temptation to break down into a blathering mess made her pause and take a steadying, head-clearing breath. "Quite so. Did you hear about it from the other teachers?"

"Nonaka-*sensei* showed me a copy of the *Tribune* article. You were on the *front page*."

"I suppose she showed everyone in the faculty room." Suki hadn't seen any newsprint exchanging hands, but her attention had been lacking.

"She's a pompous busybody if there ever was one."

Suki broke into the first true smile she'd had since receiving the news of the Tattler revelation. "She works hard?" Suki said in mock defence.

"More like hardly works." Footfalls in the hallway multiplied. Third period would be starting shortly. Suzuki-*sensei* placed a hand on Suki's. "I wanted to tell you that I love the Tokyo Tattler column. I wake up half an hour early on Wednesday mornings so that I have time to read it before work."

Shuffling and murmurs intensified outside Suki's classroom door. "Your friendship is dear to me. Whatever happens, we must remain friends," Suki said, and tears threatened to spill.

"Forever," Suzuki-*sensei* replied and took her leave.

***

"Malveaux-*sensei*," the headmaster called out when Suki returned to the faculty room after her final lesson. "Please come forward."

Teachers in the room stopped marking their attendance books and returning papers to their drawers. The room went silent, and Suki deposited an armful of papers at her desk, then stepped up to the headmaster's desk.

Bowing deeply to the man who'd made her language lessons a fundamental part of the curriculum, she spoke, "Yes, *sensei*."

The headmaster wore a placid expression; his hands were folded neatly upon his wooden desk. "It has come to our attention that you've been engaging in work unrelated to the school."

"Yes, *sensei*," Suki said, her head low, not meeting his gaze.

"We expect our teachers to make teaching their priority. Taking other employment is against our standards."

Suki fell to her knees in apology. He was sparing her embarrassment by indirectly dismissing her. For that, she would always be in his debt. Certain parents and alumnae of the school, along with a few ignorant teachers who'd yet to forgive her for being both Japanese and foreign, had probably told him to show no mercy on her. "I am truly sorry."

"When teachers pursue other endeavors, they cannot focus fully on the students, and their instruction suffers. We cannot have a teacher burdened with distractions."

"I understand," she said, her voice threatening to crack.

"You will have to leave the school."

She didn't fault him for letting her go. She'd always known it would have to be this way. Having the Tattler employed at the Ginza Girls School was unthinkable. A gossipmonger on the faculty would drag down the school's reputation. But she'd thought she'd be tired of working at the school when it happened, that somehow all the risks she'd taken in writing the column would've paid off and she'd already be a reporter. What a fool she'd been.

Keeping her face pressed to the floor, Suki struggled to steady her voice. "I understand. I will leave at once."

CHAPTER SEVENTEEN

Rosie was standing at the entrance when Suki opened the door. "Is it true?" she asked, her voice hard. "Are you the Tattler?"

Suki steeled herself. The dismissal from the girls' school had shattered her, but she hadn't earned the privilege of falling to pieces. "I am."

"I can't believe you never told me." She walked away before Suki had a chance to respond.

How many times she'd wanted to tell Rosie. She'd excused herself from revealing her *nom de plume* on the grounds that her sister-in-law was busy with the babies and would prefer not to cope with Suki's outlandish plan to become a newspaper reporter. In truth, she feared Rosie's judgment. Rosie praised her for being a talented and committed teacher and espousing lofty ideals like equal rights for women. Suki's unwillingness to pursue marriage frustrated her, but she accepted it because of Suki's higher standards. She couldn't bear Rosie thinking of her as the type of woman who relished the scintillating tidbits about which the Tattler wrote, who praised women daring enough to wear dresses with scandalous necklines and flirt unabashedly with men who caught their fancy.

Also unsettling was that Rosie would grasp the raw truth of the Tattler's warnings against foreign men: Suki was punishing them for the way her father had treated *Okasan*. And that was embarrassing.

Rosie sat alone in the back parlor, looking out the window to the garden. Grateful for the privacy, Suki took a seat next to her in the high-backed chair she'd tipped over on one of her first days living at the Garricks' home. Bounding enthusiastically around the room, seven-year-old Suki had flung herself onto the chair, causing it to fall backward. Mother Garrick's panicked intake of breath startled everyone in the room, and Suki burst into tears. Between sniffles and whimpers, Suki mustered an apology for being the family's source of distress. Mother Garrick accepted the apology, her eyes soft with love and forgiveness, and young Suki felt whole again. She needed that now.

"I'm sorry I never told you."

Rosie kept her eyes on the back garden. "How do you get your information? You rarely attend social events of note." The insult in her statement was unmistakable: Suki wasn't among Tsukiji's elites, yet she'd given the impression that she had entrée into their lives.

The words stung. But she would gladly accept any amount of stinging if it meant earning Rosie's forgiveness. "I've gotten to know a few servants. Marcelle seems to know everyone else."

"Your friend, the French maid. She helps you?"

Suki nodded.

Finally, Rosie faced her. "I could have helped you. I know a lot about what happens around here."

"You did help me, quite a few times. Like when you saw Professor Cooke fondling Mrs. Anderson's undergarments."

Rosie widened her hazel eyes. The length of her lashes added dramatic effect. "I told you, and it appeared in the Tattler the next day. The names of the parties involved weren't given, but it was exactly as I'd said. I just figured I hadn't been the only one who'd seen the professor creeping around the Andersons' garden." Her face broke into an amused smile. "I thought Mrs. Anderson would be upset when the Tattler column came out. But she never realized it was her washing that had been taken advantage of. I brought her vanilla bean cakes and stayed at her home for three hours while she complained about her children and finished every last bite."

"I feel foolish for not telling you. I should have done things differently. But I had to remain anonymous, mostly for the sake of continuing my work at the girls' school. I always knew they would dismiss me if they ever found out, and they have. The headmaster told me the column was a distraction from my duties to the students."

Rosie balled her hands into fists and brought them down on the upholstered arms of her chair. "You spent years at the school. How can being the Tokyo Tattler prevent you from teaching?"

"No one truly believes it does. It's a gentler way of calling me an embarrassment to the school." Suki gave a wry smile, then sighed. "I'm bewildered by everything that's happened today."

"If you think you're bewildered, you should see Mother Garrick."

The blood left Suki's cheeks. "She must think the worst of me for being such a disgraceful gossip."

"Not a chance. She loves the Tattler, reads every word like it's the gospel. She's just surprised."

The admission calmed Suki's nerves. Surprise was far better than outright condemnation. "What about the rest of the family? *Okasan?* Is she upset?"

"Everyone, *Okasan* included, is surprised, very surprised. They don't know what to think. They'll be even more surprised to hear you're no longer working at the girls' school."

A glimmer of hope suffused Suki. Her sister-in-law, the dear friend who'd known her for nearly all her life, was still talking to her, and her family was surprised. It was as good a response as Suki could have hoped for. "I regret not telling you and the family. Do you think you can forgive me?"

Rosie put a hand to her chest "You're like a sister to me. I'll always forgive you."

Tears welled in Suki's eyes. The sway from fear to relief, from self-condemnation to joy, had worn her down. "I can't tell you how relieved I am to hear you say that."

Charlie's high-pitched cry rang out from the second floor. In unison, Suki and Rosie turned their heads to it. The cry continued for another few seconds, then ceased. The little one had returned to sleep. "What will you do without your job?" Rosie asked.

Tension released its hold on Suki's shoulders. This part was far easier. "I'd like to write newspaper articles. It's been a dream of mine since we learned from the missionaries about women journalists in the United States who expose corrupt politicians and disguise themselves to write about conditions women face in factories and hospitals. I've always wanted to do something like that here in Tokyo. I thought I could impress Ned Taylor and become a reporter for the *Tokyo Daily News* if I did well with the Tattler."

"That would be splendid," Rosie said, at last looking at Suki with the admiration she'd been accustomed to getting from her sister-in-law.

"I haven't impressed him yet, and I don't know what will become of the column now that everyone knows Suki Malveaux, half-Japanese schoolteacher, is the one writing it."

"Everyone loves the Tattler, and everyone loves you. They'll be even more excited about reading the column. I bet you'll get tons more gossip, and invitations to balls and picnics. Will you let Mr. Spenser escort you?"

Having come up for air, Suki felt as though she'd been plunged underwater again. "I doubt he'll be interested."

Rosie furrowed her brow. "But you've been spending so much time together, and he sends you messages every day. I thought you were falling in love."

Suki pulled a handkerchief from her kimono's *obi* as tears gathered in her eyes. "Mr. Spenser harbors a special hatred for the Tattler. He has every right to bear ill will. I wrote some awful things when his wife left. Then I continued to badger him when he and Natsu Watanabe were a couple. As a foreigner who dallied with Japanese women, he was the perfect target for the Tattler, and I sent all my arrows at him."

"Then you wrote about the engagement, and that turned out to be false." Rosie grimaced.

"Suffice it to say, any tender feelings Griffith Spenser might have felt toward me are long gone."

"Has he said anything to you?"

"Nothing so far. But he doesn't have to say a word. I know he wants nothing to do with me."

Rosie crossed her legs toward Suki. "How can you be certain?"

"Trust me. There's no one in Tsukiji he despises more than the scandalmonger who put his name in the newspaper for much of the past year."

"Explain why you did it, how you wanted to become a newspaper reporter. You can tell him you're sorry for everything you wrote about him."

But she wasn't sorry for everything. True, she shouldn't have rushed to judgment about Griff or the other men she'd disparaged without consideration of their character. For that, she was sorry. A few of those men had married after her rebuking them in the column, and so far, they'd treated their Japanese wives well. But she'd observed more instances of the opposite, and the Tattler's job was to make Japanese women aware of this fact. "The Tattler is skeptical of romantic entanglements between Japanese women and foreign men. That's what she writes about. I'd be apologizing for doing what I thought was right, even though it was sometimes wrong, which isn't much of an apology."

Rosie nodded slowly. "Of course you're the Tattler. You've always been the one to raise concerns when we learned of a Japanese friend getting married or falling pregnant."

"Japanese women have also found happy lives with foreign men. The column cannot go on like this. Ned Taylor wishes for me to continue, but I'm not sure how."

Rosie grasped the woven flowers on the arm of Suki's chair. "You'll find a way. What will the women of Tsukiji do without their Tattler?"

"The Tattler's words are my words now, and if my time with Mr. Spenser has taught me anything, it's that I have to give foreign men more credit. I also have to be more careful about reporting planted stories. Did you see yesterday's column where I apologized for announcing Mr. Spenser's engagement to Mrs. Watanabe?"

"I thought it was quite big of the Tattler, by which I mean you, to admit the mistake."

"I'm thinking that Watanabe connived to get the story into the Tattler. She was asking about wedding gowns to make it look like Mr. Spenser was going to marry her in the hope that social pressure would make him succumb."

Rosie dropped her jaw. "Like Papa Garrick said at breakfast the other morning."

"I don't know what will be left of the column if I can't send barbs at foreign men." Another high-pitched cry rang out through the house. Suki and Rosie braced. The sound subsided to a whimper as the maid hurried up the steps.

Rosie shrugged. "Isn't the column mostly about fashion? Like fondled undergarments in the garden?"

"Advertisers would flee from an entire column devoted to Mrs. Anderson's drawers."

They laughed and joked about the Anderson undergarments until Rosie became serious again. "Why don't you write a Tokyo Tattler column about what a wonderful man Mr. Spenser is? Then he'll forgive you and continue sending you numerous messages a day."

Suki couldn't fathom such a progression. "I promise he never wishes to speak to me again."

"Don't the Japanese believe a sincere heart wins the heart of another? Talk to him. There may be a chance."

***

Suki spent the better part of the evening meal listening to Mother Garrick, Papa Garrick, and Roger's stories of disbelief at seeing the front page of the *Tokyo Tribune*. They spoke of friends, colleagues, and neighbors who'd been shocked to learn their Suki authored

Tsukiji's scandal sheets. Mostly, people wanted to know how Suki kept her identity secret and who her sources were, none of which the Garricks could elaborate upon since they themselves hadn't a clue their Suki was the Tattler.

Mother Garrick rested her wineglass on the table and dabbed the corners of her mouth with a napkin. "Can you tell us what you'll be writing in next week's column?" she asked.

From opposite the ends of the table, Mother and Papa Garrick, along with Rosie and Roger who sat across from her, awaited her answer with mouths agape as though she was about to spout a Shakespearean sonnet. From Suki's side, *Okasan* offered a mild, supportive smile, and gratitude filled her for their willingness to better understand her several-year deceit. "Ned Taylor and I agreed that I should take a few weeks' holiday from the newspaper. Actually, one of the reasons I started the column was to learn about journalism. The truth is I'm studying with Mr. Taylor to become a newspaper reporter for the *Tokyo Daily News*."

"A newspaper reporter?" Mother Garrick pressed a hand to her chest. "I didn't think women could be newspaper reporters."

"You've forgotten, dear, about the female reporters in the States. There were a few in Boston," Papa Garrick said.

Mother Garrick leaned toward him as though that would aid her voice in covering the distance. Everyone around the table could have told her that wasn't necessary—Mother Garrick's voice could be heard throughout the house, pretty much no matter what she said or how she said it. "But those types of women will never get *married*. Suki is young and pretty with a good head on her shoulders."

"Suki could easily find a mate and work for the newspaper." Papa Garrick leaned forward and raised his brow. "Women of childbearing age take multiple roles in their communities."

Mother Garrick lifted her chin and gave him her haughty gaze. "Maybe in the rice paddies, peasant women can plant stalks of rice in the morning, give birth in the afternoon, and pull up the weeds in the evening. But we live in the modern world, and Suki cannot do the work of a journalist while taking care of her children. Impossible!"

"I'm not having children anytime soon," Suki said in a tone she hoped would put an end to discussion.

"Have you made any money as the Tattler?" Roger asked.

Rosie twisted her head to the side and glared at her husband. "That's uncouth."

"She's my sister."

Suki cleared her throat. "I make far less than the reporters, at least I did when I started. But once the advertisers noticed the column's popularity, I began making a decent sum. Mr. Taylor has always recognized my contributions."

"Well, if a female isn't going to contribute to species continuity, she ought to do something useful, and newspaper work can be quite useful when it's done right," Papa Garrick concluded.

Feeling useful, Suki listened to Roger's suggestion that she might wish to invest in radio, a form of communication that would allow news to fly around the world. One day, he supposed, it would make newspapers obsolete.

***

After a dessert of steamed cakes filled with sugared cherries, Suki followed *Okasan* to her studio in the back garden. During the evening meal, *Okasan* had only commented that she never read the Tattler as all the English crammed on newsprint made her eyes hurt. But Suki had noticed a flash of sadness cross *Okasan*'s face, and it had almost summoned a fresh set of tears.

"I always assumed the Tattler had been hurt by a foreign man." *Okasan* smiled wearily and flattened out the skirt of a bright pink taffeta gown on her worktable. Lifting the hem, she ran a finger across the stitching, then reached for her needle.

Suki held the skirt for *Okasan* to get a better view of her stitching. "I try to warn women about what happens when their foreign lovers leave."

"You always think it's the man's fault. Men aren't always to blame." *Okasan* paused with needle and thread in hand, and her gaze took on a faraway look. "Sometimes a woman chooses to be with a foreign man regardless of his character or heart. The foreign man is a way to break free from her fate. She wants to escape a life spent at the mercy of her husband and mother-in-law, praying for a devoted son who'll eventually come to her defense. She thinks our culture, our men, deprive her of the passion she craves. Rather than wait for a foreign man who treats her with tenderness and care, she attaches herself to the wrong man." *Okasan* pulled the fabric taut and resumed her stitching.

"I've seen that, too," Suki replied, and her thoughts turned to the man who had time and again proved himself honorable in the way he treated women and the way he anticipated the needs of his niece and nephew. Griff was a man of tenderness and care.

"Such a woman pledges herself to a foreigner, knowing full well he's a debtor, manipulator, even violent. Then she's miserable." *Okasan* ran her needle under the final stitch and made a knot. "Her family has disowned her, and her neighbors won't speak to her. She has no choice but to stay with the scoundrel. Eventually, he leaves, and she suffers. She ought to have waited for the right man but didn't."

Suki realized how little she knew of her parents' relationship. From what she remembered, they'd suited. Her father had simply drifted out of their lives like a paper lantern floating downstream. Perhaps that was the easiest thing for a child to believe.

Suki picked up the gown, shook it out, and re-laid it on *Okasan*'s worktable. "Was *mon père* the right man for you?"

Okasan circled the pink gown and nodded at her work. "I was fortunate that he was a good man. But we were very different people. He was most happy when he was away from Tokyo, exploring places in Japan I'd only heard about in fantastic stories and the poetry they made us learn in school. I wasn't surprised when he left. I'd been preparing for us to be alone. Then I made that gown for Mother Garrick. We moved here, and my parents welcomed us back to their home. We've been lucky."

"It's not luck. Your dresses have been popular for as long as I can recall. You deserve this life."

"Other women are equally good. I work harder." *Okasan* placed her hands on her hips. "You had a good job at the girls' school."

"I knew they'd tell me to leave when they learned I was the Tattler. But it's been more of a shock than I'd expected. I didn't have a chance to say good-bye to the students. I wish I could've explained why I wrote the column and how much I want them to follow their dreams as I did and understand the risks involved in being an ambitious woman." Guilt and disappointment had been eating at her since she'd left the school. She hadn't meant for her work there to end in such an abrupt manner.

Okasan picked up a box of needles and pulled out a new one. "Now might be a good time to consider marriage. There are marriage brokers who can help. What about Yamashita-*san*?"

Suki dropped her jaw. They never talked about marriage. "Do you wish for me to marry?"

"It's natural for a mother to wish her daughter would find contentment with a husband and children. One day you'll regret not giving marriage a chance." *Okasan* chose silver thread from among her colorful spools.

"Have you become a romantic? Are you reading those mawkish housewife stories about love?"

"They are quite sentimental. I wonder whether a woman a few years past forty can find love as well."

Suki wished she could close her ears. "You've been making too many wedding gowns. You ought to say no to the next commission."

Okasan pulled the shiny string through the cuff. Suki was betting the stitches would soon be a flower. "I cannot deprive Tsukiji's brides of beautiful gowns for their special day. How about you assist with the next fitting and see what love does to a woman?"

Suki had a strong suspicion about what love did to a woman. Griff had made her feel that giddy joy she'd seen on brides' faces. He'd felt stirrings of love, too. She knew it from the way he looked at her and the way their lips came together. She was a cruel woman for enticing him into tender feelings while knowing the hurt he'd suffer in learning she was the Tattler. Clearly, she was not worthy of that kind of love.

Suki mustered a smile for *Okasan*. "I'm willing to assist with wedding gowns and any other commissions since it looks like I'm about to have a lot of free time."

"Good. Then you can read some housewife stories for yourself," *Okasan* said with a sly grin.

"Never," Suki replied and held the cuff taut for *Okasan* to finish stitching.

***

Suki pulled a fan from her reticule. Although it was yet early May, the sun beat down like it was late July. Waving the fan in front of her face, she picked up the sharp fragrance of basil and the penetrating heat of thyme from the American envoy's kitchen garden.

Marcelle lopped off a stem of thyme, then raised her hands, one of which held a menacing set of shears. "You cannot quit the Tattler. Everyone in Tsukiji is talking about the quiet schoolteacher turned town gossip. You're famous. Madame keeps asking when you're coming to visit." Marcelle wagged the shears at Suki. "If she knew you were in her garden, we'd have no peace."

"You don't need to wave those shears at me. I'm not *quitting*. I only told Ned I had to think about how to proceed, and I have. I'm going to continue writing the Tattler until I move into the reporters' room." Her life had been turned upside down yesterday, and, ironically, the source of the upheaval had emerged as a foothold upon which to brace herself. The lighthearted speculations on Tsukiji's romances, the incredulity over Hotel Metropolis scandals, and the extravagant comments on fashion were the voice of Suki Malveaux. Until now, she'd only shared that voice in the guise of the Tattler; going forward, it would have her name attached. The new column would still be called the *Tokyo Tattler,* but the voice was going to be less pedantic and judgmental, more…fresh and inviting, once she figured out how to write in that voice.

"*Dieu merci.* The Tattler lives on." Marcelle lowered the shears, placed them in the herb basket, and hung the basket over her arm. "Are you still investigating the baron?"

"Ned thinks I should." Suki waved the fan more vigorously in front of her face. "Monsieur Spenser sent a message two days ago that he had something to tell me about the baron."

Marcelle looped her arm through Suki's, and they ambled toward the kitchen where the cook was awaiting her herbs. "I knew he still loved you."

"This was before he learned I was the Tattler. We'd planned to meet at his house tonight. He was going to share the information then."

"What else was planned? Was the innocent schoolteacher going to lose her innocence at last?"

Suki had spent the earlier part of the week imagining that very scenario. "My innocence is no longer under any kind of threat."

"Oh, I doubt that very much. What will you wear?"

"That's not a consideration, as Monsieur Spenser has no wish to see me."

"But he's expecting you."

They reached the kitchen door. Marcelle went inside to deliver her herbs to the cook, and Suki considered the possibility that if a standing invitation meant that the invitation stood, then, yes, she was expected at Spenser's home. He hadn't sent a message rescinding his invitation. But that could have been an oversight on his part, and should she take advantage of such an oversight?

Marcelle returned from the kitchen with an empty basket. "The cook wants leeks now. Oh, the favors I do to stay in her good graces. But she makes the most magnificent pies, and always sets aside an extra slice for my late-night snack." She took Suki's arm again and pulled her toward the garden. "Then you're going to visit Monsieur Spenser this evening?"

"I suppose he hasn't sent a message telling me *not* to come to his home."

"So, your appointment remains. You must go."

"What would I say to him?"

Marcelle shook her head as though the question had passed the point of absurdity. "Tell him that you're sorry for the mean things you wrote as the Tattler, and you still wish for his ardent kisses. That's usually enough for men."

Suki swiped at a bee seemingly intent upon landing somewhere on her face. "He's angry. You were at his home last week; you heard how he talked about the Tattler."

"He'll come around. You have an attraction. Don't fight it. Go to him."

Showing up at Griff's home was going to stoke his resentment, and she didn't wish him further pain. But at least he could unleash it on her. "He's going to tell me I've been a heartless shrew, which I deserve to hear."

Marcelle tugged at a green stem and brought up the white shaft with its furry roots. "The man I met the other week is as fine a London roast beef as I've ever met, and he fancies you tremendously."

"He's a good man who knows better than to fancy a woman who has wronged him."

Marcelle pulled out another leek. "Confess from your heart, and he'll forgive you."

***

Coolness greeted Suki upon entering the house. After depositing her bonnet on the hook by the door and her shoes on the shelf, she stepped into her slippers and headed toward the stairs. She planned to spend the hour before the midday meal in her room testing new voices for the Tattler column. As she passed the correspondence table, a letter caught her eye. It was addressed to her.

A moment passed before she recognized the handwriting, and then she could only offer a wary glance at the envelope. She reached out to pick it up, then paused before taking it in her grasp out of a sudden—irrational—fear that the letter might scald her. Which it absolutely could not. With the filigree letter opener, she sliced open the envelope and read the letter's contents

Dear Miss Malveaux, otherwise known as the Tokyo Tattler,
I hope this correspondence finds you well following this week's fascinating revelations about your identity. A spinster schoolteacher and a gossip! What a pleasant surprise to learn that you have the wits to engage in respectable work. Your intelligence is reassuring. I believe you will expose the baron's misdeeds. You have failed, however, to act in a timely manner. Women's lives are at stake. You have it within your power to ensure the baron does no further harm.
Waiting most patiently for you to act.

She read it again—twice—and each time her ire rose. The phrase about finding her "intelligence reassuring" exposed a contemptuous, patronizing attitude. By banking on her sympathies toward other women, this letter-writer was trying to manipulate her into action. Between the pomposity and the blatant manipulations, Suki would guess the writer was a man, someone who either knew Suki personally, which was more frightening than irritating, or someone who knew the type of woman she was, because he was succeeding in motivating her to take action.

Last week, he'd written about victims, and now he was telling her that women's lives were at stake. Despite misgivings about this writer's character, Suki couldn't allow such accusations against the baron to go unheeded. No matter how the problem of the baron was stated, it warranted investigation. And for better or worse, it had become Suki's to investigate.

CHAPTER EIGHTEEN

Griff asked Rei-*san* to delay the evening meal for another hour. Not that he expected Suki to join him. He simply had little appetite for an earlier meal. He would eat after she left. Or, if she never came by, he'd settle into his most comfortable chair as he had the previous night and sip whisky until bitterness gave way to longing for the way things had been before Natsu had been proved right on the front page of the *Tokyo Tribune*.

The article bearing Suki's name had left him confounded. His breakfast of ham and eggs sat on his plate while he sorted out how it was possible to accuse her of being the Tattler._She must have become the victim of malicious gossip spread by a vindictive Natsu, who confused Suki's journalism lessons with employment at the *Tokyo Daily News*. He would have sent a message to Suki to inquire about her response to the article, but she was teaching. After finishing the day's tasks at the office, he'd gone to the lawn tennis club as usual and found Roger, Suki's brother from the Garrick side of her extended family, holding court in the changing room.

Roger pulled off his trousers while sharing the news. "We had no idea she was writing the column. None at all."

Griff's cubby was two cubbies away from Roger's. Pushing through the throng of players who'd gathered around him, Griff placed his bag in its rightful place and greeted Suki's brother. They'd never spoken of Suki, even though Griff supposed Roger might have heard that Suki was helping with preparations for his niece and nephew's arrival. But Griff was going to change that today. "Did you say your sister has been writing as the Tokyo Tattler?"

Roger sat on the chair in front of his cubby and removed one of his socks. "That's right, chap." He shook out a dark grey sock, which sent a mildly foul odour Griff's way. "Did you have any idea? I know she's been helping with your family arriving."

Griff averted his gaze from Roger's broad, hairy toes. "I heard she was interested in working in journalism."

Stripped to his drawers and vest, Roger sat back in his chair. "I haven't heard anything about journalism. I went home after work for tennis attire and my wife told me Suki admitted to being the Tattler. She didn't mention anything about her working in journalism. But at this point, I wouldn't put anything past our girl."

Roger's confirmation had been enough to throw off Griff's game and leave him hobbling home with a twisted ankle. He glanced up at the clock. It was a little after seven. Earlier in the week, Suki had written that she'd come by after work at the girls' school had concluded, which would be around the same time she'd come to his home the first time, and that meant she could ring the bell at any moment. Though there was little chance of her coming. There hadn't been an exchange of messages between them since the news broke. In his mind, he'd composed several missives, venting his outrage in a flurry of words he'd been unable to summon when seated before paper and ink.

His anger flared and fizzled without settling deep inside the way it had when he'd discovered that his mate at Oxford had been cheating him at Baccarat. Or when he'd found out his uncle had been using children to work the machines in his hazard-ridden factory. Learning Suki was the Tattler had struck him sideways and left him flailing for purchase. He wanted to understand why she, or rather, the Tattler, had written about him as though he were some kind of unprincipled reprobate. How could a woman who seemed so carefree and possessing of a zest for life harbour such cynicism and ire?

The bell on the front gate rang. Rising from his desk chair, he instructed Rei-*san* to bring any guests into the front parlour. Then he put on his suit jacket and went to the parlour to wait.

Rei-*san* opened the door and greeted someone in Japanese. Suki returned the greeting.

So, she'd come after all. His palms broke out in a sweat. He took a seat on the same upholstered chair where he'd sat when she'd first visited his house, and waited.

The rustle of Suki removing her shoes and stepping into the guest slippers drifted into the parlour. Griff crossed and uncrossed his legs before standing. He was a man of solid upbringing and would stand for any woman who entered his home.

Suki fell into a bow before he could catch sight of her face. "Thank you for receiving me. I wasn't certain you'd allow me to call," she said, her voice soft and even.

She stood upright, and he took in the brown eyes that seemed to capture light and send it back tenfold, the sweep of dark hair against her flushed cheeks, the lower lip he'd nibbled a week before. His body stirred. If only this was the assignation they'd planned. "Please take a seat." He'd meant for his words to come out cold and create necessary distance between them, but his voice had frayed at the end.

Suki took the chair opposite his. Folding her hands on her lap, she met his gaze. "I take it you've heard the news?"

"Of your authoring the Tokyo Tattler column? Yes, I have." *There* was the coldness he'd been aiming for.

"It must have come as a surprise."

"I was quite surprised." His voice had taken on a biting edge, but Suki's calm expression remained unchanged.

"I understand from our previous conversations that you took issue with your presentation in the column." Her words had the clarity and measured tones of a well-rehearsed speech. "I admit that I haven't always treated you or other gentlemen in your position with much generosity. I've often made assumptions based on a man being foreign, particularly when he captures the heart of a Japanese woman. Time and again, I've seen women abandoned by a foreign lover, leaving them undesirable for a Japanese husband and shunned by their families, sometimes with a baby to take care of. I've also come to realize that not all foreign men care so little about their Japanese lovers. And not all Japanese women enter these relationships with careful consideration of the man they've set their hearts upon. I've hurt many people with my words, and I know how much I've hurt you. For that I am truly sorry."

Suki had placed him in the same category as scoundrels who'd deserted their families without bothering to investigate whether he deserved to be there. "I've heard stories of foreign men abandoning their Japanese families. I find it completely abominable. Those men deserve to be haunted for the rest of their days."

"I have no doubt of your feelings in that regard."

So far, her explanation felt honest, and he wanted more. "You wrote some unpleasant things when Victoria returned to England. You said that it must have been a Japanese woman who'd come between us. Then I began escorting Natsu in public and you believed yourself vindicated. You wrote that I was like all those foreign rakes who prey on Japanese women." He clenched the arms of his chair as anger simmered in his gut. "I'd never do such a thing. I didn't want my wife to leave. I was committed to the marriage. Furthermore, I didn't seduce Natsu to fulfil some foreign male fantasy concerning Japanese women."

"I know," she whispered, her head bowed.

"I'm sorry. I didn't mean to lash out at you." He'd meant to remain nonplussed and burn Suki with his coldness; no luck.

Suki looked up and met his gaze. "I wish I could take back every one of those words. Then I wrote about the engagement. By the time you told me of your ending the relationship with Mrs. Watanabe, the column had already been printed. I requested a reprint, but it was impossible."

"The day we went to Ueno Park?"

"Yes, I spent very little time at the French bakery after you escorted me there. Unfortunately, at that point in the evening, Ned Taylor could do nothing to change the column."

Her sincerity was convincing, but it did nothing to change the fact of her deception. How could she have kissed him, touched him, made him believe they were going to have a fling, or whatever it was, when she must have known it was only a matter of time before he learned she was the Tattler? "Were you ever going to tell me that you were the Tattler?"

"I often thought about how to broach the subject. But it was never the right time, and I was scared."

Naturally, she'd been scared. Her words had caused him plenty of grief over the past year, but the deception hurt far worse. "We kissed. We shared intimate moments." He took a deep breath and let go the words that had been clamouring for release. "I was thinking about us marrying."

Silence cloaked the parlour, and regret burrowed into his heart. Yes, he'd considered the possibility of courting Suki toward marriage: she was the type of woman he should marry. But he'd let those words go because he'd wanted to throw his wounded heart in her face to show her what she'd done to him. Yet, there was no point in apologising for having spoken in anger; he was bitter. He'd meant what he'd said, and if given the chance, he'd say it all over again.

From the corner of his eye, he saw her rise. "I've damaged our acquaintance more than can be repaired. I won't take any more of your time." Her voice was clear and steady. If she'd been affected by his confession, she wasn't giving any indication. "Before I go, however, I'd like to ask about Baron Umezono. You said that you learned something, and I'd be remiss not to inquire as to its content."

Of course, she needed that information to further her career as a journalist, which must be promising after all the so-called truthful investigations she'd conducted for the Tattler column. He gritted his teeth. There was no need to brim with sarcasm. He would maintain his composure and give her what she wanted. That would get her off his doorstep, and he desperately needed Suki off his doorstep. "An acquaintance of mine from the lawn tennis club invests in Japanese rail. He told me the baron has a railway construction enterprise in Western Saitama. The new line will link commerce and travellers between Gunma and Saitama. It sounds like a stable, rather profitable venture."

Suki placed a finger on her lip in a thinking pose he'd always found charming. "Might that put women in harm's way?"

"I didn't hear anything about him using female labour on the railways. Did you hear something?"

Suki resumed her seat and pulled a letter from her reticule. "I received this message a few hours ago."

She placed a folded piece of paper on the table between them. He read through it twice, each time his anger against the letter-writer rising. Calling Suki a "spinster schoolteacher" and "gossip" rang of contempt, and the phrase about "waiting most patiently" for her to take action sounded outright threatening. Griff was left with the impression that the author was not, in fact, a very patient man. "Do you have any idea who wrote this?"

"This is the third letter I've received. The first two were addressed to the Tokyo Tattler and sent to the *Tokyo Daily News* offices. This one arrived at my home."

Someone was sending her these kinds of letters at home. That didn't sit well with Griff: he didn't wish her any harm. At least Roger was there if this arrogant letter-writer showed up in person. "The author mentions women's lives are at stake, which could be related to the railway. I've noticed that factories in Japan use female labour to a surprising extent. It's not inconceivable that women are being recruited to railway construction as well. But it is a rather hazardous undertaking."

"How so?"

"Preparing the ground for laying rail entails digging through thick, heavy earth. The equipment is large and unwieldy. Then men must hammer spikes into the flattened earth to lay the rail. All of it requires stamina and strength, which are naturally greater in men, and even the strongest of them succumb to exhaustion and the various illnesses that breed among workers in close proximity. It's difficult to imagine a woman being up to the task."

Suki's fingers tapped the arm of her chair. "How might I learn if there are women working on the baron's railway?"

"Short of going there and seeing for yourself, I'm not sure. Ask around Tokyo and the bureaucrats will tell you, or any reporter, that no such labour is being used. They'll assure you that only strong, able-bodied men carry out the very dangerous and difficult tasks of railway construction, and everyone is faring quite well."

She let her shoulders fall. "I would have to go to Saitama to learn whether women's lives were at risk?"

"To know for certain, you would have to see for yourself."

"Did you learn exactly where in Saitama the rail is being laid?" she asked with an unsettling curiosity to her voice.

She was contemplating the impossible, and he hoped she realised it was indeed impossible. "I could ask. But you cannot go there alone."

"I don't see why not. I'll tell them I'm a newspaper reporter doing an investigation about women working on the railways."

"Aside from the obvious danger you'd be placing yourself in, I doubt you'd discover anything. They'll stash away any women on the project faster than you can say newspaper. You'd learn nothing."

She paused, then gave a firm nod. "I'll tell them I'm a liaison for foreign investors. The investors I represent wish to learn more about the railway laborers."

Clearly, Suki had little regard for her welfare. A woman traveling alone to mingle with railway workers sounded, at best, risky and, at worst, like a day from which she'd never recover. "Women do not travel to Saitama alone. Besides, such liaisons are always men, and they arrive at the site with a firm idea of the bribe they wish to receive to keep the conditions of workers secret from investors."

Suki arched her brow at him. "Do you have any suggestions as to how I could learn whether there are any female workers on the line?"

Of course, he could go in her place, but he couldn't. He absolutely would *not* spend two or three days in Saitama on behalf of Suki. He was angry with her; she'd written awful things about him. She was also the woman who'd given him her first kiss, whose breasts he'd felt through her gown with his mouth. His gaze caught on the curve of her bust, and pressure grew in his trousers. Quickly, he looked away.

He needed to get her out of his thoughts and out of his life. He should never have told her what he'd learned about Baron Umezono, and he hadn't even shared half of what he knew about the bawdy baron. *Why hadn't he kept his mouth shut?*

Because he cared about her. He'd wanted her to come tonight; he'd wanted to hear her apologize, and then he'd wanted to… No, he'd been prepared to tell her to leave forthwith once she'd apologized. And here he was battling the desire to hold her and protect her and kiss those damnably alluring freckles on the top of her cheeks.

Unfortunately, he'd taken it upon himself to pass along information about the baron, and therefore he bore responsibility for its outcome. He would have to go to Saitama on her behalf. The trip would amount to only a few days, and he would learn more about railways in Japan, which could prove useful to his company and his personal financial interests. "Why don't I go to Saitama as an interested investor? Only willing to invest if the profits are high enough. Such an investor would be pleased to learn that costs were being kept low by utilizing female labour for rail construction. They could be saving a sizable amount, which they would gladly share with someone whose sole interest was profit margins."

"I cannot let you go all that way on my behalf," Suki said with a firm shake of the head.

"I mean to repay you for locating Miss Tinselly for the governess position. Thanks to your efforts, I have great confidence Marianne is going to achieve the level of education her parents wished for their daughter."

"She's a member of the Presbyterian church in Yokohama. Mother Garrick simply sent them a letter through our church in Tsukiji. Apparently, Miss Tinselly wishes to see more of Japan."

"Then I shall go to Saitama to repay a debt to Mother Garrick." Suddenly, Griff found himself enjoying the challenge of asserting his will against Suki's. "I have no doubt she wouldn't want you going there alone."

Suki folded her hands in her lap. Her lower lip jutted out, and all he could think about was sucking on that bit of petulance. His misbehaving cock responded again. *Blasted nuisance.*

"Mother Garrick doesn't have to know where I'm going," Suki replied. "I'll tell the family I'm visiting a friend." The triumph on her face was unmistakable, but she celebrated in haste.

Griff had no intention of relenting. "I simply cannot allow you to place yourself in unnecessary danger. If they're using female labour, they could press you into service."

The solution was obvious, but madness. He should have nothing more to do with Suki after the way she'd tricked him. At the same time, he owed her for helping secure a governess and maid. It really was the only way: he'd assist her in the Baron Umezono inquiry, and his debt to her would be met. Going forward, they could pass one another on the streets of Tsukiji with a pleasant greeting about the weather and not feel resentment over unfinished business. He inhaled deeply and committed to the very generous offer. "You could accompany me as an assistant. You would be my translator for the afternoon."

Suki looked at him as though he'd suggested she strip down to her undergarments and sit on his lap, which he absolutely, in no way, shape, or form, wished her to do. "That would be…" she began, and he thought for certain she was about to say "ridiculous." But she merely pursed her lips and narrowed her gaze. Small breaths puffed out her cheeks.

Her surrender was happening before his eyes.

"Are you certain you can afford to leave your business in Tokyo for a whole day?" she asked, looking very doubtful.

"We could go tomorrow. It's Saturday. I often take a leisure day before the sabbath. My secretaries will be grateful for the time off. Do you have obligations at the girls' school?"

"Ordinarily I would…" she began. Then she clenched her brow and frowned. Griff had an awful feeling about what she was readying to say. "I'm no longer working at the school. They were uncomfortable with having the Tokyo Tattler among their ranks."

"You were dismissed for writing the Tattler column?" Griff bristled at the enormity of what Suki had gone through for having been revealed as the Tattler. And all because of Natsu's spying and spreading rumours about having seen Suki at the newspaper offices. How could he have ever let someone so vindictive into his life? She was ruining Suki's over her resentment at him ending the affair. Indeed, for having exposed Suki to Natsu, he bore a degree of responsibility for the way Suki's authorship of the column had been revealed.

"They said I wasn't allowed to take work outside my duties at the school. But the truth is that I was an embarrassment to them. They could never have justified keeping me there." Her voice teetered on the brink of cracking.

Bloody fools! He wanted to march into that school and make sure they knew full well what they'd lost by dismissing a teacher like Suki. "What will you do?"

"I hope to write an article that will convince Ned Taylor to hire me as the first female reporter in Tokyo. Falling short of that, hopefully I can find work teaching at one of the schools in Tsukiji." She glanced down at the hands on her lap, then back at him. "I also plan to continue the Tattler column after a short hiatus. According to many people, the Tattler made for good entertainment. Tsukiji's women loved seeing their names in print, even when I teased them about the color of their gowns and the height of their hair ornaments.

I admit the gossip could be offensive, as you well know, but for the most part, I spoke for women and defended women, and that made the Tattler quite popular."

Frankly, he was surprised to hear that she was continuing as the Tattler. Somehow, he'd assumed that her exposure meant she could no longer write about scandals. But why would that be the case? It was who she was; it was what she did. But was it really? "Those words. They weren't you. They didn't sound like you."

For the first time that evening, she gave the amused smile that had so endeared her to him. "You mean I don't sound like a self-important, judgmental, prudish, fussy gossip?"

Griff let his misbehaving gaze travel down the dark blue dress of the woman who'd proved in his study that she was anything but prudish, and who should be in his study right now, naked and sprawled across his settee while his mouth introduced her to delights she'd yet to experience. "Not fussy," he said, his voice deep with unshakable lust. "You don't seem the type to fuss."

A pink flush sprang to Suki's cheeks. Had she noticed his wandering gaze?

"I try not to fuss. I like to get along," she said, her voice heavy with what could very well be desire, if their being alone in his parlour was having anywhere near the same effect on her as it was on him.

Fine, let her feel desire, and let her feel it thwarted. They could share the experience. "I never should've worried about the Tattler learning of our relationship."

"No," she said with a small smile, "that wouldn't have been a problem."

"Well, all that is behind us," he said with finality.

"Yes, it is."

He should be glad she so eagerly agreed. "Now that we're friends, I'd be pleased to escort you to Saitama. Frankly, if there are women workers involved in the baron's railway construction, I'd like to spread the word. Some of my friends who've invested could pressure the baron into changing his tactics. No one wants women injured doing work plenty of men are available to take."

"It's good of you to consider their safety, as well as my own. It would have been foolish for me to go all that way alone."

"I'm glad to be of service." He let his gaze take in the curve of her waist and the swell of her hips. God forbid Suki ever realized the power she had over him. One touch of her hand, one movement of her mouth toward his, and he would be at her mercy.

Vigilance was his only recourse. He needed to bear in mind that she wasn't the schoolteacher he'd spent the day with at Ueno Park. She was the Tokyo Tattler. She'd insulted his character and questioned his integrity. She'd deceived him and tricked him into imagining the possibility of taking her as his wife. He must keep in mind that Suki was a charlatan.

The problem was that she was also the woman whose tentative caress on the front of his pants had put such naughty thoughts in his head that he hadn't been able to function without frigging himself that night, and the next day, twice.

Tomorrow was going to be utter torture.

CHAPTER NINETEEN

Rain came down in a soft drizzle on the already muddy streets. Every few minutes, Suki peered out the window expecting to see a messenger from the Spenser home walking toward the front door to inform her the trip had been called off. She wouldn't be surprised—she'd hurt him terribly. Those words "I was thinking about us marrying" continued to reverberate through her with waves of anguish over the havoc she'd wrecked on him. She'd made a fool of him, and proved herself to be a careless, thoughtless, heartless woman.

If it hadn't been imperative that she ask about the baron, she would have left his home right then. But she'd asked, and Griff had once again proved himself the consummate gentleman by declaring them friends and offering to accompany her on an extensive journey. She should be pleased at being declared a friend, and she was. It was more than she could hope for from the man she'd slandered and then deceived into thinking about marrying her. At least for today, it was necessary to set aside reflection on her mistakes and his pain. She would ignore the pangs of resentment over Watanabe's callousness and the school's insistence that she leave. For Griff's sake, she would do everything in her power to make their journey a pleasant experience.

A commotion outside brought her to the window again. Several Japanese men had gathered on the street between her house and the next-door neighbor's. Their indigo cotton pants and tunics with sleeves secured at the elbow marked them as day laborers. Perhaps they were making a stir in protest at having to do street repairs on muddied roads. *Rightfully so*, Suki thought as she headed toward the dining room for a quick breakfast.

Griff rang the bell at exactly seven o'clock. Suki grabbed her satchel and kimono overcoat and bid the housekeeper farewell. It'd been quite clever of Griff to suggest she act as his translator. Her family had declared it a superb idea for Suki to translate on behalf of Tsukiji residents interested in railroad investments. Rosie had been "over the moon" and tried to convince Suki to wear the sky-blue dress with lacy sleeves that showed off her shape. She'd ended up choosing a light green kimono with a simple pattern of cranes in flight. Her hair was pulled back in a low chignon like other working women, and she'd used a single comb for decoration. The impression would be of a woman from humble origins whose Japanese and Western parentage had made her able to do translation work usually reserved for the better educated. Were there women working on the railroad, they might find her approachable.

Griff greeted her politely, then his gaze fixed on her kimono and widened as though it was his first time seeing the garment worn by nearly every woman in the country outside of Tsukiji.

Worried that she'd offended him, she asked, "Would you prefer I dress in Western clothing for the trip?"

He shook his head. "I was surprised to see you in a kimono. I hadn't seen you dressed like this since the first day we met. You look perfect…for the purposes of the trip." He looked at his feet and his face reddened.

He'd called her perfect. Heat flowered in her chest, threatening to emerge as the kind of flush that migrated upward and settled on her cheeks where it would stay for the remainder of the day if she didn't begin exercising reason and restraint.

Raised voices from the street reached the entryway. Suki peered around Griff and saw his rickshaw runner in discussion with the street workers she'd noticed earlier. "We'd better leave. I think the rickshaw must be in their way."

Griff held out his open umbrella and motioned for her to go first.

Suki stood her ground. "A woman in kimono cannot walk in front of a man. Nor can she let a man hold the umbrella."

"I suppose we'll have to follow custom today," he said with a shrug and handed her the umbrella.

Suki lifted the umbrella above Griff's head, and he left the house a pace ahead of her. As they neared the rickshaw, one of the workers asked the rickshaw runner about a woman living nearby who worked for the newspaper.

Suki stopped in her tracks. Those weren't road workers. The conservative faction, who loved to hate the Tattler, had come for her.

"Spenser-*san*," she whispered, "we should return to the house."

Griff either ignored her or didn't hear a word of what she said because he proceeded to the middle of the street next to the rickshaw runner and joined him in urging the conservatives to step aside.

A man with a scar down the side of his face pointed at Suki, who stood behind the rickshaw. "We want to talk to her." His rough Japanese made her flinch. Until this morning, these men had made sport of threatening the newspaper and the Tattler over the content of the column. They'd never come close to acting on those threats, and she'd always assumed their words were mere bluster. Apparently, she'd been wrong. Still assisting the runner in waving the conservatives away, Griff gave her a quizzical look.

She had to warn him. "Griff, don't—"

"No," Griff said in loud, clear English. "She's coming with me, and we're leaving now."

The men tracked Griff with their gaze as he walked over to Suki and put an arm around her waist. "We need to get into the rickshaw." His tone was commanding and gruff, and his protectiveness was a surprise for which she was abundantly grateful.

"Griff, these men are dangerous."

"Yes, that appears to be the case." With his arm securely around her waist, Griff led her to the side of the rickshaw and onto the bench. All the while, the conservatives muttered to one another, their words growing harsher as they circled the rickshaw.

Griff was nearly in the seat beside her when a short man with bulging eyes grabbed the back of his jacket and pulled him from the rickshaw. He snarled at Griff with large tobacco-stained teeth. "You're the reason she's betrayed her country."

Suki couldn't imagine that Griff understood the Japanese, but he most definitely understood the gesture. He yanked his coat from the conservative's grip and pushed him away with such force that the short man landed smack in the mud. Standing over his attacker, Griff glanced at Suki in the rickshaw, then back to the man on the ground, and then over to the other conservatives, who hadn't moved, but were watching with mouths agape.

Suki feared he was weighing his odds of successfully shoving each one of them into the mud. Before she could urge him to refrain from even considering the possibility, Griff came to the right conclusion and hopped into the rickshaw. "*Go*," he shouted at the runner.

The rickshaw lunged forward as one of the workers banged a shovel against its side. "It's because of the Tattler that Japanese women dream of the foreign prick. How does it feel to ride the likes of him?"

Suki gasped and covered her ears. Not only were they being crude, but they clearly hadn't read the column very closely or they'd know that she, in fact, warned Japanese women away from foreign men. But that was beside the point because the conservatives hadn't come to her home for reasoned discussion.

The rickshaw runner panted and huffed with each pull up the muddy road while the conservatives kept pace and chanted, "Out with the barbarians."

Suki braced herself for a very ugly confrontation between them and her neighbors. Fortunately, no one seemed the wiser about the rabble on their streets. But the conservatives knew where she lived. At least she'd drawn them away from her home, for now.

"What did that man say?" Griff yelled over the chanting. "The Japanese was too fast."

A conservative on the street hooted. "I say we remind her what Japanese men are made of."

"Oh, she'll love a thick Japanese daikon," his companion added.

Bile rose in Suki's throat. Their runner picked up speed as the street leveled out. The conservatives responded by hurling rocks at the rickshaw. One bounced off the backside, taking what must have been a large chunk of wood with it.

"Bastards," the runner yelled.

"Worthless gossip, spreading lies about our people. You deserve to die!" a member of the faction shouted.

Suki grabbed hold of Griff's upper arm. He placed his hand firmly on hers.

"What are those men saying?"

"Ugly words. Nothing worth repeating."

"Faster and I'll pay double," Griff yelled to the runner in Japanese.

Somehow the runner increased his speed. Even so, the conservative faction continued pounding the rickshaw with rocks while shouting about how the runner was a coward and betraying his country by serving the foreign devils.

As they approached the university district, the conservatives finally backed off and fell into the crowd of students and workers entering the foreign quarter. They knew better than to continue their fuss in front of the men guarding Tsukiji's gate.

Suki looked down at her hand under Griff's. His gaze likewise went downward, and the muscles of his arm twitched. Taking the cue, Suki released her grip. "Thank you for being here." Her voice wobbled. "I don't know what would have happened if I'd been alone."

He fisted his hand. "You shouldn't go out alone until these men have been properly kicked out of Tsukiji." He looked her up and down. "Are you hurt?"

Scared and upset, yes. And wishing she still had hold of his arm. But not hurt. "I'm fine."

She asked the runner, and he replied the same.

"I'll get those men back," the runner said, still panting. "They'll pay for the damage they did with those rocks."

"We'll pay for all the damage," she said, willing to help with repairs to the rickshaw, although she felt certain that Griff, ever the gentleman, would offer to shoulder the expense.

Griff turned to Suki. "Can you ask the runner who those men were? Who would dare enter Tsukiji and pursue foreigners in their own neighbourhood? Those men would have dragged you away to Lord knows where."

"They're from a faction that believes itself the legitimate arm of the traditional conservative political party, even though the party won't acknowledge them. They'd like nothing more than to forget the past thirty years of progress and return Japan to the feudal era."

"Are they former samurai? Like the ones we saw protesting naked that day in Ueno?"

"They could be." Suki paused to consider the type of men who joined the conservative faction. "Many former samurai support the conservative views. Some resent being forced to perform military service. Others resent that commoners can join the military and carry swords, which used to be a samurai privilege. They owe debts to lenders and taxes to the government. The spread of Christianity and Western custom disgusts them, and they want to punish their elites and us foreigners for bringing about all these changes."

"But they're not chanting naked in front of a temple," Griff replied, his jaw clenching on the words. "Those men are violent. The police need to put more guardsmen at the gates to keep hoodlums like that out. The Japanese authorities are going to be outraged at that kind of unprovoked, unwarranted attack against foreigners."

Suki could withhold the truth and hope Griff never learned why those men had been waiting in front of her home. Or she could risk Griff's ire and tell him the Tokyo Tattler had yet again placed him in an ugly predicament. Considering he'd rescued her from the baron, today marked the second time Griff had saved her from certain harm. She owed him the truth, even if it meant him calling off their trip to Saitama. "The attack was not unprovoked. They were after me."

"You? Because you have foreign blood?"

"No," she said, drawing the word out as long as possible. "They wanted to attack me because they think the Tokyo Tattler is an embarrassment to their country. I write in English about Japanese elites, which gives the foreign community a window into the elites' sometimes-embarrassing behavior. The conservatives accuse me of exploiting their countrymen for entertainment, even as they wish to strip them of power. Ned Taylor, who owns the *Tokyo Daily News*, gets letters telling him to end the column or they'll burn down the newspaper offices. As far as we know, they've never tried."

"Have they threatened you?" Griff asked in such a demanding tone of voice that the runner's head jerked around, causing the rickshaw to lean.

Suki gripped the metal bar to avoid falling into Griff's lap. "They've mentioned wishing to exact their revenge upon the Tattler's person, silence me forever, that kind of thing. Quite ridiculous. Even after today, I think they're all bluster. They could have easily overcome our rickshaw and carried out their threats, but they didn't."

"They're all bluster at seven o'clock in the morning. After a night of drinking and carousing, no one is safe, not you, not your family."

Suki shuddered at the thought, but from what she knew of the conservatives, they were more interested in shouting matches than fisticuffs. "They say awful, shocking things, and maybe throw a few rocks, but that's the sum of it. They're not going to actually follow through on any of their threats. In fact, they need the Tattler. The column supports their contention that the men running this country are sinful decadents serving their foreign masters."

"They should go after them, not you," Griff replied pointedly.

"They do. They harass those men the same way."

Griff peered out the side of the rickshaw. They'd reached the main thoroughfare leading to Shimbashi Station. "One day they're going to lose control, and people will get hurt, or worse."

Suki sighed. The conservative faction had almost hurt them both, and naturally he was angry. But she couldn't fathom them committing crimes against ordinary citizens, especially foreign ones. They'd be immediately imprisoned. "I don't think they want to end up in jail. If they aren't free to wage their protests, they're of little use to their cause."

Griff turned back to her. "We're not going to sit around and wait for them to wage another protest like that." The resolution on his face made Suki squirm. "We'll make a report to the police."

Suki feared he would suggest it. She pictured them spending the entire day making reports at the police box, and no good would come of it. "The police will pretend to listen, then do nothing. The only harm done was to the rickshaw, and our runner isn't going to lose a day's worth of passengers to make a report that will be of no benefit to him. Had those men wished to do us bodily harm, they could have. They wanted to yell at us. That was all."

Griff looked at her as though she'd lost her faculties.

Suki continued, "That's their style. Make noise and hope someone listens. Originally, I thought they were sending me letters about Baron Umezono because of some vendetta they had against him. But the letters were more sophisticated than they could pull off. Had they been sending the letters, they would have put in writing the same idle threats they issued today."

Griff leaned away from her on the rickshaw seat. "Is there something else I should know about the baron and this trip to Saitama?"

She still hadn't told him the baron was the man he'd rescued her from, nor had she told him about the baron's seedy nighttime activities, but neither of these had any relevance to their trip to Saitama. "I showed you the most recent letter last night at your home. The others were in the same vein."

"Who do you think is writing the letters?" Griff seemed genuinely curious.

"The wording is masculine, and the writing looks like it came from a man's hand. Of course, a woman could imitate a man's tone and script. I considered whether the letters might be an elaborate plan from the baroness to get rid of her husband. Then I learned the baroness was a marquis' daughter and her foremost aim in life is to ensure her sons' superiority. Exposing their father to public scrutiny would be unthinkable."

Griff nodded thoughtfully. "The letter you showed me mentioned harm to women. Might the writer be someone from Tsukiji? There are plenty of reformers and missionaries who would wish to rectify any harm being done to women."

"The letter was quite condescending, and I doubt they'd write such a letter. Nor do I think they'd send their letters to the Tokyo Tattler. They would want one of the real newspaper reporters to investigate." Gratitude at being able to share her thoughts about the letters eased the tension that had been gripping her insides, and it compelled her to share more, even if it wasn't relevant to their Saitama trip. She continued, "At first, I thought the baron had visited one too many brothels, and that was why the letter-writer had sought the Tattler's attention. Apparently, the baron has a rather sordid reputation."

Griff murmured what sounded like agreement.

"Then the letters became more serious. The second one mentioned the baron having victims. The last one claimed women's lives are at stake, and I'm beginning to think the author addressed the Tattler specifically since the Tattler is obviously a woman and would take seriously women's concerns."

"It could be one of the baron's foreign investors who's worried about his investment and wants to make certain nothing untoward is occurring at the railway construction site."

The runner stopped in front of Shimbashi Station. Soldiers with traveling sacks crowded the plaza in front of the gates. Suki and

Griff would have to wait in the rain while the soldiers took their seats. Hopefully, they wouldn't fill all the trains to Saitama.

"Would it be like an investor to mock me for being a spinster and a gossip while requesting I learn about the baron?"

"Not likely," Griff said as he alighted from the rickshaw. "Whoever is writing those letters is taunting you."

A sinking feeling gathered in the pit of Suki's stomach. Doing a questionable man's bidding while she tried to finagle an article wasn't the most advisable course of action. What had she gotten herself into? What had she gotten Griff into?

CHAPTER TWENTY

Wearing a kimono and keeping to the norms of male and female relations implied by the garment, Suki followed Griff on to the first-class compartment of the train to Saitama. He took a seat on the padded bench at the front of the car and Suki took the bench opposite. Griff immediately pulled that morning's *Tokyo Tribune* from his satchel and held it in front of him as he read. With a wall of newsprint between them, Suki's attention drifted to the headlines and the larger print on the page. She was trying to discern what the *Tribune* reporter had written under the headline "Our Collective Nightmare Realized, Women's Beloved Bloomers Invade Japan," when the paper wall between them crumbled.

"Would you like the newspaper?" Griff asked.

"No, thank you." She would like very much to know about the bloomer invasion, but even more so, she wanted him to continue reading the paper. While Griff read, he softened his posture and relaxed his shoulders. She liked seeing him comfortable in her presence. If a newspaper had that effect on him, she wanted him to have it.

So, she let her mind wander to hordes of women's undergarments roaming the streets of Tokyo, blocking the bicycles and rickshaws—truly it would be a nightmare—and gazed out the window through the misting rain as the neighborhoods of Tokyo gave way to countryside villages surrounded by fields of vegetables and broad expanses of earth sown with bright green rice seedlings.

Thankfully, the fools of the conservative faction hadn't ruined the trip. After the rickshaw driver accepted Griff's money for damages and laughed off his suggestion that they report the incident to the police, Griff had relented in his determination to make a report. Instead, he would speak with the British envoy about protecting Tsukiji from the conservatives' intrusions. The envoy might do some saber-rattling, but he wouldn't make too much of a fuss since everyone—save Griff—knew that the conservative faction only meant to alarm and insult.

The peculiar letters about the baron gave her greater pause in considering the wisdom of proceeding to Saitama. But as the distance between their train and Tokyo increased, so did her excitement at the prospect of penning a serious newspaper article. The words took shape in her mind: *Women with dirt-covered hands and unhealed fractures digging for stone purchase wherein they might lay rail to serve the greedy interests of one Baron Umezono.*

Not only would she impress Ned, but also help young women doing dangerous work as a means of escaping poverty's clutches. Mother Garrick and her social reformer friends would applaud her for taking up a righteous cause. Before long, no one in Tsukiji would associate Miss Malveaux with the Tokyo Tattler. Except Griff. He'd never forget. Nor would she ever forget how much she'd hurt him. But now wasn't the time to dwell on the rift between them. At present, they were on cordial terms, and, thanks to Griff, she was on her way to get an article on a degenerate baron.

Saitama reminded Suki of the resort towns where her *okasan*'s relatives resided, except in the plains of Saitama there were more rice paddies and fewer people. At the train station nearest the baron's railway construction, Suki paused on the platform and took in the low wooden buildings of the town center and beyond them, the plumes of steam rising from factory smokestacks. A distant hillside marked the remains of a castle from the shogunal era. The town had grown along the lines of the feudal village that had preceded it, with a main shopping street flanked by shrines, smaller shops, and homes with large gardens.

For the midday meal, they followed the train attendant's suggestion and headed down the shopping street. No fewer than half a dozen residents stopped to inquire where Griff was from and why Suki appeared not-quite Japanese. These passing conversations resulted in recommendations for the midday meal, with most residents directing them to a restaurant known for bamboo shoot and burdock root rice. Suki and Griff dined on steaming rice with warm, crunchy vegetables, tempura-fried mountain asparagus, and bowls of clam miso soup, then ventured back outside where the chilly, damp afternoon had become even damper and chillier.

Their carriage driver declared them his first foreign passengers and showed them to a padded bench behind his raised platform. Spring rains had produced numerous, rather deep ruts in the country road. More than once, Suki found herself thrown against a bracing Griff; likewise, he gripped the sides of the carriage when he was on the brink of landing in her lap.

"I'm sorry," said Griff for what felt like the thousandth time as his elbow cut into her arm.

"This is nothing. My siblings dealt out blows far worse."

They'd just bobbed up and down through a particularly large crack in the road when an obstruction sent them even higher. Griff's head scraped the brief wooden hood serving as their only protection from the rain. "That hurt."

Instinctively, Suki reached over and pressed her fingers into the thick waves atop his head, then quickly removed her hand. "No blood, but you'll have a bruise." Her cheeks stung with embarrassment at having made such an intimate gesture.

Griff, fortunately, didn't appear bothered by her touch. "It reminds me of the time my younger brother hit me over the head with a cricket bat."

A sudden bounce sent Suki squarely onto Griff's lap. She gasped. "I'm sorry."

He clasped her waist in a far more intimate gesture than her hand on his head, and blood rushed to her already hot cheeks. Apparently, *she* was not unbothered by an intimate gesture. He lifted her upward and she was almost in her seat when the carriage jumped again, sending her right back to where she'd started.

"Let me try this," she offered and wriggled her hips to help loosen her rump from atop his thighs.

"Whoa, that's…"

Suki cringed. Even spinster schoolteachers knew how a man reacted to having his nether regions crushed. "I'm sorry. That must have hurt."

"It didn't hurt necessarily. It was more… I don't think we ought to have you in that position. Perhaps you could grab that bar over there and return to your seat."

The metal bar was almost in her grasp when a quick shake of the carriage sent her flailing. Reaching for anything that would serve as anchor, she latched on to Griff's thigh, dangerously close to the place where his nether regions would be located. This time Griff looked as though he'd been struck by lightning.

Immediately, she removed her hand. But with no means of staying upright over the rocky terrain, she fell face-first onto his lap with her chignon nestled between his legs. Like a sumo wrestler tossing his opponent, Griff gave a monstrous grunt as he grabbed under her arms, suspended her above his lap, and put her down beside him.

Stunned by the horror of having burrowed her head into his lap, all she could manage was a weak apology. "I'm terribly sorry."

Griff's face was red as a berry. "It was all an accident."

The carriage reared, and Suki's shoulder made hard contact with the metal side bar. "Ouch." She winced at the pain.

"That hurt." Griff scrutinized her shoulder while she massaged the bruised area. "Be more careful," he yelled in Japanese to the carriage driver. The man responded with a hearty grunt and a wave as he had the dozen other times Griff had asked for greater care in navigating the rutty roads.

Suki's shoulder throbbed, but she put on a brave face. "It's nothing like the time Roger and Ollie were reenacting the Boshin War with wooden swords. I couldn't move my arm for a week. Hopefully this assault won't last as long."

"Our carriage ride has inflicted as much pain as decades of sibling rivalry."

"I never said this trip was going to be easy," Suki said in her best schoolteacher voice of reproach.

"First it was the conservative faction—"

"Followed by a surprisingly tortuous carriage ride."

Griff doubled over. His shoulders shook and his face turned the unholy shade of scarlet she'd only ever seen once before on a human being's face. And like that previous occasion, sounds erupted from his throat as though a small object was wedged inside.

"No," Griff said through spasmodic facial contortions. "You never said it would be easy."

Suki couldn't contain her laughter any longer. He was a ridiculous sight to behold. How could a bout of hysterics could turn a man so devilishly handsome into a sight that would make a small child rush behind her mother's skirts?

With each bounce of the carriage, Griff commenced another round of laughter, which made Suki laugh as well, until finally he caught his breath. "That's twice you've had me in stitches, Suki. I won't be surprised if you want nothing to do with me after this."

But she did. She didn't care that he laughed like a rabid pack animal. That he felt free to lose control in front of her was precious. "It was less scary the second time."

A pained look flashed across his face. Suki felt it, too, because there wouldn't be a third time. Had Griff been thinking the same?

At last, the carriage crested a hill, and Suki made out workers laying down wooden planks.

"They're putting in the sleepers," Griff explained. "That gives them a platform for laying the rail."

"Then they've just started this segment of rail?"

Griff shook his head. "Not really. Most of the work has been done already, the flattening of the land and digging drainage to keep the tracks from flooding."

"You know a lot about railroads."

"I'm an interested investor, remember?" he said with a quirk of the brow. "Actually, I think every boy over the age of five can tell you how rail is laid."

Suki told their carriage driver they would be back shortly, then lifted the umbrella over Griff's head for their walk down the pathway into the valley. The clanging of shovels and hammers and the shouts and grunts of workers responding to orders reverberated across the hillsides. Soon their steps fell in time with the workers' rhythm.

A middle-aged man in an indigo tunic and pants stomped toward them as they neared the site.

"You all lost?" he called out.

"We came to see the railway being laid," Suki replied in Japanese suitable for a woman of high rank speaking to a man of lower rank.

The man put his hands on his hips. "We're trying to meet today's quota before the rains start again. This isn't the best day for curious foreigners to be hovering around." He nodded at Griff.

"My employer is a potential investor in the Umezono railway. He's come all the way from Tokyo to see firsthand how construction is progressing. I realize the rains are making your day difficult. But perhaps you might allow him a closer look? He's interested in the methods you're using and spending on equipment and labor."

The man gestured to his workers. "I've laid rail all my life and this line is about as good as it gets. Tell that to your boss."

Suki shared the proclamation with Griff, then spent the next hour translating between the overseer and Griff, who must have been extraordinarily interested in railroads as a boy because he had questions regarding the most infinitesimal details of laying rail. The extended inquiry gave her ample opportunity to scrutinize the workers for any signs of a female face or form. Unless women railroad workers grew fantastic swaths of hair and produced noises as though their guts were being removed, there wasn't a female among them. Finally, she asked the overseer directly. "Recently, my employer has been hearing about women laying rail as a means of easing the burden of labor costs. Is this something you're doing here?"

"Why would anyone let women lay rail? They're not fast enough or strong enough to keep up with the men. I'd quit before letting any investor tell me to use women on the team. Never."

"He said there are no women working here," Suki translated for Griff, who nodded like a satisfied investor. "Is there anything else you'd like to ask him?"

Griff shook his head. "I don't have anything else. Do you have anything to add?"

Suki paused as though translating Griff's question. "Is this your first time working for an Umezono line?"

"Third time I've laid rail for the company. I have no complaints. The family does right by its workers."

"It seems that much is true."

Suki thanked the overseer and proceeded up the hillside behind Griff, dutifully holding an umbrella above him.

"I'm sorry that you didn't learn anything about the railway. It seems they have a fine operation going," Griff said sympathetically.

"I'll have to look elsewhere for the baron's misdeeds," she said to his back, not bothering to disguise the disappointment in her voice, as Griff seemed plenty aware of it.

***

Rain fell in sheets when they reached the waiting carriage. The ride back took twice as long due to the driver having to stop multiple times to extract wheels from the thick mud. Griff offered to help each time they stopped, but the driver refused the offer and exerted himself, pressing strips of wood under the wheels while uttering curses Suki refused to translate no matter how many times Griff asked.

By the time they returned to town, their clothes were soaked through, and bruising covered them from hours of being jostled about. They'd also missed the final train to Tokyo.

"We'll have to stay the night," Suki began. She'd spoken with the station attendant, who'd provided directions to several inns. "The attendant thought there'd be no problem finding one to accommodate us since the spring holiday season is over." Somehow Suki managed to keep her voice steady. The prospect of spending an evening with Griff was making her quiver with unreasonable excitement. "I'd like to stop by the post office first to send a message to Tsukiji. My family will want to know we've been delayed. Is there anyone you wish to contact?"

Griff shook his head. "My housekeeper will assume I'm with a beautiful woman, and she wouldn't be wrong."

Suki gaped. He'd called her beautiful. Again. She wasn't certain this was something men and women who were friends said to one another. Nor was she certain whether her insides should be humming from a so-called friend's compliment.

"I'm sorry. I didn't mean to offend you." Griff shrugged. "I was only stating the truth. You are a beautiful woman. Anyone would say so."

CHAPTER TWENTY-ONE

The day had been going as well as could be expected given it had started with an attack from a rogue political faction and continued with a carriage ride that had left them bruised head to toe. Griff hadn't laughed like that since the last time he'd broken down in front of Suki; twice she'd reduced him to hysterics, and twice she'd seemed more amused than offended, for which he was grateful. When he learned they'd be staying the night in the charming Saitama castle town, his delinquent mind rushed to an image of naked Suki lying on a futon, hair spread out, nipples taut from a gentle breeze blowing through a half-opened window. Then, like some horny rube, he made a flirtatious comment about being with a beautiful woman. One look at the expression on her face and he knew the line had been crossed.

He excused the errant words by claiming he was speaking in all objectivity, which was true. Suki was beautiful. Nevertheless, the comment disrupted their easygoing conversation, and Suki barely looked at him to and from the post office where they both sent messages to their homes in Tsukiji.

Rooms were available at the first inn where they inquired. The three-story wooden structure with tiled roof eaves reminded him of inns where he'd stayed during his travels in Western Japan the previous year. His Japanese sufficed to understand much of the matron's description. There were a dozen rooms of various sizes on the second and third floors. The first floor housed a tearoom where they would dine this evening and tomorrow morning. If they wished to bathe, however, they would have to leave the inn for a public bath.

The few times Griff had needed to bathe in Western Japan, he'd used the mixed-sex baths. His secretaries had taken great amusement at their esteemed foreign boss trying to keep his gaze averted. Griff's bathing time was also much commented upon as he achieved a speed not usually reached in baths where one was supposed to leisurely wash and soak.

Bathing with Suki was out of the question. He couldn't bear being in any kind of proximity to her naked body covered in soap, the water splashing over her skin as she rinsed, her breasts bobbing on the surface of the mineral-rich waters.

"Which would you prefer?" Suki tilted her head to the side. The inn's matron stared at him with eyes narrowed ever so slightly as though she'd read all the naughty thoughts in his head.

"I'd prefer not to do that," he said, not having heard a word of Suki's question but wagering that if she'd asked anything about a bath, he'd be safe.

"Would you prefer a room facing the street or the courtyard in back?"

He sighed in relief. "What do you think?"

"I think you'd prefer the back. The courtyard has several peach trees in bloom."

"That will be fine. Will you do the same?" He couldn't fathom why he needed to ask where her room would be, but the question had escaped him before he'd considered its implications.

"I'll take the front. There's a room with east-facing windows, and we wish to arise with the sun."

"Good, that's very good."

Actually, that was not good. He wanted her room next to his, or even better, she could sleep on the futon beside him, close enough for her to roll over in her sleep until their naked bodies joined under the blanket, because in his mind, Suki always slept naked.

Suki conferred with the matron, then looked at Griff. "She's suggested we take our evening meal in about an hour. Would you care to bathe before we eat?"

For the love of all that was holy, she'd brought up the bath. "Bathe? Will you?" If she wished to go, he'd have no choice but to accompany her. There was no way on earth he was going to leave her alone with men leering at her naked body. He'd knock the lights out of the first rotten degenerate who dared cast the slightest glimpse at her dripping wet buttocks.

But no one would be glimpsing at Suki because they would be doubled over in laughter over his stiffened-up Dicky Dixon following her around the bath. Thoughts about naked Suki already had Dixy trying to push his way through the front of Griff's trousers. The sight of her would send Dixy through the roof.

"Not this evening," she replied. "I'll freshen up in my room."

"That's exactly what you should do."

Suki glanced down at her wrinkled, mud-stained kimono. "I do look rather untidy."

Griff cringed. He hadn't meant to imply she looked worse for the wear. If anything, her bright pink cheeks and loosened hair only made her more aggravatingly appealing. "You look fine. It's good for us to have time to freshen up after such a long day. I'm going to do quite a bit of freshening up myself." For him, that was going to involve wringing some relief from dear Dixy.

"Then we'll meet in the restaurant when service begins?" she asked.

"Excellent, most excellent."

***

At seven o'clock, Griff arrived downstairs to find Suki waiting at the tearoom entrance. She greeted him with a cordial smile. "Were you able to rest?"

"I was, thank you." Frigging himself had provided a modicum of relief. The sight of the place on Suki's neck where he'd once run his tongue, however, was tightening up his trousers once again.

He had to reel in this infuriating desire for a woman who was supposed to be a neighbourly acquaintance at best and, in fact, was someone he should be resenting for having dragged his name through the mud. He did resent her for it, but he also understood her reasons. She'd made assumptions about his intentions based on how she'd seen foreign men treat their Japanese lovers. Her father was a Frenchman, and no longer in Japan. His leaving must have dealt a terrific blow to Suki.

Nevertheless, she could've inquired further about him before slandering his character. She might have asked Roger whether Griff was dallying around with numerous Japanese women and whether he deserved to be called a rake. Her words still stung. How could she be the malicious gossip he'd spent so long hating? How could she be the woman who let him develop feelings for her when she'd known how angry he'd been at her writing? In truth, he couldn't put his finger on who she was.

He *did* know she had strength. Anyone who'd been dealt the sort of blows Suki had been dealt over the past few days would have crumbled. She'd been dedicated to her work as a teacher and had *that* taken away from her. She'd been writing under a *nom de plume* to further her journalistic career and had *that* taken away from her. She'd been safe on the streets of her neighbourhood and had *that* taken away from her. She'd had a lead on a story about Baron Umezono and had *that* taken away from her. Still, she hadn't whined in complaint. She was strength, sense, and beauty, and he wanted her, plain and simple.

They sat on thick floor cushions with a low table between them. The tearoom buzzed with conversation and laughter, no doubt fuelled by the earthenware bottles of *sake* rice wine on each table.

216

Suki wiped her hands on the thick warm towel the matron's daughter had handed them. "I hope you're able to stomach more Japanese food. I'm afraid their offerings are limited."

"I've actually grown quite fond of the cuisine. I thought our midday meal was superb."

Suki nodded. "I've never had such delicious bamboo rice. I'm going to ask our cook if she can replicate it."

The matron's daughter brought them servings of roasted bird, root vegetables in a tangy, sweet sauce, bowls of steaming rice, and miso soup with thinly sliced vegetables and tender pieces of pork. When they finished the meal, she served a bottle of *sake* accompanied by plates of fried mountain greens and mushrooms. Soon, he had Suki laughing at his gustatory experiences when he'd first arrived in Tokyo. "I stared at the bowl, my mind blank. What in heaven's name was this dish before me?"

"Let me guess. Turtle?"

"No."

"Eel?"

"No, we eat jellied eels in England."

Suki's nose crinkled adorably. "You do not."

"Delicious."

She refilled his *sake* cup. "About this mysterious dish, did it smell fishy?"

"Yes, fishy. But it was not fish. Nor had the thing ever taken a breath of air."

"A vegetable?" Suki declared and rounded her rosebud mouth in an expression that made him want to spend the whole night giving her riddles.

"Congealed devil's root covered in dried fish flakes and a pepper sauce, but none of this was apparent at the time."

"Did you eat it?"

"I had five Japanese men staring at me, waiting for my verdict." He paused for the right words. "It was too hard to be jelly, yet easy to chew. I swallowed a bite. Then told them it was splendid."

"You liked it?" Suki's voice rose as though she couldn't believe it possible.

"Not at all."

She laughed heartily and finished her cup. Griff poured her another. "My secretary took the remainder off my plate when our guests were busy with the female entertainment."

"You dined with geisha?"

He nodded as the matron brought another bottle of *sake* along with plates of dried fish. "They were as elegant and witty as their reputation suggests. Even in translation, they were amusing companions. My glass was always full. A tobacco pipe was at hand whenever I reached for it. They played instruments of which I have no knowledge or appreciation, but sounded lovely, and their dancing was lovely as well. We Westerners are used to hearty country jigs and flying around the ballroom in couples."

"That's why the conservative faction hates our balls. Men and women touching while moving to music, *in front* of other people."

"Aren't these the same men who go to teahouses where touching and public lasciviousness is expected?"

"It's all about keeping things in their place. Aristocrats near the emperor, poor girls in the brothels, peasants tied to the land, outcasts away from sight. As for foreigners, they belong in a whole other world."

Mention of the conservative faction reminded him of the attack that morning. They were a dangerous and violent group. He'd speak with the British envoy forthwith about protecting Tsukiji's residents, but that would do little to assure him that Suki wouldn't be attacked again. The conservatives had to be stopped, and the legation had little power to act against Japanese citizens. And Suki didn't think the Japanese police would be motivated to arrest the rioters based on their having shouted insults and thrown rocks.

He poured them fresh cups of *sake* and fretted. Suki was in danger. Someone had to protect her. If neither the envoy nor the police were able to perform their civic duty, he'd have no alternative but to sit sentry by her house night and day, which appealed, provided the conservatives made another attempt at harming her. Then he could demonstrate what remained of the boxing skills he'd picked up during his university years. Better yet, he could get his hands on one of those samurai swords. One wave of the sword and Suki would never have to worry again. However, in the event that her family and neighbours objected to him brandishing swords outside her home, she had to be prepared. "What will you do next time they attack?"

"I'll turn around and walk back into our house or the newspaper offices or wherever they find me. Although I suppose I won't be spending much time at the newspaper offices." She sank into the cushion and took a sip of the sweet wine. "I believe my quest to learn about Baron Umezono has come to an end."

Griff wondered whether her disappointment would ease if he pulled her close, undid the pins holding back her thick locks, and stroked the gorgeous bounty. No, that sort of behaviour was more likely to earn him a slap. He'd have to encourage her with friendly words. "This is a single setback. There are other avenues of investigation you could pursue."

"I've been asking about the baron for over two weeks now. He's a minor aristocrat from a good family and, by all measures, an unremarkable man of business. He's never behaved badly enough in public to make him the subject of widespread rumour. Although he almost made a scene that night…" Suki put down her cup and let out a deep breath. "You've actually met him. I was questioning him that night on the Hotel Metropolis terrace when you intervened."

"You were questioning Baron Umezono? I thought that man had something to do with Mademoiselle Renaud."

"I didn't feel able to explain everything at that time."

A charge of anger ripped through Griff at recalling how Suki had her back pressed against the terrace balustrade with that man bending over her. "When I saw you with him, I thought he was too close."

"He was acting inappropriately. I'm grateful for you coming to my rescue. At the time, I was trying to ask him about enemies who might pen a letter to the newspaper about his misdeeds. He was trying to find a way beneath my dress."

"The bastard." Griff should have followed his instincts that night and throttled the man instead of letting the weasel slither back to the clubroom.

"You arrived before he did anything too horrible." Suki refilled Griff's empty cup.

"He was trying to get under your dress. That sounds horrible enough." He really should have throttled the man.

"He's an ordinary fool, by my estimate. I was able to learn through servants that he patronizes brothels. Many men do. He's also a frequent gambler, as are a number of men."

"The baron has a reputation," Griff pointed out. How could he have let a man as vile as the baron get away with throwing himself at Suki? Granted, at the time he didn't know the man was Baron Umezono, nor did he know any details regarding the baron's reputation. But shouldn't he have sensed that something was terribly amiss, as it certainly was?

"What do you mean?"

"He's known around Tsukiji as the 'bawdy baron.'" The *sake* must have gone to his head for that nickname to slip out. Once said, he'd have to provide explanation, and in no way could he describe the baron's sordid tastes to a virginal woman like Suki.

"What do you mean by 'bawdy?'" she asked, of course.

Griff steeled himself with another cup of *sake*. He could be circumspect. "The baron enjoys various activities of the sort that might offend a woman's sensibilities."

"What kind of activities?"

"It's not something you talk about with a nice woman…"

"You probably don't realize that when it comes to such matters, I'm not an innocent. The Tattler column presents readers with all sorts of indecent happenings. I have to omit parts that would offend the faint of heart. But I learn of many scandalous things taking place in Tsukiji."

He wanted to help, her but saying such things in public made him hesitate even after more cups of *sake* than he could count. He glanced around. None of the inn's guests seemed to be listening to their conversation. Usually, when Japanese people understood English, they eagerly joined the exchange. He and Suki had privacy, and she already knew about the baron's love of brothels. Indeed, the baron's debauchery with multiple persons might even be relevant to her article.

Griff leaned forward and lowered his voice. "He likes bedroom sport with many people involved."

Suki let her jaw drop then quickly covered her open mouth. "How many people?"

"I'm not entirely sure." His tongue stumbled on the words. "Probably more than a few."

"How does that work exactly?"

"I believe there are multiple…events occurring at the same time. It could be stimulating to watch others, while one is doing the same."

"Events?"

Suki was a virgin, her ears delicate, her knowledge of bed-sport little to nothing. Then again, she was also a gossip columnist who aspired to be a newspaper reporter and was currently looking into the affairs of the bawdy baron. For her own good, he should at least warn her. "There would be the usual sensual acts, kissing and fondling. The breasts and the buttocks would be manipulated by hand. Other parts as well. A man might extend his kisses down a woman's body to heighten her enjoyment."

"And the woman?"

"She might do the same to the man."

The flush on Suki's face deepened. "Oh."

Had he offended her? Or was it possible she was curious about how a woman went about extending her kisses down a man's body? He'd happily show her how it was done. They could go upstairs right now to his room, and he'd give a full and thorough demonstration of any acts she wished.

A virgin, he reminded himself. She was a virgin, and he wasn't going to deflower her in a country inn when he was too tipsy to exercise the proper delicacy. But her lower lip was suddenly moist, and she was looking at him as though she'd be amenable to some other rather naughty suggestions.

Suki's gaze drifted toward the stairs leading to the upper floors. "I'm feeling quite lightheaded at the moment. Perhaps we should take leave of the tearoom?"

Griff lowered his *sake* cup slowly. His skin sizzled with raw desire, too much for him to control around her. Their conversation had gone further than he should've allowed. He'd given her nothing useful about the baron. All he'd done was fuel his desire to run his tongue over every inch of her body. "We should do that."

He rose to his feet, his legs snagging on the underside of the low table. An amused smile played on Suki's lips. How he wanted her.

But he would not seduce her. He was going to escort her to her room, then turn around and walk down the hallway to his room. She was Professor Garrick's daughter, Roger's sister, and a virgin, very much a virgin.

Griff ascended the narrow stairs ahead of Suki. Her presence behind him brought chaos to his senses. The stairs were too narrow for him to bring her to his side, but he wanted her warm soft hand in his to secure her to him. They reached the landing, and he turned back to her. Those dark eyes gazing at him in the barely lit hallway scathed all reason. He would fall to his knees and worship if that was what it would take to keep her by his side. "Shall I take you to your room?"

"That would be perfect." Her voice was low and lusty.

He held out his arm and she placed hers in the crook. Now he had her by his side. And he absolutely could *not* be trusted around her.

They reached the door of her room, and he moved aside for her to enter.

She didn't move. "I very much appreciate all you've done for me today. You've proved yourself a good friend. But…" She let out a deep breath. "Friendship has limits, and there are times when those limits might be exceeded. Do you think tonight is one of those times?"

He needed to step away, head straight to his room, and secure the lock. But that was impossible because his legs had become suddenly, irrevocably paralysed. "Do you mean we could try to be more than friends?"

"That's exactly what I mean."

She stood before him, her gaze on his lips. What harm could one kiss do? Not much, probably. They'd kissed before, and those kisses had plunged to the depths of him. But tonight could be different; he might walk away unaffected. In any case, he'd never know unless they kissed, and the simple fact was that he'd never give up a chance to kiss Suki. So, he pulled her heavenly softness toward him and kissed her as though his life depended on it.

Again and again, in a fury of need and gratification, of pressure and retreat, their mouths came together. He couldn't get enough of her *sake*-moistened lips. There would never be enough of her lips. If he had any sense, he'd retreat to his room and wallow in regret over this slip of judgment. But he had no sense around her, and she wrapped her arms around him as her precious mouth granted him entrance.

This woman was going to be his undoing. No, she'd already undone him. Her hips took up the rhythm of their circling tongues. He reached for her buttocks and pressed her to him. Despite layers of clothing, he felt her body quiver, and it sent his blood racing.

She was meant to be his. They were meant to be together.

He found the place below her jawline where he'd watched her gentle pulse beat against her skin and pressed his lips to the warm flesh.

Suki let out an airy moan that sang with pleasure. She was enjoying this, loving the feel of their bodies together, loving what he was doing to her. He cupped the lower curve of her breast and kneaded while his thumb teased the nipple tightening under her kimono.

She moaned again, this time deeper, needier, and much louder. Griff feared that moan would be the one that gave away the tryst taking place in the second-floor hallway.

"We should go inside," she whispered.

Griff couldn't agree more. He slid open the door to her quarters. Like his, there was a small sitting room and an even smaller sleeping space with a futon already laid out. God help him, he had no idea what to do about that futon, but he had to keep kissing her.

He turned back to Suki. She slid the door shut with one hand behind her. In the moonlight filtering through the window, her dark eyes shone with hunger. Sliding his arms around her waist, he brought her to him and brushed hair away from her face to take in the breadth of her forehead and the curve of her cheekbones. She tilted her chin upwards. Her dark lips already swollen from their kisses parted, and he claimed them again, soft at first, as they were tender, then harder as she pressed into his mouth and against his body.

She weaved her fingers into the hair at the base of his neck, and electricity shot to his lower back and dug into his rock-hard erection. Stumbling, he threw them both off-balance, and Suki's back hit the wall.

"Are you hurt?" he asked.

"Not at all."

Determined to spare no inch of her, he kissed her cheeks and chin, and down her neck as far as the kimono would allow. Had he known how to tear off a kimono, the garment would already be lying in a pile on the floor. "Can we take off the kimono?"

Suki turned for him. "Do you know how to undo the sash?"

No, but he would damn well figure it out. With a few tugs and a jerk, it unravelled in his hands. She released the heavy robe from her body, and there was yet another kimono underneath. Suki's fingers moved across several ribbons holding the garment together, then shrugged and pulled until she stood before him in a flimsy chemise, her nipples studded against the translucent fabric. A low growl from deep inside him filled the air.

"Shall I?" she asked.

He wasn't certain what she was seeking to do, but he wasn't about to deny her permission for anything. "Go ahead." The lust scalding his voice was downright shameless.

She removed the pins from her hair. With a shake of her head, the thick mane tumbled down her shoulders and back, and something inside him released. He was completely at her mercy.

Then she parted the chemise.

His chest constricted as he drank in her form in the moonlight, her delicate breasts the colour of fresh milk, the dip of her waist cast in shadow, the swirl of hairs dark as night gathered between her thighs. "You are perfection."

Leaning down, he laid kisses on the top of her chest until reaching the upper swell of her plush breasts. Warm and blossoming with the scent of lilacs and oranges, they fit neatly into his hands. He caressed them, brought them together, and ran his tongue along the seam that formed between them.

Suki let out a small cry. "That is so marvelous."

"The things you are doing to me, Suki." He needed to give her fair warning. "If we go much further, I'm not going to want to stop. I'll want to be inside you."

"I understand, and I'm ready."

A virgin, the voice of reason called out through the thick haze of desire. Professor Garrick's daughter. He could take her here and now…provided they agreed to marry. That would make it right; it would make everything in his life right. Laughter collected in his throat. Marriage was the answer. That was how he and Suki were meant to be together.

He'd drunk enough *sake* to inebriate a musk ox, but he knew what his heart wanted. After the pain and confusion, the exhilaration and joy they'd experienced, their coming together tonight was a sign they were fated. She was meant to be his, for always.

True, she'd expressed a wish not to marry, but hadn't this passion between them changed her mind? How could it not?

"I want us to be together." His finger traced circles along the outer edge of her breast. He couldn't keep his hands off her. Nor did he intend to.

"As do I."

"For more than tonight?"

"Our fling should certainly last more than one night." She curled her rosebud lips into a teasing smile.

Those lips would be his; her body would be his to please and take his pleasure in return. From this very moment, if she wished. They could have a night to remember throughout their lifetimes. All she had to do was accept his proposal, and if her ardour was any indication, very shortly he would hear the word "yes."

He took her hands and brought them to his chest. "I want you beside me all the time, not for the occasional fling. I want us to be together properly."

"How?"

Bringing her hands to his lips, he laid kisses on their smooth planes, then met her questioning gaze. "We would marry."

Suki removed her hands from his, her face a picture of surprise. "Marry? I thought we were going to be lovers."

"We'll still be lovers. Let me assure you of that."

"But you wanted a fling, and now you're talking about marriage." She stepped backwards, increasing the space between them. "This isn't something I'm prepared for."

Her confusion was natural, but the way forward was clear. "It makes sense. Your family is going to become suspicious when we spend more time together. My wards are arriving next week. Simply being lovers isn't possible. Don't you want more?"

Suki picked her chemise from the floor, shook it out, and slipped it back on. "I want to be with you. I hadn't thought our being together would mean so much change."

"Marriage is the logical step for two people who feel about one another as we do." He could call it love, or the beginnings of love, but to his ears that would sound mawkish and presumptuous. Their love would grow, of that he had no doubt, and he didn't need sentimentality to prove his point. Their being together made sense: she was a virgin from a good family, and he was an unattached man of wealth and status. "It's the only way we can be together."

"You've changed the rules of our being together, and I don't know how I can agree."

Griff pulled her to his chest and wrapped his arms around her. "I want us to face the public without shame. Let's start out by telling everyone we're courting. We can wait as long as necessary before taking the next step."

Suki shrugged off his touch and picked her kimono undergarment off the floor. "That would be marriage."

"Yes, marriage would be the next step after courting." Minutes before they were kissing, ready to fall onto the futon and make splendid, passionate love. Now she was acting like marriage to him was unthinkable.

"Marrying a foreign man, or any man, isn't a decision I'm ready to make."

"Why can't we just tell our families we're courting towards marriage? Courting gives our affair the respectability it deserves."

Suki retied the kimono undergarment's ribbons. "Then everyone will talk nonstop about a formal engagement and the date of the wedding and what color hair our children will have. We'd be as good as married, and I can't marry a man I hardly know."

"You know plenty about me. You wrote about me in that column for months on end." As soon as he'd uttered the words, he knew they were the wrong ones, and he desperately wanted them back.

Suki took in a sharp breath that sent chills through him. "I thought you understood why I wrote about you. I apologized, and today you seemed to be enjoying our time together. I thought you'd moved past it. I suppose I was wrong."

He hadn't moved past it. Not yet. They'd had a terrific day of laughter and good food and drink, and he ached to have her body under his. But he hadn't forgiven her for making him the scoundrel of Tsukiji. Even so, that didn't mean he never would. "I'm working towards it."

Suki folded her arms under the breast that had been in his hands only moments before. "Would you marry me if I was still writing the Tattler column?"

"I thought you were quitting the Tattler to become a newspaper reporter."

"I plan to work as a full-fledged newspaper reporter, but I have to prove myself first, which may take some time."

One week ago, courting the Tokyo Tattler would've been as inconceivable as Suki being the Tattler herself. Now it wasn't beyond consideration, provided they had an understanding. "I'd have no choice but to accept your writing the column, but I cannot have a mere fling, sneaking around town, deceiving our loved ones, eventually getting caught. Then having to explain that we kept our relationship secret because you wanted to carry on without a proper commitment. You're not that type of woman." His words were tough, but she needed to understand what they were getting into.

Suki speared him with a glare. "Maybe I am that type of woman."

"You want to be like a geisha? And I the wealthy patron who buys you a house in town to visit when the urge strikes?"

Suki heaved the heavy kimono into the clothing basket. "Don't be ridiculous. I'm not interested in money like some kind of prostitute. It's natural for a woman to seek intimate relations."

"So you want to be like those wealthy divorcees you write about in the Tattler column? Traveling the world, having affair after affair like a wanton harlot?"

Suki gasped. "Is that what you think of me?"

"That is what you are suggesting."

"I'm only suggesting we carry on as we originally intended."

"What would Professor Garrick say about that?"

"Professor Garrick would tell me to find someone who understands a woman's basic mammalian instincts." She pushed past him and slid open the door. "I think it's best you leave."

CHAPTER TWENTY-TWO

Griff made it to the tearoom in time to see Suki rising from the table. The neck and cuffs of his shirt were still damp from the water he'd splashed on his face in an attempt to banish the pounding *sake* headache he'd earned from the bottle he'd drunk after returning to his room the previous night. Suddenly, a dreadful feeling came upon him that in the haze of his bruising hangover, he'd forgotten to put on his trousers. He looked down. Trousers were present and accounted for. At least he wouldn't have to add "unintended nudity" to his list of infractions against Suki.

Suki walked toward the entrance. *Shame me*, he wanted to say. *Punish me for hurting you, for practically calling you a harlot, for ruining what would've been the best night of my life.*

But she gave him only a mild smile. "Good morning," she said, like a teacher at the front of her classroom. "We should leave as soon as possible. The matron has your breakfast."

***

Suki took a seat across the aisle on the return train to Tokyo. Griff closed his eyes against the moving countryside and slept. When they were preparing to board separate rickshaws outside Tokyo's Shimbashi Station, Suki finally acknowledged his existence. "Thank you for accompanying me to Saitama," she said more warmly than he'd expected. "I couldn't have visited the railway site without your help."

"I was glad to accompany you." He couldn't take her in his arms and hold her until her hurt fell away. He only had words, and no words would ever capture the enormity of his regret. "I feel badly about those things I said last night. I'm terribly sorry."

A pained expression crossed her face. "There's no need to apologize. You spoke from your convictions."

Was she referring to his conviction to marry her? Did that mean she understood he'd practically called her a "wanton harlot" because he'd been smarting from her rejection? Or did she truly believe he thought her a woman of loose morals? The stern set of her mouth told him that none of those questions would be well-received. "I'm willing to help further with the article on Baron Umezono. Please let me know whatever assistance you might need."

She smiled blandly. "That's very kind of you."

The emptiness in her voice stripped him of all hope. He was going to try, nonetheless. "I can escort you home. You must be careful of the conservative faction."

"I'll manage well enough on my own. Have a good day, Spenser-*san*."

Griff watched Suki settle into the rickshaw, then turned to the runner next in line. "Ueno Park."

Ordinarily, on a Sunday afternoon, he took supper at a friend's home or explored the city. Today, he had neither plans with friends nor any desire to venture around Tokyo's neighbourhoods. He'd considered directing the rickshaw to his offices and spending the afternoon immersed in account books, but he would have ended up pacing the floor, agonizing over what had happened the previous night. He might as well be pacing outside.

Mists hovered above the park's trees, cloaking the pathways in greyness. Griff pulled up his jacket collar against the vernal chill and headed in the same direction he and Suki had strolled the park. Several couples meandered likewise, but mostly it was quiet, and Griff was grateful for the isolation. His mind drifted to how he'd wanted Suki to shame him, how good it would've felt had she called him names and questioned his character. Of course, that was exactly what she'd done as the Tattler. And he'd hated her for it.

Had his words last night been a way of punishing her for being the Tattler? No, last night he'd been shocked and hurt that she's so readily rejected a proper union for something tawdry. Granted, at the time he'd proposed this proper union, they'd hardly been engaged in innocent conversation. For some reason, he'd thought it wise to bring up courtship and marriage between fondling her breasts and taking her maidenhead. No wonder she'd been confused.

Adding to the confusion, he'd announced his desire for them to marry after having given her every reason to believe he was perfectly satisfied with a typical affair. Knowing full well her resistance to marriage, he'd nevertheless expected her to be thrilled by his proposal. He should've exercised more tact in broaching the subject. Instead, he'd laid it at her feet like a cat seeking to please her mistress with a dead rodent atop her shiny boot.

When Suki hadn't rejoiced at his grand gesture, his response had been appalling. Her preference for a fling over a courtship had felt like a betrayal, the same kind of betrayal he'd felt when he learned she was the town gossipmonger and not the innocent schoolteacher of his imagination. So, he'd implied she was a whore for not living up to the virginal image he'd made of her. He'd acted as though she'd deceived him yet again. But he'd been deceiving himself.

Just as he had with Victoria.

When she'd agreed to come with him to Japan, he convinced himself she was a willing participant in his adventures, but adventure was never in her nature. He should have acknowledged her for what she was: a young woman willing to sacrifice her happiness to be with the man she loved. Likewise, he'd spent months believing Natsu was simply a little too eager and too generous when she was maddening him with her obsessive attentions. He could've recognised much earlier they were not a match. Instead, he'd seen her based on his needs, and not for the woman she was.

Suki had shown him who she was. Yes, she was the innocent schoolteacher in the plain grey kimono, the one who'd never been kissed until that day in Ueno. But she was also a woman who thought about fashions of the day and relished a good scandal. He was familiar enough with the Tokyo Tattler columns to know she never condemned women for their intimate moments on the Hotel Metropolis terrace. She teased and tutted but never insulted or called them wanton. She was a modern woman, and he liked that about her. He certainly liked when she was modern enough to remove her kimono for him the previous night.

The Tattler column also made plain her belief that nothing good came of relations between foreign men and Japanese women. A well-justified belief. Her father had shown her firsthand what happened to women who fell in love with foreigners. No wonder she wouldn't consider a courtship with a foreigner until he'd proved himself loyal.

Griff was loyal, but he'd never be able to prove it as long as she wanted nothing to do with him. Their affair would have to be carried out on her terms, or not at all, and he couldn't bear not at all. He'd give her a fling if that was what she wanted. He'd compromise a woman from an upstanding family, a teacher, a newspaper reporter, someone he admired and respected. Maybe he'd never want a courtship and marriage. Maybe he wouldn't fall even more in love with her.

Somehow, he doubted it. He'd never been casual when it came to intimate relations. What if he became dissatisfied at her reluctance to marry and left her? What if there was a child? Would she still refuse marriage? He'd never allow that. But those were matters for future consideration. For now, he had to respect their agreement to an undetermined affair, which would never happen until he got back into her good graces.

Fortunately, as he was emerging from sleep on the train back to Tokyo, he'd realised how he might help her learn more about the contemptible Baron Umezono. This afternoon he'd make the inquiries and when they bore fruit, which they would if anything untoward was taking place in the baron's worthless life, then he'd have a basis to appeal for another chance at being Suki's fling.

CHAPTER TWENTY-THREE

Suki arrived home intent on a piping-hot bath followed by a nap that would last well into tomorrow morning. She had one foot in the entrance when Rosie appeared, cradling a very fussy Charlie. Half her hair had fallen out of its pins and dark circles ringed her eyes. "He hasn't slept more than ten minutes straight in the past twenty-four hours."

"Is it his ears again?"

"Ears or teeth coming in. I'm not certain of anything. I've barely slept." She gave Suki a once-over. "You don't look like you've slept much either."

"I haven't." Suki placed her umbrella, satchel, and shoes in their respective places.

Rosie jiggled Charlie and frowned. "You look…devastated. Come into the parlor. I'll have the maid bring us tea."

Resigning herself to a later bath, Suki followed Rosie into the parlor. A few sips of creamy, sweet tea later, she felt ready to speak. "It didn't go well. I have no leads on the newspaper article and will probably have to abandon it altogether."

"I'm sorry to hear. Perhaps you'll be able to write another story for the newspaper."

"That will be for Ned Taylor to decide. He thinks something is amiss in the baron's life. My inability to uncover whatever that might be doesn't bode well for my chances of becoming a reporter."

"But you still have the Tattler column to write. You're going to continue, aren't you?" Rosie punctuated her words with rhythmic pats against Charlie's back.

"I've decided to continue," Suki said.

Rosie gave an unamused Charlie a lift off her lap. "Hurrah. I was hoping that was the case. The women of Tsukiji would be devastated if you stopped writing the Tattler."

Suki could think of a motley group of ruffians who might not be devastated. She braced herself for Rosie's answer to a question she wished she didn't have to ask. "Did you notice any disturbances on the street yesterday morning? Did anyone say anything about a protest in the neighborhood?"

"I've heard nothing of the sort. It's been quiet as usual around here. Did you hear of something?"

The conservatives seemed to have gotten away with chasing her rickshaw down the street. While Suki believed they were all bluster and didn't wish to alarm Rosie or anyone else in the family over idle threats, she felt obliged to inform them in case they returned. "A group of conservatives chased Mr. Spenser and I down the street yesterday morning. They were posing as road workers and wanted a word with the Tattler, which I didn't give them."

"I had no idea." Rosie stilled her patting and brought Charlie to her chest, then inched away from the window. The look she gave Suki urged her to do the same: protect herself from threats lurking outside. "How did you manage to escape?"

"It wasn't that awful. Our runner got us out of Tsukiji. The conservatives let us leave, and I doubt they'll return. Mr. Spenser is going to have a word with the British envoy about increasing protections for Tsukiji residents."

"Papa Garrick will with speak with the American envoy when he learns of it." Rosie put Charlie on her shoulder and rocked. "Between Papa Garrick and Mr. Spenser, we should be well prepared if the conservatives try to enter the Tsukiji gates again."

She relaxed a little more and eased into a smile. "How was your time with Mr. Spenser? Did you enjoy his company?"

For the most part, she'd enjoyed his company immensely. The afternoon had been long and difficult, but they'd laughed through a carriage ride that stripped them of all dignity, and she'd reconciled herself to a failed inquiry that meant she had no future as a newspaper reporter. The supper conversation had been amusing, and the food delicious. She'd drunk too much *sake*, and he'd told her of the ways men and women pleasured one another, and her need for him had been overwhelming. She'd opened herself to him, and when she couldn't consent to his abrupt suggestion of marriage, he'd called her a wanton harlot. "We didn't get along as well as I'd hoped."

"How surprising." Rosie glanced around the parlor and leaned closer. "I thought spending an evening with Mr. Spenser would cement the affection between you."

Suki sighed. Griff's insult had torn the fabric of who she was, of what she believed, of whom she could trust. She wanted to hold it up for Rosie's assessment, but her sister-in-law would be shocked by what had transpired at the country inn. "He's not the man I thought he was."

"Did he hurt you?"

"No. In fact, he's a true gentleman. He wants a respectable relationship with a respectable woman."

"Then you two should be perfect together." Charlie let out a long wail. Rosie stood and bounced up and down. In a matter of seconds, Charlie's cry lessened to a whimpering hum.

"Apparently, I'm not respectable enough."

"What in heaven's name do you mean?"

Suki couldn't allow Rosie and Charlie to suffer injury from her fainting straight away upon hearing that Suki preferred an illicit affair over a courtship toward marriage. "I told him I wasn't ready for marriage, which makes me a loose woman."

"Intolerable." Rosie resumed her rhythmic pats to Charlie's back, but with more gusto. "Absolutely intolerable. That's not something a good man would say or think." Outrage must have given her the perfect degree of wallop because Charlie suddenly stopped crying and his eyelids shut. Rosie warily returned to her seat and continued the patting.

Suki wanted to be fair to Griff. After all, he'd proposed marriage to save her family from the embarrassment of their secret fling. "He apologized sincerely."

"Being unready for marriage doesn't make you a loose woman unless you lift your skirts, and I know you don't go around lifting your skirts. Right?"

"I've yet to lift my skirts."

Rosie let out a sigh. "I'm glad to hear. If I learned you were the Tattler and a loose woman in the same week, I would have to question whether two plus two still equals four."

"I kissed him."

"That's absolutely fine, as long as no one else knows," Rosie said as though it were an obvious truth. "But if you've already kissed him, then you must find him desirable. You've said yourself he's a gentleman. Why not marry him?"

"I can't marry the first man who catches my fancy, especially when he's a foreigner. I need more time before I can put myself in the same position as all those other women who think they're in love with a foreigner. Their lovers leave them and the children they fathered. Eventually, they return to their home countries, at least most of them do."

"I cannot image that a gentleman such as Mr. Spenser would abandon a commitment."

"I suspect Mr. Spenser is such a good man, but I don't yet know for certain. It's too soon to think of marriage. I'm not opposed to the idea of being married," Suki said. She'd just never imagined herself finding a man, Japanese or foreigner, who could overcome her anxieties about their future life together. There was a possibility

Griff could be that man. He was right that they made sense as a couple. But before she could truly devote herself to a union, she had to shed misgivings, large misgivings, about marrying a foreigner. That would take time. "I suppose I'm opposed to rushing into a marriage, although Mr. Spenser did offer an extended courtship for as long as I needed."

"*That's* perfect. Then we'll have plenty of time to plan the wedding brunch, and you can begin making changes to his house."

"That's the problem. Once we mention marriage, it's practically done. I thought he might be willing to try a different kind of courtship. More like a private friendship."

Rosie shook her head so many times Suki feared she would get a neckache. "A private friendship will not suffice. A man like him wants children before he's forty."

"He's thirty-one."

"Then he'd better get to it," Rosie said, her voice carrying the shrill warning of an aged matriarch.

Suki laughed as usual at Rosie's imitations, and the piercing sadness and insufferable frustration that had taken hold since the last night loosened its grip.

Rosie beamed at her. "Griffith Spenser wishes to marry you. This is a rare opportunity."

"I can't face him again after what he said."

"A man will speak in anger when the woman he loves refuses an offer of courtship."

"You think he loves me?"

"Why else would he offer a courtship?"

So he could commit carnal acts at a country inn while preserving his sense of chivalry. He certainly hadn't mentioned anything about love the previous night. His desire for a courtship could be borne from pressure to satisfy social dictates. If that was the case, theirs would be a courtship of obligation, much like the courtships of foreign men who felt obliged to marry their Japanese lovers for the duration of their time in the country.

Yet she knew in her heart that Griff wouldn't make a lifetime commitment, or any other kind of commitment, unless he intended to fulfill his commitment in every sense. Indeed, the man welcomed commitments: he had wards arriving; he practiced daily at the lawn tennis club; Rei-*san* was fiercely loyal to him, and he to her. Most telling, he'd parted with Natsu because he'd been unable to make a commitment. Griffith Spenser stood by his word. If he wanted a courtship toward marriage, then marriage in its fullest sense, a marriage of mutual love and devotion, was his intention.

And to have his love made her feel as though she was stranded on the shoreline while a typhoon swirled the unruly seas. What if she could never trust him enough to love him fully in return? She would end up hurting him, yet again. "I believe he has deep feelings for me. I can see how it must have disappointed him when I expressed opposition to our courting."

"He spoke in haste, which is always a mistake, especially when angry, but not an unforgivable one."

It'd been horrible, but it wasn't unforgivable. "I was angry as well and might have responded to his proposal in a way that was insensitive to his feelings."

Rosie widened her eyes. "What kind of fight did you have with Mr. Spenser?"

"It was uglier than the gown Mrs. Larson wore to the foreign officers' ball."

Rosie let out a sharp laugh. Her gaze darted to Charlie, who looked like an angel snoring softly. "Then an apology should suffice for his speaking out of turn. You must reconsider a courtship. Mr. Spenser would make an ideal husband."

Griff's wealth and social standing alone made him an ideal husband. She also knew him to be generous, charming, intelligent, and adventurous, all of which made him ideal for her. Then there was the way he made her feel. The mere thought of his touch sent a sublime heat coursing through her body.

He'd said she could take as long as needed before they walked down the aisle. In the meantime, they could be together however they desired.

"I may reconsider the courtship. Please—"

Rosie held a finger to her lips. "I won't say a word."

***

Following a short but restful nap, Suki dressed for supper and arrived downstairs to find a message addressed to her on the correspondence table. Her heart fluttered at the sight of Griff's hand.

Dear Suki,

I trust you have rested well after the long journey.

I pray you will not think me intruding into your investigation of Baron Umezono, but I took the liberty of speaking with an acquaintance who I thought might have information on the baron and learned something that may be of interest to you.

Please inform me if you wish to receive this information, and how you would like to receive it.

Sincerely,

Griff

Suki pressed the letter to her chest. Griff had inquired about the baron on her behalf. In the letter, he'd used their Christian names. The article about the baron was likely a lost cause, but Griff's tenderness was yet hers. Of course she would meet him, and she knew exactly where she wanted them to meet.

***

The following evening, Suki opened the front door and scanned the dark street for fanatical conservatives preparing to hurl insults and street debris her way. Not that she anticipated any more encounters with the faction. That afternoon Papa Garrick had received assurances from the American envoy that additional guards, specially tasked with preventing conservatives from entering the foreign quarter, would be placed at the Tsukiji gates. But she would err on the side of caution; she had a feeling Griff would want her to exercise utmost safety on her way to his home.

All appeared calm, but the more she gazed down the dark street shrouded in trees, the more her skin tingled as though she were anticipating an unseen menace about to pounce at any moment. She could ask Roger or Papa Garrick for an escort. She'd told the family that Mr. Spenser sought her and Marcelle's opinions on the rooms he'd designed for the wards. But were she to ask one of them to accompany her, whoever it was would accept Griff's inevitable invitation to stay for a drink. Before long, her escort would realize that Marcelle wasn't coming, and Suki had been less than forthcoming about her evening at the Spenser home.

Griff had been right about the toll a love affair's deceits would take on them—yet another reason to give their fling the respectability it deserved. The prospect of seeing his surprise, and hopefully joy, when she told him of her decision to engage in a proper courtship lightened her step and carried her through the front gates to the sidewalk.

She kept up a brisk pace and listened carefully for the sound of footfalls around her. A rustling sound from one of the maple trees had just caught her attention when across the street, a hearty greeting rang out in her direction.

Her heart thundered in her chest even as she recognized the rotund gentleman. "Professor Billings. Good evening to you," she called back. To hurry past any colleague of Papa Garrick's would be highly irregular and impolite. To hurry past his dear friend, Professor Billings, was impossible. Suki crossed the street and offered overdue congratulations on his son's nuptials. "How is your son enjoying married life?"

They chatted for several minutes about the young Mr. Billings's good fortune at finding a wife who shared his love for seaweed pressing. Then Professor Billings tugged at his moustache and raised a suggestive brow. For a moment, Suki wondered if she'd be wise to flee the suddenly lecherous family friend. But he didn't attempt to close the distance between them. "Do you think my new daughter-in-law could make an appearance in your column? She spends a lot of time on dresses and whatnot."

The previous few evenings, Mother Garrick and Roger had regaled her with numerous such requests from friends and neighbors. Accommodating these requests would make the Tattler column Tsukiji's forum for presenting the merits of young women seeking husbands and resolving disputes involving missing rain chains, pets, money, and kitchen help. "Thank you for the suggestion, Professor Billings. I'll have to see if there is room in the column."

"You ought to put more good news in there. Readers like to learn about the good fortunes of others."

No, they didn't. They wanted the headiness of moral superiority or the vicarious experience of a scintillating scandal. Truth be told, they wanted both.

Suki passed the American envoy's house and headed down the street with the grandest homes in Tsukiji. A swishing sound from a row of rhododendrons made her spin around in fear she was about to come face-to-face with a fervent conservative. But when she turned, only a row of motionless trees stood, staring her in the face. Likely, the sound had been rabbits or mice chasing one another through the shrubbery.

As she neared the crossing to Griff's house, she could've sworn she heard a rustle behind her. Like before, she turned toward the sound, and it ceased.

Griff's house was still halfway down the block when Suki's body prickled with certainty that she was being pursued. Ignoring murmurs from the bushes skirting the sidewalk, she ran as fast as her boots would allow. Not bothering to pull the bell, she opened Griff's front gate and stepped into the garden. Beneath the lantern she stopped to catch her breath.

The gate creaked. Suki turned toward the noise and gaped at the sight of Watanabe striding into the garden like a haughty apparition. Straightening her dark kimono, she pulled a rhododendron leaf from her hair and patted down the offended strands. "I thought this was where you would end up, Mademoiselle Tattler." The word "mademoiselle" flowed from her glistening lips without a hitch. Watanabe had been practicing.

"Were you following me?"

"I waited outside your home today because I knew you'd go to your lover. You and Spenser-*san* are lovers, aren't you?"

Watanabe's sneer dispelled the relief that had come over Suki in learning that her imagination hadn't been playing tricks on her. Indeed, she had been followed, and whatever instinct had alerted her to a pursuer was now shouting "danger." Griff was somewhere inside the home. She could call to him. But that would risk alerting the neighbors and raising embarrassing questions about why two women were locked in confrontation beside his azalea bushes.

She'd have to deal with Watanabe directly. "You're mistaken, Watanabe-*san*. Spenser-*san* and I are not lovers." In truth, they hadn't fully consummated their affection.

Watanabe eyed Suki as though she'd attempted to gift her a basket of rotten plums. "You spent the night together in Saitama. How could you not be lovers?"

"How did you know we were in Saitama?"

"Sources. You know all about sources, don't you, Mademoiselle Tattler?" Watanabe gave her a conspiratorial wink that made Suki's stomach churn. "So tell me, do you find Spenser-*san* satisfying?"

"We're friends."

"Friends who spend the night together? There's no such thing."

"He was helping me with a newspaper investigation." There was no need to defend herself to Watanabe. But despite Watanabe's cruelness in the way she'd exposed Suki as the Tattler, Suki pitied the woman. After all, Griff had only recently ended their affair. She must be seeking clarity as to its demise. Why else would she have waited outside Suki's home all day and followed her into his garden?

"The Tattler has an investigation in Saitama?" Watanabe chortled. "Don't lie to me. I know the truth."

"If you believe we're lovers, and nothing I say will dissuade you, then why are you asking?"

"I must hear your confession. I must hear how he left me to be with you. Then I can end it all."

Watanabe reached into the reticule dangling from her wrist and pulled out a revolver.

Suki hopped backward, aghast at the sight of the metal piece.

Watanabe grinned wildly and waved the gun about, which did little to ease Suki's nerves. "The gun belongs to Spenser-*san*. I took it while you were in Saitama. His maid loves me, unlike that devil of a housekeeper, Rei-*san*. That dear little maid told me he had to stay the night in Saitama, as he was assisting a young lady. I knew it was you, Mademoiselle Tattler, the woman he claimed to hate more than any other in Tokyo. I cannot understand. You must make me understand."

Seeing as it was unclear whether the gun was meant to threaten or achieve some other effect, such as murder, Suki could only think to placate Watanabe. "You're overreacting. Spenser-*san* was helping me with an article."

Watanabe narrowed her eyes at Suki. "Tell me your secrets. How do you seduce a man who thinks you're utter filth? What kind of magic does the half-breed possess?"

She might have paid heed to Watanabe's insult had the woman not been brandishing a deadly weapon. And since Suki had no desire to become better acquainted with said deadly weapon, she needed to act. She could call out to Griff, but what if that only agitated Watanabe further? Well, the woman wouldn't have come to his home bearing his revolver unless she was already thoroughly agitated. "Let's summon Spenser-*san*, and you can speak directly to him. He'll tell you everything you wish to know."

Watanabe tilted her head back and laughed. "Spenser-*san* never listens to me. That's the problem. But I need to know before I shoot myself." She pointed the gun at her midsection.

Suki froze. "Please, Watanabe-*san*, don't do anything rash."

Watanabe looked down at the gun pressed to her gut, then twisted it side to side as though readying to play with its lethal possibilities.

Suki's insides twisted into knots. "What do you want, Watanabe-*san*?"

"What I want is the truth about your affair. Did you find him an adequate lover? He was always a little too gentle with me. A bit of a novice, truth be told. I offered him all manner of delights, but he satisfied himself on the most basic acts. Alas, not very interesting at all. But your half-breed spells must have aroused his most barbaric desires. Tell me about the sexual deviations you tantalized him with. I must know what stimulates his serpent before I end it all."

Suki couldn't keep her eyes off the gun. "Don't do it, Watanabe-*san*. You're young and beautiful, a war widow. Everyone in Tsukiji adores you."

"It makes no difference. The one man I wish to adore me adores a vexation of nature, a scourge on humanity, a woman whose existence is the product of a demon's curse."

Suki steeled herself and adopted her most severe teacher's voice. "Give me the gun. I'll return it to Spenser-*san* and tell him I found it in the garden. He'll never know you were here."

"Mademoiselle Tattler would stop me from taking my life in Spenser-*san*'s garden? Imagine the column when this is over. I'm giving you the biggest scandal Tsukiji has ever seen. You'll be even more famous. Just tell me what you have that I don't. Why did Griff-*san* choose your ugly body over my beauty? Tell me." Watanabe raised the gun and took aim at Suki.

"*No.*" Suki shouted loud enough to wake neighbors a street over.

"How dare you?" Watanabe whispered through clenched teeth. "I'm not going to shoot you. I only want you to confess. Tell me."

The front door burst opened, and Griff came out. "What the *devil* are you doing here, Natsu?" he hollered.

Watanabe turned the gun back toward her midsection.

Before Griff reacted, Suki pulled back her fist and struck her square in the jaw.

The clang of teeth slamming together filled the garden. Watanabe reached up to her face, and the revolver fell from her hand. "*How dare you.*" Launching herself at Suki, she sent them both to the ground. They rolled across leaves and rocks until Watanabe claimed the upper hand by gripping Suki with her thighs. Twice she slapped Suki's face. Her hand was about to make contact for a third time when Suki caught her wrist. Using her free hand, Watanabe dug her long nails into Suki's cheek.

Griff was upon Watanabe before she could press any further. Flinging her aside, he pointed to the gate. "To hell with you. Leave here now."

He knelt next to Suki as she sat up. "*The gun*, you have to get the gun."

"It's right here," he said, patting his jacket pocket. He scanned her face, his gaze full of concern. "She really scratched you. There's blood. Are you otherwise injured?"

Suki could still feel Watanabe's hand against her cheek, and the back of her head hurt from smacking the hard ground. But she was otherwise unharmed. "I believe I'm fine." She looked around the garden. "Did Mrs. Watanabe leave?"

"Apparently so. I can't believe she had my gun."

"She stole it when we were in Saitama."

"How?"

"Your maid let her in."

Griff stiffened his jaw. "Rei-*san* will handle the maid. We need to get you inside and take care of your face." He wrapped his arm around Suki's waist and helped her to stand.

"I'll be fine. You need to go to Mrs. Watanabe."

"Never," he said and tightened his grip around Suki's waist as he led her to the house. "I'll strangle the woman if I get anywhere near her tonight."

"She said she was going to kill herself. She meant to do it here, in your garden."

"Utterly ridiculous. Natsu loves a spectacle. I can assure you she would never kill herself. She's trying to manipulate me into giving her another chance."

Suki suspected that was the case, but what would happen when Griff didn't give her the chance that she wanted? "We have to help her. She's not in her right mind."

Griff let out a sharp laugh. "Natsu has never been in her right mind. She'll snap out of this tantrum soon enough. I can't imagine her ending her life when she has so much havoc left to wreak on the lives of others."

"How can you know for certain? What if she gives up her quest for your affection and throws herself into rushing water or takes arsenic? We'll bear responsibility for not stopping her."

"That's exactly what she wants us to think."

"You don't want her death on your conscience. I don't want her death on mine."

Griff muttered what Suki supposed was the sort of profanity proper gentleman only ever muttered under their breaths, then opened the front door. Rei-*san* stood in the entrance. "Please help Miss Malveaux clean the wound on her face and give her whatever she needs."

Suki's panic receded. "Then you'll go to Mrs. Watanabe?"

Griff nodded. "Will you wait for me?"

"I won't go anywhere."

CHAPTER TWENTY-FOUR

Griff tugged off his boots in the entrance and bit back a curse at Natsu for ruining what was supposed to have been an evening of apologising to Suki and telling her the story of how the idiot baron had ended up with his arm in a sling. Then he was going to hold Suki and kiss her and make sure she knew how much she meant to him and how much he wanted her in his life.

But the violent, deceitful she-devil Natsu hadn't been anywhere he'd looked, and he'd looked everywhere he could think of. He'd inquired at Natsu's apartments, at the homes of several friends, at her favourite teahouse, and at the Chinese restaurant she frequented. He'd heard the Tokyo Players were presenting an encore performance of *The Importance of Being Earnest*. Even though the idea of Natsu attending a play she never liked in the first place after having threatened to end her life seemed quite absurd, he'd gone to the Tsukiji Playhouse all the same. Finally, he'd checked the Hotel Metropolis bar and strolled the infamous terrace.

Failing to locate Natsu was probably for the best. The urge to wring her neck would've been difficult to suppress.

Rei-*san* scurried to the entrance. Before she could open her mouth to greet him, he asked, "Is Suki here?"

"In the study," Rei-*san* said, and nodded reassuringly, her loosely tied grey chignon moving in tandem.

His mood brightened considerably. "How is she?"

Rei-*san* raised a large-knuckled finger to her cheek and made a circle. "Her face should heal in a few days. Fortunately, we had marigold in the garden. I ground the flowers and added aloe and ginseng to make a poultice. There shouldn't be any scarring."

Japanese medicines were a mystery to Griff, but he had faith in Rei-*san*, and she had faith in flowers and herbs, which was good enough for him. He thanked her and walked down the hallway to his study. Slowly, he pulled the door open so as not to disturb a sleeping Suki and found her reclining on the settee, a book in hand. Despite the rather large cloth over her cheek, she seemed well: skin was flushed pink and her eyes glimmered in the firelight.

"Did you find Mrs. Watanabe?" she asked.

Griff crossed the study towards Suki. "I went everywhere I could think of. I walked along the Tsukiji waterfront, back and forth, but found no sign of her. I bullied the maid into allowing me inside her apartments, but she wasn't there. Nor did I find a diary, letter, or any indication of a plan to end her life. I checked the homes of friends, the teahouse she favours, even the Hotel Metropolis. But she was nowhere to be found."

Suki set the book on the side table and moved over on the settee. Griff sat gently and studied the thick cloth secured to her cheek with a strip of fabric circling her head. "Are you in any pain?"

"None. Rei-*san* applied herbs and oils and covered it soundly. There shouldn't be any trace of injury in a few days."

Griff gritted his teeth so as not to offend Suki with the profane curses he wanted to direct toward Natsu. "I can't believe she hurt you this way."

Suki rested her elbow against the back of the settee and leaned against the palm of her hand. "Watanabe-*san* was distressed. She could have hurt me and you, much worse. Perhaps you were right that her threats were idle."

Griff was relieved to hear Suki coming around to his thinking. "I can't imagine Natsu taking her life when there are so many men in Tsukiji she's yet to badger into becoming her husband."

Suki brushed the settee as though removing a fine layer of dust, then looked over at him. "A widow like Watanabe needs a husband to protect her. Any day, the government could change its rules on war pensions and leave her with nothing. Or her father, grandfather, or brother could claim it for themselves. As heads of her family, they have that right. They'd probably leave her destitute for the crime of having humiliated them by being involved with foreigners. Many families think like that, especially ones that reside outside Tokyo. I can understand her desperation."

Griff knew Natsu was desperate, but he hadn't fully grasped the severity of her situation. "Hopefully, she'll find the right fellow, and they'll both be better off."

Suki placed her hand on top of his. He laced his fingers between hers and they sat in silence, his thumb caressing the back of her hand and the crease of her thumb, the fire crackling as it let off a puff of steam. Gone was the piercing sense of loss at having driven Suki away with his words, gone was the irritation of being on Natsu's wild-goose chase. Suki was beside him; he had everything he needed, so he surrendered to a languid sense of peace.

Suki squeezed his hand. "Please tell me if I should leave. You must be exhausted."

Suki leave? He never wanted her to leave. He eased over on the settee until their sides touched. "I want you here, for as long as you wish."

She settled their clasped hands on her lap. "I'll stay as long as you'll have me. I'm not expected home for another hour or so." He loved the tentative question in her voice.

"Then I shall keep you through the duration." Easing his hand from hers, he placed his arm on the back of the settee. Suki shifted to face him, bringing his knee within the folds of her skirt.

He gazed into her dark eyes and wondered whether they should talk about what he'd said at the inn and how he didn't care about marriage or a courtship as long as they were together. Or whether he should just kiss her.

Suki made the decision for him. Bringing her hands to rest along his jawline, she closed her eyes and gave him a gentle sweep of a kiss that tasted of sweet tea and butter biscuits. Her lips were like a caress of silk, and they soothed his soul. He drew her nearer, and they kissed in a gentle tangle of open mouths and seeking tongues.

Purring sounds arose from within her, igniting a need for them to be nearer still. He placed a hand on her nape and wove his fingers between her lightly curled hairs. Moving away from her lips, he touched his forehead to hers. Their gazes met and he let go in the warm depths of Suki's eyes no fire could rival. Then he brought his thumb to her cheek without thinking and brushed against her bandage. Instantly, he pulled away. "Did that hurt?"

"Not at all," she whispered against his lips before playing her tongue into his mouth in a velvety swish. Her body rose and fell, and before he recognised her intent, she was sitting sideways on his lap, her skirts pressed against his swollen cock. If he could have her anywhere, that was exactly where he would have her.

Griff raised his chin, seeking her generous mouth. And it came down on him, open and enticing. With one arm around her back, he used the other to take in the swooping arc of her hip and the shallow dip of her waist. Reaching the underswell of her breast, he cupped it, then gently kneaded. Those light purring sounds rose once again from her throat, and they spurred his desire to get closer to Suki, to please her.

The peaks of her nipples dotted the front of her dress. Griff drew a thumb back and forth across her nubs while Suki squirmed in his lap and exhaled heat into his mouth.

Would she mind doing that all night?

After pulling away from their kiss, she turned in his lap and presented him with the back of her dress. "Can you unbutton?"

"Yes," he grunted. It would be his pleasure to undo every one of her buttons. He started at the top, removing fabric from the pearly circles. The citrusy, floral scent of her wafted up. He pressed his forehead against her chemise as he undid the rest and inhaled the divine, delectable scent of Suki herself.

After finishing the last button, he stopped, readying himself for the rush of hot desire that would course through him when the dress fell from her shoulders. And it came as she pulled her arms from the sleeves and he took in the curve of her shoulder and fine line of her arm. Then it multiplied in strength as she faced him and the soft fabric settled at her waist.

A light corset lifted the swell of her breasts under her thin chemise. The sight enflamed him, driving his erection against the side of her hip. Then it took him back to that night in Saitama when he'd feasted on the sight of her peaked nipples before acting like such a fool.

Having her on his lap deprived him of the eloquent apology he'd planned to deliver. But he had to say the words. "I'm sorry for everything I said at the inn." God, he hoped he wasn't ruining this. "I only want for us to be together, however you'll have me."

"That's what I want, for us to be together. I know you're sorry, and I forgive you."

The words dissolved the heavy mass that had lodged in his chest.

Suki loosened the string at the stop of her chemise, and the translucent fabric fluttered off her shoulders. Firelight danced across her lustrous skin, and breath caught in his throat. He could stare at her like this for hours.

But she'd forgiven him, and he wasn't going to spare a chance to show her how much her forgiveness meant. Tugging down the top of her corset, he released her breasts, so perfectly round and ripe. *This* was how they were meant to spend the evening. "You're breathtaking," he murmured.

Suki arched her back, raising her chest before him. Her nipples were like dollops of caramel; he tasted each one with a flick of his tongue, then covered them with his mouth. The more he kissed her warm skin and tongued the peaks of her taut nipples, the more she wriggled her backside in his lap. For his cock, it was relentless torture. For his raw need to please her, it was a salve. And he would please her, but there was something he needed for them both: her bare skin against his.

He met Suki's gaze. "Would you mind if I do the same?"

Suki furrowed her brow.

No, he wasn't making any sense. But that couldn't be helped. "Would you mind if I took off my jacket and shirts? I want to feel us together."

She smiled with such delight that he almost congratulated himself. "I would love that." Her gaze shifted to his jacket, and she moved a hand under his lapel. "May I?"

"Absolutely."

Her touch was light, magical. Then tentatively, she drew her fingers across his chest. He exhaled slowly, willing himself not to lose control at her touch. Her hands went to his shoulders, and he responded by pulling up his elbow. She removed his arm from the sleeve; then together they removed the other. Her heavenly touch, her breath against his cheek, her breasts dragging the fabric of his shirt sent molten heat through him.

"And your shirt?" Suki asked.

Yes, that needed to come off too. "Please."

While Suki undid the buttons, he took her breasts in his hands. How perfectly they rested in his palm. Then he kneaded and teased. Her backside in his lap pitched side to side; the sensation was heaven and hell. He ached to spread his legs and let her movements take him, but that was not how they were meant to spend the evening. It was supposed to be about Suki.

He placed light bites along and down the curve of her neck to her shoulder and she fumbled on the buttons, then stopped altogether; her mouth parted, and a sigh filled the firelit air around the settee.

"Is something the matter with the buttons?" he asked in all innocence, though his gravelly voice was full of sinfulness.

"I can't undo the buttons while you're touching me like that." She pouted, but her eyes twinkled with delight.

"Then let me." Griff released the rest of the buttons and pulled his shirt along with the linen vest beneath it over his head.

Suki's eyes fell to his chest and widened. Had she ever been this close to a man's bare skin? She drew her fingers through the swath of hair at the top of his chest, then down to his abdomen. Her touch nearly breached his guard. He wanted her hand down the front of his trousers, finding the length of him, with that awed expression of discovery on her face and her breasts undulating inches from his lips. When she finally reached the top of his trousers, reason prevailed. He took her hand in his.

"I can't have you going any lower, Suki. Not now." So he kissed her on the mouth, letting their tongues mingle slowly, languidly. Tonight was about Suki.

He shifted her from his lap and eased her down on the settee, taking care to avoid jostling her bandaged cheek. Then he took the space beside her and circled her in his embrace. The bare skin of her chest against his was joy in grief and peace in anger. And it made him harder than he'd ever been in his life.

He planted kisses everywhere he could: on the delicate bone of her jaw, on her downy cheek, on her succulent lips. Then he moved his hand down the length of her skirt and lifted the silk fabric. Warmth and the secret, musty scent of a woman's desire greeted him, then beckoned. Drawing a hand up her petticoats, he marvelled at the shape of her lithe thigh and the curve of her arse.

Suki gasped into his mouth, a light sound of pleasure and the wish for more. He circled her buttocks, matching his touch to the movements of their tongues. Thank God the bulk of her skirts gave him pause to consider his actions, or he would have faced an ungodly struggle to keep himself from pushing his erection against the thin cotton layer covering soft, damp quim.

Griff moved his touch to the top of her mound and lightly stroked her drawers over the bone of her pubes. One of her purring sounds fell against his cheek as her hips rose to meet his hand. "I had it in mind to touch you here. Would you like that?"

"I would," she said, her voice weighty.

His head spun with the thrill of conquest, but he would be foolish to think for a second that he'd conquered Suki when she'd so clearly conquered him.

After he pulled down her petticoats, he ran his hand over the swell of her thigh to the crease that held the edge of her drawers, then slid a finger under the thin cotton covering. Arousal slicked her thick curls.

Suki gasped.

Had he hurt her? Was he going too fast? She was a virgin who'd given him her first kiss. "Would you like me to stop?"

"No," she rasped, and relief poured through him.

Venturing to her folds, he stroked and circled while she kissed him in hot breaths that filled his mouth. The bulb of her sex pulsed under the pad of his thumb. He gave it a gentle nudge, and her hips surged forward. He could practically feel himself buried inside her. One day, he'd get there. *But not tonight.*

He found the entrance to her sex and slowly inserted the tip of his forefinger into her snug sheath. She slackened her jaw, and her lips fell open. "Oh Griff, what are you doing?"

The truth that had gathered within him since he'd sat down beside her on the settee poured from him. "Studying you, Suki. Learning everything that will keep you coming back to my bed."

Teasing her entrance with his finger, he ran his thumb through her folds and around her bud, returning to each place that made her legs quiver and her entrance clench around his touch. She drove herself against his palm, her need growing for release, then furrowed her brow and squeezed her eyes shut. Even with her face half-covered in a thick wrap, Suki had never been more exquisite. Her panting turned into moans as the prize of her orgasm soaked his fingers.

Yes, this night belonged to Suki.

Her gaze, glittering and wild, met his. "What did you do to me?"

He brought her head to his chest and kissed the top of her hair. "I gave you a small hint of delights to come."

She pulled her head back from his chest and looked up. "That wasn't small."

"No, it was not." She'd come with a ferocity he was determined to experience on many parts of his body. "You're a passionate woman, Suki."

Her heavy breath stirred the hairs on his chest. "I must be."

Griff pulled her to him, willing Dixy into retreat so he could revel in the comforting warmth of their bare chests joined. Suki settled her head in the dip of his shoulder. Her breath rose and fell in a steady, slow rhythm, and with his arms full of her, Griff drifted off, complete.

***

Griff awoke to an empty space beside him, the fire's last embers casting their light on the place where Suki had rested beside him. He pulled on his undershirt and wandered from the study. An envelope with his name written in Suki's hand sat on the table by the entrance, and he picked it up.

Dearest Griff,

I had a delightful time in your company tonight. I apologize for departing in haste, but I thought it best to return home before Roger knocked down your door demanding to know my whereabouts.

Although I am uncertain of any worth in pursing the wretched Baron Umezono, I am curious about what you have learned.

Please feel free to call on us tomorrow.

Yours,

Suki

With a small glass of whisky poured from the drinks cabinet in the kitchen, he returned to his study and penned a letter for Rei-*san* to send out the following morning.

My dearest Suki,

I look forward to calling on you at home. However, if we are to discuss the baron, who I will forever wish I'd pummelled on the terrace that night, your home might not be the best place. What I learned, and how I learned it, is scandalous enough to offend the delicate ears of the women in your home.

We could take a stroll at the park adjacent to the lawn tennis club, if that suits.

Fondly,

Griff

CHAPTER TWENTY-FIVE

Stretching under her covers, Suki woke to midmorning rays of sunlight streaming through her windows. She'd slept later than usual because she'd stayed awake late because, well… She gave a contented sigh as her mind alighted on the memory of Griff's hand moving up her thigh and into her drawers already wet with yearning for the mysterious, magical tricks she'd somehow known those hands were capable of. He'd made her squirm, and summoned the most desperate noises from her throat, then took her to the clouds and rain, the heights of which she'd never quite imagined. Now she understood the swollen feeling between her legs when she thought of Griff. What would it be like when they were lying next to one another, naked, in bed?

Passionate and loving, especially within the space of a courtship toward marriage, the experience of losing herself with Griff had brought forth unexpected feelings of vulnerability. When they'd lain together, their lips joined and their bare chests touching, she'd turned herself over to him. It had been an act of faith in him and a surrender of herself, and it had felt like freedom. Within a courtship they were free to lose themselves—free to take from one another—because they trusted their commitment.

Suki rose to sit, and the muscles of her back protested with sharp pains. She lifted the hem of her nightdress and sought out the place on her hip that had been red and hot to the touch when she'd returned home from Griff's. A bruise was already forming where she'd hit the ground after Watanabe had sent her reeling backwards.

She reached up to the bandage on her cheek. Two questions came to mind, both of which dampened her mood: how was she going to explain this to her family, and where *was* Watanabe?

Last night, she'd arrived home after the family had retired for the night. Today, she would give them the story about running into branches not visible in the shadows of Griff's garden. She'd have to send a message to Griff informing him of her explanation in case Roger mentioned something at the lawn tennis club.

The other question was more vexing. Griff believed Watanabe's threats of suicide were a dramatic bid for attention, and he was probably correct. But Suki couldn't forget the desperate, troubled woman she'd seen in his garden. How close had Watanabe come to hurting herself? To hurting Suki?

Suki grimaced as she took her steps around the room but kept moving in the hope that her cramped muscles would release. Taking off her nightdress and reaching her back to lace her corset hurt in ways it usually did not, but her thoughts kept returning to Griff and the previous night, and a delightful tingling sensation through her body eased the aches and pains.

Over the course of the morning, Suki exchanged several messages with Griff. He'd heard nothing from Watanabe, nor had he received any news concerning her whereabouts. Mostly, their messages concerned plans for meeting that afternoon. Because of the offensive nature of his information on the baron—and how could news about the baron be anything other than offensive—they decided to meet at the lawn tennis park for a private discussion. Given her fortunes with the baron story, Griff's information would probably only amount to another salacious rumor unworthy of journalistic inquiry. Even as she prepared herself for the disappointment, it smarted.

After Griff told her about the baron, she would tell him about her decision regarding their courtship. Then they would return to her home, and Griff would speak with Papa Garrick about their plans to court. Once the cat was out of the bag, Griff would probably spend the remainder of the visit being fawned over by the women in her family while he and Roger regaled them with tales of lawn tennis victories and she endured excited side-glances, discreet hand squeezes, and knowing looks. Much to her surprise, she was actually looking forward to her family's excitement at learning their Suki had found a beau.

She was redoing her chignon after the midday meal when Rosie brought a message to her room. Expecting Griff's upright penmanship, it took her a moment to place the slanted writing. A foul taste came to her mouth, and for a moment, she considered waiting until she was safely beside Griff before opening the letter. But there was no reason to think a piece of paper would hurt her even as the sight of it made her hairs stand on end. Finally, curiosity prevailed, and she slid the opener across the seal.

Dear Miss Malveaux,

I request your forgiveness for calling the Tokyo Tattler's attention to Baron Umezono's past. Obviously there is nothing to investigate. I have been accused of being overly suspicious, and in this instance, curiosity got the best of me. The baron is clearly a man of upstanding character and unblemished career.

Please refrain from any further investigation.

My sincerest apologies.

From the very first letter about Baron Umezono, the author had treated the Tattler as a servant who needed urging to perform her duties. Clearly, he didn't realize that Suki wasn't in the employ of anonymous letter-writers. She'd decide whether the baron investigation warranted continuation, and she'd make that decision based on information Griff would share with her shortly.

Indeed, the request, arriving on the heels of Griff having learned new information, begged examination. Had Griff discovered too much? Did this new information somehow implicate the letter-writer?

Suki inserted a tortoiseshell comb into her chignon and chose a reticule to match the cream lace day dress she'd put on to meet Griff at the park. For the first time since he'd told her about having news of the rotten baron, Suki found herself intrigued to learn what he'd uncovered.

***

Standing by the park gate in a brown tweed coat and matching hat, Griff was easily the most dapper gentleman in Tsukiji. And one day this dapper gentleman would be her husband. Suki trembled with fiery anticipation at the thought of what being Griff's wife would entail. He caught sight of her, and a wicked smile spread across his face.

It reminded her of the look he'd worn after she'd spiraled out of control on his settee, right before telling her that was only a hint of what was to come. Suki reached for the fan in her reticule.

"I've been thinking that we might stroll through this park as we did in Ueno," Griff said with a wink.

That would mean kisses, blissful kisses. She could feel her cheeks turn a darker shade of pink. "I'd like that very much." An unnerving sensation, like the neckline of her dress was constricting her breath disturbed her equilibrium. She waved the fan in front of her face a few more times and basked in the refreshing air. Kisses would have to wait. First, they must talk.

Suki placed her arm in the crook of his elbow, and they passed through the gate into the brief woodsy respite on the south end of Tsukiji. Southern breezes rustled the fan-shaped leaves hanging from the gingko trees and added warmth to the late afternoon sunshine dappling the stone pathways. Tsukiji's residents used the park mostly for leisurely strolls and gossipy chats. Today was no different. Matrons separated by the lacy rims of their parasols had taken their conversation to the pathways, along with older gentlemen on their daily constitutionals and a group of young mothers engaged in lively chatter while children dashed around their skirts.

Suki looked up at Griff. "May I ask whether you've had any news about Mrs. Watanabe?"

"I sent one of my secretaries to Natsu's home earlier this afternoon. The maid said her mistress had yet to return. My other secretary inquired at the police box and learned nothing with respect to Natsu."

"That's good news, don't you think?"

"Natsu is quite resourceful, and I have no doubt that wherever she has escaped to, there are friends at her beck and call."

"Then she was merely playacting in your garden?" Suki asked.

"I believe so," he said and gave her arm a pat. "The lengths to which Natsu will go to achieve her aims are far greater than ours." His gaze rested on Suki's bandaged cheek. She'd replaced the large covering with a more modest plaster, and the swelling had gone down. "How is your face healing?"

"Remarkably well. It should be fine by tomorrow."

Their gazes met, and warmth suffused her body. Had they been alone in his study, she would've been tempted to throw herself bodily at him. Two older matrons strolled by on the pathway, and Suki buried a grin. The clatter of their canes and the formidable eaves of the imperial palace looming over the treetops constrained much of her desire to make a spectacle with Griff. "I'd like to hear what you've learned about the loathsome baron."

"I'll tell you everything, provided I can steal a kiss or two after I've finished. And we can find a location with a bit more privacy." He nodded at the strolling matrons and gave Suki a wink.

"I believe that can be arranged," she said, and an image came to mind of Griff's kiss once she told him of her desire for a courtship. The neckline of her dress once again became snug. Griff—or rather, heated thoughts about kissing Griff—was distracting from the main purpose of their meeting. "So, what scandals have you turned up about the dreadful baron?"

"He is a truly dreadful creature, because of his behaviour on the Metropolis terrace. What I've learned more recently has only confirmed the impression. After our trip to Saitama, I recalled a connection between one of the fellows at the lawn tennis club and a group that deals in the more unsavoury aspects of social life."

"A *yakuza* gang?"

"Please don't hold it against my friend. He has an agreement with the head of one such group. My friend employs men from this group to transport goods when his regular workers are unavailable. In their dealings, my friend and the head of the group have become rather friendly themselves."

Suki made a mental note to request an introduction to the lawn tennis friend's associate. Ned believed women incapable of fostering connections in Tokyo's underworld and therefore unfit for the newspaper business. She'd very much enjoy proving him wrong. "I won't hold it against your friend."

"He'll appreciate that. On my behalf, he inquired about Baron Umezono and learned the baron is a man about town, as you well know. He seeks out card games and women well above what his wits can handle. Not long ago, he caused a stir at a club in Asakusa and had to be escorted from the premises. While tossing him into the street, the young men guarding the club, also *yakuza*, liberated his shoulder from its socket."

Suki stopped her fanning as she made the connection. "That would explain the sling."

"Exactly what I was thinking. I remembered seeing his arm in a sling the night I should have thrown him into Tokyo Bay."

Suki's mind whirled with the implications of the baron's expulsion from the club. "The sling appeared new the night at the hotel, which would've been shortly after the anonymous letters regarding the baron began arriving at the *Tokyo Daily News*. If that is the case, then the baron's 'misdeeds,' as the letter-writer put it, could have something to do with this club. Do you have the club's name?"

"The Purple Lilac. I was thinking that I could go there and inquire among the patrons about what they knew of the baron. My secretaries could act as translators."

Being the gentleman, Griff probably felt obliged to make such an offer. The thought of her being exposed to the unsavory aspects of social life must have roused his chivalrous nature. But this was her investigation. "While I appreciate your offer, a journalist needs to hear statements for herself. People often tell falsehoods, and I have a responsibility to determine when a witness is being forthright."

Suki paused to consider the wisdom of sharing the letter she'd received before leaving the house. It might make Griff wary about her continuing to pursue the baron. But if they were to have a courtship, and more, he needed to get used to her taking risks in the course of an investigation. "This afternoon I received another letter from the letter-writer who tipped me off about the baron. He wishes me to stop the investigation. He says the baron is unblemished. Having received this letter after you learned of the baron's expulsion from the club, I cannot help but think these events are related."

Griff stopped their stroll and took both of Suki's hands in his. "That would mean this letter-writer has connections with the underworld. This investigation of yours could prove dangerous. What if the *yakuza* came after you? You've already had the conservative faction hurling rocks in your direction. I simply cannot allow you to put yourself in harm's way."

Griff was sincere in his generous concern for her safety, but there was no reason to think she'd be threatened in the pleasure quarters. True, *yakuza* gangsters had stakes in the entertainment districts, but they were fastidious about not harming ordinary citizens. It was why society tolerated them. "I'll take Marcelle, and we'll be fine. Please don't worry about us. Your niece and nephew are expected in two days, and I know you're busy with preparations for their arrival."

"All is ready for Marianne and Lucien."

"Splendid," Suki replied dryly. She wasn't going to give up. There was a story here, and Griff would have to understand the necessity of her pursuing this lead.

Silence settled between them as they came full circle to the park gate and headed down the pathway for another revolution. Griff pulled her to his side. "I'm pleased you'll be able to accompany me to meet them at the ship."

In messages exchanged earlier that day, Suki had responded positively to Griff's request that she be present for his niece and nephew's arrival. Neither Mademoiselle Toutain, the French maid, nor Miss Tinselly, the governess, were able to take residence in Tsukiji for another few weeks. Until then, Suki was going to make herself available to help. "I'm looking forward to meeting Marianne and Lucien."

"They'll be grateful to have someone who understands their language. Marianne might have questions she'd feel most comfortable asking you."

Suki was happy to see Marianne and Lucien settled on their first day in the new city, especially since she and Griff were about to be in a courtship, which she planned to tell him forthwith. But once she told him, he'd want to speak with Papa Garrick, and the ensuing congratulations from the family would dominate their evening. There would be no way to escape for a clandestine visit to the Purple Lilac, and if she didn't go this evening, she might not have another chance. Once Marianne and Lucien arrived in Tokyo, she'd be busy attending to their needs. She also needed to start writing the Tattler column as Suki Malveaux, which meant she had to begin collecting gossip. It was tonight, or never. "I'll be available whenever Marianne and Lucien need me. But tonight, I must go to the Purple Lilac."

Griff's jaw tightened. "What will you do there?"

Foremost, she wanted to speak with the women who worked there. The waitresses, however, would take one look at proper Suki Malveaux and assume she'd come to test them for venereal diseases.

Which might be the perfect cover. "I'll pose as a health worker. They're always visiting these clubs to ascertain whether the waitresses are spreading diseases of the night. I'll tell them I've come to ask questions, not to conduct any kind of personal examination. That should put them at ease."

"Might I accompany you to the club under the same premise?" He sounded so hopeful, but a foreign male presence would only dissuade anyone inclined to speak with her.

"I don't think so."

A group of young schoolboys playing a game of chase cut across their path. Suki and Griff stopped, and he turned to face her. "Could I wait for you outside?"

Waiting outside seemed like a fair compromise, although she wondered whether Griff could bear a night in Asakusa; the prostitutes and their pimps weren't going to leave him alone. "You could wait in the area. Marcelle and I may be inside for several hours, depending on the number of waitresses. I'll have to uphold the pretense of asking about their health concerns. Once I have them in my confidence, I can broach the subject of unruly customers who happen to be members of the nobility."

Griff furrowed his brow. "You're determined to take this course of action."

"I think it's the best way," she said brightly, hoping he'd note her confidence.

"You wish to do it tonight?"

"Yes, and later in the evening is better. That's when they'll be serving the greatest number of patrons, and the madam will be too busy to inquire closely of my credentials. Marcelle can be an international observer, as the French are curious about Japan's success in combating the spread of venereal diseases. In truth, I'd feel safer having her with me."

"And I'll be grateful knowing Marcelle is inside the club since you're not going to allow me in." He spoke in a teasing manner, but his downward gaze betrayed his hurt.

Having Griff hover outside the club would give her an added sense of security while she attempted a rather complex ruse. But having him accompany her on every newspaper investigation she undertook wasn't a situation they could sustain. Eventually, she'd have to carry out investigations on her own, and he'd have to trust her judgment. "Thank you for understanding and thank you for making inquiries about the awful baron. Because of you, I might get a story worthy of newsprint."

Griff took her hand in his and placed his other one on top. "I almost lost you after those horrible things I said in Saitama. Your forgiveness has been an undeserved blessing. I want you to know that I've accepted that our courtship can wait until you're ready, and if you're never ready, I'm perfectly content with a fling."

Suki savored the expectant look in his eyes before replying, "If it's all the same to you, I'm of the opinion that a courtship at this time would be preferable."

Griff widened his eyes and let his jaw go slack. Then he grabbed her by the shoulders. For a moment, she thought he was going to lift her off the ground. But he loosened his grip and grinned broadly. "You'd like a courtship?"

"My family would approve, and Marianne and Lucien might find it curious that I spend so much time at your home, especially after their governess and maid arrive."

"You think that your family will approve?"

"I know they will. Papa Garrick will want to hear your intentions."

Griff glanced toward the park entrance. "Shall I go to him now?"

Suki placed a hand on his arm. "Let's wait a few days. I need to prepare for tonight's visit to the Purple Lilac, and then Marianne and Lucien will be here."

"Whenever you wish," he said, the grin still creasing his face. "Once we tell your family, I imagine all of Tsukiji will know the Tattler has a sweetheart."

"They might be surprised to learn the sweetheart is the man I once dubbed an incorrigible rake."

Griff leaned down to her ear. "I can be a rake. I have plenty of rakish schemes in mind."

"To be carried out on me?" she asked with feigned surprise.

He pulled her to him. "It's almost all I think about."

Her gaze went to his mouth, and she wished for one of those kisses that made her legs quiver and knees buckle.

He put a finger under her chin and tilted her head upward. "Once those ladies over there stroll by, I'm going to take you behind a tree and find out whether a rakish kiss makes Suki swoon."

Suki let a smile creep in. "I have a feeling it will render her senseless."

CHAPTER TWENTY-SIX

To play the role of health inspector, Marcelle disciplined her unruly locks into a tight bun and conceded to wearing one of Suki's plain, wool dresses even though it presented an "unforgivable insult to a Frenchwoman's sensibilities." Suki merely had to tighten her chignon and put on one of her teaching kimonos. After bidding the family farewell to attend a speech on laws for the rights of women workers, a far better explanation for their late-night excursion, she and Marcelle walked to the Tsukiji gates without confronting either rock-throwing conservatives or gun-wielding former lovers. Griff had already commandeered two rickshaws for the ride to Asakusa. He boarded the first, and Suki and Marcelle took the one behind.

Their runner stopped at the entrance to Asakusa's pleasure quarters and scrutinized the two severely dressed women. "Are you certain this is where you'd like to be let off?"

Suki nodded. "Indeed. We've come to inspect the working conditions of young women at the clubs."

The runner quirked his lip slyly. "Then I ought to charge you double."

"We're not here to collect bribes. We're here to ensure modern standards are being implemented at all levels of society."

He nodded several times. "In that case, I wish you luck." One fooled rickshaw runner boded well for the rest of the evening.

Tangy notes from the three-stringed *shamisen*, along with bursts of laughter, clapping, and song, poured out of Asakusa's clubs, giving the streets a festive atmosphere, although there were few carousers outside. Waitresses and pimps attached themselves to passersby like vultures to the kill. Several waitresses draped in loose kimonos made rather weak attempts to summon Griff. The two priggish women accompanying him likely tamped down their enthusiasm for his patronage. Suki doubted he would get away so easily once she and Marcelle were inside the club.

The Purple Lilac occupied a large space at the end of the block. Light from the *chochin* paper lanterns strung along the street flattered even the most run-down establishments and made the Purple Lilac all the more outstanding for its freshly cut wood exterior and brightly painted sign.

Griff stopped half a block before the entrance. "I'll leave you here, but I promise to be nearby at all times. Shout for me if anything unseemly occurs."

"I promise we'll be fine. Although I'm afraid you may be accosted by those young women charged with finding patrons."

Griff gestured as though shooing away a pesky insect. "I can handle them."

Several men jostled Suki in pursuit of a waitress in a Western-style ball gown that had been fashioned to give her breasts maximum freedom. Griff sneered at the ruffians, and they immediately raised their arms in apology. "I'm storming the Purple Lilac if that group ends up there."

"We'll have nothing to do with the customers. Clubs keep their health inspectors well out of sight."

Griff kept his gaze trained on the men as they pushed through the *noren* curtain of the club next to the Purple Lilac. "Good thing," he muttered.

Suki and Marcelle bid Griff adieu and circled the block to the back alley. Behind each club ran a small dirt garden leading to the service entrance. Several gardens were occupied by young women in satiny kimonos, smoking tobacco and laughing with one another and their young male admirers. A woman with lovesick eyes handed a small, wrapped package to a man standing beside a cart of empty sake bottles. In return, he gave her rear-end a squeeze and whispered something that made her face break into a radiant smile.

As they approached the Purple Lilac, Suki took a breath to steady her words. "Are you certain you wish to do this?"

Marcelle set her lips in a grim line. "Of course, I do. I'm a devoted French health inspector who cares deeply for the health and safety of the young women employed at this establishment."

A small giggle escaped Suki before she covered her laughter with a cough. "I only hope to carry out my duties with the same vigor as my French colleague."

Suki straightened up and gave the Purple Lilac's back door several authoritative knocks. After half a minute passed with no response, she tried again, and at least a dozen more times before a girl of no more than ten years of age opened the door. She wore a maid's simple cotton kimono with the sleeves tucked at the elbows, and her hands were red and cracked. After looking them up and down several times, she asked them to wait while she fetched her mistress.

A few minutes later, a petite woman in a shimmering sea-green kimono appeared at the door. Rouges and powders failed to conceal saggy, splotchy skin, marks of a youth spent flirting, flattering, pouring *sake*, and drinking her share. "How may I help you?" she asked, each syllable attesting to the weight of her dismay.

"I'm Mako Yamamoto of the venereal diseases prevention department in the Ministry of Health. This is Sophie Bernard. She came to Japan from France. Her country is interested in how we Japanese control venereal diseases."

"I'm Yume Okuda, owner of the Purple Lilac." Eying Suki up and down, the madam let out a small yawn. "What can I do for you, Yamamoto-*san*?"

"We've been tasked with conducting a brief inquiry among young women working at the Purple Lilac."

"An inquiry?" Okuda tilted her head to the side. "Naturally, I insist my girls adhere to the highest hygienic standards. The timing of your appearance is quite irregular. Ordinarily, we expect your visits outside business hours."

"This particular set of questions concerns young women's alcohol consumption. Alcoholic intoxication can cause women to fail in taking protective measures against venereal diseases. Proprietors, yourself included I'm sure, are concerned about the amount of *sake* young women are drinking. Conducting interviews during evening hours gives us a chance to ask questions while making additional observations."

Suki held her breath. Okuda could easily turn them away for disturbing business or ask that they come another evening. Then again, she might welcome an inspection from two women who looked as though they would sooner lick her floors than demand a hefty bribe.

Finally, Okuda broke her interrogating stare with an obliging smile. "My girls never drink more *sake* than needed to satisfy our customers' demands. Collecting the yen comes first, and girls who are full of cups forget their priorities. We welcome your questions and observations. Please come inside," Okuda said and turned into the club.

Suki exhaled such a heavy sigh of relief that she feared Okuda would turn around and call out her ruse for what it was. But she didn't, and Suki followed her inside.

The back area of the club comprised a hallway of private rooms, a small kitchen where several girls, including the one who'd answered the club's back door, were washing earthenware dishes in a large tub, and a small room next to the kitchen. Okuda led Suki and Marcelle there. Futon mattresses, blankets, and towels were piled on the tatami flooring; there was barely room for the three of them to stand. Like the hallway and kitchen, the scents of stale *sake* and damp tobacco smoke filled the space. "I'll ask the maids to remove the futons, so you'll have room for your interviews."

On orders from Okuda, the kitchen girls removed the mattresses and linens and filled the space with an *adana* lantern, cushions for sitting, a low table, a pot of tea, and two cups. "Please wait here while I send the waitresses back to speak with you. How many waitresses would you like?" Okuda asked with a toothy smile.

Suki hazarded a guess that the question was one Okuda frequently posed to the Purple Lilac's patrons. "As many as possible and one at a time would be best. Bernard-*san* will wait outside to ensure privacy for the interview."

Okuda gave Suki and Marcelle a perfunctory bow before leaving the storage room.

Suki took a seat at the table and Marcelle followed suit. "That went far better than I expected," Suki said in French.

"It went perfectly," Marcelle replied.

Suki disagreed. "Madame Okuda is suspicious. She's right that inspectors wouldn't come at night. They're at home with their families."

"Or in the front room of the club."

"The inspectors must get curious about the young women they interrogate."

Marcelle narrowed her eyes. "I bet they become mad with lust when the nymphets spread their legs for inspection."

"How horrid for the waitresses."

"If there's any justice in the world, the waitresses make good money from those perverts. At least a health inspector knows to wear a condom."

"The waitresses deserve better." She sounded like Mother Garrick and Rosie, who pledged a crusade whenever they heard stories of suffering.

Marcelle shrugged. "Some prostitutes make good money for their families and eventually marry, usually to a laborer of some kind. Then they'll have children, in addition to the ones they birthed while working in the brothels, provided, of course, they haven't become barren from the pox. For others, it will not turn out as well."

Suki shuddered. Whatever happened with this story on the baron, she wouldn't use these young women merely to further her career as a journalist. Somehow, she would do right by them.

She pulled out a list of questions and set them on the low table. In the hour she and Marcelle had spent readying for the evening, Suki had decided that asking about *sake* consumption might be more productive than delving into whether a waitress scrubbed her genitals with sand or washed with whale oil soap after intercourse.

Someone flung open the door. Suki looked up from her questions and found a furious Madame Okuda. "Who are you and what business do you have coming here during the busiest time of the night when my waitresses need to be making money?"

Suki stood and folded her trembling hands. What could possibly have happened to make Okuda suspicious? "I don't know what you mean."

Although inches shorter than Suki, Okuda managed to stare her down. "A foreigner just entered my club seeking the company of two foreign women. His Japanese is wretched. From what I understand, he took issue with my fishmonger."

Griff. Why had Griff come to the club? And why had he taken issue with the fishmonger? "May I speak with him?"

Okuda nodded to the back door. "You may speak with him once you leave these premises."

Suki pictured Okuda's men treating Griff's shoulder the same way they had the baron's. "Where is he now?"

"I directed him to the alleyway where I'm sure he'll be waiting for you." Okuda spitted out her words.

"Is he hurt?"

"Of course not. Do you think I'm interested in ruining my chances with foreign customers? We'll take so much yen from them, they'll leave with their pockets empty."

Relief washed over Suki.

Okuda gave Suki a twisted smile. "I assume he's your lover." Then she glared at Marcelle. "Or your lover? Or perhaps he services you both?"

"We're courting," Suki replied.

Okuda crossed her arms. "I'm not releasing you until you tell me who you are and what you're doing here. I cannot fathom why a half-breed and a foreigner would wish to speak with my waitresses unless you're planning to steal them away to a club in Ginza or Tsukiji. In that case, I'll have to familiarize you with what I do to people who steal from me."

Suki took a deep breath. Hopefully, those who deceived the madam fared better than those who stole. "The truth is I'm a newspaper reporter and I'm investigating Baron Umezono for a newspaper article. I heard he suffered injury at the Purple Lilac."

Okuda smirked. "Why are you interested in that wretched excuse for a man?"

To her credit, Okuda possessed a highly accurate opinion of the baron. "I heard the baron has made victims of women. I'm endeavoring to write a newspaper article that will ensure no more women become his victims." Okuda raised her brow as though Suki had proposed to scale Mt. Fuji in her drawers. Suki continued, "We must hold men like him accountable for their actions. If the baron goes unpunished, there's no hope for our sex. We must stand up for ourselves."

Okuda huffed. "Society doesn't care about women who work at the Purple Lilac."

"I'll make them care."

Okuda looked away, but before she did, Suki could have sworn she saw tears pooling in the madam's eyes. When the older woman turned back, her gaze was unperturbed. "Come here tomorrow, around noon. I'll tell you a story about the baron."

Was it possible Suki had gone through the charade of pretending to be a health inspector when she could have simply approached Okuda in the afternoon hours? Suki half-expected a traveling musical troupe to enter the room and poke fun at her unnecessary deception. "I'll be here tomorrow. I'm terribly sorry for the way I conducted myself. I didn't know you'd be so accommodating to the newspapers. Sometimes it's necessary for us to take a more covert approach to our subjects."

Okuda waved a hand at Suki. "My innocent do-gooder, you possess the audacity to come here in disguise and commandeer my waitresses' time when they should be entertaining guests, which means you may actually possess the strength of character to do as you say and punish the baron. Now leave the Purple Lilac and let us make our money."

"I'm looking forward to visiting tomorrow."

"No doubt you are," Madame Okuda said and left the room without a backward glance.

Suki and Marcelle swiftly departed through the back entrance. At the other end of the alley, Griff hurried toward them. Suki and Marcelle likewise quickened their pace in his direction.

"I'm not going to say anything to Griff about meeting with Madame Okuda tomorrow," Suki whispered to Marcelle, who raised a brow in response. "I wish to speak with Madame alone," Suki replied. Tokyo had been her home for every one of her twenty-three years. She could navigate the streets of Asakusa in broad daylight without a foreign escort. And fishmongers, as far as she knew, didn't pose a problem she couldn't solve well enough on her own.

The look on Griff's face was pure contrition. Thankfully, the rest of him seemed unhurt. "I'm terribly sorry," he said. "A man with a long knife entered the Purple Lilac, and he had tattoos. I worried that he was a *yakuza* gangster who'd come to harm you. One of the club's patrons spoke a little English and explained that the man in question had in fact come to deliver fishes."

Touched by his concern for her safety, Suki nevertheless felt compelled to emphasize that his actions had been unnecessary. "We were fine. By the time you arrived, the madam had already granted us permission to interview the waitresses."

"Did you have a chance to speak with any of the waitresses?"

Suki shook her head. "I'll have to pursue another lead on the baron." This wasn't exactly a lie since she was pursuing an interview with Madame Okuda the next day; it was a significant—and necessary—omission.

"I'm terribly sorry. I ruined your chance to interview the waitresses. Why don't I go back to my friend and ask him for more information on the baron?"

"Let's wait. Perhaps I can come up with another way to ascertain why the baron was expelled from the Purple Lilac."

"If anyone can devise ways to obtain information, it would be the Tokyo Tattler," he said with a teasing grin.

Already, Griff was joking about her being the Tattler. He'd let go of resentment for the terrible things she'd written about him, and tonight he'd accompanied her to the pleasure quarters to support an investigation he'd deemed dangerous. The prospect of a lifetime of his kindness, care, generosity, and humor made her a most fortunate woman. She should be brimming with gratitude.

Instead, she was planning to deceive him, again.

CHAPTER TWENTY-SEVEN

Suki walked through the Purple Lilac's *noren* curtain at exactly noon. Okuda sat before a low table in the front parlor. A breeze from the open windows lifted pages from the ledger before her. Pressing the pages down, she scratched out a few numbers and shut the book. Her face bare of cosmetics and hair pulled back in a simple chignon, she appeared all of her forty, or more, years.

"Good afternoon, newspaper reporter. Please take a seat." Okuda gestured at the thick cushion opposite her.

Suki eyed the pattern of gold swirls on a navy background and thought about the Purple Lilac guests who'd been seated on the same cushion the previous night, sweating and spitting, spilling drinks and all manner of fluids.

"The cushion's cover was replaced this morning," Okuda said.

"Of course it was," Suki said with a bright smile and seated herself. "I was admiring the design."

"Our customers are mostly from the new salaried class, men of business and law, the usual bureaucrats. Last night, we had an architect who is drawing plans for a new hotel near the emperor's palace, if you can believe it. They make excellent customers, these salary-men, but they madly aspire to be treated like aristocrats, at least when they're in the presence of delicious *sake* and pretty girls. So, I give them cushions stamped with royal men's crowns for their asses." Okuda's burst of laughter sent the cloying odor of spirits across the table. Exhaling a long stream of tobacco smoke, she ran her gaze across Suki's face. "What shall I call you, newspaper reporter?"

"I'm Suki Malveaux. I apologize for not giving my name last night."

A maid whisked away Okuda's teacup and brought a fresh tea service along with two small plates, each containing a gelatinous rice ball stuffed with bean paste. Okuda handed her ledger back to the maid. Setting the pipe aside, she poured Suki a cup of tea. "I'd been wondering whether anyone would ask about Baron Umezono. Behold, it was the health inspector who'd come to inquire about my girls drinking *sake*." Okuda's broad grin revealed spaces where several back teeth had been. "You could've just asked about the baron."

"I apologize. I hadn't realized such a generous woman ran this establishment." Suki gave Okuda an admiring smile. Flattery was a potent elixir.

"Would you like a job here? You sound like one of my girls vying for extra money on the side." Okuda's words seemed to stick to the top of her mouth. Suki wondered how much of the madam's cup had contained tea and how much had contained something more intoxicating.

Okuda refilled her pipe. "I know I'm generous, and I don't appreciate being deceived by newspaper reporters." She lit the pipe, took a drag, and placed it back on the table. "I'll tell you about Baron Umezono. He is everything I despise in a man." Okuda shifted in her seat and looked around the room.

Suki guessed she was looking for something stronger than tea. If Suki wanted coherent responses to her questions, she'd better get started. "What exactly is your relationship to the baron?"

Okuda looked at Suki long enough to make her wonder whether there was something stuck between her teeth, then she shouted orders for the maids to prepare the afternoon meal. When the din of clanging pots commenced, Okuda leaned across the table. "Baron Umezono killed one of my girls. Let me clarify. I don't know that he actually killed her. That's beyond my knowing. He is, however, responsible for her death."

Suki swallowed hard against the shock. The baron had killed a waitress. Facts had to be obtained; notes had to be taken. She retrieved paper and pencil nub from her satchel and began writing. "What makes you think he's responsible?"

"A few weeks ago, some men came to the club and enjoyed an evening with the waitresses, including our Haru-*chan*." Okuda's voice broke at the name. "They wore Western-style suits, and one of them had the most exquisite gold pocket watch. He was fortunate to leave the club with that treasure in his possession. In my younger years, I wouldn't have let him get away so easily.

"The following day, one of those men visited the club. His name was Yasuda. He'd been impressed with Haru-*chan* and requested her company at a gathering he was attending that evening. Haru-*chan* had an average face, but her manner of speaking was polished, more so than any of the silly imbeciles I've got working here. She must have had some education. I thought this was an opportunity for her to take a wealthy lover and quit the Purple Lilac. Then I could hire a proper imbecile in her place. Yasuda gave me a large sum for Haru-*chan*'s services. I dressed her in my best kimono, sent her off with Yasuda, and never saw her again."

Okuda refilled her pipe and took a drag. "At first, I was certain Yasuda had been a secret lover, and the request for Haru-*chan*'s company had been an elaborate hoax to free her from my clutches. Really, I'm not that terrible, no matter what the girls may say. There are far worse than me. I don't force my girls to bend over for every man who requests them for the night. They protest a man's company, and I do my best. I'm fair, and I was upset that Haru-*chan* had deceived me like that. As for the waitresses, they were deeply upset their dear sister hadn't told them of her plans. We were all angry with Haru-*chan*."

Tears formed in Okuda's eyes. She pulled a flask from her *obi* sash and poured amber liquid into her teacup. In a single gulp, it went down her throat. "Please excuse me. I'm not a hard woman. Spirits fortify me. Fortunately, your people have given us whisky. For that, I'm grateful." Okuda's head cocked to the side. "You're foreign, aren't you?"

"I'm half French."

"I take it you don't indulge in spirits."

Suki shook her head. "Do I look that innocent?"

"Your complexion is pure as snow, save for that scratch on the side of your face."

"A cat got me," Suki replied. It seemed that Okuda might be rushing to judgment about the waitress's death. "Haru-*chan* sounds like a good woman. But might there be a chance she ran off with Yasuda?"

"That's not what Baron Umezono said. He came to the Purple Lilac with Haru-*chan*'s ashes in a vessel befitting a samurai. Utterly ridiculous. He told me she'd died in an unfortunate accident." Okuda's lips curled into a sardonic grin. "Of course, that always happens to women whose work is fulfilling men's most base needs. It's never the man's fault. Always a terrible, unfortunate accident when a woman's neck is squeezed a bit too hard, when she teeters off the veranda, when she contracts a disease that drives her insane before dealing its death blow."

Suki felt as though the air had been sucked from her lungs. She knew that women in brothels had short, difficult lives. Everyone knew, but no one ever spoke of their fate in such vivid terms.

Okuda poured herself a fresh cup of tea. "The baron ordered me to return the ashes to her family. I refused. How could I do such a thing? I had no idea how she died, or what prayers were said over her body. What would I say to her parents? I told him Haru-*chan* had come from a village near Utsunomiya, and her family name was Abura. He'd have to find someone else to take her ashes home."

Then it was quite possible Haru-*chan* was dead. A weight settled on Suki's shoulders. A dead waitress and a baron clutching her ashes would make the front pages of the *Tokyo Daily News*. And if the baron still had her ashes, the Abura family might not be aware that their educated, well-spoken daughter had died. Suki would have to tell them before Ned published the story.

Suki scanned her notes. "You said the baron was responsible for Haru-*chan*'s death, but that he might not have killed her. Why not?"

"The baron is a lush and a wastrel. I know the type. They love *sake* and women. They want life to be an unending ode to pleasure. When such men hurt women, they feel badly. They must convince themselves it wasn't their fault. They explain it. They weep. They bow their heads in shame for whatever role they played. Had Baron Umezono killed Haru-*chan*, his spirit would have shown the effects of his actions. But I saw nothing of the stark guilt possessing a man who has sent a woman to her death. Even so, he had her ashes. He was taking responsibility for something."

"Then you think this Yasuda might have killed her, the one who summoned Haru-*chan* that night?"

"Short of a visit from Haru-*chan*'s ghost, how could I possibly know?" Okuda said with an exhale of tobacco smoke directed at Suki.

Suki circled the name Yasuda. Along with the baron and the writer of the baron letters, that made three men who had knowledge of what had happened to Haru-*chan*. How would she find them? How would she convince them to speak with a female reporter?

"Did you tell the police or anyone who could investigate Haru-*chan*'s death?"

Okuda opened her mouth wide with laughter. "The police wouldn't do anything but paw around the club, ruin business, and then expect to get off under my waitresses' kimonos."

"I understand why you would hesitate."

Okuda contorted her lips into a sneer. "You don't understand anything about me and my waitresses."

Suki winced. Okuda was right, she had no idea what it was like to be a waitress. "I apologize for my presumption."

Okuda excused the apology with a roll of her eyes. "Write this newspaper article. Tell people how Baron Umezono marched in here with Haru-*chan*'s ashes as though her life meant nothing. As though I would thank him profusely, then speed away to Utsunomiya to reunite yet another dead waitress with yet another confused, distraught family. As though I do this every day. I want men like him to know shame for what they've done. I want them to know that ordinary people care. You said you were going to make them care." Okuda's eyes fluttered shut and her head lolled forward.

"Readers will care, I promise." Suki jiggled Okuda's arm. "Please, Okuda-*san*, I only have a few more questions, if you could bear with me."

Okuda rubbed her eyes and gave Suki the sheepish smile of a student who'd drifted off during class. "I'll do my best."

"Can you tell me why you had the baron thrown out of the Purple Lilac?"

"I threw him out of the club because he had the nerve to ask if he could have a cup of *sake* with one of my waitresses. He was carrying Haru-*chan*'s ashes in one hand and planned to use the other to squeeze a cunny. My guardsmen treated him with all the respect the putrid piece of shit deserves." Okuda's venom dissolved into a broad yawn. She emptied more of the whisky flask into her cup. "I must take my rest, or I won't make it through the night, and my imbecile waitresses will give all our *sake* to their lovers. I'll never see a yen in profit."

Suki looked over her notes for anything else she needed to ask before Okuda's head hit the table. Then she heard the madam grunt as she gripped the sides of the table and pulled herself to standing.

"Okuda-*san*…" Suki watched the woman walk across the parlor and disappear through curtains leading to the back of her establishment. Several minutes passed, and Suki was readying to ask one of the maids to rouse Okuda from whatever futon she'd landed upon, when the club's madam sauntered toward her. Okuda placed a rectangular box covered in crisp white silk on the table and nodded for Suki to untie the knot.

Resting inside the box was paper currency issued by the United States of America. Suki counted ten one-hundred-dollar bills. "Where did you get this?"

"From the baron, of course. Compensation for Haru-*chan*'s death."

Compensation for the death of a waitress was unsurprising, especially since it was given in the course of returning Haru-*chan*'s ashes. What surprised Suki was the sight of American currency. This brought the investigation back into the foreign community where it had started with the anonymous letters postmarked in Tsukiji. The twisted knot of the baron's story had tightened. "Why did he pay you in American currency?"

Okuda reached for her pipe. Putting a pinch of tobacco inside the bowl, she lit it and inhaled. "I haven't a clue. I opened the box after he left the club and found foreign currency. One of my waitresses recognized it as American."

"This is an extraordinary amount of money. Why haven't you changed it into Japanese yen?"

"I was going to exchange it when I found someone I could trust to handle it on my behalf, as I have no idea how to ascertain its value. But that day isn't likely to come anytime soon." Okuda pushed the box closer to Suki. "I no longer want it. You take it."

"This is a large sum. You must keep it."

"It's tainted with Haru-*chan*'s blood," Okuda said with a dismissive wave. "Misfortune will come to the Purple Lilac if it remains here any longer. Bring shame on the baron with your newspaper story and have yourself a nice reward."

"I don't need a reward. You must use this money to help your waitresses."

"This money will ruin us. It's bad luck. If you don't want it, toss it in the river."

Madame Okuda's mind was made up. Suki knotted the silk and placed the box in her satchel. Once she knew what had happened to Haru-*chan*, she'd know what to do with the money. Of that, she felt certain.

***

Suki boarded a rickshaw outside the Purple Lilac. The runner shouted warning to a group of young women with rouged cheeks and babies strapped to their backs, then took off through the narrow streets. Barely avoiding a group of youngsters hauling leather schoolbags, the runner weaved through crowds gathered at the temple entrance and entered the wide thoroughfare leading to Ginza.

Releasing her grip on the rickshaw's sides, Suki's thoughts turned to her conversation with Okuda. The baron bringing ashes to the Purple Lilac, the mysterious Yasuda, and the American money were the most unbelievable parts of Okuda's story and the ones for which there were eyewitnesses and physical proof such as the silk-wrapped box in Suki's satchel. Okuda might have been intoxicated and distressed over the loss of Haru-*chan*, conditions that encouraged sources to exaggerate and deceive, but her story held.

The *Tokyo Daily News* would sell like freshly roasted sweet potatoes with a banner headline reading *Waitress Dead, Baron Pays off Madam with Extraordinary Sum of American Dollars*. Suki envisioned a series of articles on Haru-*chan*'s death, each one adding details about the tragedy and raising new questions that Suki would explore until the truth prevailed. Ned would expect her to interview Baron Umezono before penning the article. Tomorrow she'd have to track him down. Tomorrow was also the day of Marianne and Lucien's arrival.

A sinking feeling gripped her. If she joined Griff at the port, she could forget about interviewing the baron. Obtaining his address, requesting the interview, making him understand the urgency of their speaking, and hopefully speaking with him would take all day. She would have to excuse herself from meeting the ship, which meant explaining why she was excusing herself, and that meant telling Griff about having gone to the Purple Lilac. He was going to be upset. The previous day, he'd insisted on accompanying her and Marcelle to interview the waitresses out of concern for her safety. When she told him about having gone alone to the pleasure quarters this afternoon, he wouldn't be pleased. Her determination to interview the degenerate baron would only further incense him.

The briny scent of the bay grew stronger as the rickshaw neared Tsukiji's gates. Inhaling deeply, Suki willed her panic to recede. She should be pleased by his protectiveness; it showed how much he cared. She had every reason to believe he was falling in love with her. She, too, felt love's presence, and she was coming to trust it. A small part of her was yet wary of his foreignness, yet unsure whether he might have one foot in Japan and another back in England. The rest of her protested that she was foolish to doubt him. Griff was above all loyal and compassionate. He'd forgiven her for letting their relationship grow under false pretenses; he'd moved past his anger over what she'd written about him. She owed him honesty and greater consideration of his feelings. How could she have risked this precious bond between them with another deceit?

A gust of wind swept across the thoroughfare. Suki grabbed the front bar as the rickshaw leaned and the runner skidded to brace the conveyance. Sweat broke out under her kimono.

Abandoning the investigation into Haru-*chan*'s death would likely ensure Griff's forgiveness for her neglecting to inform him about her meeting with Okuda. She could tell the police everything she knew about the baron and let Ned assign the story to one of his reporters. Then Griff would no longer have to worry for her safety.

But doing so would effectively put an end to any serious inquiry into the circumstances of Haru-*chan*'s death. Neither the police nor a male reporter would do justice for Haru-*chan*. She would be treated the way they always treated women of her station, like a disposable night worker who'd died in an unfortunate accident.

Suki was the only one who'd put forth the effort required to uncover the truth. Unlike the police or reporters for the *Tokyo Daily News*, she wouldn't sympathize with a fellow whose nighttime entertainment had come to an unfortunate conclusion. She'd expose him without remorse.

Griff was a reasonable man; he'd understand why she kept the visit to Okuda a secret and why she had to spend tomorrow tracking down the baron. She'd go to him this evening after reporting her findings to Ned. Learning the truth about Haru-*chan* had become her fate. Griff would understand.

CHAPTER TWENTY-EIGHT

Dispensing with the usual protocol of ringing the bell and waiting for the maid to escort her inside, Suki walked straight into the *Tokyo Daily News* offices. Several reporters sat behind desks in the room across from Ned's office. Suki gave them a nod. One of them raised a brow in return. No, she wasn't Ned Taylor's lover here for a late afternoon tryst. She was Suki Malveaux, someone they presently knew as the Tokyo Tattler and someone they'd soon know as a full-fledged reporter.

"Suki. What a delightful surprise." Ned stood when she entered his office.

Suki slid the door shut on prying eyes from the room opposite. "I trust this is a good time."

He returned to his desk chair and gave her figure the usual perusal as she took her seat. The man was abominable, but at least he had faith in her journalistic abilities. "Are you submitting the next column early? Has there been a scandal that cannot wait? Give me the word and I'll put it on the presses tomorrow, evening edition."

Suki took her usual seat in front of his desk. "Actually, I've got something else for the presses."

"Baron Umezono?"

Suki told him about what she'd learned from Okuda. After she finished, he leaned back in his chair and steepled his fingers. "You have a missing young woman, who you presume is dead, a drunk madam, an injured baron, and a thousand American dollars in your possession. I'm overwhelmed, truth be told. Is it possible your Haru-

chan ran away with this Yasuda? Perhaps the baron was playing out the fiction of her death to give the lovers a chance to run away together. Maybe the baron owed Yasuda a favor, and he had American money from his railway investors that he was willing to part with. So, he took the ashes to the Purple Lilac and paid the madam himself."

"A thousand American dollars is a large amount for playing out a fiction."

Ned raked a hand through his hair. "Agreed, but the fact is that you don't have a dead body."

Suki didn't think she'd have to work this hard to get Ned enthused about an article that would have Tsukiji, and all of Tokyo, clamoring for his newsprint. "Baron Umezono brought a vessel to the Purple Lilac with her ashes inside. Then asked Madame Okuda to take Haru-*chan*'s ashes to her family. No Japanese would lie about possessing someone's remains. The baron wouldn't dare offend his ancestors or risk angering malevolent spirits with such a ruse. He's a profligate, neither evil nor insane, which is the only type of fool who would expose himself to the wrath of the supernatural."

Ned pushed a long exhale through his front teeth. "I don't see an article here. We have a missing woman whose disappearance implicates a baron directly, and most men in Tsukiji indirectly as there happens to be a thousand American dollars involved. Print any word of it and we're in trouble."

"We're Tsukiji's foremost newspaper, and it's our responsibility to hold the foreign quarter accountable. This is a story meant for the front pages."

"I'll give you another story. How about that? Work on the Tattler column, and when you submit those pages, I'll have something else you can sink your teeth into."

Ned was being a fool. Any editor would jump at the chance to have the baron scandal on their front pages. "How can you abandon this story entirely?"

Ned shuffled the foreign newspapers on his desk. "There's nothing here worth reporting."

"I disagree. A young woman is dead, or at least, she's disappeared. These kinds of stories appear all the time in the newspapers. I daresay editors such as yourself love them."

"Not this one. There's nothing here besides vague suspicions and a whole lot of conjecture."

Suki ground her teeth. Ned's reluctance to touch the story was contradicting his oft-professed beliefs. "You've always said journalism deals in speculation. That's why we verify the information we do have and let the facts tell whatever story they will. As you can see, I have plenty of verification. Tomorrow, I'm going to find Baron Umezono and hear his side of the story."

"Back off, Suki. You're on a wild-goose chase. People could get angry at your asking questions. You don't want to put yourself or your loved ones in harm's way, do you?" Ned's voice was full of concern, but his words were the type one used for making threats.

Why was he being so resistant? Granted, she had hurdles to clear before the story was complete. But that was the point of journalism: print what you know and continue to gather information. Newspapers got people talking, and the more people talked, the more they filled in the missing puzzle pieces. That was the way Ned had always operated. What had changed? "By any chance, did you receive a letter about ceasing the investigation into the baron? I received one telling me to do exactly that, which is what you're telling me to do now."

"I've received no such thing. But you did?"

"I received the letter yesterday, written in the same hand as the other letters about the baron. I disregarded it."

Ned ran both hands through his hair. "Let this investigation go. You have no idea who you're dealing with. This author could be a very dangerous man."

"I have no reason to believe I'm in danger other than from the conservative faction. They came after me and Griffith Spenser the morning we went to Saitama to visit the baron's railway. All because of my work on the Tattler. There's danger in that, too. Isn't danger part of being a journalist?"

Ned squinted at her. "You went to Saitama with Griffith Spenser? And you were attacked by conservatives?"

"They threw rocks at our rickshaw and shouted awful things. But given their lack of attention in recent days, I believe they're satisfied at having said their piece."

Ned tapped on his desk. "Suki, I can't have you getting hurt, or worse, in the course of working for my newspaper."

She wasn't giving up, no matter how worried Ned might be. "I'm going to continue to pursue this story wherever it takes me. Tomorrow, it's taking me to the baron. If you don't want my report, I'll inquire at the *Tokyo Tribune* about whether they might be interested."

"Please. Don't be a fool."

"I'm going to speak with the baron tomorrow. Do you want the story?"

Ned sighed and leaned back in his chair. "Come to me after you talk to Baron Umezono, and we can review what you've learned. At that point, there may be an article that belongs in the newspaper."

Suki stood and raised a hand to keep him in place. "I can show myself out."

Every reporter in the room opposite was staring when she emerged from Ned's office.

"So, you're the infamous Tokyo Tattler," one of them said with elongated vowels that marked an American Southerner.

"My name is Suki Malveaux, and I do write the Tokyo Tattler column. It's a pleasure to meet you."

"Pleasure is ours," he replied and introduced himself along with the other men in the room. "We caught a bit of what you were saying to Ned. Not that we were listening, but voices were raised. Sounds like you're trying your hand at investigative journalism."

Suki was pleased they asked. Forewarning might make relations easier when they were working alongside one another. "I'm looking into a young woman's death."

"That's a big leap for the Tattler," a voice called out from the far side of the room.

"As it turns out, Mr. Langley, I've been studying journalism under Ned's tutelage and following the work of women journalists in the United States who are doing remarkable investigative reporting from hospitals and mental asylums."

Langley gave a drawn-out whistle. "It's a tough business."

"Not just indecent necklines and kisses on the terrace," another reporter added to chuckles from the others.

Suki gave a sporty laugh; she could find humor in the superficiality of the Tattler column. "Funny, wasn't it, how much the newspaper's popularity increased when Ned introduced the Tattler column? He thinks it's the reason the *Tokyo Daily News* remained standing when the *Sun* and the *Herald* folded last year. By all indications, female readers are keeping newspapers afloat."

Langley pulled the tobacco pipe from his mouth. "Then we owe you a big thanks, Miss Malveaux. I, for one, am looking forward to reading about this death you're investigating."

"I'll try not to disappoint," Suki said breezily and bid them good evening. She walked to the front door with measured steps that ensured the *Tokyo Daily News* reporters would have to wallow in silence longer than they might prefer before commenting on the Tattler's visit.

***

Suki slowed her steps as she approached the end of the block where she would turn toward Griff's home, then stopped.

She wanted nothing more than to leap into his arms and take comfort in his embrace. Learning of Haru-*chan*'s death had overwhelmed her. Ned's attitude had been confounding. She needed

Griff to help her make sense of it, and she needed him to stroke her back until she purred like a kitten.

But going to Griff would mean confessing the trip to the Purple Lilac, and he would be angry. She had her reasons, which a reasonable person should understand. The visit took place in the safety of daylight hours. She'd wanted to speak with the madam without having to worry about a zealous beau fretting over the fishmonger. There had been no need for him to be involved.

Even if he forgave her for neglecting to tell him about going to Asakusa, he was going to object to her spending the day locating the baron, and he was going to be disappointed at her missing Marianne and Lucien's arrival. After Ned's dismissal of what she'd learned at the Purple Lilac, she couldn't bear any more rejection.

Suki took the road home. A message from Griff waited in the entrance. It began with the usual pleasantries, then expressed hope she'd spent the afternoon resting after last night's adventure in Asakusa. He looked forward to their welcoming Marianne and Lucien together. The letter ended with his desire for them to find time alone the following evening, preferably in his study in the same manner as previous occasions.

Suki's throat swelled with the onset of frustrated tears. Shouldn't she be able to conduct a newspaper investigation as she saw fit and do unmentionable things in Griff's study? That wasn't a question she could answer on her own. She'd go to him tomorrow morning before tracking down the baron and tell him everything. Then she'd learn whether the affection between them had any hope of surviving.

CHAPTER TWENTY-NINE

The sound of Suki greeting Rei-*san* at the entrance broke through Griff's concentration on the refrigeration company's prospectus. He checked the clock. There still a few hours until he was supposed to be at her home. From there, they were going to take a rickshaw to the port for Lucien and Marianne's arrival. What could possibly have brought her here?

He buttoned up his jacket and headed to the front door, not caring if Suki had come to tell him she had a new obligation that prevented her from greeting his niece and nephew. Plans changed. His feelings for her weren't changing, and he still felt terribly about having sabotaged her interviews at the Purple Lilac.

He'd spent yesterday smarting with humiliation over mistaking a fishmonger for a gangster and stewing over his need to protect her. Naturally, a modern woman like Suki resented it. He'd seen her annoyance the other day at the park when he'd discouraged her from going to the Purple Lilac. But he couldn't help himself. Suki was a woman, and women were vulnerable whether they were directing trains, laying rail, or investigating loathsome barons for a newspaper report.

Or were they? Certainly, they weren't vulnerable in every instance of assuming the same responsibilities as men. He had to face the truth: all this worry about her journalistic investigations was less about her following leads around Tokyo and more about his fretting over losing her. She'd taught him what he desired in a woman: someone who shared his zest for adventure, who found work outside the home exciting, who mingled with people of all classes and types. And unlike his previous relationships with Victoria and Natsu, he wasn't in love with an idealized version of a woman. Suki had her faults—attraction to danger being the most prominent among them—just as he had numerous faults of his own. As far as he could tell, neither of them possessed traits that would doom their future together. He only hoped Suki felt the same.

She was removing her wooden *geta* sandals when he reached the entrance. He couldn't help but grin like an enamoured schoolboy at the sight of her. She'd fastened her chignon with lacquered clips and wore a light pink kimono cut from a silk that even he recognised as one of the finest money could buy. Hell, had she been wearing an oat sack, he'd still have found her stunning. He could spend hours taking in the contours of her face, her high, straight nose, her arched brows. Each time they met, desire for her pulsed in his veins, and his thoughts centred on how long until they were alone and how he'd kiss her when they were.

"I apologize for calling unannounced," Suki said, her voice lacking its usual brightness. Fumbling to place her feet in the guest slippers, she managed to right herself without taking Griff's offer of a steadying hand.

"You're welcome to call any time you wish," he replied, hoping she'd soon share whatever had set her out of kilter, because it was making him break out in a sweat.

She looked up at him with a steady, serious expression. "I wanted to speak with you before you left to meet Marianne and Lucien."

They were supposed to meet Marianne and Lucien together. Had she reconsidered their plans? Their courtship? His heart hit the pit of his stomach. "We can speak in the back parlour." He sounded as disappointed as he felt. How could he not be disappointed? He loved her.

It was late morning and sunlight flooded the parlour. Before he could ask whether she wished for sandwiches with their tea, her arms were around him and her head pressed against his chest.

"I can't bear to lose you," she said, her voice ragged.

Relief steadied him and he pulled her closer. He couldn't bear losing her either. Resting his cheek on her head, he took in the fresh scent of lavender and lemons. Calm settled into his bones. "Lose me? You're not going to lose me."

Stepping back, she looked up at him. "Yesterday afternoon, I returned to the Purple Lilac to ask the madam about Baron Umezono. The other night she invited me to return, but I didn't tell you because I wanted to go alone, and I thought you'd object."

She was right—he would have objected. Had she told him of her intention to speak with the madam, he would have discouraged her. "You went yesterday afternoon?"

"I took a rickshaw from Tsukiji and spent a few hours in Asakusa. It was the middle of the day and I felt confident in going alone. Then I went to the newspaper offices. I had meant to call on you afterward, but I wouldn't have been good company. Ned Taylor wasn't encouraging in my pursuit of this story."

Suki seemed to encounter endless obstacles in her investigation of the baron, Griff among them. "I made a fool of myself when I went with you to Asakusa. You had good reason not to trust my instincts. And I'm trying to trust yours." Her eyes shone as he spoke. Somehow, he'd managed to say the words she'd wanted to hear.

He continued, "As you said, the visit was in the afternoon, and the Purple Lilac was one of the finer-looking establishments. Perhaps under those circumstances, you were safe." He ran a finger down her downy cheek and along her jawline. She was so precious to him. "I care about you, and I don't want anything to happen to you. In the future, I ask that you tell me what you're planning to do, where you're planning to go, and I'll do my best to understand."

Suki pulled a handkerchief from her kimono *obi* and wiped the tears from her eyes. "I worried you'd never forgive me."

"We're coming to trust one another. There are bound to be missteps along the way." He wrapped his arms around her, and they stood in the middle of the parlour awash in light. Griff was basking in the seamless way their bodies fit together and the heat building between them when a thought upset his reverie. "Why didn't Ned encourage your story about the baron?"

"Perhaps we should let Rei-*san* bring us some tea," Suki suggested.

Over tea with milk and sugar, exactly the way she liked it, Suki told him about what she'd learned from the Purple Lilac madam and Ned's response.

"I would think Ned Taylor would place that story front and centre," Griff said after she'd concluded. "Why do you suspect he's hesitating?"

"I wonder whether the writer of the baron letters might have scared him off. Ned's wariness increased when I noted the letter-writer also didn't want me to continue the investigation."

Griff eyed the expensive kimono Suki was wearing. "But you still intend to interview the baron?" The idea of her speaking with that piece of filth—especially alone—did not appeal. But he had to start trusting her.

Suki nodded. "I'm afraid the task will consume the bulk of the day, which means I'll miss welcoming Marianne and Lucien."

"How do you plan to locate the baron?"

Suki shrugged. "I'm going to inquire at the post office about the location of his home and go there. If I can get past his maid, or whoever he sends to the front gate, I'll tell him what the Purple Lilac madam said about his bringing Haru-*chan*'s ashes to the club and my intention to write a newspaper article about her death."

Griff squeezed the arms of the wingback chair. It was easy to imagine the degenerate baron getting rough when threatened. Suki, however, was unlikely to get the baron's ear in the first place. The baron had nothing to gain by speaking with a newspaper reporter about a waitress's death; it was in his best interests to ignore Suki. Griff, however, might know of a way to keep the baron from ignoring Suki. "I believe I can help you get the baron's attention."

Suki gave him a quizzical look.

"I have friends in the conservative faction. From what I understand, they're notorious for getting the nobility's attention."

Suki let her jaw drop. "You have friends in the conservative faction?"

"After returning from Saitama, I was determined that those men stay out of Tsukiji and away from you. I had my secretaries find out where the conservatives met and who their leader was. I considered various ways of approaching them, most of which involved samurai swords and guardsmen from the British Legation, but my very wise secretaries suggested I was more likely to achieve my aim with a bottle of *sake* and an attempt at mutual understanding. Suffice to say, it worked. Their leader, Sasaki-*san*, vowed his faction would never again throw stones at rickshaws in Tsukiji. Nor would they bother the Tokyo Tattler. I woke the next day with the worst *sake* hangover of my life."

The look of incredulity remained on Suki's face, but her eyes shone with amusement. "How I wish I could've seen you negotiating with the conservative faction."

"My secretaries did the translating. I have no idea what they said on my behalf, but Sasaki-*san* and I are apparently in accord on many things. With his distaste for debauched nobility, I wonder whether Sasaki-*san* knows where the baron lives and would be interested in compelling him to speak with you. As you are well aware, the conservatives are fond of shouting expletives at those they deem a threat to their nation's integrity."

"That would be wonderful," Suki said, a flush coming to her cheeks. "The baron would be more likely to speak with me if he feared the conservatives' chants. They can be quite offensive."

Griff hated that he was about to let his protectiveness take over, but she had to be prudent. "I don't want you to think that I don't trust you, but I sincerely believe it wouldn't be wise for you to approach the conservative faction on your own. Their headquarters are located in a run-down part of town, and they are a rather motley group. I truly cannot in good conscience let you go there without an escort, and since I already know Sasaki-*san*, it would make sense for me to accompany you."

Suki placed her hand on his. "I wouldn't dream of approaching the conservatives on my own. Nor do I wish to speak with the loathsome baron alone. I'd be grateful if you were to accompany me both places. But what about Marianne and Lucien? We might be late to meet them."

Griff had already sent one of his secretaries to the port this morning, and the shipping company had confirmed that Marianne and Lucien's ship would arrive on schedule. He and Suki would never make it in time. His secretaries were competent young men, and Marianne and Lucien were experienced travellers. They'd be fine in his secretaries' hands. "My secretaries can meet the ship."

"But they're expecting you. You have to meet them. They'll be disappointed not to see you. We can go another day."

Suki was being considerate in giving no hint of disappointment at the prospect of postponing her interview, but he knew she wished to speak with the baron as soon as possible. "They'll think it's a fine adventure to be escorted through Tokyo with two Japanese citizens who speak English."

Suki beamed at him. "Thank you for coming with me, and thank you for understanding why I went to the Purple Lilac yesterday." She glanced toward the wide-open parlour doors.

Unless he was mistaken, she was curious about whether they had enough privacy to kiss, and he was curious about how a grateful Suki planned to kiss him. As for reservations about Rei-*san* or the new maid witnessing their kiss, he had none.

He pulled her to standing and brought her into his embrace. Placing a hand behind her neck, he leaned down until their lips met. Then he let her take over. The kiss was gentle, an almost shy caress. Then her mouth spread into a grin, much like it had their first time in Ueno Park. Tightening her grip around him, she parted her lips, and he entered with a tender stroke. Blood rushed through his veins as their tongues circled and her softness pressed into him. No man in the world was as fortunate as he. Suki was his.

CHAPTER THIRTY

Suki and Griff's runner let them off at an older house in a neighborhood on the outskirts of Nihonbashi's busy commercial district. The wood of the home's exterior was bloated and dark with soot, and its partially rotted gate hung at a slant.

A lively group of children gaped at their alighting from the rickshaw. Between her foreign features and *Okasan*'s exquisite kimono, Suki doubtless made for a curious sight. Griff, in his obvious foreignness, seemed to attract no fewer wide-eyed stares.

"We're here," Griff said.

"Spenser-*san*," a man called from an open window. A long scar marked the side of his face. Suki recognized him from that morning at her home. "What has brought you here?"

"We've come to beg a favour of you and your men," Griff replied in rudimentary Japanese.

"I'll let you in," the man called and shut the window.

"That's Sasaki-*san*, the leader," Griff whispered.

Sasaki-*san* appeared at the door and bowed deeply before looking directly at Suki. "I understand from the fine gentleman, Spenser-*san*, that our faction has offended you deeply with our coming to your home. I apologize." He fell into another low bow.

Suki appreciated Sasaki-*san*'s sincerity. For a Japanese man, particularly one of Sasaki-*san*'s ilk, to humble himself in apology to a woman was no small feat. Griff must have made him feel terribly about that morning. "Your apology is accepted."

Sasaki-*san* welcomed them inside his home, and over green tea that made Griff's nose twitch, he eyed Suki.

Griff started to speak, but Sasaki-*san* shook his head at him. "Why are *you* here?" he asked Suki.

She let her lips curl into a smile. "I have a bit of gossip for you."

"From the Tattler?" He let out a hearty laugh echoed by the conservatives who stood around the room taking in the unusual encounter. "I'm all ears."

***

Rickshaw runners deposited them on a residential street of urban villas set behind high stone walls and wrought-iron gates.

Sasaki-*san* had been more than familiar with the Umezono clan's decadent Western ways and after raging about the baron's betrayal of his heritage, he'd eagerly agreed to help them. He'd sent several underlings to obtain the baron's home address and several more to summon additional help for the day's mission.

With Sasaki-*san* and his men in tow, they now stood outside the baron's home in the hilly Yamanote district. Sasaki-*san* spat on the ground. "A neighborhood of minor aristocracy," he said. "All of them worshiping the Western ways."

"I'm beginning to think Sasaki-*san* doesn't think too highly of Western culture," Griff said with a raised brow.

Suki stifled a giggle; even so, the jest provided respite from her nerves. Thus far today, she'd let Griff take the lead, but now it was her turn. With the threat of the conservative faction making a lot of unwelcome noise, she felt certain the baron would speak to her. And with Griff by her side, he wouldn't do anything untoward. They'd left her well-positioned to get information on Haru-*chan*'s death.

Sasaki-*san* led them down the street to a gate that appeared much like the others and addressed Griff. "This is the house. Would you like us to start chanting?"

"Not yet," Suki replied on Griff's behalf and pulled the bell.

Moments later, a maid appeared at the gate. Her gaze moved and widened between Suki and Griff—no doubt foreigners—to the ruffians dressed in the conservative faction's brown kimonos.

"Please tell Baron Umezono the newspaper reporter he met at the Hotel Metropolis would like to speak with him," Suki said. "I have a feeling he'd also appreciate knowing that members of the conservative faction are present to ensure his readiness to speak."

The maid bowed and scurried away. Not long thereafter, the baron arrived at his gate. Sasaki-*san* and his men, who'd been bantering about the idea of starting their own gossip column to condemn the despicable elites, fell silent at the sight of the baron and regarded him with obvious disgust. Bleary eyes and a bloated face gave the impression of the man having only recently awakened after a long night in the company of many *sake* bottles. The sling was gone, but the baron appeared in no shape to order them and their conservatives allies away.

Suki bowed politely. "Baron Umezono," she said in English for Griff's benefit.

"I am," he replied in equally well-articulated English as he looked Suki up and down. "I recognize you from the Metropolis. You look different in kimono."

Suki had worn one of *Okasan*'s finest kimonos as a means of establishing a common heritage and building rapport for the interview. But the baron hadn't noticed the fine garment for its thick, lustrous silk; he'd noticed the garment because degenerates like the baron set their gaze on a woman's figure first. She doubted she'd be getting an apology for the baron's assault on her nipple, like the polite apology she'd received from Sasaki-*san* when it came to nearly attacking her on the street. "I'm here with Griffith Spenser."

Griff took the cue from Suki and offered his hand for the baron, which must have been difficult given his desire to cause the baron irreversible injury.

"I recognize you from the hotel as well," the baron said. His forehead gleamed with perspiration. "And these are your friends?" He nodded at the conservatives.

"This is Sasaki-*san*, leader of the conservative faction," said Suki. "His men are here in the event you experience any reluctance to speak with us."

The baron eyed the conservatives with undisguised disgust. "What have you come to speak with me about?"

"I believe you know what happened to a waitress from the Purple Lilac."

Perspiration poured from the baron's temples and his pallor took on a grayish hue. "Who have you been talking to?"

"Madame Okuda of the Purple Lilac."

The baron nodded at Sasaki-*san*'s men. "Are they the ones who chant about removing body parts of nobility who take too many pleasures of the flesh?"

Suki nodded gravely. "The very ones."

The baron sighed. "Very well, then. Please, come inside."

Suki would've wagered that the baron's redbrick home had been built fifteen years ago when redbrick was de rigueur for the nobility and the earthquake had yet to make citizens question the wisdom of European construction. She and Griff removed their shoes before stepping onto the parquet flooring. On one side of a wide staircase was a spacious dining room. On the other was a receiving room filled with gilt-edged chairs and glass-fronted cabinets full of vases. The baron led them there.

Sasaki-*san* and his men surveyed the receiving room like a pack of hungry wolves. He nudged Suki. "Which chant should we start with first?"

Suki didn't want the chanting disturbing her interview with the baron, but she did want him aware of the sort of chanting favored by the conservatives. "Something he'll remember for weeks to come. But in a soft voice."

Sasaki-*san* nodded and sat on a wingback chair that Suki doubted had ever made contact with a threadbare, stained kimono

"Your friends can wait here," the baron said with a sigh at the conservatives. "Our maid will bring them refreshments."

He took Suki and Griff to a smaller parlor down the hallway. A tapestry of gold and pink flowers covered one wall. Paintings of woodland creatures, and children chasing woodland creatures, covered the others. "I've asked the baroness to join us. She'll be here shortly."

Suki and Griff sat on a sofa, and the baron took a chair opposite. They waited without comment for the baroness as waves of tobacco smoke filtered into the parlor along with remarks about degenerate nobility and the betrayal of their nation by those who collected Western flowerpots.

A maid brought in a tea service and was preparing their cups when a woman in a pea-green dress and broad lace collar presented herself with a low bow. The baron introduced the baroness to their unexpected guests. In soft, steady English, she inquired about Griff's country of origin and Suki's parentage. She directed questions to Griff about his impressions of life in Tsukiji and the Japanese foods he'd found pleasing.

Griff had just finished explaining how using chopsticks had been difficult at first, but with practice, he'd become accustomed to taking meals with the implements, when Suki interjected, "Baron Umezono, I'm about to write an article for the *Tokyo Daily News* about your involvement in the death of a waitress from the Purple Lilac. It's for your benefit that I'm asking you to comment on what occurred."

A low rumbling chant about avenging samurai ghosts and the guts of noblemen festering in the streets filtered into the parlor. The baron ran a finger under his shirt collar. "How much louder do those men in the other room get?"

"I believe it's loud enough to wake the count napping at the other end of the street."

"I thought so." The baron pulled air between his teeth. "Are you planning to confide in the police what I tell you?"

"The police can read the newspapers," Suki replied.

The baron lowered his head toward the baroness, whose vaguely amused expression befitted a conversation about cultural differences in eating utensils. "You're not going to be pleased," he said to her.

The baroness might have blinked a response, but Suki couldn't tell for certain, so she proceeded to address the baron. "Why did you go to the Purple Lilac on the night you injured your shoulder?"

Baron Umezono grimaced. "I went to the Purple Lilac on behalf of a foreigner who wished for me to deliver a waitress's ashes to her family. She'd been the foreigner's guest at his hotel."

Suki responded with the name of the first hotel owner who came to mind, the one who'd been acquainted with the baron, the one who'd told her about the baron's arm being in a sling. "Are you referring to Mr. Chase Norton of the Hotel Metropolis?"

"As a matter of fact, I am."

The baroness exhaled loudly through her teeth, a surprisingly unladylike gesture.

The baron stiffened and continued, "Mr. Norton and I enjoy a reciprocal relationship. I keep quiet about his less savory business dealings. In exchange, he very generously extends loans that fund my…pastimes."

Suki recalled the charming, confident man she'd met at the hotel. He'd known exactly where the baron had been gambling. "When you say that you're keeping quiet about Mr. Norton's unsavory dealings, does that mean you're blackmailing him?"

"Nothing so vulgar as that. It's more of an unspoken agreement between gentlemen."

"My husband joins Mr. Norton in evenings of pleasure," the baroness said and wrinkled her nose. "These include taking the opium pipe, of which I fear my husband will grow fond. He has difficulty controlling himself. I forbid him to take it, but he participates in Mr. Norton's festivities, nonetheless." The baroness pursed her lips as though she'd sucked the juice of a yuzu fruit. "I will not tolerate the evil pipes. They have no place in the emperor's Japan. We're having enough trouble curing the Taiwanese people of the horrific plague."

Suki had never heard of opium in Japan, in Tsukiji no less. "Are you suggesting that Chase Norton imports opium to Japan?"

"That's precisely what I'm suggesting," the baroness replied.

The conservatives switched to a chant about grave misjustices carried out on the bodies of noblewomen whose husbands insult their nation's founding achievements. The baroness paled.

"When are they going to cease this?" the baron asked. "We're speaking with you."

"They're taking advantage of your acoustics. Can you blame them? The noise does travel well," Suki replied. "Please continue."

The baron grimaced. "Mr. Norton owns hotels across the Asian continent and brings the opium to Japan for himself and his friends. I'm not among such friends. I don't take the pipe, as my wife doesn't allow it."

"Last year my maid found a bit of the substance in the baron's jacket pocket," the baroness clarified.

Baron Umezono clenched his jaw. "I have no idea how the opium got into my jacket."

The baroness refolded her hands in her lap. "I accept that men engage in many useless activities, but I will not accept the opium."

"I'm fortunate to have a strict wife. Once a man gets used to the pipe, that's all he wants. I'll take a bottle of *sake* and my chances at the tables."

Suki cleared her throat. While she appreciated the Umezonos' openness in conducting their disagreement in her presence, she was here to question him about Haru-*chan*. "Baron Umezono, you mentioned earlier that Mr. Norton asked you to deliver a waitress's ashes. Do you know what caused her death?"

The baron shifted in his chair. "This is not something for women's..." He blinked several times at Suki as though she'd suddenly appeared in his parlor. "The night I met you at the Hotel Metropolis, you said someone had been writing letters to the newspaper about my dealings?"

Suki nodded. "At the time, I'd only received one letter. But consequently, I received several letters urging me to investigate your person. Do you know who wrote these letters?"

The baron gave a short laugh. "Norton, of course. He wants me to take the blame for the waitress's death. That's why he had me deliver the ashes to the Purple Lilac and sent those letters to the newspaper. I know too much of what he's done. What a clever scheme to get rid of me."

Griff, who'd been observing the conversation like it was a game of lawn tennis, gave Suki an admiring glance. Indeed, she was scoring points. But she would prefer scoring them on Haru-*chan*'s behalf. "Did you have anything to do with the waitress's death?" Suki asked.

"That's what Norton wants you to think. But I was not present when she died. I only handled her ashes later."

"But you know how she died?"

The baron looked at his wife, who sat ramrod straight in the wingback chair, her expression stern.

Suki continued, "If you don't tell me about the waitress' death, then I'm going to write an article about your bringing her ashes to the Purple Lilac with one thousand American dollars to compensate the madam for the loss of her employee."

The baroness gasped. "You gave the club madam one thousand American dollars?"

"It was Norton's money," the baron retorted, then looked at Suki. "I'll tell you how she died. Then you can write the truth in your newspaper article. I'm not going to have my family's name dragged through the mud for Norton's crimes. At least the truth may permit us some dignity when we're shamed out of Tokyo and forced to live in the countryside."

The baroness let out a sharp cry.

The baron didn't even look in her direction. "The waitress died at one of Norton's opium parties. He likes to have a waitress by his side when he takes the pipe. He gives it to her too. Then she gets dizzy and sleepy, and he treats her as her profession warrants. Each time, he takes a waitress from a different part of the city. The woman has no idea what's about to happen. He likes to surprise them. Usually, they leave the next day with a large sum in their purses. Not the one from the Purple Lilac. She took the pipe and never woke up."

Grief for a woman she'd never met and whose name she'd only learned the day before made Suki's throat swell. Then, just as quickly as the grief had come, it transformed into a clenching anger. Chase Norton had murdered a woman. The baron had known and never informed authorities who could bring justice to bear on her killer. "How did you learn about her death?"

"I'd won a large sum at the tables and wished to repay a portion of my debt to Norton. It was quite late. Dawn broke soon thereafter. Most of his guests had left. Those who remained were in the opium stupor. I don't know if any of them realized what had happened to the waitress. Norton was walking back and forth across his hotel rooms. The waitress lay on a sofa. She had passed."

Suki pictured a young woman on Norton's sofa, dead at the hands of the depraved man. "What did Norton do with the waitress's body?"

"He had her cremated. He couldn't have anyone asking questions about how she'd died. Then he gave me American dollars to take care of the ashes and compensate the madam and her family for their loss, enough money to keep them quiet." The baron ran his hands along the side of his armchair. "You see, Mr. Norton receives various currencies from selling opium to his friends. He runs into difficulty exchanging large sums with officials he has yet to bribe. I took part of the American money as payment for delivering the waitress's ashes. After changing my portion into yen, I couldn't exchange the remainder of the money without raising suspicions. So,

I gave half to the Purple Lilac madam, and the rest to the waitress's family."

"In Utsunomiya?" Suki asked.

"How did you know?"

"Madame Okuda of the Purple Lilac told me. I'll be sure to let her know Haru-*chan*'s ashes are in her family's hands."

"Her name was Haru-*chan*?" the baron murmured.

Hearing him voice the name of the woman to whose soul he'd shown so little regard filled Suki with the desire to let the conservatives make good on their threats. Fortunately for the baron's nether regions, Suki was a patient woman and would wait for her newspaper article to destroy him. "She was a well-spoken young woman who was seeking a way out of her life in the club."

Suki looked down at her notes. Ned couldn't possibly have any misgivings about publishing the story. It was going to be the biggest scandal in Tsukiji's history and an international incident since Norton was American with businesses all over Asia. "Do you have anything to add, Baron Umezono?"

The baron shook his head. "I'm glad to have told you about what happened to the young woman. I want to be done with Norton and his hotel. We'll go live in the countryside, leave this hedonistic city behind."

The baroness's posture somehow straightened even further. "We'll do no such thing. Your sons are going to be educated in Tokyo, and you still have those railway projects your cousins promised you." The baroness turned to Griff. "Please assure your foreign friends their investments will yield the great dividends we promised." Then she turned to Suki. "Don't forget to take those…men in the receiving room with you. They were quite persuasive in getting your audience's attention."

CHAPTER THIRTY-ONE

Before bidding the conservative faction farewell outside the baron's gates, Suki told Sasaki-*san* about how Chase Norton was bringing opium into Japan. An outraged Sasaki-*san* swore his men would tear Norton and the Hotel Metropolis to pieces for his crimes against the emperor's people. Suki wanted Norton to suffer extreme punishment for killing Haru-*chan*, but she didn't want Sasaki-*san* and his men to hang for exacting that punishment. Finally, Sasaki-*san* agreed to chant night and day outside the hotel until Norton fled Japan, went insane, or the police arrested him.

At Tsukiji's gates, Suki and Griff headed in separate directions, him to ascertain Marianne and Lucien's whereabouts and her to tell Ned what she'd learned. The newspaper offices were empty when she arrived. According to the maid, Ned was at the presses, and the reporters had departed in pursuit of their sources. Suki waited in Ned's office, all the while formulating opening lines for an article about a murderous hotelier, a dead waitress, and a corrupt baron who should have reported the hotelier to the police but eventually told a journalist the truth. Between Madame Okuda and the baron, all the claims in Suki's article had verification. Ned was going to be pleased. She'd done a thorough investigation; her article was going to be the talk of Tokyo.

Her dream was coming true, but she couldn't celebrate. The unfair fate that had befallen Haru-*chan* had sown seeds of anger and a desire for justice. Going forward, she would use her journalism to expose the wrongs done to all of Tokyo's women no matter the circumstances of their birth, the conditions of their work, or whether society believed they'd earned their misfortune. She'd fight for them, and in this way, honor Haru-*chan*'s memory.

Ned breezed into the office. "Apologies for keeping you waiting. The evening edition was late getting off the presses, which means we're going to be up half the night finishing the morning edition."

"I suppose I'll be aiming for tomorrow's evening edition with my article about the Purple Lilac waitress's death." Suki tapped the notes in her lap.

"Tell me what you've learned." Ned sat behind his desk and crossed his arms.

Suki recalled the events of the day from summoning the conservatives to the baron's statements about opium parties at the hotel and the circumstances of Haru-*chan*'s death.

Ned nodded as she spoke, then ran a hand through his hair. "You've done good work. Let this be a lesson on how to conduct your investigations going forward. But we can't publish any of it."

Suki felt as though the wind had been knocked out of her. "Whyever not?"

"Chase Norton would have us shuttered in a fortnight." Ned spoke as though it was an obvious outcome, but she could not comprehend how that would be the case.

"A woman has died. Norton killed her. He's bringing opium into Japan. Won't an article to that effect destroy him, not us?"

Ned let out a cold, empty laugh. "Nothing will destroy Norton. He'll declare every word of your article a pack of lies and tell his friends in the communications ministry to close us down." Ned leaned back in his chair. "Suki, you don't understand how things work in this city. Norton has more bureaucrats in his pocket than anyone in Tokyo thanks to what goes on at that hotel. He orchestrates it himself. He dangles temptations before a man until he gives in, then uses those sins to keep him in check. He does it to all of Tokyo's elites."

"Including you?"

"Let's just say I would be putting myself and a married friend, or two, in peril were I to anger Mr. Chase Norton."

Suki couldn't look at Ned. He'd been on a rampage to slay the demons that had been haunting him since he'd had his heart broken in Hong Kong. The way he carried on with women disgusted Suki. Even worse, he was in cahoots with Norton. Like Norton, he'd pressured her to stop investigating the baron. Indeed, Ned must have known all along that Norton had penned those letters urging her to investigate Baron Umezono. "Why did Norton want me to stop investigating Haru-*chan*'s death?"

"Norton was concerned about Spenser being involved in your investigation of Baron Umezono. I presume that's because Norton has nothing unsavoury with which to threaten Spenser."

Suki wasn't surprised to hear as much. "So, what had Norton hoped to accomplish by sending me those letters about Baron Umezono in the first place?"

"I know little of Norton's motivations. Nor do I care to know. As you said, the baron believes Norton was setting him up to take the blame for the waitress's death. I imagine Norton wanted the Tattler to discover that the baron had taken the ashes to the Purple Lilac and then write a sensational column about the depraved baron. That would've been sufficient to ruin the baron without involving police or making enemies of the Umezono family."

Norton was as clever as he was evil. "The shame would've been the death of him; he might have ended his life. Then Norton would no longer have to put up with funding the baron's pastimes, and Haru-*chan*'s death would never be traced back to him."

"Norton is always two steps ahead of the rest of us," Ned said with a wry smile.

Suki looked him straight in the eye. "Norton is a murderer. Let me tell the story of Haru-*chan*'s death, and let him try to stop us. We'll bring him down with the truth." If Ned was committed to justice for women as he claimed, he would be galvanized to see Norton pay for his crimes. But might justice for women be something he associated with the woman he'd loved and lost? Was he denying the chance to bring Norton down as a way to punish her?

Ned ran both hands through his hair. "Forget about Norton. You conducted a brilliant investigation. You're ready to be a reporter."

Once again, Ned was seeking to manipulate her with the prospect of reporting for his newspaper. Enough was enough. "I'll take the article to the *Tokyo Herald*. Perhaps their editor has integrity."

Ned shook his head. "He'll never publish. Norton would retaliate at the *Herald* the same way he would here."

"Fine. I have no choice but to go to the police. I'll tell them everything I know."

"I wouldn't do that, Suki. It'll be your word against his, and he owns enough men at the top to make your complaint go away."

Suki considered whether Baron Umezono might assist her in bringing Norton to justice, but the notion was ludicrous. The baron was going to be thrilled when her article never came out.

Ned sighed. "You have a career as a reporter ahead of you. Don't cross Chase Norton and you'll be Tokyo's first female journalist."

"And spend the rest of my career writing stories to please Chase Norton. Won't that be tremendous?" There was nothing more to say to Ned. He was Norton's sucker, and she had no intention of becoming the same. She stood to leave.

Ned raised his hand. "Don't go just yet. Let's come to an understanding. You're meant to be a newspaper reporter. You have a good sense for the story; you know what readers want. This is what you're meant to do."

"I'm meant to stand by while a bully like Chase Norton gets away with murder? Let me give you some understanding, Ned. I'm a half-breed living in a society that isn't certain whether I'm fully human. Bullies are everywhere and indulging their cruelty is not how you deal with them. I'm going to do everything in my power to ensure that Norton pays."

Reaching the door, Suki turned back. "And I'll never write another word for this newspaper, not as the Tattler and not as a reporter. I'm through with cowards like you."

***

Griff had reached the entrance of St. Luke's Hospital, his mind ruminating on his impressions of Marianne and Lucien, when he caught a glimpse of Suki and flashes of her pink kimono coming toward him from the university district. His niece and nephew had been at home when he'd checked there after parting from Suki at Tsukiji's gates. Their spirits had been bright, and their enthusiasm for exploring Tokyo would have him and Suki escorting them all over the city for the coming weeks, if not months. They seemed to be faring so well that he excused himself to meet a friend who would be joining them for supper. They didn't miss the sparkle in his eye and teased their *oncle* about how often they'd be dining with this friend and whether they might expect this friend to become a more permanent fixture in the home. Marianne and Lucien had inherited their parents' humour.

Griff waved as Suki came into sight. Head down, shoulders sagged, she didn't acknowledge him. Whatever had occurred at the *Tokyo Daily News* offices must have been a terrible disappointment. He increased his speed and waved again. This time she looked up. Upon seeing him, she increased her pace until she was barely a foot away, then flung herself into his arms.

Griff felt her breath slow and her body melt into his. "Would you like me to carry you home?"

"I'm afraid the injury would leave you abed for days," she said into his chest.

"As long as you were by my side..." The idea of being in bed with Suki for days caused him to momentarily forget that as he held her in his arms, she was upset. "What happened at the newspaper offices?"

Suki stepped from his embrace and smoothed down the sleeves of her kimono, a gesture he'd come to learn signalled her upset. "Ned Taylor is in Chase Norton's back pocket. Apparently, Norton knows the dirty secrets of everyone in power." She told him of her failed efforts to get Ned to publish the article about Haru-*chan*'s death. "Norton is going to win. He's going to get away with killing a woman."

"He's not going to win. We'll find a way to get him." Griff's gut twisted at the thought of Norton coming after Suki for what she knew about Haru-*chan*'s death. There was no way he'd let the rotten bastard get to her as well. If he had to kill him with his bare hands to keep her safe, he'd do it. But he couldn't discuss this with Suki without giving her more cause for distress. "If we don't get to him, the conservative faction no doubt will."

Suki let out a small laugh. "They might be the only ones who bother trying." Wrapping her arms around his midsection, she nestled her body into his. His chest swelled with the now-familiar sense of satisfaction at having found the piece missing from him.

He reached down and angled her chin upwards. "Tell me what you need me to do, and I'll do everything in my power to help."

A smile lit up her face. "I need you more than I've ever needed anyone or anything. I love you, Griffith Spenser."

The words rang in his ears like a thousand tinkling bells. Suki loved him. He wanted to lift her off the ground and swing her around for all the world to see his prize. But given her current state, she might appreciate something less dramatic. A scandalous kiss on the streets of Tsukiji would have to suffice. He brought his lips to hers and she graced him with soft, probing kisses that unfurled into bold kisses that sent a rush of heat through him. He broke the kiss when the words he'd been summoning finally came.

"I know we've only been in a courtship for a few days, so I hope you don't think I'm being hasty." He looked into her eyes and saw all the tenderness and care he felt toward her reflected back at him. "Suki, you are warm and generous, witty and intelligent beyond what any man should hope for in a wife. I love you for all the things I've learned about you, and I love you for all the things I've yet to learn. I love you, Suki Malveaux, and I want you to be my wife."

Tears formed in her eyes, then trailed down her cheeks through a radiant smile. "I believe you've just given me the best marriage proposal ever offered on the streets of Tsukiji." The smile faltered as she pulled a handkerchief from her kimono sash. Dabbing her eyes, she looked away, and the muscles of his chest clenched. It had been too soon to suggest marriage; she'd only agreed to a courtship a few days before. Once again, he was saying the wrong thing and pushing her away.

She looked up; her chin trembled. "I never considered the possibility of marrying because I didn't think I was wise enough to recognize a man who would stay true to his commitments. I adored my father and trusted him with all my heart, then he left and never returned." Suki gripped Griff's hand as though to steady herself. He placed his other hand on top of hers and gazed at her with the earnestness and respect she deserved from her father, from Ned, from him.

"All my life I let a wounded heart be my guide. I'm not going to do that any longer." Suki dabbed her eyes again. "Haru-*chan*...she died before she could have a better life. I'm not going to let the misgivings of a wounded heart sway me into giving up a chance to have the life I want. I know you are a man who honors his commitments. You aren't going to abandon me. I trust that today and I'll trust it forever, and I absolutely accept your proposal." She threw her arms around his neck, and he lifted her until her face pressed into the curve of his neck. Then she pulled back and met his lips with a kiss that rang with unabashed love.

As the kiss eased, Griff recalled that in less than half a block, they'd be at his home and face-to-face with Marianne and Lucien. Clearing his throat, he summoned the gravest of tones. "I hope you're ready to meet my niece and nephew. I'm sorry to report they're atrocious, and I'm afraid that as long as you're with me, you're going to have to bear their misbehaviour."

Suki looked up at him with narrowed eyes, and he couldn't keep from grinning. "How dare you tease your future wife like that?" she said with a playful tap to his chest.

He'd teased his "future wife." His face threatened to break from the grin those words summoned. "You'll have to see for yourself. You won't believe the horror."

"Then we should hold off announcing our marriage so as not to tempt them into terrible mischief."

The idea of sharing their intentions with family pleased him to no end, but he was unsure whether either of them had the stamina to bear the deluge of congratulations. "Should we tell everyone tonight?"

"I want to tell the world. But after today's events, I might prefer to celebrate our announcement another time."

Griff nodded. "After the shortest courtship in the history of courting, a secret engagement seems quite fitting."

***

Marianne placed her fork and knife on her plate and leaned back on her chair. Despite his niece's protestations otherwise, the day seemed to have exhausted her. "What will you do about this Norton fellow, Suki?"

Suki rested her elbows on the table and folded her hands. "I'll speak to the police and hopefully they'll take action against him. For now, I think that's the best course of action."

One look at Lucien and Griff bit back a smile. His nephew fought staring at Suki, her elegant kimono and slightly lopsided chignon only enhancing her charms. Lucien looked back at him with an incredulous expression. Did his nephew not think him worthy of Suki? Griff would have to enlighten him about winning a stunning women's adoration another time. Tonight, he wanted to celebrate that win with his fiancée. He addressed Lucien. "You and your sister look like you could use a good night's rest."

Marianne opened her mouth as though to protest, but before she could speak, Lucien addressed her in rapid French. Griff caught the words "love," "privacy," "tomorrow," and "sleep." That sounded about right. "Good night, *oncle*," Marianne said with a kiss to Griff's cheek. She had her mother's honey-coloured tresses, her broad, welcoming smile, and manner of tilting her head at the end of a question. How Griff wished Suki could have met his brother's wife. They would've become fast friends. "Sleep well and we can plan tomorrow's activities in the morning, depending upon how you feel."

Marianne beamed at Suki. "Will you be joining us tomorrow?"

"I wouldn't miss it," Suki replied.

Marianne clasped her hands together. "Rei-*san* said the weather would be perfect for exploring the city."

Lucien finished the sweet wine Griff had served for a digestif in keeping with the French custom. "Might we see some of those woodblock prints we've heard so much about? The many views of Mount Fuji, and so forth."

Much to Griff's surprise, all things Japanese had been the rage in Paris for the past few decades. Marianne and Lucien knew more about Japanese porcelain, kimonos, and castle architecture than most of Tsukiji. "I believe there's an art museum in Ueno with a large collection. We can go there tomorrow if you like."

Lucien stood. "Excellent. Good night, *oncle*." He turned to Suki. "Good night, Mademoiselle Malveaux," he said in gracious French that Griff imagined had won his nephew the hearts of more than a few young women.

After Marianne and Lucien left the dining room, Griff sat down next to Suki and took her hand in his. "I was wondering if you might be interested in celebrating our betrothment in my study?"

"And what might this celebrating entail?" A flush sprang to her cheeks, and she lowered her gaze. He'd seen the same expression on her face the last time they were in his study. As he recalled he'd just pushed down her corset and pressed his face into the seam of her lush breasts.

"Glasses of champagne? Some time on the settee?"

"Monsieur Spenser," she said with a suggestive raise of the brow, "you're reading my mind."

CHAPTER THIRTY-TWO

The empty champagne flutes sitting on the small table glinted in the firelight, and Suki ran her hand down Griff's shirt sleeve, letting her fingers rise and fall with the swell of his muscles. She gazed back up at him, and he kissed her again, deeply, hungrily, which was exactly how she'd wanted to be kissed. He'd gotten good at reading her desires, or at least responding to the indecent looks she directed at his lips.

Lounging on the settee with the champagne lingering on her palate and Griff's warmth enveloping her, she should have been free of all bothersome thoughts, but her mind wouldn't stop churning over the events of the afternoon and what they meant for the future: she'd never spend another day working at a newspaper. Not only would she never be a newspaper reporter, but she'd also never write another Tattler column. She'd given up her dream. But soon she'd be married to Griff. That thought, at least, thrilled her.

Every time she took in Griff's woodsy, masculine scent, she felt as though her heart would burst with joy. Being married to the man she loved, having his children, and delighting in their years together was a dream she'd never dared embrace, and it was coming true. But this dream threatened an essential part of her. She was a modern woman with aspirations beyond the home. Truth be told, she still wanted to be a newspaper reporter. "Griff?"

His gaze met hers, and her body responded as it always did with a tremble of longing to be taken by him. "I was wondering if I could ask about your hopes for our marriage."

"Of course." He squeezed her to him.

Suki took a deep breath. "More than anything I want to be your wife. I want us to have children, and I'll do everything in my power to raise them well. I'll ensure that they have the best education and watch after their health. And yours."

Griff cocked his head to the side. "I'm glad to hear you say that. I plan to watch over you and our children very carefully. Considering my unfortunate tendency towards overprotectiveness, I'll probably drive you all mad with my attentions."

"I also want to work." Relief poured out of her with the words. "But with Norton's hold on Tokyo's newspapers and newspapermen like Ned unwilling to stand up to his bullying, there is no place for me. I'm a modern woman and I'd always thought that I would contribute to society beyond my role in the household. I'd thought to become a newspaper reporter and work toward bettering relations between the Japanese and foreign communities. I felt that was my calling in life. I still do. I don't know what that means for the type of work I'll be able to do, but I don't want to give it up."

"That's one of the many things I love about you, Suki. You care about society and have a plan for making your country a better place. I won't object to your working."

His tone left no doubt as to the strength of his sincerity, and she felt almost embarrassed for having asked. But she'd needed to hear those words. "I had a feeling you would say as much. But I wanted to be sure."

Griff laced his fingers through hers. "There's nothing you can say or do that will cause me to leave. You said before that you felt you could trust me, and you can. Our marriage is forever."

Suki sighed out fears and anxieties that had been lingering at the edge of her awareness. She hadn't realized how much she'd needed to hear those words, but Griff had known. He cupped her face and used his thumbs to brush away tears that had fallen to her cheeks. Then he kissed her languidly, adoringly. Her body turned to liquid in his arms, and with each swirl of their tongues, with each press of his hand into the small of her back, with each kiss trailed down her nape, that liquid turned molten.

Griff moved from the small of her back down to the swell of her buttocks. Through the thick silk of her kimono, his strokes and squeezes teased with their lightness. She wanted a firmer grip. Even better, she wanted him gripping her skin.

Suki stood and tugged at her *obi* sash.

"Wait," he said and caught her hand. "You have to be home shortly. We shouldn't get carried away." His hungry eyes waged war against the proper words.

She gave him a suggestive pout. "We have a few more hours. I thought we were going to spend them as we had before in your study."

Griff stood alongside her, their bodies almost touching. The electricity between them grew stronger, even more palpable over the short distance. "In that case, how do you feel about spending them in my bedroom? Our bedroom? I think you'll find the bed more comfortable than our settee."

"Our bedroom?" The breath caught in Suki's throat. The bedroom was the sort of place where innocent schoolteachers lost their innocence. "I would like to see this bedroom."

They took the stairs without a word, their footfalls light on the wooden floor. Griff opened the door to a large room with a four-poster bed. The drapes on the bed and curtains framing two sets of large windows had been cut from gold and dark blue silk. Likewise, the walls had been papered in stripes of the same colors. No pictures or paintings adorned them, and the side tables were bare. She couldn't discern any mark of his former wife, nor did it seem that Griff had made this space his own. It was a shell of a room, and Suki had the distinct impression it had been waiting for her.

Griff stood at her side, his gaze taking in her reaction. "I love our room." She faced him and brought her hands to his shoulders. Their bodies came together, and she reveled in the oneness they created.

"I want you to make this room a place you never want to leave." His voice was almost a whisper. Was he being careful not to wake Marianne and Lucien? Or was he as overcome as she with curiosity and yearning to discover what this night would bring?

"I already never want to leave."

Standing in the center of their room, they exchanged tender kisses like wishes for their future. And hot, tantalizing kisses that flowered on her lips and neck and the shell of her ear like wishes for the sinful delights of the present.

Their bodies swayed to the hum of the fire and the bay winds rustling the garden's leaves. Wanting to be closer, needing to feel that heat that their bodies created together, Suki drew her hands down the front of Griff's shirt, over the rise and fall of his chest and abdomen until she reached the top of his trousers. Freeing his shirts, she roved the warm skin below, taking in the wiry hairs that blossomed at the top of his chest, and the smooth sides of him that narrowed to his hips.

"Your touch…" he rasped, "is the most wonderful thing I've ever felt."

"I want yours," she said, amazed at the effect of her words in bringing Griff's hands to the small of her back where her *obi* rested.

He turned her in his arms and made surprisingly quick work of lengthy silk. Then he slid the outer kimono from her shoulders and ran his lips over the length of skin between her nape and her shoulder's curve, leaving little bites that made her head arch back against his chest and compounded the pressure between her legs.

Her mind was a blur, but she couldn't neglect *Okasan*'s priceless kimono. She took a step away from Griff, and he responded with a protest.

"I cannot let the kimono end up in a heap on the floor."

He responded with an expression of feigned hurt that earned him a roll of the eyes.

She folded the gorgeous silk and placed it on one of Griff's empty side tables. "Shall I remove the undergarment as well?" she asked.

"That would be most welcome," he said, and his pout loosened into a desirous gaze.

She undid the ribbons of the cotton kimono undergarment and let it fall from her shoulders and off her body. Sill in her chemise, she stood before him, loving the way his eyes roamed her skin and the appreciative murmur that fell from his lips. Her breasts tingled for his touch, but before she could move toward him, he raised a hand.

"Your hair."

She marveled at how the insistence in his voice made her hasten to do his bidding.

Pulling off the lacquered clips, she let her chignon unravel in wavy locks that fell over the front of her chemise and down her back to the curve of her waist.

Griff let out a hard breath. "And the chemise."

She unlaced the garment and it fell in a swirl of cotton. They gazed at one another, him with his shirt untucked, and her in flimsy drawers.

"Your shirt," she said with that same insistent tone he'd used with her, and like her, he wasted no time in doing her bidding. And like him, she gave an appreciative murmur while she took in his broad shoulders, his brownish nipples, and the tapering of his torso at the top of his hips.

Griff closed the space between them with a look of raw desire that made Suki swell with anticipation. He took a strand of her hair and threaded it between his fingers then twirled it while spreading kisses along the edge of her jaw and into her mouth. As his head moved down to her chest, she guided him to the raised peak of her nipple. There he lapped and suckled exactly as she'd wished, and the pressure between her legs built to such a frenzy that her moan echoed through the bedroom. Both she and Griff went silent. Moments later, there was still no response from the bedrooms down the hall.

"I didn't mean to be so loud."

"Oh, you'll get louder, much louder," he said and moved to the other nipple with his licking and lapping. "I plan to hear those noises on a nightly basis, Mrs. Spenser."

Excitement bubbled within her at the thought of being with Griff like this on a nightly basis. "What will Marianne and Lucien think?"

"That you are a brazen woman."

Suki shifted backwards toward the bed, pulling Griff along with her. "You make it easy to be brazen."

"Then I'm doing exactly what I intended." The bed caught the backs of her thighs, and she shimmied onto the soft coverlet. Griff took the space beside her. Without giving thought to the brazenness of her actions, she straddled his lap and explored the breadth of his shoulders and chest. Like hers, his nipples grew hard under the pads of her fingers. A giggle escaped her. Who knew a man's nipples did that?

"I'm glad you're enjoying this." Griff's beaming smile amplified her enjoyment by miles. "Because this might be the best thing that's ever happened to me."

How she wanted to make it even better for them both. His erection pressed against her inner thigh, and she recalled how he'd groaned then pulled away the night of the headmaster's dinner when she'd touched his stiffness. This time she wasn't going to let him get away so easily. She brushed her hand against his erection, and he let out a guttural sound that could have been pleasure or pain. She tried pulling away, wary that she'd hurt him, but he caught her hand and brought it back.

"Don't stop," he said, his eyes gleaming with need.

"But you were so loud, Mr. Spenser," she protested in a sultry voice. "You could wake the neighbors."

"You're making it easy to be loud."

"Oh, you'll get louder, much louder," she replied. Running her hand along the trouser fabric, she located the swollen tip of Griff's erection, then coddled and caressed it. His breath grew heavier, tickling her neck and sending shivers down the length of her. When she palmed the side of his shaft and moved her hand up and down, his hips tilted back and forth, matching the pace of her strokes.

"Are you going to take off your trousers?" she asked.

Griff swiped his hands over his face and leaned back on the bed. Lowering his hands, he grimaced. "Once the tiger is out of the cage, it's going to want to be inside you. You're a virgin. I need to know that you're ready."

Suki lay down beside him and propped herself up on her elbow. "I'm as ready as I'll ever be, and I know it's going to be wonderful, provided, of course, we don't wake everyone in the house."

Griff faced her. His gaze roved her nakedness as he caressed the swell of her hip. "You're beautiful. More beautiful than any woman should be."

The words thrummed through every part of her being. "That's how you make me feel."

Griff swirled his tongue through her mouth as he tugged at the strings of her drawers until they disappeared into the coverlet's folds. Air cooled her hot sex. And Griff and his touch, which had brought her so much pleasure before and which she'd been dreaming of since, moved to the inside of her thigh. Parting the folds of her inner bouquet, he grazed the delicate flesh already wet with need.

Shockwaves sent her hips reeling. The muscles of her legs loosened and spread. How open she was to him. He pressed against her nub, teasing, stroking, kindling that sublime pressure. "Stay silent, Suki," he murmured into her neck, the vibrations of his lips taunting her skin while his fingers unraveled her.

"Griff, I'm going to lose myself."

"Not yet, Suki. You'll scream and wake the whole house."

She giggled at his rough tone. "You think you're better than me at keeping quiet? What if I do this?" She felt for the front of his trousers, but before she had him in hand, he rolled off the bed.

He gave her an amused smile under hooded lids. "You win."

His trousers fell from his hips and onto the floor in a heap. The front of his drawers jutted out and she stared in wonder as he undid the string and pulled them from his body.

His erect penis was longer and thicker than anything she'd seen at the baths. Its tip glistened with wetness. "That's extraordinary."

"You do it to me every time we're together. Even when we're not together, and I start thinking of you, it happens."

"Does it hurt?"

Griff resumed his place beside her. "Not usually. It's only doing what God and nature intended. I'm just wondering," he said, his voice dark, "what you want to do with it."

That was easy. "I want to touch it."

He released a stream of air. "That's what I was hoping you'd say."

Suki ran her fingertips along the soft, yet taut flesh. He folded her hand around the shaft, and together they squeezed firmly and moved up and down his length. Griff let out a hot breath, then eased her hand away and dragged the coverlet to the end of the bed. Returning to her side, he stroked the length of her, his fingertips leaving a trail of tantalized nerves, while she took his maleness in both hands and explored the length of him, circling the tip and fondling his heavy balls. He sighed a kiss into her mouth, and somehow his erection seemed to grow even fuller.

"Will that…when we're together, will it…work?"

"I believe it will," he said and moved a hand up her thigh.

Knowing where he was headed, Suki wanted him there desperately. When he reached the delicate wetness, she shuddered in his arms. He slipped a finger beyond her entrance, and her insides squeezed down on him as though laying claim.

"I believe it will fit just fine. But I ought to take a closer look."

"A closer look?"

Since Griff had said he was going to take a closer look, Suki wasn't surprised to feel the roughness of his cheek on her chest or his breath whirl against her belly. Nor was she shocked by kisses on her navel that sent undulating heat across her skin. But when his mouth settled on the place where his hands had been, the sensation was utterly unexpected. It tickled; it taunted; it begged a demanding cry for Griff to never cease, and a demanding cry for him to release her from its grasp.

"I'm going to scream, Griff. You have to stop or everyone in Tsukiji is going to know exactly what is happening in our bedroom."

He rose from between her legs and gave her a silly grin. "You'll just have to cover your mouth." Then he returned to where he'd been—thank the gods of East and West—and continued licking and sucking until the orgasm broke her. Her back arched; her mind shattered; and her body throbbed as wetness poured from within.

Her breaths peaked and dipped on waves of exquisite pleasure. As they steadied, she found Griff sitting on his knees, his eyes shimmering with deep affection and fundamental need. Opening her arms, she welcomed him to her, and he fell into her invitation.

"Suki?" he asked, one hand resting on his elbow, his breath grazing her forehead.

"Yes?"

"Can you tell me what you want?" His voice was low and hoarse. In his gaze was aching vulnerability. In her hands was his pleasure, his need.

"I want you inside me," she said, her gaze never leaving his.

He took her mouth in a deep kiss that penetrated her to the core. "Are you ready?" he asked.

"I am."

He drew the tip of his erection against her swollen, tender loins. Still they throbbed at his touch and her pelvis rose in response, bringing him to her entrance. He pushed into her, and a strained, cloying pain bloomed from her sex. Her hands found the bedsheets and twisted them against the sensation.

"Suki, you feel…magnificent." Lips parted, he breathed in short gasps as he eased into her.

Her body reached out to his fullness and the pain transformed into pressure that mounted with each seductive glide of his hips. She surrendered to the movements of his body, to the rhythm of their breaths, and the blissfulness of their pairing overcame her in an orgasm that sent heat radiating through her and flashes of light dancing before her eyes.

"God, Suki." At the sound of her name, she clasped the muscles of his upper arms and held on as a fiery tension seized him, then unfolded on his features in a cascade of fury and surprise, of deprivation and rapture. A light curse spilled from his lips as he thrust a final time and filled her with his hot seed.

Slowly, Griff pulled away and fell onto the bedsheets. Suki placed a hand on the center of his chest, and he topped it with his, securing her to him as his breath evened out.

When he recovered, Griff pulled up the coverlet and turned toward her. With his knees, he parted hers, and their legs were entwined. "Was that as you'd hoped?" he asked

"It was the most passionate, most overwhelming, most anything I've ever done."

He ran his fingers over a strand of her hair. "I'm very much looking forward to married life with you, Mrs Spenser."

Her name. She beamed at the sound of it. "I had no idea marriage presented such awe-inspiring obligations."

"Usually, these obligations end up being much louder."

"It was difficult staying quiet," she conceded.

Griff pushed a strand of hair over her shoulder. "We'll take a long trip after marriage, tour the length of Japan, and make all the noise we want."

"A grand idea, Mr. Spenser."

Suki rested her head against Griff's chest and her thoughts drifted to places they'd discover together. And they drifted toward the horizons she'd chase for the sake of giving women a voice, women like Haru-*chan* whose voices had been forever silenced. Crude and painful, but also powerful, truth would prevail. Suki would see to it.

CHAPTER THIRTY-THREE

Six months later, November 1897

Suki ran her hand across an inaugural copy of *Tokyo Women's Magazine: Reading for Women of the New Century*. Tomorrow, the magazine would debut in train stations, street-side kiosks, hotel lobbies, and the homes of several dozen Tsukiji residents who'd subscribed in support of their Tokyo-Tattler-turned-magazine owner and editor. She lifted the copy and reveled in its satisfying weight.

After opening to the table of contents, she glanced down the list of articles: "Japanese Midwives Delivering Tsukiji's Babies," "Women Vendors at Shimbashi's Market Fight for Space at the Front," "Competing in a Male-Dominated Lawn Tennis Club," and "One Woman's Journey of Love with a Member of the Conservative Faction." There were entries for short stories submitted by the Tsukiji Literary Society and for the society pages authored by Marcelle, wherein she picked apart the dresses, hairstyles, and accessories of Tokyo's most prominent citizens, and reported on their pairings, breakups, and other engagements.

On the cover was an inked sketch of a Japanese woman wearing a Western-style day dress, a beret perched at a fashionable slant, and an expression of jaunty confidence. Griff had taken one look at it and applauded Suki for putting a picture of herself on the cover.

"It's not me. I'm only half-Japanese," she'd protested.

"She dresses like you and has your smile."

"I asked the artist to imagine a Tokyo woman of the twentieth century."

Griff made a sound as though she'd proved his point. "Your artist chose the founder of Tokyo's first women's magazine, and I think it's perfect."

"May there be many more of us in the new millennium."

The all-consuming labor they'd put into the first issue far outweighed its seventy-three pages. In the days after Suki had departed the *Tokyo Daily News* offices for the last time, an image began taking shape in her mind of a monthly magazine for women, by women, with the entirety of its contents in English and Japanese. It would be a bridge between the communities: Japanese women would learn about the concerns and experiences of foreign women, and foreign women would gain understanding of what life was like for Japanese women. Suki invested her savings from years of teaching and work as the Tattler, and Griff provided the remainder of the capital needed to purchase writing equipment, rent space on a printing press, pay for article translations, and hire Marcelle as her assistant and advertising saleswoman.

Still, Suki remained a resident of her childhood home. Starting the magazine had been the daunting challenge she'd anticipated. Griff understood that she didn't want to marry until the publication was on solid ground. Then they could take a leisurely wedding trip and relish the joys and difficulties of cohabitation. Nevertheless, she spent most evenings at the Spenser home, dining with Griff, Marianne, and Lucien, often accompanied by Marcelle, who mused with them about the differences between France and Japan and the many reasons she was never returning to her home country. And most evenings, Suki and Griff retired to the study for private discussions about their upcoming nuptials and to practice the intimate obligations associated with married life.

Griff entered *Okasan*'s studio, half of which she'd ceded to *Tokyo Women's Magazine* for their headquarters, and wrapped his arms around Suki. "The magazine is going to be the talk of Tsukiji."

Suki vented her frustration on a large squeeze around his midsection. "I've found three errors that don't belong to the printer."

"Better than most dailies I read," he said with a nuzzle of her neck. "Your family and friends are gathered in the house, ready to celebrate with you. The Baron and Baroness Umezono sent an outstanding flower arrangement to honor your new venture."

Suki rolled her eyes. She would never accept Baron Umezono's reasons for helping Norton cover up Haru-*chan*'s death but gave the baron credit for corroborating her story to the police. She told them everything she'd learned about the circumstances of Haru-*chan*'s death, and they proved better listeners than she'd hoped. Within a week of Baron Umezono confirming her statement, the authorities shut down the Hotel Metropolis. By then, Chase Norton was long gone. Rumors swirled that a motley group of conservatives forced him onto a boat destined for somewhere in the northern part of the Asian continent.

Naturally, the police ignored the baron's role in aiding Norton because Haru-*chan* was a woman who'd worked on the fringes of society and the nobility was its core, or so society believed. "The baron's flowers are another of the baron's attempts to atone for the error of his ways," Suki said, her teeth grinding at the injustice.

"Speaking of atonement, the Jinzai Nunnery sent a rather large flower arrangement."

Suki had gifted the money from Madame Okuda to the nunnery, which had recently opened its doors to women who no longer wished to work in Tokyo's nighttime entertainment districts. Suki had been surprised to learn their newest devotee, Natsu Watanabe, had started the charity after arriving on the nunnery's doorstep several months before. On the day Suki visited the nunnery, Watanabe greeted her with a placid smile and told Suki helping pitiful young women had cleansed her spirit and set her on a path toward glorious rebirth. Suki had almost believed her.

"Was there a message from Natsu?" Suki asked.

"Only from the nunnery."

"We'll have to host a charitable event this spring for their benefit, once the magazine has settled into a workable rhythm."

She caught Griff's wince and knew its reason. He was good about not pestering her for a wedding date, but sometimes remarked how much he looked forward to the days when their private time together didn't have to be so limited. Seeing as the magazine would be ready by spring for her to host a charitable event, perhaps it was time to fulfill her marriage promise. The thought of announcing a wedding date to family and friends at tonight's party danced in her head.

"Has Madame Okuda arrived?" she asked.

"When I left, she was telling Papa Garrick about her present for you."

"A present?"

"I hope you're interested in archery."

Suki widened her eyes. "She brought me a bow and arrow?"

"Several copper arrows inside a lacquered quiver case. She said it was a family heirloom."

Suki doubted such a valuable item had been part of Okuda's inheritance. "I wonder from whose family. Madame Okuda has mentioned on several occasions the creative means she uses to obtain gifts from her lovers."

"But why an arrow?" Griff asked.

"To aim for my dreams."

"I say you've already achieved all your dreams." Griff wrapped her in the kind of snug embrace that righted her world.

"Not quite. I'm still waiting for the man of my dreams to set a wedding date."

His face broke into a smile. "Me?"

"I'd been hoping you would agree to a spring wedding, an early spring wedding. But if you'd rather wait…"

"Wait?" he said with all the mock outrage she'd expected. "You know I'd marry you tomorrow if I could."

Their lips joined, and his kiss swept her away to the place of togetherness that had become familiar and cherished. "You have a delightful way of saying yes."

Griff replied with another yes, and then another.

HAVE YOU READ THE PREQUEL?

Scandals of Tokyo

AND

How the devil did Natsu end up at a nunnery?

Visit https://www.heatherhallman.com/ for a short story about what happened to Natsu after she departed Griff's front garden.

Turn the page for a sneak peek at

Toast of Tokyo

TOAST OF TOKYO

Monsieur Koide's department store was an extraordinary accomplishment, unlike anything in Tokyo. *La France Boutique* couldn't hold a candle to it.

As they neared the staircase to the upper floors, the crush of patrons ceased moving. Marcelle followed their gazes to a man of formidable proportions holding court on the red-carpeted stairs. Tall and robust, he filled his elegant black suit with a commanding presence. Newspaper reporters assembled around him called out questions.

"Koide-*san*," one of them shouted over the others. "What was your inspiration for the department store?"

Monsieur Koide shifted toward the reporter, giving Marcelle a view of his impressive profile. He had a smooth, regal brow, bold jaw, and the hooked nose of samurai warriors she'd seen in woodblock paintings. His black hair had been cut short and shaped with a light pomade. Rough and refined, he appeared impervious to—and master of—the carnival of glamor surrounding him. "My father, and grandfather before him, spent a great deal of their careers abroad, learning foreign customs …"

Marcelle leaned forward to make out the cut of Monsieur Koide's suit. An expert tailor had sewn the jacket to emphasize the length and breadth of the monsieur's torso. Indeed, there was no sign of suspenders. The tapering of his jacket at the waist suggested the presence of a belt beneath. Only a man daring in his haberdashery would employ belt loops on his trousers. Monsieur Koide knew fashion.

She stretched farther for a better view of his lapels. Round. Another nod to present-day trends.

A searing pain, somehow twice as dreadful as the one from which she'd barely recovered, struck the muscle between her neck and shoulder.

"*Mon Dieu.*" She grabbed her nape.

Monsieur Koide paused in the middle of whatever he was saying, and Marcelle's heart stopped as he gazed upon the crowd.

She ducked behind Yumi-*chan*, which was no easy feat since Yumi-*chan* only reached the top of her chest. The movement sent pain straight into her fingertips. Biting the inside of her cheek, she suppressed a whimper and gave her muscle a furtive massage.

Yumi-*chan* peered back at Marcelle. "Again?"

"Don't look at me," Marcelle hissed. "Look at Monsieur Koide. Pretend I'm not here."

Yumi-*chan* faced forward. "But he's looking this way."

"I know that. Ignore me." Marcelle drove her fingertips deeper into the muscle, inflicting enough pain to overcome her embarrassment.

ABOUT THE AUTHOR

Heather lives in Tokyo with her professor husband and two young daughters. Once upon a time, she earned a doctoral degree in cultural anthropology for her thesis on adolescent friendship in Japan. Presently, she writes witty, sensual, contest-winning romances set in Meiji-era Japan (1868-1912).

Heather spends her free time translating ancient Japanese poetry and observing the passing of seasons while sipping green tea. Just kidding, she has no free time. But she does watch something that makes her laugh while she does the dishes.

Perennial obsessions include the weather forecast (she checks three different apps at least three times a day, as no single app can be trusted), Baltimore Ravens football (hometown obsession), and making smoothies that taste like candy bars.

Feel free to chat her up about any of her obsessions, or even better, about historical Japan—any era is fine, she loves them all.

She also enjoys exchanging book recommendations, discussions about the craft of romance writing, and stories about life in present-day Tokyo. You can reach out through Instagram, TikTok, Facebook, Twitter, or her website.

Connect with Heather:

website: heatherhallman.com
FB: /hallmanheather
IG: @heatherhallman_author
TikTok: @writing_romance_in_japan

www.BOROUGHSPUBLISHINGGROUP.com

If you enjoyed this book, please write a review. Our authors appreciate the feedback, and it helps future readers find books they love. We welcome your comments and invite you to send them to info@boroughspublishinggroup.com.

Follow us on Facebook, Twitter and Instagram, and be sure to sign up for our newsletter for surprises and new releases from your favorite authors.

Are you an aspiring writer? Check out www.boroughspublishinggroup.com/submit and see if we can help you make your dreams come true.

Love podcasts? Enjoy ours at www.boroughspublishinggroup.com/podcast

Made in the USA
Middletown, DE
14 October 2023

40802701R00201